D0951911

Praise for *Skipped Parts*

"There is no more compelling subject than young human males and females coming together in the spring of their lives...A thoughtful, surprising and delightful entertainment."

—*St. Louis Post-Dispatch*

"A sparkling tale...*Skipped Parts* offers some big helpings of western wit, down-home adult humor and once-in-a-while sorrowful truths...It's a classic story of the well-read, old-before-his-time young teen and hip mom learning to cope...Excellent."

—*Indianapolis News*

"Wittily told...reminiscent of Larry McMurtry's *The Last Picture Show*."

—*Library Journal*

"Chock-full of wonderful characters and good writing."

—*Dallas Morning News*

"This witty, often touching portrayal of a dirt-streetwise youth's coming-of-age sparkles with intelligence."

—*Booklist*

Praise for *Sorrow Floats*

"A raucous, surprisingly original tale."

—*New York Times*

"Unforgettable…*Sorrow Floats* has a multitude of gifts to offer—laughs, real people, high drama, and a crazy cross-country journey that makes it hard to put aside for long, if at all."

—*West Coast Review of Books*

"Sandlin understands that the best black comedy is only a tiny slip away from despair, and he handles this walk without a misstep."

—*Dallas Morning News*

"A zany road trip across America starring an engaging heroine and two AA devotees occupies talented novelist Tim Sandlin in *Sorrow Floats*."

—*Cosmopolitan*

"Able storytelling and an engaging cast of dysfunctional modern American pilgrims animate this winning tale of the road… Sandlin fashions a convincing tale of redemption."

—*Publishers Weekly* (starred review)

"A rousing piece of Americana…rowdy, raunchy…A total delight."

—*Library Journal*

"Funny and poignant…Sandlin's sustaining insight and faith in humanity give the book compassion and hope."

—*Winston-Salem Journal*

Praise for *Social Blunders*

"A story of grand faux pas and dazzling dysfunction...a wildly satirical look at the absurdities of modern life."
—*New York Times Book Review*

"A weird, funny, raunchy novel that veers wildly from pathos to slapstick and back again, and it's surprisingly effective."
—*Booklist*

"Wild, wonderful, and wickedly funny...Highly recommended."
—*Library Journal*

"Downright superb...wickedly funny...richly rewarding."
—*Milwaukee Journal*

"Sandlin is the only novelist I've read in the last two years whose prose forced me to laugh out loud.
—*The Bloomsbury Review*

"Tim Sandlin only gets better. *Social Blunders* is an affecting book, now sprightly, now sad, as his characters experience the common upturnings and downturnings of life. It is fiction to be savoured."
—Larry McMurtry

"Ribald...comic and bawdy...oddly endearing...an effective blend of flippancy and compassion."
—*Publishers Weekly*

Also by Tim Sandlin

Lydia

TIM Sandlin

sourcebooks
landmark

Published by Sourcebooks Landmark, an imprint of Sourcebooks, Inc.
P.O. Box 4410, Naperville, Illinois 60567-4410
(630) 961-3900
Fax: (630) 961-2168
www.sourcebooks.com

Library of Congress Cataloging-in-Publication Data

Sandlin, Tim.
  Lydia : a novel / Tim Sandlin.
      p. cm.

  1. Dysfunctional families—Fiction. 2. Mothers and sons—Fiction. 3. Older women—Fiction. I. Title.
  PS3569.A517L93 2011
  813'.54—dc22
                          2010043340

Printed and bound in the United States of America.
SB 10 9 8 7 6 5 4 3 2 1

I wrote this book for

Steve Ashley
*Books will get you through times of no money better than
money will get you through times of no books.*

In memory of
Karol Griffin Young
Who knew my people better than I do. We miss you.

And, of course,
Carol

I am that I am.

—GOD, EXODUS 3:14

I yam what I yam.

—POPEYE, IN HIS SELF-JUSTIFICATION TO OLIVE OYL

What's time to a hog?
What's dynamite dope to the pope
Or religion to a brown groundhog?

—DEAN WEBB/MITCH JAYNE

NORWOOD DEGARMO SAT PERCHED ON A CANVAS STOOL IN A *Venice Beach sidewalk curio shop, doing his best to ignore two guys in* PROPERTY OF MONTANA STATE ATHLETIC DEPARTMENT *T-shirts who wanted a dollar off on a five-dollar pair of wraparound sunglasses.*

"*Look at the crack there.*" *The bigger one with a shaved head showing irregular skull plates shoved the glasses into Norwood's face. There did seem to be a hairline fracture in the nosepiece, but Norwood wasn't sure. The glasses were too close for him to focus.*

The other one—skinny, sneaky, probably a quarterback—said, "I don't see how you can even sell cracked sunglasses. You ought to give 'em away."

Norwood closed his eyes. His brother Timmy was in charge of tourists from east of I-15. They had a deal, and Timmy would just have to handle it.

Timmy said, "You put that crack there yourself. I watched you on the surveillance camera."

The big one looked around in faux disbelief. "What surveillance camera? You got a cigar box for a cash register, what would you be doing with a surveillance camera?"

"*Hell,*" *the quarterback said. "This sty don't even have electricity."*

Norwood wished Timmy would sell the sunglasses for whatever the idiots wanted to pay. The glasses were stolen anyway; it was pure profit. Besides, Norwood had taken three Ativans and a Librium, and he wasn't in the mood for antagonism. Much more of this and he'd be forced into pulling pepper spray, which would cause a scene and destroy the point of the pills.

"We got a hidden surveillance camera," Timmy said. "Hidden means you can't see it."

The big one stared at Timmy through the sunglasses in question. "Guy two booths down sells them for three."

The beaded curtain door rustled, and a deeply tanned and tattooed man stepped through. Norwood's skin prickled as if the temperature had dropped ten degrees. The man wore no shirt or shoes—nothing but an unzipped pair of canvas shorts. His ribs stuck out like bones on a shark carcass.

He murmured, "You boys have to leave now."

The big jock took off the cracked sunglasses. "I haven't made my choice yet."

The shirtless man moved into the booth, close to the tourists. Norwood smelled bad shrimp. No, it was more like an overflowing outhouse, the plastic Port-A-Potty you hold your breath to go into at concerts.

"Here's the choice." His voice was two shades above a whisper. "The glasses are free if you walk away in the next five seconds."

"And what if we don't?" the quarterback asked, but his buddy was already heading for the door, with the cracked glasses. The big one had a fighter's instinct; he knew when it was best to get out. The shirtless man stared at the quarterback, while Norwood wished he had a cell phone so he could call 911 and get this cleaned up before his drugs kicked in.

The quarterback slid around the wall and started for the door. Before he left, he said, "If this was Montana, somebody would shoot your ass." Then he scooted out the curtain.

Norwood dropped his right hand into an LA Clippers gym bag at his feet. His fingers closed on the pepper canister. This wasn't cheap spray designed for stunning ethnic minorities, this was grizzly bear repellent—not even legal in California. He said, "You owe us five dollars."

"Anything you bring out of that bag, you're going to eat."

Norwood weighed the risks of five dollars versus what might happen if this guy was half as tough as he thought he was. His fingers groped below the pepper spray and came up with a package of Hostess Sno Balls. "You want one, Leroy. They're kind of squished."

Timmy couldn't take it anymore. He didn't care how mean the son of a bitch was—this was Venice Beach, for Christ's sake. He'd been raised on mean sons of bitches. "Who the hell you think you are, busting into our legitimate business and coming on like Sean Penn?"

"It's Leroy," Norwood said. To Leroy himself, he said, "Ever'one thinks you're dead."

"Ever'one's wrong." Leroy strolled to the sunglasses rack and pulled off a pair of wireless silver lenses. Sunglasses were all the DeGarmo brothers sold, except one card table full of two-dollar T-shirts they'd found in a Dumpster behind the Third Street Promenade.

"That's not Leroy," Timmy said.

Norwood tore cellophane off the cupcakes. "Check out the tattoo." Leroy had a tattoo across his chest showing a Green Beret firing a flamethrower. The flames looked like wings until you looked close and saw the tattoo wasn't angels; it was burning babies.

Leroy's odor wafted ahead of him like a cirrus cloud of stink as he crossed the booth and took a Sno Ball from Norwood's hand. "Where's my boy?" Leroy said.

Norwood tried to hide his disgust. "What boy?"

"The boy I left with you two short peckers. The boy you said you'd hang on to till I got back."

"Jesus, Leroy, that was ten years ago."

Timmy said, "Twelve."

"It was ten," Norwood said. "We were in Tucson, and Leroy said he had to run over to Bogotá for a week."

Leroy popped the Sno Ball into this mouth and talked through a wad of pink paste. "I told you it might be more than a week but I'd be back for the boy."

Timmy said, "We couldn't hold the boy for twelve years."

"Ten," Norwood said.

"Besides, you were dead."

"I wasn't dead." He took the other cupcake and shoved it in whole also. Norwood shuddered. Leroy hadn't even finished swallowing the first one.

"Where were you?" Norwood asked.

"Where do you think?"

"Jail," Norwood said.

Timmy stared hard at Leroy. "No wonder you don't look like yourself. I've heard those Colombian jails are worse than state pens down South."

Leroy barked a laugh that held no humor. "Timmy, you don't have enough imagination to dream what I been through. Now, where's my boy?"

Norwood said, "Gone."

"Don't tell me that."

Timmy's voice rose to a whine. "But you were dead. We couldn't raise a boy."

"I told you to hang on to him." The tan drained from Leroy's face. His rope muscles drew in on themselves, and a drop of saliva appeared at the corner of his mouth.

Norwood nodded toward the canvas walls of the booth. "There's lots of people outside. Don't go Branch Davidian on us, Leroy."

To Norwood, the struggle for control was visible on Leroy's face. It was as if his brain flipped a coin—heads, I kill everybody in sight; tails, I wait till later. The coin came up tails.

"How long after I left did you keep him?"

The DeGarmos looked at each other and shrugged. Timmy said, "Couple of weeks."

Norwood jumped in before Leroy's brain decided to go for two out of three flips. "We took him to Mary Beth."

"Who?"

"Mary Beth. Your Mary Beth."

"In Boulder?"

Norwood nodded. "She was living outside Nederland. Little cabin by a creek there. Looked real pretty."

"I didn't tell you to take the boy to Mary Beth."

"You were dead. Wouldn't you rather her raise him than us?" Norwood said. "We're not responsible parties."

"She still have him?"

"We haven't talked to Mary Beth since the night we dumped the kid, but I wouldn't think so. He'd be grown by now."

Leroy took off the silver-lens sunglasses and turned them by the earpiece, thinking. He said, "Corporal balance says if someone brings harm to another human being, such as me, the balance must be refit for Earth to maintain a proper axis. Until the world-state is brought back into corporal balance, there will be earthquakes, typhoons, and plagues upon the people. That boy owes me a life. Until the debt is paid, the planet will be out of whack. Nothing will fit."

Norwood said, "The whole planet? That's a bit harsh."

Leroy stared at Norwood. "If I do not find my boy and bring chaos to order, I promise you two I will come back here and slice your livers out and eat them." He stood so close that the smell triggered Norwood's gag reflex. "Do you believe I will do that?"

Norwood said, "Yes."

"How about you, smart fella?"

Timmy said, "Yes."

Nobody blinked for a full five seconds. Then Leroy dug into his pocket and pulled out the filthiest five-dollar bill Norwood had ever seen. "I'll buy these," he said.

"They're yours," Norwood said. "Complimentary. You can keep your money there."

Leroy looked at the bill in his hand.

Timmy said, "Complimentary means free."

"I know what complimentary means. Bogotá jails don't make you stupid."

"I wasn't sure," Timmy said.

Leroy stuffed the bill back into his pocket, put on the sunglasses, checked himself in the mirror, and left. The stench, however, stayed behind. Norwood desperately wanted to run to fresh air, but he was afraid Leroy might be standing out front on the boardwalk. Instead he pulled a cardboard box out from under the table and started packing T-shirts.

Timmy hadn't moved. "How can he possibly find Mary Beth? She's more than likely moved three, four times since then."

"He found us, didn't he?"

Timmy considered this. "What're we going to do?"

"You can do what you want, I'm out of the retail business."

"Where you going to go?"

"What difference does it make?"

1

MY MOTHER, LYDIA CALLAHAN, WALKED OUT OF THE DUBLIN, California, federal women's penitentiary at noon on Mother's Day 1993, a free woman, with nothing but the clothes on her back and a Lands' End fanny pack full of credit cards. She took a taxi to the Holiday Inn in Walnut Creek, where she checked in as Lydia Elkrunner and gave her address as hell. Then she washed her hair in complimentary Pert and fell asleep. Lydia was fifty-eight years old; in her dreams, she was twenty.

The next night, she telephoned my daughter Shannon in Greensboro, North Carolina.

Lydia said, "I'm out of stir."

Shannon said, "Stir?"

"Prison. They let me go."

"That's wonderful, Lydia. I can't wait to see you."

"I want you to pick me up at the airport Thursday afternoon. I don't know what flight I'll be on, so you'll have to meet them all."

"Which airport is this where you want me to meet every flight?"

"Jackson Hole. I want you to be the one waiting when I come home. No one else."

"Lydia, Dad lives right there, almost next door to that airport, and I live two thousand miles away."

"Are you going to do this for me or not?"

Shannon said, "I was being practical." Then there was silence. In the past, before going underground, Lydia would have flown into a tirade at the suggestion that practicality might take precedence over her will. But prison had taught her the power of silence. Noisy intimidation works on men; women respond to a quieter approach.

After twenty seconds, Shannon said, "I'll be there."

Lydia said, "I would also like you to organize a community get-together. No use sneaking back into town."

"You want a welcome home party?"

"Put up a notice at the GroVont post office. Tell them chicken wings and shitty beer for all. That'll bring the yokels out."

"Anything else, Grandma?"

"What?"

"Lydia."

"Dress nice. This is my triumphant return. I don't need to come off the airplane and see a slob."

———

Lydia's phone call came while Shannon was in the process of breaking up with her tenth boyfriend in ten years. This one's name was Tanner. They had made love with a device Tanner bought for seventy-five cents from a machine in the truckers-only washroom at the Dixie Land service center near High Point. Tanner was proud of his device, and in his mind, he had just given Shannon the sensual experience of the epoch.

Tanner kissed her left breast and said, "My God, that was great."

Shannon rolled over on her back to face the ceiling. "I don't feel the way you're supposed to feel when you're in love."

Tanner said, "Yeah, but the orgasm makes up the difference."

"There's more to love than orgasms."

Tanner was confused. His belief system was based on the concept that sexual prowess and popularity go hand in hand. "What the hell does that have to do with us?"

"I do not love you, Tanner. You're interchangeable with others."

"But I'm here now."

Shannon rolled back to look at Tanner, who had a little scar on his chin she was fond of. She realized the scar was why she had chosen him in the first place. It lent Tanner a sense of fragile danger, but fragile danger is not enough in the long haul. "Tonight was fun," she said. "I want you to move out tomorrow."

He said, "No."

At that point, the phone rang.

———

Tanner pouted throughout Shannon's conversation with Lydia. After they said their good-byes and hung up, he said he was sorry he wasted his youth on a woman with the emotional capacity of a mud flap. He asked her if their time together meant nothing to her, and she said, "That's right." He asked her if she was made of stone. Shannon realized Tanner would not leave her until tears flowed and glass shattered. She would have to make him believe the breakup was his idea, and at the moment she simply didn't have the energy. Instead she telephoned her father, Sam. This is where I enter the story.

———

I answered midway through the first ring.

Shannon said, "Grandma's out of the slammer."

There followed a moment of silence as I adjusted to the idea of a free mother. It's not as easy as you would think. "I knew it was happening this month; I wasn't sure when."

"They let her go yesterday. Seems strange to do it on a Sunday."

"We express mailed her a loaf of pumpkin bread for Mother's Day. Do you know if she got it?"

"Lydia didn't say." Tanner flounced off to the bathroom and slammed the door. Shannon knew he was angry, but it was hard to take him seriously with a condom dangling between his legs. "She did say I'm supposed to pick her up at the Jackson Hole airport Thursday afternoon."

I said, "I can be there."

"She said I have to be the one. Nobody else." Shannon could hear Tanner's electric toothbrush. First thing after sex, Tanner always brushed his teeth. "Grandma's nuts. Prison hasn't changed her."

"I didn't think it would."

"She wants me to organize a party at the GroVont house."

"Am I invited?"

"I guess so. She didn't say invite everyone but Sam." Tanner came from the bathroom, minus the condom. He picked his jockey shorts off the floor, snatched the seventy-five-cent device from the nightstand, and left the room.

I said, "Will you need a ride from the airport yourself?"

"Leave Lydia's BMW in the parking lot with the keys behind the gas cap cover. I'll pick it and her up at the same time."

"The BMW hasn't run in ten years."

"Better have someone look at it. Grandma's coming home."

The next day I drove out to the TM Ranch. I found Maurey Pierce sitting on the top rail of a buck-and-rail fence, watching a pasture filled with pregnant mares named after movie stars. It was an ideal day—high-altitude blue sky, room temperature, no humidity to brag about. Days like this are rare in the muddy, sluggish springs of the West. I should have been basking in the glory of good weather, but Maurey had permed her hair over the weekend. Changes of any kind, and especially in Maurey Pierce, throw me for a loop. You should know that about me. I hate change.

"How long till it grows back out?" I asked.

"I'm glad to see you too, Sam."

"I mean, your hair looks nice and all, I just like it the way it was—when you were a teenager."

"That was twenty-five years ago."

"What's your point?"

Maurey patted the rail, indicating that I should climb up beside her. Maurey's been my friend since I came to Wyoming. We're so close, we don't have to talk to communicate. She said, "Lydia called this morning. She's a free bird."

I settled in next to her. "She phoned Shannon last night. You think by calling everyone in the family but me, that she's trying to make a point?"

"Lydia's not in my family."

I started to disagree but decided I wasn't going to convince her of anything new. Maurey is Shannon's mother; I'm Shannon's father; Lydia is my mother and Shannon's grand-mother: that makes the whole bunch of us family in my book. And this is my book. One of the mares knelt on her front legs and flopped sideways. Since Maurey didn't seem concerned, I figured it was normal behavior.

Maurey said, "Uma Thurman will drop first."

"Which one's Uma Thurman?"

"The sorrel. Drew beat her by ten hours last year." Maurey nodded toward a black horse with white feet and a white wedge running down her nose. "But my money is on Uma. She's set to pop. God, look at her. I'm glad I'm not pregnant."

We watched Uma for a while, expecting her to pop at any

moment, although I wasn't sure I was watching the same mare as Maurey. I know brown and pinto, palomino in a good light, but sorrel is beyond me either as a color or a horse.

"What did Lydia say this morning?"

"She's in San Francisco on a shopping spree."

"Shannon told me Lydia's coming home Thursday."

Maurey nodded. "That's why she called. She's throwing a prodigal mom party. Pud's supposed to barbecue a pig."

"Shannon thinks she's supposed to organize the home-coming bash."

"Lydia changed her mind. She doesn't trust Shannon to get it right, not that she thinks we'll do better."

I said, "Lydia has high standards when it comes to parties thrown by other people for her."

"She wanted a fatted calf on a spit, but that's where I drew the line."

My eyes went from the horses in the pasture, across the river line, to the red mountains in the distance. Somehow, the older I got, the less I was able to deal with the difference between nature and people. I'd recently been feeling almost paralyzed by the unlikelihood of life.

Maurey said, "Pud's over in Idaho Falls now, looking for a butcher who sells whole hogs."

"Why not buy a live one and slaughter it yourself?"

Maurey's nose wrinkled. "Yuck, Sam. Do you want to stick a pig?"

"Not me."

"That's one of the many reasons we run horses instead of cattle—I don't have to kill the inventory."

"You've raised cattle before."

"No need to throw the past in my face. Do I throw the past in your face? Do I say, 'You once owned a golf cart company,' which is sure as hell nastier than feeding cows?"

"Sorry."

"You never know when to back off and let it alone. When I met you, you wore Dickeys and thought hooters were people from Indiana. But do I hold it against you? No."

After decades of multiple apologies per conversation, I had adopted a policy with women of saying I was sorry once, then keeping my mouth shut till they ran down. In my job, I dealt almost exclusively with women, and the policy served me well.

"What are you going to do about Lydia?" Maurey asked.

"Nobody can do anything about their mother."

"Got that right." She grabbed my arm and pointed. "Michelle Pfeiffer's water just broke."

"That's nice."

2

RIDING AIRPLANES MADE SHANNON FEEL EVEN MORE vulnerable than she usually felt, which, she thought, might be more vulnerable than almost anyone else. She wasn't sure. Shannon sometimes spent entire days on the edge of hysteria, but she hid it so well that she suspected others around her were doing the same thing. Once, as an experiment, she snapped, *"Boo!"* to a rude teller at the Wachovia Bank, and the teller burst into tears. After that, Shannon realized it wasn't fair to test the hard asses.

Vulnerability in others cannot be judged. It's like my theory on colors. I told Shannon each person in the world sees colors differently, only this is impossible to discuss, because there's nothing to compare it to. Color blindness can be quantified since that's one color against another. But intensity, depth, and vibrancy are isolated in the individual. When I say, "The Coke can is red," I mean an entirely different thing than when she says, "The Coke can is red."

Shannon couldn't see how it mattered, so I tried to explain the relevance. "There is no common ground," I said.

Shannon said, "What did you expect?"

Airplanes made Shannon feel extra vulnerable, and not just because the passengers have absolutely no control over whether they live or die. There was that. But also, Shannon had no control over who sat next to her. For some reason, my daughter brought out the chattiness in humanity. If there was a Scientologist or past-lives regresser or even a bathroom-fixtures salesman who really loved his job, the airlines plopped Shannon down next to him. Or her.

On the flight from Greensboro to Atlanta Shannon sat next to a girl who believed there is a secret code in the Bible that explains all mysteries—such as why her boyfriend was in prison in Reidsville, Georgia, for selling counterfeit travelers' checks.

As the girl ate Shannon's free peanuts, she said, "A man in Florida knows the code. He'll give it to me for a two-thousand-dollar love donation."

"Which version of the Bible has the code in it?" Shannon asked.

"The King James, I guess. That's the one God wrote." Then the girl showed Shannon a photograph of her boyfriend. He had white hair and a T-shirt that said FUCK OFF, WORLD—I'M A SENIOR. "We're getting married—soon as he makes parole. I'm flying down today to tell him I'm preggers."

Shannon felt so vulnerable, and the Atlanta airport was so crowded, that she decided to telephone Tanner. Harsh words had been spoken before she left, and Tanner had gone into a sulk. Shannon wanted to tell Tanner that he was a fine man and her inability to love him the right way was not a reflection on him personally. He wasn't any worse than anyone else.

"I have to be totally honest," Tanner said, on the phone, after she told him it wasn't personal. "I believe in honesty above all else. You can ask anyone in Carolina. I tell the truth, first, last, and always."

Shannon looked down the concourse at the line coming through the security checkpoint and wished she were there instead of on the phone. She knew, whenever a man says he has to be honest, he's fixing to inflict pain.

Tanner said, "You need to lose some weight."

"What?"

"No man is going to marry you if you're fat."

"Is that your best shot?"

"No. Your pussy smells bad."

"Tanner."

"It's like bad clams down there. I wouldn't tell you if it wasn't for your own good. I would heavily advise that you never let a man go down on you again. You'll make them sick."

———

I loaded the Madonnaville Suburban with three pregnant teen-agers, a nurse practitioner, Gilia, and Baby Esther—who was terrible two and Gilia said we had to stop calling *Baby* soon—and drove down to GroVont to Lydia's getting-out-of-prison party. The math here adds up to six females and one male, which is the general proportion I am accustomed to living with. It leaves me with a permanent sense of feeling put-upon.

"I can't believe you had the low class to buy Gilia tires for Mother's Day," Eden Rae O'Connor said. At nineteen, Eden was the oldest of the present batch of Unweds. She was also the farthest along—eight months—so she'd appointed herself spokesperson. The other two were fairly new to the Virgin Birth Home for Unwed Mothers, and it usually took a few weeks for the girls to adjust to the point where they felt comfortable criticizing me.

"New tires will give her peace of mind when she drives Esther into town," I said. "Peace of mind is the most precious gift of all."

My wife made a snort noise that sounded like a cross between *hmph* and *bullshit*.

Eden said, "You can give peace of mind on a weekday. On Mother's Day, you're supposed to give flowers."

Honor Edmonson stopped playing with the radio. It didn't

get but two stations anyway. "Face it, Mr. Callahan, the romance has left your marriage. The tires are for you." Honor was the nurse practitioner. She'd been an Unwed seven years ago, one of our first. Then, after her baby was born, she went to school for her nursing degree and came back.

"My daddy always buys Mama things he wants for presents. He says she'll hate whatever he picks out anyway, so it might as well be useful." Angel Byron, who sat in the way back, had just come to Wyoming a couple days ago. Angel hadn't yet decided whether to abort, offer for adoption, or keep the baby, and these were her first nonessential words. Talking was a good sign. It meant Angel was emerging from the scared silly stage.

The company policy is to avoid putting any pressure on the girls either pro or con as to abortion, but nurturing without pressure is stressful in itself. Gilia and I are always tense until the initial decision has been made. After that, the adoption-or-keeping question can go right down to the wire. Sometimes well past the wire.

"I don't understand why your mother was in prison in the first place," Eden said. "I heard she was a feminist force for justice in America."

I glanced in the rearview mirror at Gilia, who sat next to Esther's car seat, staring out the window at the red cliffs along the river, pretending not to listen. It would be just like her to feed Eden that *feminist force for justice in America* line. Although we'd been together almost ten years, I still had no clue as to when Gilia was being sarcastic. It seemed like an important thing to know.

I said, "Mom FedExed a poison chew toy to Ronald Reagan's dog."

Charlie, the third Unwed in the van, whistled through the ring in her nose. "That's totally spooky."

"Lydia thought she was doing good for humanity," I said.

"By poisoning a dog," Gilia said, as if the girls hadn't heard it right the first time.

After a moment of semi-stunned silence, Eden said, "Now I see why you're so squirrelly."

———

"Look at all those cars," Honor said. "It's like they're going to a baseball game."

I said, "Maybe someone is having a garage sale."

Cars were pulled over on both sides of the street. People unloaded lawn chairs and coolers, a few baby strollers. Dogs sniffed each other's crotches and peed on each other's pee; kids pretended to hit their friends; women hugged everyone in sight, as if they hadn't seen all these people yesterday. It had that feeling you get in the parking lot of a bluegrass festival.

"They're headed to our house," Gilia said.

I said, "Are you sure?"

"Well, look, for God's sake."

I eased between the double rows of cars, narrowly avoiding killing a couple of children, until the view opened up on Lydia's house and lawn covered by Wyomingites doing what Wyomingites do after a long winter. Everyone even vaguely close to the legal age held plastic cups of beer. Several kids from up in Buffalo Valley were playing a game where you shake up a can of Coca-Cola and open it in another kid's face. The men were split evenly between one group at the kegs and another group gathered to watch Roger Pierce and Maurey's husband, Pud, standing on either end of a fire pit, turning a greasy pig on a spit.

Eden said, "Look at Roger."

I said, "What about Roger?"

"Nothing. Just look at him."

So we did. Roger was a slender, tall boy wearing jeans and an old cowboy shirt with the sleeves scissored out. He had a tie-dyed bandanna wrapped across his forehead like an Apache, and as we watched, he dipped a mop into a washtub of barbecue sauce. When the mop was good and slathered, Roger wiped it back and forth over the shiny pig.

"You think that mop is new?" I asked.

Honor opened her door. "This is going to be a hoot."

I repeated what I had said earlier. "Are you sure?"

As the females unloaded, I sat watching the front door of the house where I had grown up. "You guys go ahead. I have an errand."

Gilia stopped unlatching Esther's child seat. "What kind of errand?"

"I should run into Jackson for potato chips. This is a bunch of people, it would be a shame to run out of potato chips."

Not one of the five women bought the gig. Even Esther knew I was lying through my teeth.

"What's your husband up to?" Eden asked Gilia.

"I've found you save a whole lot of time if you don't try to figure that out," Gilia said.

As the pregnant girls huffed their way out of the van, Gilia came around to the driver's-side window. She leaned in and kissed me on the tip of my nose.

"The tires are okay," she said.

"I could have done better."

"Listen to me." I listened. "Your mother will take all the guilt you have to give. Don't waste any on this."

———

The whiny kid banged on the bathroom door again, but Shannon ignored him. He could just go piss on a bush like everyone else in Wyoming. The whole state thought nature was one big commode, the way they acted. The kid would have to find a way, if it was the emergency he claimed it was.

Shannon was sitting on the toilet in Lydia's cabin with her head down between her knees, trying to sniff her crotch. She knew Tanner had only been trying to hurt her, he probably said the same thing to every woman who had the gall to split up with him. She knew he was lying. And yet, the seeds of insecurity had taken root.

Why did men have to go and wreck whatever good memories were left when a relationship ended? That was the eternal question. She and Tanner had been close once—two months ago—so close it was hard to conceive of being apart. They laughed together. They talked all night and held hands in public. There had been deep trust, and now, simply because she wasn't in love with him, Tanner was smashing every warm moment from the past. You only hate the ones you sleep with. Shannon suspected this was a Southern attitude. Californians didn't automatically hate everyone they stopped having sex with.

She sniffed again, exploring for rankness. Fish. Sweat socks. She'd read people can't smell their own body odors, which is why some people get into crowded elevators smelling like week-old roadkill. Deodorant companies spend millions of dollars on advertising for the sole purpose of making us paranoid. Shannon considered this inhumane, right up there with clubbing baby seals. The world is ridiculous enough without commercially caused anxiety.

The kid banged the door. "I gotta go."

"Stick it in a jar."

The kid kicked the door.

Shannon gave it up. There was no way to tell if she smelled, and no one she could ask. She stood, pulled up her panties and jeans, and crossed to the mirror to study her face for signs that she was turning twenty-nine in August.

The trip out from Carolina had been a royal pain in the butt. From Atlanta to Salt Lake, she was trapped next to a man whose stomach gurgled. He pretended it was her making all the racket, like a kid in third grade who farts, then blames the girl sitting in front of him, minding her own business. The other passengers believed him.

Then, from Salt Lake to Jackson Hole, it was a woman reading—out loud—from a book called *Attacks of the Grizzly*. "Listen to this, way back in 1923, two cowboys on horses roped a bear, and an idiot Yellowstone Park ranger rammed into the grizzly with his motorcycle." The woman had Certs breath and leaned into Shannon as she ranted on. "The bear ripped the ranger apart and started to eat him, but one of the cowboys finally killed him. The bear. The ranger didn't pass out or anything. Just laid there under the bear's dead body until the cowboys set him free."

"You think that's true?"

"In the '30s, there was a decapitation. Decapitations fascinate me. Do you think the eyes keep working for a while afterward? I don't see why not. Imagine what it must feel like to see your own body without a head."

And while the woman went into an hour drone on the subject of blood, guts, and gore, Shannon sat next to the window and stewed over the stupid amount of energy she'd wasted deciding what to wear when she met Lydia's plane. Shannon's grandmother was impossible to satisfy, so it was senseless for Shannon to work herself up over clothing. Lydia criticized. Maurey said it was an evil habit Lydia fell into years ago, and she didn't mean to be mean. Shannon should take it as a lesson on what not to do when she grew up, which you would think would have happened by now, if it was going to.

"We need bad examples even more than good ones," Maurey said.

"Yeah, but why do I have to be related to so many of them?"

Shannon chose a white turtleneck, black Wranglers, Nike running shoes, and earrings Hank Elkrunner made in the prison jewelry shop from two #12 Royal Coachman dry flies. She changed in the airport restroom, ran out to the parking lot to find Lydia's BMW, threw her bag into the trunk, then ran back into the airport in time to meet the next flight. Lydia wasn't on it.

Shannon settled in to read the pile of catalogs she'd brought from Greensboro, but visions of Tanner kept getting in the way. She came up with at least ten things she should have said, most of them having to do with the size of his penis. Then the shape. Then his ability to use it effectively for anything other than a whiz in the wind. Given two days to write several drafts of her phone call's last line, she could have made him feel like such a loser.

Lydia was on the next flight up from Denver. She had bought herself a first-class ticket, and she came off the plane wearing a flowing white broomstick skirt with a silver conch belt and matching bracelets, looking like honorable mention in the Isadora Duncan lookalike contest. Her hair was jet-black like vinyl seat covers. Shannon had been braced for the rejection of no hug after not seeing each other in two years, and she was shocked when Lydia grabbed her around the shoulders.

"Let me give you some advice," Lydia said. "Don't ever go to prison."

"I'll try not to."

"Prison makes a woman stronger, but it isn't worth the trouble." Lydia released the hug as the economy-class passengers parted and flowed around them like rocks in a river. "You look nice. Did Hank give you the earrings?"

Lydia hadn't said, *You look nice*, to Shannon since middle-school graduation. "He sent them to me for Christmas. Are you okay? You want some water?"

"I'm perfect." Lydia headed for the baggage carrel. "But we'll have to do something about those shoes before the party."

They waited by the baggage carrel for Lydia's four brand-new suitcases, then passed through the glass double doors into the Wyoming sunlight. Lydia almost kissed the asphalt, probably would have if Shannon hadn't been standing there looking like she expected a slap. It was all Lydia could do to keep from sounding happy.

"Are you still working in the little frame shop at the mall?" she asked.

Shannon was having trouble with the bags. Lydia thought about offering help but was afraid it might set a precedent.

"I don't think so," Shannon said.

"Don't think so?"

"I broke up with the owner right before I left Greensboro. He doesn't seem like the type who can work with an ex."

"You were sleeping with your boss?"

Shannon set three bags on the pavement and dug for Lydia's car key. There wasn't much to say, beyond the obvious.

Lydia said, "That is so asinine."

"I know that now."

"You should have known it earlier. When I was your age, girls had long since stopped sleeping with their boss."

Shannon said, "When you were my age, you were a grandmother."

Lydia reached for the key. "It's nice to see you haven't completely lost your spunk. I was afraid you'd gone meek on me."

3

LYDIA HAD BEEN SPUNK PERSONIFIED ON THE PLANE. NOTHING like spending a few thousand dollars on clothes to give a woman back her confidence. And she did relish flying first-class, up there ahead of the rabble. It may have cost an extra five hundred, but by God, her wine came with a cloth napkin. An executive with his cutting-edge ThinkPad tried to strike up a conversation, and she cut him dead. She was in control.

Then came the steps and the walk across the tarmac. She held up like a champ through all that. She was home. The county should have sent a brass band. Then she saw Shannon, and Lydia's illusory bubble burst. In one breath, she became the ex-con limping back to the cave after doing her time. In her breasts, from which Lydia thought all emotions spring, she knew she was a cliché. It was Shannon's earrings that did it. Hank had made them. She didn't want to think about Hank, not today. Hank brought on the ache of loss—lost people, lost years. The entire last ten years had been a write-off. She was free and home, and he wasn't. She felt like Dorothy, waking up in her own bed in her own room in Kansas, surrounded by Auntie Em and Uncle Henry, only to discover Toto had been hit by a truck.

And Shannon—Shannon looked like cold soup. Girls should wash their face after they cry. Hard times should improve your posture, not wreck it. Lydia had been set to establish her authority, but one look at Shannon and she took the girl in her arms.

Lydia said, "You look nice." She would never have said that if it were true.

At the house, twenty or thirty locals milled around the yard, their attention split between meat and beer. They didn't rush the car and welcome her back into the bosom of the community. A couple old codgers who looked vaguely familiar cut their eyes her way, but they were checking out the antique BMW more than her. Except for Pud and his cousin Rowdy, she didn't see anyone whose name she knew. Pud grinned and waved, making signs like he would come over and hug her, but he was stuck at the barbecue pit. Lydia waved back and waited for Shannon to carry her bags into the house.

Later, after Shannon finished the obligatory fussing with the bags and pointing out where things were, as if Lydia were the guest instead of the owner of the house, Lydia sat in her room and wept. She couldn't remember the last time she'd cried. Not in all the years on the run, not during the arrest or the trial or the nights in prison. She didn't cry when her father died. Maybe a pet death way back in childhood. The week after she stopped smoking there'd been a tire commercial that made her dewy-eyed, but Lydia blamed that on nicotine withdrawal. And the night Nixon was elected the second time, she almost cried but got drunk instead. But now, when it was over, she was bawling like a baby. That was the shits of it all—it was over. Lydia looked into her future and saw one long playing out the string. She would be going through the motions from here on out. She'd lost her turn.

After a while—a short while, considering it was her first cry in forty-five years—Lydia dug in her purse for her emergency panties and blotted the tears off her cheeks. She stood and walked to the mirror and looked at herself, thinking what every middle-aged person thinks when they look in the mirror—*Where did it all go?*

She sneaked from her bedroom to the bathroom, but Shannon was locked in and wouldn't come out, so Lydia had to wash her face in the kitchen sink. She was thorough. Scrubbed clean, she doubled back to the bedroom and reapplied her makeup, careful not to overdo it like an old lady. Then she went back to the mirror. Now, she didn't think, *Where did it all go?* Now, she thought, *Take no prisoners, bitch. Let's mingle.*

———

I showed up carrying a dozen daffodils wrapped in brown paper. Lydia was the first to spot me.

"Sam."

The tanning-booth tan threw me off. The last time I'd seen Lydia, six months ago in Dublin Prison, her skin had been rice white, the same rice white it'd been—with the exception of her fugitive year on the reservation—since my birth.

"Mom?"

"The flowers are sweet." Lydia swept the daffodils from my hand.

"They're not for—"

"Your hair is turning gray, Sam. I want you to run straight to Kmart and buy Grecian Formula."

"Is that what you did?"

She sniffed the flowers. "Daffodils are my favorites, next to orchids. Shannon."

Shannon came over from the dessert table, where she'd been talking to a white Rastafarian. I hadn't seen my daughter in almost as long as I hadn't seen my mother. Shannon looked grown up. I realized with some shock that if I were single and we weren't related, Shannon was probably too old for me to date.

Lydia said, "Shannon, be a dear and find these poor flowers some water."

Shannon smiled at me as she took the flowers. "Hi, Daddy." The hug was hampered by the daffodils, but it was still what I lived for.

"How you been?" I asked.

"Terrific."

"You're not bulimic, are you?"

"Daddy!"

"I can feel your bones."

Lydia said, "Stand up straight." Shannon stood straighter and decided her family was the most boorish bunch in America. There wasn't one thing they were incapable of saying.

Lydia went on. "Bulimic, my eye. Wouldn't hurt you a bit to lose ten pounds."

Maurey and Gilia walked up. Maurey's newly permed hair was piled up under a cowboy hat, and she wore a long-sleeved white shirt with a yoke. Gilia had Esther propped on one hip. "I think Shannon's weight is perfect," Gilia said. She passed Esther to me and took the daffodils from Shannon. "Thanks so much, Sam," she said. "You're a prince."

Maurey said, "If anything, five more pounds would make her look healthier."

Even at her strongest, Shannon could barely deal with a family gang-up. Right now, she'd been up since 4 a.m. Carolina time, flown on three airplanes, and been told her pussy stank. "Would you tactless wonders stop discussing my weight?"

"How's your sex life, then?" Maurey asked. "Still having that dry problem?"

Shannon fled for the house.

Lydia, meanwhile, had been eyeing the daffodils. She'd

known they weren't meant for her, but she was the guest of honor here. It was her Goddamn party.

"I think those are for me," she said to Gilia.

I did the only thing I could to keep the peace. I offered up my child. "Mom. Lydia. Meet your granddaughter Esther."

Lydia peered at Esther, who broke into a beatific smile.

"Wherever did you come up with that name?"

I said, "You like it?"

"It's Jewish."

Gilia almost bristled. "So."

"Only pretentious twits pretend to belong to ethnic groups they don't belong to. On the reservation, you couldn't turn over a rock without finding a pasty white girl calling herself Running Dove or Dances in Sunshine."

Lydia bent down for a closer look at Esther. I had been training Esther for this moment for three nights—hours after supper and during bath time. It was the moment I'd been planning since Esther's birth.

Esther said, "Yo, Grandma."

Lydia smiled. "She is charming. I can see the Callahan eyelash line."

Maurey made a sucking-air sound. "My God, you said something nice."

"I can say nice things if they're true."

"Prison softened you, Lydia."

"It did not. And don't for a second think I don't remember who finked to the Secret Service in the first place."

"I'd do it again in a heartbeat," Maurey said.

———

Lydia's first arrest was only for threatening the president's dog. She wrote Ronald Reagan a letter saying if he didn't appoint a woman attorney general, she would assassinate Rex. The

Secret Service called the local sheriff, who threw Lydia into the county jail for the weekend. Monday, they offered to release her on her own recognizance, but Lydia refused to leave, because the men's cell had color TV and the women's was black-and-white.

I bought the women a color TV—without Lydia's knowledge—she went home, and everyone but Lydia thought the incident had run its course. Unfortunately, Reagan, always the idiot, appointed a male attorney general. Lydia soaked a Ken-L Ration chew toy in Raid for two days, then sprinkled it with d-CON. She wrapped the poison chew toy in a Hershey's candy-bar wrapper with the ends stapled shut, bought a dog birthday card from the Hallmark store in Jackson, wrote a nice note explaining how this is a gift for Rex from the grateful American people, and FedExed the package to the White House.

Her mistake was she told Hank Elkrunner, who told Maurey Pierce, who telephoned the Secret Service. Even then, Lydia almost came away clean. Federal Express lost the package. Lydia took this as ineptitude, while I saw it as proof of God's existence. Whichever, the miracle lasted three months before the package was found holding up the short leg of a dispatcher's desk in Hannibal, Missouri. FedEx called to say the dispatcher was fired, Lydia's money would be returned, and the package would be delivered by three p.m.

Lydia and Hank disappeared by noon.

The ethical question discussed at family gatherings from North Carolina to Wyoming was: did Maurey do the right thing? Which led to the splinter question: would Lydia have been nailed anyway? The Reagans get a signed threat from GroVont, Wyoming, followed by an anonymous poison chew toy, also from GroVont, Wyoming. How much brains does it take? Lydia contends that without Maurey's warning, the White

House person in charge of gifts would have thrown the sticky chew toy in the trash. Shannon and Pud side with Maurey. As usual, I straddle the fence. I admit Lydia did an awful thing and deserved to be caught and punished. But she's my mom, for Chrissake. Nobody wants to see their mom in prison.

————

Over by the barbecue pit, a lively discussion broke out on how you tell if a hog is cooked. Words like *trichinosis* were being bandied about. And *New Age pansy*. I drifted from the potluck table—cheese pesto and red Jell-O with suspended cling peaches—to a table of open wine bottles. As I poured myself a glass of zinfandel, a woman standing next to me said, "Zinfandel doesn't go with pig."

She was early thirties, dressed in a bureaucratic sweater-skirt combination with open-toed, sensible shoes.

"Are you one of Lydia's authors?" I asked.

"What makes you think I might be?" Her hair was that unnatural copper-tubing color favored by Yankee women.

I said, "You're not."

"A second ago, you thought I was."

"An Oothoon Press author would have used *fuck* in the answer."

The woman studied her fingernails on the edge of her plastic cup. The nails were painted the color of liver.

"Fuck off, fuck no, or fuck you," I said. "Lydia's authors say *fuck* whenever they can. It's a sign of empowerment."

"You must think you're pretty empowered."

"Oh no. I never say *fuck* except when I'm quoting others. Lydia taught me the confident man doesn't have to curse."

"But the confident woman does?"

"That's how life works."

She sipped her own wine, which was close to the same shade as her fingernails. "You must be her son."

I held out his hand. "Sam Callahan."

"Brandy Epstein. I'm Lydia's parole officer."

"Oh."

"I hope you don't mind me joining the party. I came out to introduce myself and saw all these people here. The whole town must have come together to welcome your mother home."

"More like the whole state."

"She must be a revered personage."

I couldn't detect sarcasm, but you never know with women. "Would you like to meet her?"

"That's what I'm here for."

———

Brandy insisted we first check out the dessert table, which proved to be an excuse for her to snag a big piece of chocolate cake with chocolate icing. She ate as we made the rounds of the other tables, drink stations, and horseshoe pits and finally found Lydia in the side-yard parking lot, standing next to a mid-'60s GMC truck with two Indian teenagers. Lydia cradled a rifle in her hands; it appeared we'd walked in on negotiations.

"Sam," Lydia said. "Meet Terry and Little Jim. They're Hank's cousins, twice removed." Terry kept his eyes on the rifle, but Little Jim glared at me as if I were the icon of white impunity.

To put Little Jim at ease, I said, "Custer had it coming."

Lydia almost smiled. "Social faux pas. Little Jim's a Crow."

The significance of that slipped right over my head, but Brandy caught it. "The Crow were on Custer's side."

I said, "Oh."

Lydia rotated the rifle bolt and checked the lever action. "You don't see many of these," she said. "Remington center-fire pump action. Thirty-thirty. This should keep the peasants at bay."

Brandy said, "Firearms are off-limits to felons."

Lydia's face flared. "What the hell is it to you?"

I said, "Lydia, this is Brandy Epstein. She's your parole officer."

Lydia kind of shifted her weight back on her heels. She looked from Brandy to the rifle, then, casually as passing the salt, she tried to hand the rifle to Terry. Only he wouldn't take it. Terry was in no position to touch a rifle in front of a parole officer. The rifle hung there between them for a moment until Little Jim threw it into the truck.

He muttered, "White women."

Lydia said, "I hope you're not one of those live-and-die-by-the-book bureaucrats."

Brandy cupped her cake from the top and took a bite off the bottom. She seemed intent on either avoiding the icing or saving it for last. "I'm afraid I am."

Lydia flounced. "I've got better things to do than driving into Jackson once a week to put on a dog-and-pony show for you."

Brandy wiped a crumb from the edge of her lower lip. "I've got better things to do than watch your dog-and-pony show, Mrs. Elkrunner."

"The name is Callahan." Which wasn't always true. Lydia went by whichever name was convenient at the moment.

"I don't care what you call yourself," Brandy said, "but weekly contact is my job and part of your sentence."

"Why can't we ignore the unpleasant? I won't tell if you won't."

"Can't be done. I have to document your five hundred hours of community service."

"You're not going to hold me to that?"

"It's a condition of the parole."

Terry and Little Jim had disappeared. One moment they were flanking Lydia, and the next they were gone. Hank used to pull that stunt all the time, which led me to think it's an Indian skill.

Lydia twisted the GMC driver's side mirror to look at herself.

She bared her teeth, checking for bits between her incisors. "I'd hoped the community service was only a formality," she said. "Couldn't you write down that I was available to give advice for five hundred hours?"

Brandy finally went for the icing.

Lydia said, "If you want true community service, you'll help me get my press back in operation."

If there is one thing I delight in, it's watching women deal with each other. Any women are interesting, but the levels of complexity between heterosexual women go on forever. Sometimes I get so wrapped up in subtext, I miss the conversation.

"I have found something I think you'll enjoy," Brandy said.

"Not if the word *service* is involved."

"Oly Pedersen turns one hundred this August. The county library asked me to have someone make an oral history of his life and adventures. That sounds right up your alley."

A picture of Oly formed in my mind—huge Adam's apple, visible thyroid gland, spots on his forehead, hands you could see the veins through. He'd been ancient thirty years ago.

"I could have sworn Oly died," Lydia said.

"Nope." Brandy shoveled in the icing. "They're planning Oly Pedersen Day. He presents the town fathers the oral history, and they give him the key to GroVont. There'll be an old-timers' rodeo and fireworks."

Lydia sighed. "Don't you admire the Eskimo ritual of leaving their elderly behind on an ice flow. I always thought that was so poignant."

Brandy swallowed the last of her icing. "Did you bake this cake yourself?"

———

There aren't many advantages to traveling with three pregnant women and a baby, but one of them is you can beg out of social situations early, before cleanup. As the sun turned pink and dipped into Death Canyon, I said our good-byes, while Gilia rounded up the infanticipating charges.

I found Shannon talking to the white kid with Rastafarian hair. He called himself Chuck-O, had a spider tattoo crawling on his neck, and was one of those boys who shake hands with everyone they meet. He called me *sir* and said it was quite a thrill to meet me, because when he was little, he read all my novels. "You're the best, man. I used to model myself after Bucky Brooks."

I said, "I hate Bucky Brooks." The Rastafarian thought I was kidding.

"Chuck-O is going to teach me snowboarding this winter," Shannon said.

Lydia was explaining the federal prison system to three women from the Southern Baptist Golden Rule Club. They'd come out to invite Lydia to join the club but, after seeing her in person, changed their mind.

Lydia clamped a hand on my wrist and led me out of Golden Rule earshot. "Do you think Maurey was right?"

"Of course," I said. "About what?"

"That prison softened me. What if I've lost my anger, Sam?"

"Your anger is you, Lydia."

"I have always defined my self-image by my fire."

I could tell she was thinking about something. "What's the matter, Mom? You're home, out of prison. You should relax for a few days."

"I can't relax. That silly twit accused me of baking a cake."

"She's a parole officer. They're trained to deal with hard cases."

Lydia released my wrist and brushed the bangs off her forehead. "Maybe she's blind. Some blind people hide it real well."

"I don't think so."

"My greatest fear is I might lose my anger."

"I think you're safe on that one."

"Thank you, Sam."

———

I got into the van and buckled my seat belt. As Gilia shifted gears, she looked over at me and said, "You look like you've seen a ghost."

"Lydia said *thank you*."

Gilia put the van back in neutral. She turned to stare through the twilight at Lydia, who was teaching Roger the proper way to clean a spit. She had him stretched out over the cold coals with a sponge and wet rag.

Gilia looked back at me and smiled. "Don't worry. She didn't mean it."

4

MY WRITING CAREER STARTED IN THE FIELD OF YOUNG ADULT Sports Fiction. Mountain-climbing books. Not that I ever climbed a mountain myself, but no one expected Agatha Christie to murder people, I don't see why they would expect an author of mountain-climbing fiction to climb mountains.

I created the Bucky Brooks series—*Bucky Climbs the Matterhorn, Bucky on Half Dome*. You've probably heard of them. Bucky and his sidekick, Samantha Lindell, fight evil and wrong thinking while conquering the major peaks of the world. Only, I found Samantha more interesting than Bucky, so I finished the sixth book in the series by throwing Bucky off Mount Rainier. My editor wouldn't let me kill Bucky. She said it would traumatize introverted young adults, so I let Bucky go into a long, unrecorded career in wheelchair racing.

I left Young Adult Sports Fiction and moved on to a romance subgenre, technically known as *Plucky Women in Jeopardy*. I took on the pen name of Patrice Longfellow. Samantha and I had fun zipping her in and out of tight spots without breaking the primary rule of PWJ, which is the heroine has to save herself. No rescues by Prince Charming or any other male. The Patrice book wasn't very successful. My editor said I fudged on the sex scenes—cut straight from foreplay to breakfast. You can't do that in romance, even in the subgenres. Harlequins don't skip parts.

At the urging of my agent, I left *Plucky Women* for the *Moral Private Eye*. This is the man or woman with an amazingly strict personal code who never compromises an inch, no matter how vile the consequences. My private eye was RC Nash. Slimeball land developers cheated his family out of their Nevada ranch, driving his father to suicide and his mother to California. RC hitchhiked into Las Vegas and started wasting real estate agents—always in self-defense. After the first book—*Craps Is for Killers*—RC opened his own private investigator business, specializing in helping tourists swindled out of their nest eggs.

RC lived in a one-room trailer on the edge of the desert. He was a vegetarian and a chess master, and his girlfriend worked at a legal prostitution ranch thirty miles out toward the nuclear test range. Her name was Samantha Lindell. Whenever a mystery stumped RC, he drove his '57 Willys Jeep to the Spruce Goose Ranch and asked the hookers' advice. Because hookers are in touch with the dark underbelly of America, they almost always gave RC an insight that helped him solve the case.

That's the part that steamed Lydia.

"You're nothing but a man," she said.

"I resent that."

"You men writers all make up the same hookers—nice girls who just happen to turn tricks. The male idea of a whore is Julia Roberts in *Pretty Woman*."

"She seemed okay to me."

"Have you ever been with a real whore?"

"Mom."

"Have you had a single conversation with a real whore?"

"Maybe. I wasn't sure what she was."

"Your whores sit around the parlor discussing life like

they're at an existential Tupperware party. Prison is full of real whores, and they don't quote Hegel."

"Only one of my whores quotes Hegel."

"The hooker's heart of gold is a male fantasy. Ninety-five percent of all whores think men are scum."

"My stories are entertainment. They aren't supposed to reflect reality."

"Why write them then?"

I was carrying a plaster bust of Flannery O'Connor from my old room, through the living room, and out to the Madonnaville van. Lydia had telephoned at 7:30 that morning.

"I'm hauling this junk to the dump. If you want any of it, you better hurry."

"My good stuff?"

"I don't see anything worth holding a garage sale over."

So I jumped in the van and drove down to GroVont to save my prize possessions. Lydia stood in the living room, delivering comments on the quality of the goods.

"Gilia has appalling tastes," Lydia said. "Are you certain you want to be associated with her?" She said this while glaring at a *Cannery Row* movie poster—Debra Winger playing a hooker with a heart of gold.

"This is the stuff she wouldn't let me keep at home," I said.

"So you turned my house into a storage unit for the ugly?"

"I used the house as my in-town office. I wrote here."

"You wrote those books in my home?"

Which led to her literary criticism of the RC Nash legacy and male authors' shoddy treatment of prostitutes.

She said, "Not one woman on that ranch of yours is a lesbian or drug addict. The prototypical prostitute in your books is an art student from the Netherlands earning an honest living while exploring her creative potential."

The part of the discussion that floored me was that Lydia

had actually read the RC Nash books. "I can't believe you read me," I said.

"I read a lot in prison—every book written by anyone even vaguely connected to Jackson Hole, and after I exhausted the rest, I ended up on you. There wasn't that much else to do except pump iron and watch network television. Does Maurey still have that dumb boy at the ranch?"

The question went right over my head. "What?"

"The boy her friend Mary Beth dumped on her? She had an ex-husband or something named Freedom who got killed and his friends left the kid with her and she passed him along to Maurey."

"Roger?"

"I knew his story, but I forgot his name."

"Roger was at your coming-home party the other day. Remember the kid mopping the pig. Sleeveless cowboy shirt. Tie-dye bandanna he seems to sleep in."

Lydia didn't remember anyone mopping a pig at her party.

"Roger started talking again," I said. "Years ago."

Lydia's fingers kind of fluttered, as if brushing away a fly. "That's nice."

"Why are you asking about Roger?"

"I was just wondering what happened to him."

"Roger is okay. Maurey raised him. He works for me now, at the Home."

"I read a book about a traumatized child, and I couldn't help but wonder why I came out okay and so many others didn't."

"Maybe because you weren't traumatized."

Lydia's eyes focused somewhere else. "I thought I was, until I met the prostitutes in prison."

———

Lydia—in a powder blue jogging suit and red tennis shoes—drove to Haven House, where Teton County's oldest pioneer lives. Haven House is one of those new deals for senior citizens that's part apartment complex and part nursing home. Their stationery says INDEPENDENT LIVING IN A CONTROLLED ENVIRONMENT. There's a central cafeteria and rec room and a van that ferries the old-timers to the drugstore and post office, but they each have their own studio apartment where they can hang pictures on the wall and feel self-sufficient. It's like a college dorm without the keg.

Lydia found Ellis Gill standing on a chair in his office, pulling the clear plastic insulation sheets off the windows. Ellis wears socks that match his ties—in this case, green stripes—which you wouldn't normally notice unless you caught him standing on a chair.

"Spring is upon us," he said in explanation of his actions.

"Where's the old fossil?" Lydia asked.

Ellis's face went cloudy underneath his conspicuous whirl-pool comb-over. "We cannot approach our residents with that attitude, Mrs. Elkrunner. They can sense condescension, like dogs and children."

"First, it's not Mrs. Elkrunner. Marriage didn't change me."

Ellis came down off his chair and retreated behind his desk. Most bureaucrats feel a need to keep furniture between themselves and Lydia.

"Second," Lydia went on, "I'm here by court order, and I don't give one hoot whether Oly Pedersen senses condescension or not. As a matter of fact, I feel condescension and it would be less than honest to hide my true feelings."

Ellis stood awhile, as if adapting to something unpleasant. Then he reached over and pushed an intercom button. "Eden, come in here."

Yes, it was my Eden. The Madonnaville girls are urged to find jobs in the personal-service industry while they await labor. It acclimatizes them to the idea of putting someone else's comfort above their own.

Eden stuck her head in the door and looked from Ellis Gill to Lydia. She smiled at Lydia.

Lydia said, "You must be one of Sam's."

"I met you at the coming-home party."

"Has my son taught you that pregnancy is political? You think your condition is empowerment, but little do you know, it is the exact opposite."

Eden said, "I've never cared enough to vote."

Ellis averted a lengthy yet standard lecture by jumping into the conversation. "Eden, have you seen Oly since luncheon?"

Eden looked back at Ellis, no doubt wondering what kind of putz calls lunch *luncheon*. "He's playing Yahtzee with the Crone Patrol."

Now Ellis was concerned. Ellis's self-image is that of a man who puts out fires. "Didn't I make myself clear when it came to the subject of Yahtzee?'

Ellis charged out from behind the desk, past Eden, and through the door. Lydia followed, then Eden herself.

"He promised he wouldn't gamble," Eden said to Ellis's back.

Ellis turned on Lydia. "The loved ones have been complaining. Oly is hustling the other residents out of their spending money. Winnie Crawford's daughter complained quite bitterly. Said Winnie stole money from her purse to cover her Yahtzee losses."

"Oly promised he wouldn't gamble," Eden said again.

Ellis made a sound like *tut, tut* and headed down the hall. Just before they reached the rec room, he stopped for Lydia to catch up.

"Do you have your recording instruments with you?" he asked.

Lydia patted her leather purse, which was shaped like a woman's old-time sidesaddle.

"Mr. Pedersen tires easily," Gill said. "I'd appreciate it if you limit your interviews to an hour apiece."

"You think this will take more than an hour?" Lydia asked.

"He has ninety-nine years to cover."

"I know for a fact he hasn't done a thing the last thirty."

———

Oly sat at a card table, buck naked except for his tennis shoes. He stared at five dice—three twos, a six, and a five—and a Yahtzee sheet. The woman across from him was fully clothed, but the two at his sides were down to bras and panties. One of them wore an adult safety diaper. We're talking eighty, if they were a day.

Eden Rae said, "Yuck."

Ellis Gill said, "Mr. Pedersen."

"Oly's not near as good at strip Yahtzee as he was when we played for money," the dressed woman said in a New Orleans accent. Even seated, it was clear the woman was exceptionally short. "I wonder why that is?" Beside her on the floor, she had neatly stacked four or five sweaters, a couple of vests, and a pile of jewelry. She had come to the game prepared.

"Mr. Pedersen, you go too far." Ellis moved to cover the two women in bras and panties. The one wearing a diaper giggled, and the other looked sad.

"I wanted to age with dignity," the sad one said.

"Oh, Winnie, why?" the giggler said. "Elder dignity is just some idea young people made up so we'd stay quiet and out of the way."

Winnie pleaded with Ellis. "Don't tell my daughter-in-law. She'll send me to the nursing home in Pinedale." She looked more depressed than ever. "They don't have cable in Pinedale."

Throughout all this, Lydia stared at Oly, who, in turn, stared at the dice. At first, she thought he was catatonic. Lydia claims to be repulsed by flesh in general, but Oly was beyond repulsive. Except for some liver-colored discs on his face and the backs of his hands, he was the color of a filthy commode.

Loose skin hung from odd places, not just under his arms and chin. It was as if his skeleton had shrunk and left the skin to fend for itself.

A deep purple scar, like an implanted rope, snaked down his right thigh from crotch to knee. Another scar, this one black and thatched, ran across his left shoulder. He wore thick glasses and a hearing aid and there was a blue tattoo of a columbine on one hip. The balls had no hair, but thankfully, his penis had retreated from sight. Lydia had the sensation of standing before a skinned lizard.

Oly's eyelids blinked slowly behind the lenses of his glasses, and he turned his head to stare at Lydia. He said, "You're wearing my shoes."

Lydia looked down in horror. Oly was wearing red tennis shoes with untied laces, exactly like hers.

The clothed woman clamped a hand around Lydia's wrist.

"He's mine," the old lady whispered loudly. Hissed might better describe it. "Don't you get any notions."

"My God, what are you talking about?" Lydia asked.

"Oly. I know what you have in mind, and it won't pick cotton."

"Oly is ninety-nine years old."

The man in question had returned his attention to the Yahtzee dice, oblivious to anything that didn't fall into his immediate focus. The woman wearing clothes looked Lydia over with eyes recently released from cataracts.

She said, "You're no spring chicken, honey."

Lydia fled.

———

Monday was check-in-with-your-parole-officer day.

"Oly's waiting with his oral history," Brandy said. "You have to go back."

"Over your dead body."

"Murder is a revocable offense."

Lydia faced Brandy Epstein across a government-surplus laminated desk surrounded by government-surplus file cabinets. Brandy was wearing a forest green career-woman suit. Lydia wore cutoffs, a T-shirt, and clogs. The Isadora Duncan look had been temporarily abandoned.

Brandy rustled a form. "This is your needs-and-risks assessment. We use it to determine the level of control exercised upon a parolee. That's you."

"I'm not a child."

"Then don't act like one."

There was a tense moment of extended eye contact. Imagine two female praying mantises poised over the dying husk of a mutual lover.

Brandy said, "You can be placed in any of four categories, ranging from high, where we meet twice a week, and I observe while you urinate in a cup, to minimum, where you and I are virtual strangers."

"What hoops do I jump through to get minimum?"

"No hoops. You only have to cooperate on your community service assignment."

"But Oly is senile. He doesn't know what century he's in."

Brandy gave Lydia the parole officer's give-me-a-break look, which is much like Lydia's own give-me-a-break look, only more world-weary.

"I spoke to Oly Saturday. He's as alert as you are."

Lydia knew she'd been insulted, but for a change, she didn't trash-talk back. She'd met women like Brandy Epstein in the pen. They considered themselves tough broads and were basically unaffected by anything short of a chair up against the head.

"I don't like old people," Lydia said. "I wish old people would go away." She studied her fingernails in a moment of quiet self-examination. "It would be gratifying to load all these geezers onto a spaceship and blast them into orbit around some other planet."

"You know, you're getting fairly close to the senior demographic yourself," Brandy said.

"If one more person tells me that, I'm going to break a window."

Brandy put on her half-glasses with the cord connecting the earpieces. She picked up a three-ring binder and flipped pages. "Wee Ones Day Care needs a volunteer in diaper changing."

"I'd rather die."

Brandy turned to another page. "You know anything about pouring concrete?"

"Of course not."

"Then you must go back to Oly."

———

There was a mop bucket in the hall, and Ellis Gill raised his hand to touch Lydia's arm, to guide her around it. But he couldn't do it, and she knew he couldn't do it. She knew he had tried to touch her arm and failed, and that brought Lydia pleasure.

"Will you be staying for snack?" Ellis asked. "I'm sure some of the folks would like to meet you. It's not every day we're visited by a famous feminist."

"I won't be staying for snack."

Ellis's head bobbed up and down in acknowledgment. It's a strange head, shaped more like a little boy's, with rounded planes and no definition. Like a junior high yearbook photo with an old face.

"I hope you don't mind if Mrs. Dukakis is present during the interview. She insisted, and I just couldn't say no."

"I can."

"Mrs. Dukakis is Oly's special friend. We like to encourage our residents to have special friends. It gives them a feeling of youthful exuberance."

45

Lydia raised an eyebrow. "You mean she's his girlfriend?"

"That's what we would call it if they were younger. It's comparable to children pretending to go steady. We encourage it."

Lydia stopped and turned on Ellis. "What are you running here?"

His neck turned a purplish shade. "I beg your pardon?"

"You think because half of them wear diapers, you can treat them like toddlers."

"Why, no. Of course not."

Lydia stared a moment, then whirled and entered the solarium.

———

The solarium had originally been a sunroom full of plants, but they had some problems with allergies and one elderly woman who ate ferns, so the real plants had been replaced by fake ones. Because three walls were glass, the solarium stayed about ninety degrees, which was fine by the old-timers who'd lived through eighty Jackson Hole winters.

Oly sat rigid in a pink dining-room chair—that unnatural pink they paint the fingernails of department-store mannequins. He was wearing a long-sleeved white cowboy shirt buttoned all the way to his goiter, gray slacks, and sandals with black socks. A woman was pinching back buds on a fake wandering Jew. Lydia recognized her as the tiny crone with the New Orleans accent from the Yahtzee game. She was dressed for church—rayon dress, white gloves.

Ellis said, "Lydia, this is Irene Dukakis. I don't think you two were properly introduced the other day."

Irene said, "I'm watching you, missy."

Lydia ignored Irene. Instead she went about setting up the Radio Shack voice-activated tape recorder with the accessory microphone on a stand. Oly didn't blink or move his head in any way. There was some question of rigor mortis.

Ellis fussed over Irene. "No need to cut back the plants, Mrs. Dukakis. They're plastic."

"I know they're plastic. I'm not stupid, dear."

Lydia studied the mike setup and spoke without looking at Irene or Ellis. "Then why are you cutting them back?"

Irene lowered her white-gloved hands. "Because they're gangly."

"Does she have to be here?" Lydia asked, still without looking at anyone.

Irene walked over and sat next to Oly. "I'm his chaperone."

"Chaperone?"

Irene straightened Oly's silver and turquoise collar corners; it's hard to say if he noticed. She said, "I'm here to make certain Oly isn't abused. According to the *Phil Donahue Show*, there's more abuse in retirement homes than day-care centers."

Lydia stared at Oly, taking particular note of his goiter. "I wouldn't touch this man with latex gloves."

Oly's mouth worked like he was chewing. Then he croaked, "I was born in Dover, Delaware, in 1893."

"Hold on, hoss," Lydia said. "The tape's not rolling yet."

Oly returned to his catatonia imitation. Irene brought a Kleenex out of her bra strap and dabbed at a tiny bit of saliva in the corner of Oly's mouth.

She said, "Oly is the only eligible bachelor over eighty-five from here to the Montana border. All the women are after him."

"That's the saddest thing I ever heard," Lydia said.

"Unless you count Lumley McConnell, which I don't, because he hasn't bathed since his wife passed over."

Lydia leaned toward the microphone. "Testing, one, two, three, four, community service is a frigging bore."

Irene looked down at her white gloves. She seemed suddenly overcome by depression. "You read in *Redbook* about girls who are sexually active in their eighties and nineties, but what I don't understand is who they're sexually active with."

Lydia pressed a Rewind button, and the tape whirred, then she pushed Play. *"Testing, one, two, three, four, community service is a frigging bore."*

Ellis Gill said, "My presence is needed in the crafts room. I'll drop back by to check on you kids later."

Lydia said, "Whatever."

Oly did the chewing thing again and started over. "I was born in Dover, Delaware, in 1893."

"We don't need the filler material," Lydia said. "You should skip growing up and start when you first came to Teton County."

Oly's head slowly rotated, and he glared at Lydia, giving the effect of an irritated tortoise.

"Oly has it all straight in his head," Irene said. "He can't skip around."

"Jesus," Lydia said. "No one's interested in childhood memories."

"I was born in Dover, Delaware, in 1893."

"Jesus," Lydia said again as she hit the Record button.

5

I WAS BORN IN DOVER, DELAWARE, IN 1893, THE ONLY BEGOTTEN SON OF Jan and Portia Pedersen. My father was of the second generation out of Uppsala, Sweden, and my mama was of so many generations out of Bath, England, the family had lost track or wouldn't say. Suffice it that since well before the American Revolution, the Wiggins people had crouched flush up against the Atlantic Ocean, as far east as they could be and still not leave Delaware. They owned a company that made iron beds and tin chamber pots.

Granddad Wiggins viewed anyone who come to Delaware after his first ancestor as riffraff. And my father was the worst sort of riffraff, that is, the kind who marries Granddad Wiggins' daughter. I don't recall Mr. Wiggins except for his mutton-chop sideburns and irate eyebrows. Facial hair. I don't recall the man. Dad called him the Slop Bucket King.

Dad was a barber by trade, and a good one. After Mom and Dad had already been married some years, enough that I had come along, Mr. Wiggins formed a plan of arrogance and malice. He took it to mind to drive my father out of barbering and into the family business, never dreaming for a minute that my father might choose to leave Dover, and my mother might choose to go with him. No Wiggins in history had left Delaware, except to graduate from Dartmouth, which was fine, so long as they scampered home afterward. What the family forgot to reckon with was Jan and Portia were in romance love.

Mr. Wiggins convinced all those of his social set to take their tonsorial business elsewhere. His buds at the bank cut off Dad's credit, then called in his shop loan.

Therefore, on the century turning, Dad moved us to San Francisco. I do not know why he chose San Francisco. Maybe he read an article or maybe some ship's captain came back from California and told him of a barber shortage. Mama cried because she had to leave her piano, but myself, I was tickled pink. Young ones in Delaware wore knickers then, and I'd seen enough picture books to know cowboy youth did not wear no knickers. The general belief at the time being that folks west of Chicago had to be either cowboy or heathen. It didn't strike me to consider the Pacific Ocean had sailors, same as the Atlantic, and I knew nothing of miners or Chinamen.

We like to didn't make it West on account of old Mr. Wiggins told the state police my father had stolen bonds from his desk and a pair of gold cuff links. The police yanked us off the train in York, Pennsylvania. They put Dad through a hard time until they come to realize the throwdown—it was only a Delaware millionaire trying to impose his will. That disgusted the Pennsylvania police to the point where they apologized to Mama and gave me a sack of horehound drops and put us and our belongings on the next train to San Francisco.

We lived in a yellow house south of the slot there. We had a parlor with a three-piece furniture set upholstered in green plush. I used to love pushing my face into the plush. Dad rented a corner of the Oddfellow Building, where he barbered, only the Oddfellows called for a dime apiece off their haircuts, which was normal thirty-five cents. Shaves was fifteen cents. Dad got the idea to shave Chinamen's heads around the pigtail, which they referred to as a queue. He wanted to charge twenty-five cents, only the Oddfellows wouldn't let him. Oddfellows didn't like Chinese. When an Oddfellow rode his carriage down the street, if a Chinaman stepped in front, the Oddfellow would just as leave pretend not to see him and run him down. I saw it happen more than once. The Oddfellows didn't see me too good neither.

I liked the Chinamen 'cause they wore shiny pajamas outdoors and their talk was like birds. One time, my dad took me to a Chinese funeral parade. The deceased had been a general or somebody important and dignified, and these white policemen tied his queue to a hitch post and hit him with sticks. The Chinaman was so ashamed that white people had done this thing to him he went home and gassed himself from the light fixture. You cannot gas yourself from a light fixture now, but you could then.

They had a parade with just about all the important Chinese in San Francisco in it. Dad and I watched from the third-floor balcony of a hotel on Clay Street. Or maybe Dupont, I forget. Dad put me on his shoulders so I could see the thousands of Chinese all wearing white and carrying banners and riding horses. Some rode in cars. It was a big event to them.

Dad told me Chinese wear white for mourning instead of black like us because China is on the opposite side of the Earth and everything is backwards there. Up is down, and if you could read the letters on the banners they'd be backways. He said in is out, and I said what's that mean? He said if a Chinaman tells you he is going inside, it means he is going outside. And vice versa. I do not know where Mama was that day. I think she had a headache.

San Francisco was pert near paradise for a lad of ten to twelve. The streets were chaos, and I did enjoy my chaos. There were cable cars and horse cars and streetcars; automobiles started showing up in bunches, yet most folks still went by horse carriage, only they had no stop signs or stoplights or any of these modern rules the government imposes on road travel nowdays. Ever intersection was a test of wills. That's why so many, especially Chinamen and Indians, got run over. I saw a fat man in a white suit drive his carriage right over the top of a Mission Indian over to Market Street. He stopped his carriage and looked back and said, "At least it weren't nobody white."

The Indian's legs were broke, but he didn't show no pain. I don't what come of him.

Mama hated me running the streets, on account of the Chinese and Indians, but I never saw neither bunch hurt a soul. It was sailors you had to keep a lookout for. A bud of mine got shanghaied, hauled away and turned into a sailor against his desires. He was only eleven years old. It like to ruined his family.

I was supposed to be in school, but I didn't put much stock in it. There was too much excitement outside to study Latin and cipher. I only went to school when it was cold. For one thing, the teachers weren't hardly older than me, and half hadn't gone past eighth grade their own selves. They mostly read us *Uncle Tom's Cabin* and *Kidnapped* and drew pictures on the blackboard they copied from the science book. I liked the stories, but spelling and grammar are not my strong suits, and I didn't pay attention to science at all, which I'm glad for now, because fifty years after I left school, ever'thing they tried to teach me was proven wrong. Ever'thing children have been taught about science since the beginning of time has later proved false. There's no call to think today is different. We shouldn't even teach science since it's all gonna be wrong in fifty years.

After a bit, Dad told the Oddfellows to go to heck and moved his shop over to Kearny Street. I had a job sweeping the hair up each day at 5 p.m., but he didn't pay me nothing. Just made me work free.

At first, Mama liked being someplace where you were not judged by your last name, but then after a year or so, she didn't. It's hard when you have been important to not be important. She said the California fog smelled bad. So she would relax, Dad bought her a twelve-dollar fiddle and bow, and she took lessons from a man with the biggest mustache I ever saw. He would shout at Mama for playing the notes wrong. She wound up not relaxing after all.

April of '06, our lives changed between breaths. One breath we were this way and thought we always would be, and the very next breath we were more different than we ever thought possible. Change has come on me often like that. Maybe that is the main lesson I have learned in the last hundred years—it can all go to hell in a single breath.

I'd just woke up and was laying in bed, wishing I didn't have chores, when the earthquake struck. The house shook like a dog shaking a rag doll—side to side, up and down. This wasn't no rolling wave like I've heard earthquakes described since. It was a thorough shake. I held the bed with both hands to keep from being flung out, and listened to the dishes and knickknacks break. Pictures jumped off the walls. Plaster fell from the ceiling, making it quite a problem to breathe.

As soon as it stopped, I ran into Dad and Mama's room. Dad was somewhat composed, considering, but Mama was pale and could not catch her breath. I went to find her a cup of water, but all the cups was broke, so I filled a Ball jar and took it in. I didn't tell her the cups was broke. When she got her breath she took to crying and could not stop.

There was enough gas left in the pipes to make a pot of coffee, which Dad and me drank from jars, then we went out to see the street. Our block wasn't so bad except for windows and a chimney or two had fallen. But when we looked away downtown to see where City Hall was you could see right through it. The sun was bright red, red as fresh blood from all the dust and smoke in the air. A big fire was blazing downtown, and our neighbor said Alameda had fell into the ocean. I don't know how he knew that, but it turned out not true.

The fire grew, even as we stood in the street watching. All those gas light fixtures in the hotels had broke loose in the earthquake and then blew up. People were coming in a steady stream, leaving the fire district with trunks and blankets and what food they could find, making for the hills. Even the smallest of children carried bundles.

Little quakes kept up as the morning passed, so no one wanted to stay indoors. Dad and me took Mama to a park and found some women she knew. We left her there wrapped in a blanket. Dad wanted to see to the barbershop, and I wanted to see the fire, though I didn't say so out loud. The streetcars hadn't run, and it took a long while to walk to the business district, on account of waves of people coming at us. A number of the flee-ers was carrying talking machines. Phonographs. That seemed the possession they chose to save first, except some women who had ironing boards and irons.

The closer we came to downtown, the more glass was broke. Whole buildings lay on their sides, and some had fell into their own basements. Mission Street was in flames. We passed the Oddfellow Building, and it was all gone. I found out later some Oddfellows had been asleep in the rooms upstairs and they all expired. I wasn't sorry about that.

When we reached the barbershop, the fire was almost to Kearny Street. The keyhole was too hot to put the key into, and

Dad and me were so worked up over the flames that at first we didn't notice the glass window was gone, so we needn't use the door, anyway. We went in to save what we could. Dad got his clippers. There was no time to move the cash register or barber chair. I grabbed one bottle of hair tonic, and we ran.

Later, we went up on a hill and watched the barbershop burn.

———

The fires went two days. They stopped three blocks short of our yellow house, so we were spared much of the pain that befell others. If we had lived up by the Oddfellow Building, I guess I would have died when I was twelve, and the rest of my life would have been somebody else's dream.

———

After the earthquake, Mom wouldn't stay in California. She wouldn't go in a building or stand at the bottom of a slope. She didn't sleep at all. We were on our way back to Delaware, where Dad was supposed to stop the barber life and go into furniture, but in Billings, Montana, life changed—once more in a single breath. We got off the train to overnight in the Shamrock Hotel, and Mama was killed by a boiler blew up in the middle of the night. Dad and me was thrown clear, or we'd of been killed too. I landed on a porch of 139 Imeson Avenue, which was across two streets from the hotel.

"Hold on," Lydia said. "You flew two blocks and landed on a front porch?"

Oly rotated his head and glared at Lydia, who said, "You expect us to believe that drivel?"

"Let him tell the story," Irene Dukakis said.

"It's a waste of my time if he's going to lie."

"Oly doesn't lie," Irene said.

Oly blinked slowly, cleared his throat with a disgusting rattle, and started over. "I was born in Dover, Delaware, in 1893."

Lydia panicked. "Wait! Stop! You already said that part."

Irene straightened Oly's already straight collar. "If you interrupt, he'll lose his place and have to go back to the beginning."

"Wait a minute." Lydia hit Rewind, then Stop, then Play.

> Dad and me was thrown clear, or we'd of been killed too. I landed on a porch of 139 Imeson Avenue, which was across two streets from the hotel.

Lydia punched Stop again. She and Irene both looked at Oly. Would he recapture the moment? Oly blinked again and gave a half nod. He cleared his throat once more.

> I landed on the front porch of 139 Imeson Avenue, which was across two streets from the hotel. That is how I come to meet the Coxes.

Lydia's sigh at this point is quite clear on the tape.

> Mrs. Cox walked out on the porch and found me laying there with a broke leg and she said, "What are you doing on my porch?" and I said, "I don't know, ma'am, I was asleep," and she hit me with a broom.
>
> Mr. Cox come out and said, "Can't you see the boy is hurt?"
>
> Mrs. Cox said, "That's no excuse for calling without an invitation."
>
> They took me into the parlor and laid me out on a red velvet sofa and gave me lemonade sweetened with molasses. My leg was hurting pretty good and I'd hit my head on the porch railing, so when Mr. Cox suggested a doctor be sent for I said okay.
>
> Only the Billings doctors was busy taking care of those in the explosion, especially those that were expired such as Mom, so no

one got time to treat me till the next morning. My head ached to the extent where it affected my vision. Mr. Cox had me drink a little laudanum that he'd bought from the Chinese for emergencies—which is somewhat a coincidence, considering how Dad turned out later—and I spent most of the afternoon and evening either asleep or incoherent, I'm not certain which. I dreamed Mom was fixing a breakfast of slab ham and coffee, with her hair up on her head held in place by two chopstick-looking sticks. She smiled in my direction.

Later that night, I come to with a wet cloth over my eyes and a girl of no more than eight years setting next to me on the divan reading a Monkey Ward Wish Book. After she took the cloth off my eyes, she showed me a drawing of a ribbon there on the page.

"What do you think?" she asked. "Would it look pretty next to my hair?"

I said, "Has anyone seen my folks?"

"I imagine they're blown up with the hotel. What's your name?"

She had freckles and tiny teeth. Eighty-seven years later, I still can call up a picture of those tiny teeth.

I said, "I don't recall."

She laughed like this was queer, which I guess it was, for a person not to know their own name, but I took offense anyway. I said, "You fly through the air and land on your head and leg and see how much you remember."

She said, "I wouldn't forget my own name," and I said, "Which is?" That's when she told me: "Agatha Ann Cox."

"Is this your family's house?"

"All except Bill, he went south to be a cowboy."

I wondered if I was supposed to know who Bill was. When a person is incoherent, they can be told things that later they don't recall.

Real solemn-like, she said, "My father is Mr. Cox."

I didn't know what to say to that, and talk hurt my head, so I didn't give a rejoinder.

She went on anyhow. "Mr. Cox owns the bank downtown. He takes care of the money."

"You think he might give me some?"

She screwed her mouth up like she was considering the proposition. "I don't know," she said. "I'll ask him. There might be a thousand or so laying around with nobody's name to it."

I said, "I'd appreciate that."

———

Mr. Cox found Dad at the Saint Vincent Hospital where the Sisters of Charity had taken Mom and the others. Three or so bodies had been scorched to the condition you couldn't recognize who they'd been, and Dad thought one of these was me, so when Mr. Cox told him of my whereabouts, Dad was greatly relieved. I heard later he cried and made a scene to the point where the other bereaved were not comfortable.

They brought Dad to the Coxes', where I was sitting up on the divan eating breakfast with Agatha and Mrs. Cox. It was only oatmeal. There wasn't coffee on account of the Coxes being Anabaptists. Dad's pupils were tiny pushpin prick holes, and his fingers trembled when he hugged me. I would normally be made sheepish to have him hug me in front of the Cox women, but this time I didn't mind much. After all, Mom was dead, and he'd thought I was along with her.

He said, "Your mama didn't suffer." I don't know how he knew this. Or even why it mattered so much to him. She was dead either way. A big lead mirror frame had fallen across her and broke her neck in half. He said, "She never even woke up."

I said, "That's for the best," because I knew he wanted me to say so.

I felt real bad about Mom being dead and all, but more for

me than her. She was too scared of life to enjoy it. When you wake up each day fully expecting to be killed, the coming to pass finally is a relief.

While we talked, the doctor appeared on the Coxes' front porch. Billings had three regular doctors, a female doctor, and a Chinese fella did medicine with needles. Dr. Harriet Clarke, the female, had eyebrows you could clean a chimney with. She'd been awake since the explosion the morning before and had performed several amputations since breakfast, so she didn't waste no bedside sympathy on a boy with a broke leg.

She set it quick. There was a flash of white pain, then I was okay. For my concussion she rubbed my skull with a liniment made from ammonia, prairie-chicken eggs, and a pair of secret ingredients. It was white, kind of like milk of magnesia, and smelled of sulfur. Whatever the secret ingredients were must of done the trick, because my head pain fled and I could see normal again.

Before Dr. Harriet took her leave, she said to Dad, "You'd better lay off the stuff."

Dad said, "I lost my wife Portia," and Dr. Harriet answered with, "That's reason enough today, but this boy will need tending tomorrow."

I did not know then, but the cause for Dad's pupils being pushpin prick holes was opium. To this day, I suspect he'd discovered opium in San Francisco, which is why he knew so much about Chinatown and the Chinese ways. Whenever he started doesn't matter so much. The truth is, my father became an addict, just as bad as any in a magazine. I think the grief drove him so he didn't want to feel or think straight ever again. That was his choice. I do not wish to speak poorly of my dad, but, so far as living goes, his life ended with Mama's.

In that deep, dark place that Mary Beth alternately *thought of as her guts or her heart, she never truly believed Leroy was dead. Everyone from the days when she'd been with him said he was dead. A man named Dolf told her he saw Leroy's body, riddled with bullets, every bone in his right hand broken. Dolf said the Colombian cartel threw Freedom into a village well, in hopes the rotting decay would make the peasants sick.*

"If he was so riddled with bullets, how could you tell it was him?" Mary Beth asked.

"The tattoo on his chest. Only one man in the world has that tattoo."

Mary Beth nodded her agreement, but in her dark place, she knew better. Some people don't die. Like Elvis or Jesus. Or more like Butch Cassidy. Exactly like Butch Cassidy, because they both of them went to South America to get killed—or not killed—when it could just as easily have happened at home.

Over the years, she moved from Boulder to Telluride and on to Houston. In Houston, she married Lonnie Bath. They moved to Santa Fe, where Jazmine was born, followed eighteen months later by Meadow. Mary Beth found a good job as a chiropractor's receptionist; Lonnie went into construction. And every day of the journey, she expected Leroy to walk through the door and claim her as his own. She didn't speak of him to anyone, not even Lonnie, and the few friends she kept up with from the freak days didn't say a word about the possibility, but Mary Beth knew—her happiness was an illusion. It was temporary.

She refused to buy more than one roll of toilet paper at a time, and her family made do with the travel-sized tube of toothpaste. She never subscribed to a magazine, always paid full newsstand prices. Mary Beth knew better than to tempt God. She knew that if she took the future for granted, Leroy would rise from the dead and bite her.

And then, one day, he did.

She was driving home from the Suds'n'Duds Laundromat, where she'd washed eight loads, an entire week's worth of clothes in a single organized attack involving almost one hundred quarters. Meadow was strapped in the back, sleeping, Jazmine sat in the front seat next to Mary Beth, jabbering about a boy at her day care who could eat Play-Doh.

"It turns his poop blue," Jazmine said.

"If your poop came out blue, I'd rush you to the emergency room and have you irrigated," Mary Beth said.

"What's irrigated feel like?"

"You won't like it."

And there he was, leaning against a stoplight with his hands in his pockets, his back slouched as if he had no intention of crossing the street, even if the light did change. He'd lost weight, his head had been shaved in the last couple of months—when Mary Beth knew him he'd had hippie hair—his face had more pockmarks, and his nose had obviously been broken since she had last seen him, but Mary Beth didn't have a doubt. It was Leroy.

She instinctively ducked an inch, but it was too late. He'd seen her the moment she saw him. Their eyes locked as Mary Beth's car glided through the intersection. Leroy didn't move; his face gave no sign that he recognized her.

"Mom!"

"What?"

Mary Beth saw the bread truck a moment before it was too late. She swerved hard right and hit a parking meter. Both girls broke into loud tears. A man ran from a computer store toward her car. Steam hissed from under the hood. Mary Beth twisted in her seat and looked back at the intersection, but Leroy had disappeared, as if he'd never been there. But he had been there. It was Leroy, and he wasn't dead.

6

"ROGER, YOU MUST KNOW MORE THIRD-TRIMESTER POSITIONS than anyone else on the planet," Eden Rae O'Connor said to Roger Talbot.

"I've never been with a girl who wasn't pregnant."

"You should write a book."

At the moment, Eden's third-trimester position involved a buck-and-rail fence and two pails. Roger stood behind Eden, counting the various tints of pink in the sunset as five Canada geese flew in single wing formation from the ridge behind Grizzly Lake. Snow on the Sleeping Indian gave off a nice watermelon glow, more from within than any reflection of sunlight. The Sonny Rollins soundtrack to the movie *Alfie* played in Roger's head—fourth track, the tune where Kenny Burrell lays down the guitar equivalent of a waterfall.

"Oh my *God*," Eden squealed. "Just as I gazzed, the baby jumped up and kicked."

"Are you sure you know what an orgasm is? Nobody comes that quick."

"Back up. I think the baby is trying to tell me something."

"But I haven't squirted yet."

Eden stepped off the pails and lowered her skirt. "Don't be selfish, Roger. The baby is more important than your off."

"Wasn't more important than yours."

Eden turned and sat on the middle rail of the fence, with her forearms propped across her great belly. "We'll bonk again in a minute. Maybe it'll make me go into labor."

Roger pulled his jeans up from his packer boots and tried to button his fly, but it wasn't comfortable. "You want to go into labor this early?"

"I love you dearly, Roger, but all I want right now is to have this baby, give it away, and go home to Pasadena."

Later on, as they walked across the west pasture back toward Roger's cabin, she entwined her fingers in his free hand. Roger liked this. He wasn't used to much display of affection after the fact.

Eden said, "You know when we're doing it, do you feel any emotions?"

Roger considered the question. "Do you want me to?"

"I was just wondering what you feel while we're scrogging."

"I felt peaceful back there. The sky was a pretty color, and you're easy to be with. So I would say I felt comfortable."

"That's nice. I'd rather you be comfortable than any of that other emotional gunk boys talk about after they get off." They walked on across the sagebrush. Eden held her belly with her left hand and Roger with her right. "Honor told me that when you first came here, you couldn't talk."

An owl hooted down by the river. Roger thought it was a female barn owl, but he wasn't sure. Owls had never been his strong suit.

"Is that true?" Eden asked.

Roger pulled his tie-dyed bandanna low over his eyebrows. It gave him the look of a Grateful Dead roadie. "I wish Honor was the one who can't talk."

"Was it you couldn't, or you wouldn't?"

"Didn't seem much difference, at the time."

"Why did you stop talking?"

Roger thought before he answered. He liked Eden and

didn't want to fall back on the quick, smart-aleck answers he usually gave such questions. "As I understand the deep mental crap, if I knew why I quit, I wouldn't have quit."

"How long did you go without talking?"

He shrugged.

"You can't remember?"

"Nope. Don't want to either."

She stopped and looked at him. Most late-pregnancy teenagers can't see beyond their own bodies. Roger had the feeling that six months after they went home, not one in ten even remembered what he looked like. But now, in the soft evening alpenglow, Eden was staring right at him. "I'll bet you had something God-awful terrible happen in your past, made you forget and stop talking."

"No shit, Sherlock." Roger walked on, immediately regretting his words. I once told him that being flippant is how men sidestep intimacy. If Roger had a tragic flaw, it was his innate talent for sidestepping intimacy. He had recently promised me he would never answer a sincere woman's question glibly, yet here, the first test out, he'd failed. God knows with girls sincerity is hard, but you've got to try.

Eden hurried to catch up. "Don't you want to know what it is?"

"I hadn't thought about it one way or the other."

"How could you not think about it?"

"There's a reason people forget terrible things. If everybody remembered every detail about their past, the whole world would go insane."

"But what if you're Princess Di's illegitimate son, given up at birth the way I'm giving up my baby? Or you're the next Dalai Lama?"

"If I was the next Dalai Lama some monk from Tibet would drive up the river and tell me."

"I know!" Eden's face lit up like the watermelon snow on the Sleeping Indian. "You witnessed a grisly murder, and the murderer is someone famous who's been on TV, and unless you remember, he'll get away scot-free. Only he knows you know, and when you remember, his goose will be cooked, so he's hired a band of private detectives to search the countryside, and when they find you, he'll slit your throat."

Roger smiled, which wasn't something he did on a regular basis. "Your story makes as much sense as any of the others I've dreamed up."

"Why did you start talking again?"

"Don't know that either." Roger stopped to hang the pails on the side of the snowmobile shed. "Yes, I do. At supper one night, I wanted cornbread, and Auburn was whining about hockey or something, and Maurey wasn't paying any attention, so I thought to myself, this pointing-and-signing stuff is stupid.

"Is that when you started talking?"

"I said, 'Please pass the fucking cornbread.'"

Eden's right hand went to her mouth. "What'd your family do?"

"They passed the fucking cornbread."

———

Roger and I had spent a lot of time together recently, discussing what life means and which parts matter and which don't. I firmly believe lying to women is the same as lying to God—or the Great Whatever. I believed that then, and I still do. If this is true, Roger was lying to God when he told Eden he never thought about what had made him stop talking. Some days he didn't think about it so much, but other times it was practically all he thought about.

Somewhere back in his childhood, he had been royally gypped—screwed out of eleven or twelve years of memories. He'd read enough books and seen enough movies to know you don't simply lose those years; they exist somewhere, sealed in by scar tissue. But repressed-memory retrieval scared the beJesus out of Roger. He'd researched it. He knew when people did remember lost childhoods, the memories could not be trusted. These days thousands of wanna-be victims were clearly recalling horrible Satanic cults and baby sex-abuse experiences that hadn't happened at all but were remembered anyway. What was the point of remembering unless you knew for certain the memory was true?

Not remembering held its own anxieties. On Maurey and Pud's satellite television, he saw a movie called *Sybil*. It starred Sally Field as a girl with seventeen or eighteen personalities, and some of them didn't like each other. The real Sybil would disappear for long periods of time while other girls with names like Erica or Judy lived in her body. For months after he saw the movie, Roger walked around expecting to turn into someone else. He imagined a jock named Bubba Joe would take over his body. Bubba Joe hated Roger and would try to kick him out of himself. Roger had trouble relaxing.

Then, last winter, the dreams began. They weren't specific dreams; he wasn't tied to the piano till he peed his pants the way Sally Field was. They were feelings dreams. Dreams where he was terrified and trapped. Great weights on his third-eye dreams. Or the rush of a roller-coaster drop. Flying a thousand miles an hour through space with no one to hold him.

By Easter, there was a man in his dream. A true villain with bad teeth, cracked lips, and a smell of rubbing alcohol. The man didn't do anything; he just stood too close. Roger knew not to move when the man looked at him. He knew the pain was real. Roger woke up from the man dreams quivering, soaked in sweat, blood gushing from his nostrils like his brain had been skewered.

Smells triggered the dream feeling, even when he was

awake. A blown-out match gave him a Freon feeling in his spine and stomach. Intense and terrific sadness. A dry well on the steam table at Dot's Dine Out sent him into two days of spinning suicidal remorse. Suicide was the concrete fear. He was afraid he wasn't the one in control of the question; that Bubba Joe or the dream man might make him do things he didn't want to do. He was afraid if he remembered, he might go back to wherever he had come from.

———

I know all this because he talked to me about it. "Do you think it's possible that a person can lose control over what they do?" Roger asked.

I tried to come up with the answer least likely to screw him up, and couldn't, so I fell back on the truth. "I suppose so. Last summer, I lost my temper and rammed a pickup truck that went straight from a left-turn-only lane."

"I mean more along the lines of having an alien take control of your body."

One thing you have to give me is I always take whatever people say seriously. Others ignore the bizarre statement. Not me. "Like that guy in New York who said his dog made him murder random strangers?"

"The Son of Sam."

"You can't blame me for that one."

"I'm wondering if irresistible acts are truly irresistible."

I nodded. "You're talking suicide."

Roger pulled his bandanna down over his eyebrows.

I said, "A clinically depressed person might think he has no choice in the matter, but he does."

"I'm thinking of the shattered personality."

"You saw *Three Faces of Eve*."

"*Sybil*."

We were drinking brandy and coffee in Roger's cabin. I came up whenever the pressure of living with a pack of females got to be too much. About once a day.

I said, "You're afraid you might kill yourself?"

Roger crossed the room to put another stick in the woodstove. "I worry about psychological clutter making me do stuff I don't want to do."

"I could ask Shannon. She studied this in college."

"Don't ask Shannon."

"She had a job at a mental hospital once. Nurse's aide to the catatonics."

"I wish you wouldn't talk about me to Shannon."

"I'd think you'd want expert advice if you're really worried about losing control of yourself."

"Nurse's aide to catatonics doesn't make Shannon an expert on suicide."

———

On account of the not-talking thing and general spookiness, Maurey kept Roger out at the ranch his first year in Wyoming, so when he finally started GroVont Middle School he was older than the other kids in his class. He followed a year behind Auburn at Jackson Hole High. They rarely spoke to each other at school. Auburn was popular with the football and hockey crowd, while Roger kept to himself. Roger knew he embarrassed Auburn, and at first he enjoyed causing embarrassment, but soon the thrill wore off. Auburn's senior year, the boys treated each other like the Hong Kong flu.

Auburn graduated and went on to the university at Laramie. Roger graduated and went back up the river. He wasn't ready to take on the wide world quite yet, but he was also sick of feeding horses at 5 a.m. in below-zero weather. The only nonranch work on the upper Gros Ventre River was my Virgin

Birth Home for Unwed Mothers at what had been the Bar Double R, a mile and a half upstream from the TM.

I had been bungling along, doing my own maintenance, and it was only dumb luck I hadn't burned the place down. Gilia wasn't any better. While she was brilliant when it came to decorating the lodge, if the generator went down, she was no more competent than me or the pregnant girls. Roger spent his post-graduation summer building himself a one-room cabin a couple hundred yards up the creek from the unwed mothers' compound and moved in.

He liked it there, alone, with his jazz CDs, his woodstove, and my books. It was the ideal situation for a kid who wanted to avoid pavement.

Roger soon discovered his job came with perks. Virgin Birth housed from two to maybe six pregnant girls at a time. Some had babies, and some had abortions. A girl leaning toward an abortion was not roomed with a girl leaning toward having the baby. It might cause sadness. Most of the girls were sad, anyway, and some were flat miserable. Some cried for six months, until Roger thought the baby would grow up split, like Sybil. A few of the girls—at least one in each batch—had led creative, active sex lives before pregnancy and were in no rush to give it up. Since I practice monogamy with Gilia—we should stress that fact—by default, Roger became alpha male of the compound.

It started less than a month after Roger moved upriver. He'd been working on the kitchen-stove vents all afternoon, and in the evening, he took a shower in the main house, then walked to his cabin and built a fire in the woodstove. Brother Jack McDuff wailed on the CD player. Pud had given Roger a left-handed Orfeus bass guitar for a graduation present. He'd set up a music stand to hold his book so he could pluck his bass and read at the same time. He was reading a novel he'd borrowed from me called *The Moviegoer* by Walker Percy. I collect books and have a huge library, but I haven't read 10 percent of the books I own. I want them there on the shelves in case the road avalanches and I'm stuck at home for two decades. Roger read more of my books than I did. Fresh out of high school, Roger's ambition in life was to sit by the stove, playing jazz bass lines and reading.

The Moviegoer was quite a good book, and Roger was as at peace as Roger ever got, when his door opened and Coffee Kennedy slipped in.

She said, "We need to talk."

Roger said, "What about?"

Coffee was from New Mexico and pregnant with her second child. Her mother was raising the first, with no intention of taking on number two, so Coffee had been shipped to the Home. Coffee's problem was she loved sex more than responsibility. Some people do. When Coffee slipped through Roger's door, she was a woman on a mission.

The second girl didn't even want copulation. Amelia said, "I can't sleep. I haven't slept in a week."

"What can I do to help?" Roger asked.

"Hold me."

Roger stayed awake, holding Amelia all night while she slept with the innocence of a child. His arm was dead as day-old hamburger by morning, but Roger didn't care. He'd had sex with a girl before; he'd never seen one sleep.

Tammy Lynn was eight months along and had a secret horseback fetish. When Tammy Lynn yelled, "*Heigh-ho, Silver!*" Roger fell off the back of Debra Winger, who stampeded across the field with the naked Tammy Lynn hanging on and laughing like a hysteria patient at a state mental institution.

Roger didn't mind the girls sneaking into his cabin in the middle of the night. He looked forward to it. The girls who came after him were experienced, yet young and nimble. Since they were already pregnant and had been tested for disease, there were none of the usual fears that go with teen coupling. Roger was in the unique position—sex without consequences.

In May, Roger decided he needed even more privacy, so he built an outhouse down the hill from his cabin, away from the creek. The outhouse itself was no problem for a man with tools and know-how, but the outhouse hole was a different matter. It doesn't take know-how to dig a hole on the upper Gros Ventre; it takes a strong fool with time on his hands. The site Roger chose was three inches of red dirt over a mountain of cobbled rocks put in place by glaciers and packed down by a million years of gravity.

Ten hours of pouring sweat in the high-altitude sun got Roger blisters on both hands and a four-foot hole in the ground, which was nowhere near deep enough for an outhouse. The next day he found an iron bar—called a pig sticker—in the toolshed and proceeded to smash the rocks rather than dig around them. At five feet, a salamander popped out of the hard-pack wall and fell down the back of Roger's jeans. That brought him out of the hole in a hurry. He danced on the slag pile as the salamander slid down his leg and out the bottom where Roger stomped it.

The stomp came before thought, and Roger immediately regretted his action. He stood, hands on hips, unblinking, staring down at the squashed salamander. It had happened so quickly. Roger didn't even remember jumping out of the pit. One moment he had a squirming *thing* in his jeans, and the next it was dead in the dirt. Roger's boot print was impressed on the ground around the salamander with a little moon of waffle track on the head. The body looked plump and alive, but the head was flat as corrugated cardboard.

Roger picked up a baseball-sized rock and threw it hard as he could into the hole in disgust. He sat on the dirt pile, his hands now fists. The problem wasn't so much that he killed the salamander—he hated killing animals, but you don't grow up on a ranch without knowing how. The revulsion came from how quickly he'd killed. He'd had no time to choose. No premeditation. The deed had been beyond his control.

———

I found Roger sitting in the same spot on the dirt pile, only by the time I arrived, he'd buried the salamander and set up a cross made from chinking slats held together by a leather shoelace cord. Roger's lips were moving, and as I leaned closer, I heard him whispering the poem that starts, "*Now I lay me down to sleep.*"

"Odd choice of funeral prayer," I said.

"*Amen.*" He glanced my way. "It's the only prayer I know. Maurey taught it to me, back years ago when I used to have bedtime terrors."

"You still have bedtime terrors."

He nodded, more to himself than me. "I never like the 'If I should die before I wake, I pray the Lord my soul to take' part. Seems against the point of calming the child down to remind him every night that he might die in his sleep."

I knelt to inspect how he'd tied the cord around the knot. A Boy Scout couldn't have done better, but Roger had never been social enough to join Boy Scouts. "What was it?" I asked.

Twin tear tracks ran from the corners of Roger's eyes, leaving worm-like trails in the dust on his face. "Salamander. Did you know they live underground? No light, no tunnel, I can't figure out how he came to be where he was."

"Did he have a name?"

Roger gave me a look to see if I was teasing. Of course I

wasn't. I don't tease. "Not that I know of. He only lived a couple seconds after I freed him."

"Then tell me this. Why are you so upset over the death of a salamander? Random animal empathy is fine, but if taken to extremes, it makes trivial the emotion you might need later when something personally tragic happens."

Roger blinked twice and leaned over to pick up the shovel he'd used in the burial. "I killed it before I thought about killing it." He paused, deciding how far he could go with frankness. "What if I'm built for violence? I don't know my birth parents. They could be serial killers. God knows that would explain a lot."

"Such as not talking, and the nightmares."

"And killing helpless animals."

———

We observed a minute of silence. Roger had always been somber, fairly detached, but he'd never come across as sad. He struck me as more consciously flat. A kid who played bass guitar alone. I knew there was something I should be saying—"You're not bred to kill" or "Let a smile be your umbrella." Everything I could think of came across as fatuous nonsense. He was right. A kid doesn't stop speaking without a violent reason. The odds were high that he had been spawned from a bad seed. That didn't mean he was doomed to badness. Where would I be if I bought the heredity-forms-us line?

So I said what I'd walked up the hill to say in the first place. "You know my mother, Lydia?"

Roger's tore his eyes from the salamander grave. It turned out I'd said the right words to get him to move on. For most terrible thoughts, distraction beats introspection every time.

"We haven't been introduced exactly. At the barbecue, she

told me I was cooking with a dirty bandanna on my head, that I should show more pride in my appearance."

"That's Lydia."

I stood and dusted dirt off my hands. "Lydia got pulled over Friday for not having brake lights."

"That's happened to me twice."

"She refuses to get them fixed because it would be giving other drivers too much information."

Roger said, "My fuse went out."

"Yeah, well, Lydia's driver's license expired six years ago."

"Isn't she on parole?"

I leaned over to check the outhouse hole. It needed more depth. "Now she can't drive, and she's supposed to go down to Haven House this afternoon to record the oral history of this old-timer. He's turning a hundred in August, and everyone expects him to die right after that, so they're in a hurry."

"Your mother should apply for a new license."

"That's what I said. In the meantime, she wants you to drive her to the interview."

Roger looked over. "Why me?"

"You'll get along better with Lydia if you don't use the word *why*."

"But she said my name? She said, 'Get Roger'?"

I nodded again. "Sort of. I offered to come give her a ride, and she said to send the boy Maurey took in, the one who couldn't talk when she lived here before."

"I'll have to clean up first. You want to finish my hole?"

I said, "The Earth will fill it back up in a few thousand years. I can't see the point in digging a hole just to have it filled in again."

Roger said, "It's for my crap."

Roger owned a '79 Datsun pickup truck he paid thirty-five dollars for, even though it wasn't worth that much. He called the truck Cindy and Cindy should have been ranch-bound. She wasn't the sort you would take on asphalt if you had a choice. Lydia answered the door, barefoot, with her head cocked to the side as she slid a silver hoop into her right ear.

She saw Cindy out by the mailbox and said, "We'll take my car." Her BMW was actually older than Cindy and had more miles, but so far as Roger knew, it had steering, lights, and brakes. "You know how to drive a standard?" Lydia turned and walked back into the living room.

"Yes, ma'am.

Lydia stopped before a five-yard lineup of shoes—boots, sandals, slippers, running shoes, hiking shoes, lick-me heels, and pumps. Ever since she'd worn the same shoes as Oly, Lydia had been obsessed with footwear.

"Didn't my son ever tell you what happens when people call me *ma'am*?"

"No, ma—"

Her voice rose into a scream. "*I fly off the handle!*"

Other than being loud enough to shake the windows, she didn't look off the handle to Roger. She seemed calm, balanced on her left leg, slipping her right foot into a squared-off, black high heel with straps that went well with her black tights and blood red cowboy shirt.

"How do you address the girls out at the sanitarium, or whatever Sam is calling it this week?"

"Generally, I say *You*."

"You?"

"'You need anything from town?' 'How are you this fine day?' We don't get personal enough for names."

Lydia kind of smirked. Roger had a flash that she and everyone in Wyoming knew the story.

"No doubt that causes tingles to run up and down their spines. *'Hey, you!'* Okay, other boys your age—what do they call girls?"

Roger's mind went back to high school. It was the year before last, but it felt like nostalgia. "They call the girls *Babe*."

"That's fine then. Call me Babe."

Roger tried to hide the recoil in his eyes, but he wasn't quick enough.

Her voice was quieter than before, more menacing. "I'm too old to be a babe?"

"No, ma'am." Mistake. "I mean, you're a fox, for your age. But I never called anyone Babe. That was the other guys. I thought the word wasn't polite."

"What did you call your female friends?"

"I didn't have female friends."

"Are you trying to piss me off?"

He shook his head No. It seemed like the time not to say anything aloud.

"What did you call your male friends?"

He didn't have many of those either, but Roger knew better than to say so. He thought about what Auburn's gang of jocks called each other. "Last names. Most guys used last names."

"Thusly, you would call me Callahan."

"I guess so. Thusly."

"Try it."

"Yo, Callahan."

"Use it in a sentence."

"Hey, Callahan, you ready to ride or what?"

"Yes, I am." Lydia picked up her purse and waited for him to gather the taping equipment. "See how easy it is when you do things right?"

She stood by the passenger door while he set the equipment in the backseat. Roger got in, then got back out and walked around to open Lydia's door.

She said, "Thank you," and slid into the car.

Roger had trouble finding reverse, but Lydia didn't comment. She sat quietly while he ground the gears. She waited until they were on the GroVont Road before starting the conversation.

"Has my son been filling you with gobbledygook about the purpose of life?"

He sneaked a peek at her face; she was wearing Vuarnet sunglasses. "Now and then. It's something he likes to talk about."

"Talking about the purpose of life is the single biggest waste of time in human society. It's worse than television."

"I suppose so."

"I know so. I'd rather Sam watch the Miss America Pageant than talk about the purpose of life."

Roger wasn't sure what they were discussing. "Maurey and Pud have a satellite dish, but Gilia won't allow TV at the Home."

"You call your parents Maurey and Pud?"

"They've only been my parents since I was thirteen or so. I never got used to saying *Mom* and *Pop*."

Lydia sat in silence until he turned onto the South Highway and headed toward Jackson. As they passed the elk refuge, a small group of silver males moved toward the river. The leader had velvet stumps growing to replace last year's horns.

"What does Sam claim is the purpose of life?"

"It changes. Last week he said life is a Saturday-morning cartoon meant to entertain a God who tends to sleep late." He glanced over at the sunglasses. There was no reaction from the visible parts of her face. "I think what he meant was God generally misses the show, but we have to put it on anyway."

Lydia said, "Have you ever wondered who you are?"

Roger took that four different ways, then gave it up. "What?"

"Who your other parents are? The ones before Maurey and Pud, before you came to Wyoming?"

Roger knew this wasn't a woman he could lie to like a pregnant teenager. "Sure, I wonder."

"If I had the power to tell you, would you want to hear, even if it isn't pretty?"

"I always figured it couldn't be pretty."

"Because you were struck dumb when you arrived at the ranch?"

"Because I wasn't raised with my normal family." He turned right again, toward Haven House. "You know who I am?"

"I have an idea. Of course, I can't say for certain; it's more a theory than an actual fact, but the important thing here isn't who you are and where you come from."

"It's not?"

"It's do you want to know the truth."

He stopped the BMW between the fake Greek columns that framed the Haven House door. "Do you?" Lydia asked.

Roger stared at his hands on the steering wheel. She probably didn't know. Hell, she'd been underground or in prison for years, how could she know something Maurey and Pud didn't?

"I'll think about it."

"You do that. Go for a drive, or whatever it is you do when you think, then pick me up back here in two hours."

He got out and opened Lydia's car door. She looped her purse under her left arm and gathered the taping equipment. He opened the Haven House door and waited while she walked in, then he closed the door behind her. Roger got back into the BMW and started the engine, but he didn't drive away. For a moment, he was sorry he had started talking again.

Mary Beth spent the next week in a trance of waiting. Whenever she dropped Jazmine or Meadow off at day care, she hugged them to her chest and said good-bye as if this was the last time. She wrote Lonnie a nine-page letter on pink paper, then hid it in her hope chest where he would look only after she was gone. She glided through her days, thinking, I may never see this Payless shoe store again. She stopped flossing. There didn't seem to be any point.

The other boot fell Tuesday morning. Mary Beth slipped out of bed at five thirty and went downstairs to watch her exercise class on TV. After seeing Leroy, she'd stopped actually exercising with the sparkly PBS babes who bounced on rubber mats on a beach in Hawaii, or maybe Malibu, but Mary Beth still watched. She liked being up before everyone else. It was the one time of day no one wanted a piece of her.

She flipped on the TV and padded barefoot into the kitchen for her carrot-and-artichoke-heart energy soda, and at the kitchen table sat Leroy—no shirt, no shoes, baggy canvas shorts held up by clothesline cord—his cracked hands folded around a mug of coffee.

They stared at each other. Mary Beth saw Leroy'd lost his teeth. His face collapsed in on itself. He had that homeless tan so different from the tan you get at a tanning salon or a beach or even working outdoors. His skin shone like wet denim.

She said, "You better hope Lonnie doesn't wake up and come down here."

Leroy cocked his head, as if listening. The aerobics teacher chirped from the living room. "Tuck in your tailbone, align those shoulders, and kick on the four count—left foot first!" Carly Simon burst forth, singing a song about anticipation.

"You're the one better hope Lonnie doesn't wake up and come down here," Leroy said. Mary Beth shuddered. Leroy said, "Have some coffee." It wasn't a question.

Mary Beth poured herself a cup from the Mr. Coffee. Leroy'd made it stronger than she liked. She looked into the refrigerator for an open can of condensed milk, but when she poured the milk into her coffee, her hand shook. She looked up to see if Leroy noticed.

He said, "Sit here." He patted the chair beside his. Leroy had moved Meadow's booster seat to the floor.

Mary Beth looked from Leroy to the lime green refrigerator, where the girls' Crayola drawings of stick people and dragons were held on by magnets shaped like Navajo talismen. She wondered what Meadow and Jazmine would grow up to be like without her. Lonnie ate beef and didn't buy into crystal therapy. She didn't doubt for a moment that he would sell her collection of love poems.

"Critter, sit," Leroy said.

Mary Beth sat. "No one's called me Critter since I left Oklahoma," she said.

Leroy glared at her. He was too close. His fish-gone-bad breath took the place of space around her. His black-rimmed fingernails looked magnified.

"Where's the boy?" he said.

Mary Beth blinked. It wasn't what she'd expected. "I'm afraid I don't follow you," she said.

"You're not as stupid as you pretend to be," Leroy said.

"Do you mean that in a good way?"

"Where's my boy?"

There was some chance Mary Beth might swoon from the fumes. She wondered if that would be a negative. He might carry her off before Lonnie or the girls came down. She'd given up on herself. All she could do now was protect her family.

"Norwood and Timmy said they brought him to you," Leroy said. "Those two jizz-for-brains don't have the balls to lie to me."

"Are you talking about the little boy we kidnapped?"

Leroy backhanded Mary Beth, knocking her to the floor, against the dish-machine vent. "My boy. The boy taken from me by his cunt of a mother."

Mary Beth flattened her palms against the linoleum and looked up at Leroy. His eyes had that stallion-in-a-burning-barn wildness she remembered from the old days, right before he was set to explode on someone. She knew better than to argue with Leroy about the past, but she'd been there when he grabbed the boy. She drove the van. It was the one experience from the bad years that still gave her night sweats. That day was the reason she and Lonnie slept in the same room as the girls.

"Get off the floor," Leroy said. "We know each other too well for you to play victim."

Mary Beth made it to her feet, slowly, but she didn't move any closer to Leroy.

He stared into his coffee mug. Then he cleared his throat with a sound that came out something like a sigh. "No more games, Critter. Where's the boy?"

She brought her hands together, intertwining the fingers, chest level. "He's not here."

"I can see that. I'm not an idiot." Leroy's eyes violated her. "Did you raise him up?"

She shook her head. "I couldn't. I didn't have any money."

"Who had him then?"

Mary Beth didn't answer.

"I'll make this easy for you. You can give up the boy, or you can give up those pretty little girls."

"You wouldn't hurt my daughters?"

Leroy waited while Mary Beth supplied the answer to her question.

"I thought you were here to claim me," she said.

Leroy snorted. "Look at yourself. You're elderly. I got no interest in you."

The relief made Mary Beth dizzy, but it was followed by a hint of a letdown. All these years, she'd thought he would return like a vengeful demon to carry her away—that, or kill her—when the truth was, her existence didn't matter.

"You want me to go upstairs?" he said.

"I took the boy to Wyoming."

"Where in Wyoming?"

"I heard about a woman with a ranch where people could go when they were in trouble. I drove the boy up there and left him. That was ten years ago."

Leroy leaned down, snaked his hand up the right leg of his canvas shorts, and scratched his scrotum. It was a purely natural act. He said, "Address."

Mary Beth said, "I don't understand you."

"Give me the damn address."

She dropped her hands. "How'm I supposed to remember that, after all this time?"

Leroy pulled his hand out of his shorts. He swiveled in the chair to face her directly. "I'm losing patience here, Critter. You don't want me to lose patience."

"The address was a box number in GroVont, Wyoming. I would need time to look for it, but the place where I left him is up the river there a few miles. The TM Ranch. You should be able to find it."

"You best pray I do." Leroy drained his coffee, tipping the cup to get every drop. His Adam's apple rose and fell like a rat in a snake.

Mary Beth watched in wonder that she could have ever been romantically involved with this carnivore. He wasn't even human. Had he been human when they met? It didn't seem possible. She was seventeen *then, a Georgia runaway in a halter top, looking for shelter disguised as adventure. Kids that age often mistake meanness for charisma. Mary Beth swore her girls would never grow up to be like her, even if she had to chain them to their beds.*

"The boy is a grown-up by now," Mary Beth said. "What're you going to do when you find him?"

"Nature's balance is undone because that woman spoiled my peace of mind. She owed me a life, and killing herself moved the debt to the boy."

"But that child is innocent. He never did a thing to you."

Leroy stood quickly. Mary Beth winced. He said, "I aim to kill the bastard."

Mary Beth's breath caught in her chest. "Why would you do that?"

Leroy's eyes did the crazy snap thing. He appeared to be grinding his gums. "Earth cannot continue spinning properly until I've hurt that dirty slit more than I did when we took the boy. I don't care if she is past the grave."

"You can't hurt a person more than what we did," Mary Beth said.

Leroy smiled. Without teeth, it came off as a grotesque mockery of a smile. He said, "Watch me."

7

DAD SENT A TELEGRAM TO GRANDDAD WIGGINS BACK IN DOVER, BUT WE never heard nothing from that side of the family. I guess they forgot Mom soon as she left Delaware. There wasn't any point in going anywheres else, so Dad bought us a thirty-dollar shack back of the train depot, and we moved on in. On account of the explosion, there was a stiff competition amongst the Lutherans, the Congregationalists, and the Presbyterians for who could best take care of us. Believe me when I tell you this—Congregationalist women cook circles around Lutherans. Lutherans are fine with greens, but they fry the hell out of everything else. The Presbyterian folks give us a wooden table with legs that didn't set proper and one chair but not two. They were fixing to come across with a second chair, only Dad nodded off while cutting the pastor's hair and sliced his neck and it became apparent to one and all that Dad was an addict. After that, the Christian element pretty much wrote us off. Dad picked up some work dipping outhouses, but he didn't do no real labor the rest of his life.

I could have pulled us through the summer, but come winter, I imagine Dad and me would have starved if Mr. Cox hadn't taken an active interest in my welfare. He brought us flour and side meat to get by, then, soon as my leg healed, he hired me to clean up his various establishments, including the bank and the Bluebeard Cafe. He gave me his son's cast-off clothing and a red harmonica I still have. Nobody said more about me and school. My formal education came to a close at thirteen.

I know you may wonder why Mr. Cox showed such kindness as to give me clothes and a job when there was plenty of others equally poor as myself. I have had a long while to think about this, and I have come up with superstition as the answer. Mr. Cox was a forward-looking man with no fondness for the nineteenth century—folks in those days didn't think the past was superior to the future. That's a new thing—yet he played poker two nights a week, and thusly he had become deeply superstitious. I think he saw me flying through the air and landing smack on his porch as a sign. Mr. Cox viewed his role as that of dynasty patriarch; his son wasn't living up to expectations, then I dropped from the heavens into his lap. I was the draw he got to fill an inside straight. So to speak.

In later years, Bill claimed Mr. Cox took me as the cheapest labor to be found and took advantage, but I pointed out his acts of charity began even before I could be of any use to him—such as the Fourth of July. Fourth of July I'd only been without crutches a week and still couldn't walk any distance, and Dad was sick like usual, so the Coxes came around and gave me a ride to the carnival grounds in Mr. Cox's new Maxwell. On account of the picnic food, I had to ride on this platform strapped off the back end, but that was okay. I felt good anyway.

Fourth of July was the biggest of holidays back then in Montana. All others came in the cold part of the year, when about the best you could hope for was a dance. Fourth of July was an all-day outdoor event with potato-sack and three-legged races, a rodeo, and a baseball game. Carnies set up booths where you could throw hoops at milk bottles or shoot little targets with a .30-.30 that had a crooked barrel. There was a booth where men threw balls at a bull's-eye, and if they hit it, this mechanical chair dumped a fancy woman backwards off her perch far enough so if you looked quick, you got a peek at her drawers. Imagine now-days a gang of men spending their money and effort to glimpse a woman's undergarments.

We ate dinner under a pretty little grove of cottonwoods, and there was hot dogs, fried chicken, ham hock, cold potatoes and onions, lemonade, and chocolate cake. Afterward, Mr. Cox treated me and Agatha to blue cotton candy. I got sick and haven't eaten nothing blue ever since.

———

Just after dark, I had to see a man about a dog. I did my privy business and was coming back to the tree where Mrs. Cox had a quilt spread, walking along the row between the booths there, when the first firework exploded smack in the sky over my head. Orange spires shot off every which way like a dandelion gone to seed in the wind, then at the tip end of each spire a white flash popped. I stopped dead in my tracks to look up at the effect, and somebody walked into my backside, knocking me forward and sending a pain up my bad leg.

A voice yelled, "Look out, you stupid oaf!"

I turned to face a cowboy, not much older than me, in one of them little Butch Cassidy hats and Spanish spurs. He had black, water-slicked hair and a scrawny mustache no thicker than his eyebrows. I hadn't been in a fight since Mama died and my leg broke, and I guess I was spoiling for one. Whatever caused my hackle to rise, I took one look at the cowboy and decided to knock his block off.

I said, "Look out yourself, pecker head," and we lit into each other. He hit me a time or two and I hit him back; then we commenced to roll around on the ground, neither one getting

87

enough distance to land a proper punch. He raked my bad leg with a spur; I stuck a thumb in his eye. It was nothing but boys feeling their oats, the way they do, and I was having a pretty good time until we broke loose from each other and he pulled a pistol.

"What's this?" I said.

"It's what I aim to kill you with," he said. It was a one-shot derringer about the size of his palm. It looked like a toy, but it wasn't.

"You wouldn't kill a man 'cause you tripped over him," I said.

He said, "Like hell I wouldn't."

Just then Agatha Cox hollered from behind me, "Bill!" and she ran between us. "You put that gun away. This is my friend Oly. Do Mama and Daddy know you're here?"

He looked like he wanted to shoot me real bad, but his sister was right in the way, jabbering like we were at afternoon tea. "Mama'll be happy to see you. The last letter we got you were in Manitou Springs. How'd you get back from there? Ain't no trains going south."

"I rode my horse," he said. The derringer disappeared into whatever hidden pocket where he kept it. "Ain't that my shirt?"

"Daddy gave it to Oly. His clothes got blown up."

"Well. I want my shirt back."

At that point, I became disenchanted with Bill Cox. Agatha had been talking about him like he was Natty Bumppo of the high plains; even Mrs. Cox seemed to think her son was above-board, but anybody would try to shoot a man for stopping to look at a firework, then demand the shirt off his back wasn't no Natty Bumppo, far as I was concerned. In front of Agatha and a crowd of mixed-gender carnies, I yanked Bill's shirt off and threw it to the ground.

"Take your old shirt," I said and walked off, doing my best not to show any limp.

He laughed in a mean fashion and called after me. "Them pants look like mine too."

———

A year and a half later, Christmas, Mr. Cox introduced me to Bill again in the Bluebeard Cafe. Bill shook my hand and asked where my people was from, polite as could be, as if he didn't recall me from Adam. Maybe he didn't. Maybe he went around threatening to shoot so many folks that he couldn't bother to remember them. Or maybe he held himself in check 'cause his father was present.

I wasn't in no position to start trouble with Bill then, on account of my own father was in county lockup that day, and I was vulnerable to insults. A Chinese man name of Hoo Sue Kong had got into a street shoot-out with police and been killed out front of a saloon on Minnesota Avenue. Afterward, the police searched the saloon and found an opium den in the basement, with my father in it. The other hopheads had cleared out soon as the shooting begun, but Dad was not in shape to climb stairs, so he got caught.

They locked him up for three months, which was probably for the good, it being December and all. I doubt he'd of made it through the winter outside of jail, and he didn't make it through the spring. April 11, my father, Jan, fell asleep on the railroad track out by Coulson and the Burlington Number 41 squashed him. Nobody ever figured out how he come to be out by Coulson. I think maybe he tried to walk home to Sweden.

I was at the roller skating barn when they came to tell me my father had been smashed. I didn't like skating so much as watching cowboys fall on their rear ends. Their legs aren't shaped proper for the roller wheels; not a one I ever saw was any good at it. That woman doctor was sent to tell me the news. I don't know why they sent her. She didn't have no sympathy for Dad nor me.

I sat on this narrow bench by the skate floor, watching cowboys flail their arms and fall, and I thought about us leaving Dover for the West. As a rule, people go west in hope and east in defeat. On days like that one where Dad died, I think perhaps there is a life on the other side; the rest of the time, I don't worry myself over it. Mr. Cox gave me an advance for the coffin, and once again, the various Christian groups outdid themselves with cakes and casseroles and such.

———

August of 1911, two days after my birthday, the Anglican Church there had a hayride down to Bitter Creek, where we built a cottonwood bonfire and played charades and roasted up an antelope. There was two wagons full of twenty-five young people, ranging in age from eight to twenty, and some chaperones that snuck off on occasion to nip the bottle.

I rode in the older kids' wagon where we hunkered under blankets, pretending it was cold but in reality holding hands and carrying on—tame by what young ones do today out in public, but fairly scandalous for the time. You have to recall Montana wasn't like Nebraska.

Anyway, they were singing "Bishop From Pike," but I wasn't; I never had no voice I cared to show off. Instead I pretended to yawn so's to shift my weight over closer to one of the Pease sisters on my left—I forget which one, they was both somewhat horsey—when I felt soft fingers on my right hand and looked up to see Agatha Cox smiling sweet, right at me.

She said, "You can be my beau."

Which nonplussed me no end. "You're a little girl," I said.

She pouted her lower lip out, and I must admit she was pretty as a button. "I'm thirteen. If I was Arapaho, I'd have three babies by now."

I had no idea what being Arapaho had to do with holding my

hand under the blanket. I tried a new tack. "Mr. Cox trusts me not to take advantage."

She smiled. "It's fine. When I'm nineteen and done with school, we'll get married."

Nineteen back then was practically an old maid. "Why wait till nineteen?" I asked. See how she switched me around. One minute I'm saying she's too young, and the next I'm asking why we have to wait. Agatha always did have that affect on me.

"Because I don't want to be biggered till I'm done with school." *Biggered* meant pregnant. I knew that, even though it wasn't really a Montana word. I'm not certain where Agatha had heard it, probably from a book. Agatha read books, so there was never was any telling what she might say next.

I said, "So, little girl, you're planning on us courting for six years?"

She took my upper arm with her other hand and said, "We'll know the joy of love."

———

I never discovered whether Agatha played a part in my improved prospects or not, but soon after this Mr. Cox raised my position to that of bank steward. No more mopping out the Bluebeard kitchen at midnight. Now I wore a collar and necktie and worked in daylight. At first, I mostly filled inkwells and stoked the furnace, but before long I was numbering checks, posting statements, and taking mail out. Once I was sent to repossess a buggy, but when I got there, the man had burned it up. In the evenings, Agatha taught me numbers and improved my reading skills. She taught me how to talk more like a gentleman. She wanted me to advance in life so we could have a house with electricity and indoor hot water. She said she wasn't bringing no papoose into my dirty shed.

I applied myself with gusto and soon I was dealing firsthand with customers. I helped farmers fill out loan papers, even though I never got permission to approve loans. I'd of given money to anybody needed it to survive, and in the banking business, you don't loan money to those that need it.

The first time Mr. Cox turned me loose behind the teller window, he showed me a .36-caliber brass-handled pistol they kept on a shelf under the money drawer. He told me sooner or later someone would attempt to rob me.

He said, "Act meek. Say, 'Yes, sir, here's the money, sir,' and give them whatever they want. Then, when they leave you follow the bastards into the street and kill them."

"I never shot a pistol. I'm not certain if I know how."

"It's simple. Point this end at the robber and pull the trigger."

"What about the safety?"

"Do you see a safety on this gun?"

"No, sir."

"Point it at the robber's rib cage and pull the trigger. If there's more than one robber, keep pulling it until six of them are dead. Then you can quit. If you're not willing to do this one thing for me, I'll have to find a man who will."

"I'm willing," I said, although secretly, I had no such intention. I told Agatha, and she accused me of not loving her.

"If you truly love me, you won't let a robber take my daddy's money."

"I guess not."

"Someday that money will belong to us."

My raise in position did not come with much of a raise in salary, only enough to pay for the clothes I was required to wear to the bank, and the Chinese laundry that kept them clean. In point of fact, without access to the Bluebeard kitchen, my added expenses went higher than my added income. I saved almost every penny in a hole under my shed floor—I didn't trust the bank not to fail—and within three years I was ready to take a loan on a little rock house on West Fifth Street.

But then, before I had time to fill out the papers, as it had so often in the past, my circumstances turned upside down.

———

The winter of 1913 lasted just about forever, with snow covering the window of my shed and wind you got permanently stooped trying to walk against. One day in late March, Mr. Cox and Frank Lesley left me alone in the bank while they took their dinner down at the Bluebeard. That's how we generally did it, then they would come back at 12:45 and relieve me while I ate out in the alley from a pail. I did not mind this arrangement, on account of ofttimes, Agatha took advantage of the hour when I was alone to sneak into the bank and we'd spark if there wasn't any customers.

This one day, though, the moment Mr. Cox and Frank Lesley was out the door, old Mrs. Hitchcock come through to root around in her safe-deposit box. She did this three, four times a week. Once, when I was helping her with the keys I peeked in and there wasn't anything but newspaper clippings from the Civil War and a couple of medals. I guess they mattered to Mrs. Hitchcock.

The only trouble was you had to escort her into the box room and stick in a special key while she turned her key, and that left the cage unguarded, which meant if she come at lunch, I was forced to lock down the entire bank until I had her settled.

I tried to hustle back quick, but this particular time, Mrs. Hitchcock wanted to tell me about a liver procedure she'd had described to her—she seemed to care about my opinion—and when I went back to my post I found someone in my money box.

It was the Cox boy, Bill. I said, "How'd you get through that locked door?"

He said, "How do you think?" And he held up a key for me to look at.

"Does your daddy know you have a key to the bank?"

He ignored that and went on counting my ten-dollar bills, getting them all mixed around, with some Benjamin Franklin's face right ways and some Benjamin Franklin's face the wrong ways.

Bill gave me his gunfighter stare-down that I know he practiced looking in the mirror. It wouldn't have scared a ground squirrel.

He said, "What are your intentions toward my sister?"

I was temporarily thrown off. "Agatha Ann?"

"I only got the one sister."

"My intentions toward Agatha Ann are none of your affair."

His left hand crept toward the vest pocket where I knew he kept his little muff gun. "I can make it my business," he said. "Agatha says you two plan to marry."

She had not mentioned marriage to me in years, not since the hayride where she first brought us up, and I thought she'd forgot all about that part of the plan, but that's just like Agatha to tell someone it would upset before she tells the person who's involved. I said, "What if I do?"

"My daddy's been swell to you over the years, in spite of your line being dope fiends. I won't have you repaying his trust by taking advantage."

"Taking advantage is not the way I see matters."

"You only want Agatha for my father's money. She's too homely for anyone to want her for real."

Now, Agatha was not homely in the least. She had a button nose and freckles acrost her cheekbones. Her hips were a bit slim for bearing children, but like I say, she was not homely, and I took offense at Bill for saying she was.

He went on before I could sock him in the jaw. "You got a soft deal here," he said. "But if my daddy knew you were dipping Agatha, he'd fire you in a flash."

"Your sister is a lady. I have not dipped her in any way."

"Mr. Cox won't believe that when I tell him. He'll fire you and put you out of that pigsty you call a house."

That's when Mrs. Hitchcock came from the deposit-box room. She kind of trilled, "Thank you, Oly," as I unlocked the door, but before I could shut up behind her, three men pushed their way through. Two men and a boy, really. The two men smelled like mule skinners, and the boy had a case of nervous hives. You could see his hand quivering on the buckle of his belt there.

One man come over to the cage as I walked around. He said, "We want to make a withdrawal." I already knew it was a holdup. These weren't customers with ready accounts.

Bill said, "How much, pard?" like he owned the bank instead of his father, Mr. Cox, and they pulled sidearms. The one who'd talked before said, "All of it."

The men cleaned my teller drawer, then went to work on the safe. They must have been watching the bank awhile, because they knew exactly how long till Mr. Cox and Frank Lesley would be in from dinner.

The boy—he was nervous and soon I saw Bill was too, and I knew he wasn't going to let this end with no trouble. I kept behind the cage there so I could either drop when gunfire commenced or reach under the counter for the loaded .36 caliber.

The men came from the safe with their hands full loaded so they'd had to holster their pistols. The uglier of the two said, "Cover us, Shad," and headed for the door, only Shad was scared so he headed for the door himself. With no gun on us, Bill pulled his and plugged one fella square in the back. The other fella dropped his money and went for his gun. He cleared holster, but before he shot Bill I shot him. The bullet entered at his voice box and exited from the back of his neck. Before long, he was on the floor, gurgling blood.

The boy threw his pistol down and surrendered. He didn't really have to because Bill was out of bullets and I wasn't about to shoot nobody else. It made me sick to shoot the first fella. I couldn't help but think of his mother.

The boy spoke as if resigned to his fate. "They'll hang me for certain."

I walked over to view the gurgling man. He stared up at me like a landed trout for a few seconds, then he expired. I said, "They don't hang for bank robbing anymore. Unless you kill somebody."

The boy said, "Then they'll put me in prison for life. I'd rather be hung."

After Bill'd shot the first one, he turned white as an antelope's ass, but now, he commenced to recover.

He said, "We'll tell the sheriff you wasn't with them."

The boy and I stared at Bill. I don't know what Bill's plan had been in the first place, shooting a man in the back when you only have one bullet and there's three men. I don't imagine he even had a plan—just saw a chance to kill someone and went for it.

He said, "We'll claim you were a customer, caught in the cross fire."

The boy said, "Why would you do that?"

I said, "Yes, Bill, why would we do that?"

Bill's brain was working so fast you could almost see it go, like a cash register dinging and binging. "This boy don't deserve a life in prison. He was led astray by these blackguards."

The boy said, "Blackguards?"

"What's your name?" I asked.

"Shadrach Pierce. My mama died in childbirth and I had no proper guidance. I fell in with the wrong crowd." As an example of the wrong crowd, he pointed at the dead fellas bleeding out on the bank floor.

I said, "My mama died, and you don't see me robbing no bank."

Bill turned to face Shadrach close in the eye. "Promise to do what I say from now to eternity, and I'll lie to the sheriff. You'll be spared a life in prison."

"What about him?" Shadrach asked, indicating me.

"He works for my dad. He'll do what I say." Which wasn't

true, and saying so almost got that boy sent to prison, but I felt sorry for him. Ever'body makes mistakes, and I hoped his partners being dead might scare the meanness out of him. Besides, that thing about the dead mother touched me. If not for Mr. Cox, I could have gone bad when Mom died, just like Shadrach.

All this thought took place in a heartbeat. "I'll back you," I said to Bill, "but not because you threatened me. The boy needs a second chance."

So that's what we did. Sheriff Nowlin didn't believe us. He kept asking what Shadrach's business had been in the bank if he didn't have money, and which of the dead fellas was carrying the third gun and how it got way over by the door. In the end, though, there wasn't much choice for him. Shadrach was let go.

8

LYDIA FLOUNCED OUT OF HAVEN HOUSE IN THE STATE OF irritation that Oly generally triggered. She found Roger sitting in the car as she had left him. Even the hands on the wheel hadn't moved. One would have thought he'd been frozen in time while she recorded history, except the BMW had 110 new miles on the odometer, a fact Lydia noted immediately.

"That petrified rock of a human is a complete waste of my time and talents," she said as Roger pulled away from the curb. "I'd rather be back in the joint than suffer any more of his drivel."

"His story isn't interesting?"

"His story isn't true. He's making up every word, and I have to sit there in silence because if I so much as point out a single historical inaccuracy, he starts over at birth." Lydia twisted the rearview mirror sideways to check her hair for uneven bangs. "And there's no consistency. Half the time he talks like a South Carolina clay-eating hick, and then he'll say a word like *nonplussed*. I've never used *nonplussed* in conversation in my whole life."

She grabbed Roger's arm above the elbow. "Pull in the A&W. I feel the need of a root-beer float."

They went inside, on account of Lydia's view that drive-up

food denigrates society. Roger ate a double cheeseburger while Lydia polished off her float and his french fries.

Their table overlooked a muddy creek where six fuzzy ducklings followed a female mallard in and out of the willows. The babies made interesting patterns of independence and need as they flowed around their mother.

"Do you have any concept of how much I missed the call of a migrating Canada goose while I was locked away?" Lydia asked. "There were days I would have sacrificed my future to see one, even for an instant."

Roger chewed his cheeseburger and considered telling Lydia the bird she would have gladly sacrificed her future for wasn't a Canada goose; it was a duck.

"You never appreciate the details of a way of life until you lose it," she said. "You want that pickle?"

"No."

When she took the pickle, he noticed the veins on the back of her hand. Instead of blue and thick, the way you would expect, they were red and thin—spidery veins like you see in the cheeks of a drunk.

"Well," Lydia said. "What do you think?"

Roger said, "I think you're a crackpot."

Her color shifted slightly, but otherwise, Lydia gave no response.

Roger went on. "I think you had too much time on your hands in prison, and if I listen to you, I'll get my hopes up, and I'd rather not get my hopes up for nothing."

She sucked root beer through a paper straw. The Jackson A&W was possibly the last fast-food restaurant in America giving out paper straws. "So, you do not wish to hear my theory concerning your origins?"

"Yes, I want to hear your theory. I just want you to know I think you're a crackpot."

Lydia stared at him a full ten seconds. He stared back. Both

Lydia and Roger would have chosen public humiliation over blinking first. Finally, Lydia said, "Fair enough."

———

"Between hiding with Hank and the time of incarceration, I was unable to see the valley that I love for ten long years. Imagine being banished from home for ten years."

Roger folded his arms and watched the ducks. He had trouble picturing Lydia as homesick but supposed it was possible. Maybe behind that wall of scorn lived a sentimental sop.

Lydia pulled a pocket mirror from her purse and checked her teeth for residual french fry. "I came up with the idea of reading every book written about Jackson Hole or written by an author who lived in Jackson Hole—every book with any vague yet tenuous connection to Jackson Hole and GroVont. As you must know, I once owned a press here in the valley, specializing in feminist ecological philosophy."

"Does this have anything to do with my roots?"

"Are you in a rush? Got a busy schedule out there at the Home, servicing the needs of over-ripe little girls?"

Roger glared at her but didn't speak, so she waited for the testosterone level to settle, then she went on. "I devoured everything, all the way from Owen Wister and his recycled cowboy-as-Ivanhoe stories to that sentimental hogwash my son passes off. There's a bookstore in Portland with more titles than the Library of Congress. They can send you anything."

Roger had read Owen Wister, not just *The Virginian*, but also *Lady Baltimore*, and he could have argued the cowboy-as-Ivanhoe crack, but he was afraid to go there for fear of knocking Lydia off her train of thought. Lydia's train of thought didn't appear capable of dealing with distraction.

"I found several books by a man named Loren Paul who used to live up Ditch Creek."

"The screenwriter?"

"You've heard of him?"

"Sam told me about a novelist up past Antelope Flats who sold out his ideals and moved to Hollywood to spew pabulum for the movies."

"Sam's one to talk about pabulum."

"I'm just repeating what he said."

"Yeah, well, *Bucky on Half Dome* is no more serious literature than *Dukes of Hazzard*."

Roger instinctively knew the best way to keep Lydia on track was to shut up.

She said, "Loren Paul made his reputation off a piece of horse dung called *Yeast Infection*, which was nothing but a woman-bashing polemic disguised as satire."

"I mostly read books by dead guys, so I haven't gotten around to that one yet."

"Don't bother. Loren had an earlier book, after the Westerns and before the commercial crap, called *Disappearance*. I have one of the few copies still in existence."

She reached into her saddle purse and withdrew a narrow green hardback. Turning it in her hands, she showed Roger the word *Disappearance* embossed on the cloth cover. "It's about his stepson who disappeared at a campground on Jackson Lake." She passed the book to Roger.

Roger said, "And you think the stepson might be me?"

Lydia shrugged. "The years match up. The description of the boy fits what I imagine you might have looked like at five."

"Any description fits what I might have looked like at five." He opened the book and studied the title page. It was signed by the author: *To my good pal Marcie VanHorn, in memory of her Cornish game hen.* The signature was indecipherable.

Lydia said, "There are odd details, names, and places that come across as more than random coincidence, to me, anyway."

Roger turned to the copyright page. "Callahan, this is fiction."

"So?"

"Fiction means *not true*."

"You don't know that."

"Look it up."

"This is a personal story. Read it and tell me you don't believe this man lost his stepson."

"It might be based on a true event, but fiction means the names are changed. The descriptions and locations. All those odd details you think are coincidence connecting the story to me would be changed."

Lydia stared at him across her purse. This wasn't what she'd expected. She'd expected wonder and curiosity, perhaps awe at her detective skills. Instead he was smack in denial.

She said, "When you first came to Maurey's ranch, you were quite a mystery. Practically intriguing. You don't remember, but you and I spent time together. You were a spooky little boy."

"And that makes you think this kid is me?"

"Read the damn book, Roger."

Roger turned over another page, to the first chapter. "What's the kid's name?"

"Fred.'

He read the first sentence. *Sometimes I have these gaps which are amazingly like being dead except that they don't last, and I have an awful feeling that being dead lasts.*

Lydia said, "Fred. But his mother called him Buggie."

Roger said, "Fred or Buggie, I don't know which is worse."

———

Roger and Lydia found Shannon rocking in a wicker glider on the front porch of Lydia's house. She was barefoot, wearing a sleeveless blouse and cutoffs, eating a candy bar while she read a magazine. She looked up from the magazine with a vague smile on her face and sent them a four-fingered wave.

"Look at her," Lydia said. "All the oomph of an old biddy."

Roger parked the BMW beside his truck. "She looks pretty nice to me."

"At your age, a fence post with knockers and a knothole would look pretty nice."

Roger helped Lydia load up her equipment. "You want me to carry that stuff in for you?"

"I've got it."

"Wouldn't be any trouble."

"I said I've got it." She started toward the house. "Don't forget your book. I'll call next time I need you."

Roger said, "You're welcome," but he said it so quietly he was fairly certain she didn't hear. She gave no sign of hearing him.

As Lydia crossed the yard toward Shannon, she admired the balance of new purchases on and around her front porch. Since she'd come home, she had installed the glider, three hanging plant baskets, and a hummingbird feeder. Last time she lived in this house, she'd taken it as a temporary arrangement—for twenty years. This time she planned to stay.

Lydia hit the steps, talking. "That boy has all the subtlety of an elk in rut."

Shannon glanced up to see Roger pulling a three-point U-turn before heading back up the mountain. He double-clutched the gear changes, which made the truck cough.

"Roger?"

"You know they have a word for girls your age who seduce boys his age."

"What is it?"

Lydia paused, momentarily thrown off her roll. "I forget. But I wish you wouldn't flaunt yourself before him. After all, he is related to you in some bizarre, labyrinthine fashion."

TIM SANDLIN

"He's a half brother, sort of. I don't think Maurey ever legally adopted him because he got too old before the birth-certificate thing could be worked out. And I wasn't flaunting. I was sitting here alone, reading and eating a candy bar." As if to prove her statement, Shannon licked chocolate off her fingers.

"Let's see what you're reading." Lydia took the magazine from Shannon and flopped it closed, losing Shannon's place. The magazine was *Cosmopolitan*. The cover showed an anorexic junkie with lip implants and huge, artificial breasts. The word *sex* appeared on the cover three times, *orgasm* twice, and *love* once. *Love* was used in the banner head: "Tom Hanks Knows What Love Is."

"I'll tell you what love is," Lydia said. "Love is systematically lowering your standards until you find someone who has systematically lowered their standards down to you."

Shannon tucked her bare feet up under her thighs. "Is that what you did with Hank?"

Lydia sniffed. "Hank and I were the exceptions. Neither one of us had to lower our standards an inch."

"Why is it you always get to be the exception? All these natural laws you come up with apply to everyone but you."

"I'm different. You could be different too, if you didn't pig out on candy bars in the middle of the day. I haven't had a bite since breakfast, but you don't see me bombarding my blood sugar level with chocolate goo."

Shannon turned sideways with her back against the swing's arm. She watched Lydia fuss with a flower basket. Lydia was humming quietly, and it sounded to Shannon like the theme from *Green Acres*.

Shannon said, "Grandma, do you think I could stay here awhile?"

"You've been staying over a week."

"I mean live here—with you."

Lydia bit her lower lip, then said, "How long are we discussing?"

"I don't know. Until I get back on my feet."

"I wasn't aware that you are off your feet."

Shannon straightened her legs in the swing. Several of her toes showed a chipped light blue polish. "When I think about going back to Carolina, my mind shuts down. I have no life there, no job. Nothing I want to see or do."

"If you have no life, it's because you define yourself by men, and when you don't have one, you are an empty pot."

"I've lived without men before."

"How long?"

Shannon tried to remember. It had been a long time ago.

Lydia said, "What's the longest you've ever gone without a man on your mind?"

"I went four months without sex once."

"That's because you were in love with a married geek who was too racked with guilt to screw you but not racked enough to avoid leading you on."

Shannon thought about that one—Wyatt. He'd taken an amazing amount of energy. They'd shared more tears than any of the guys she actually slept with.

She said, "Don't you want me to live here?"

Lydia considered the question honestly, and honestly, it was nice to have Shannon around. Not that she would admit it. "That's up to you," she said. "Why would you choose me over your mother and father?"

"I think you'd be a better influence."

Lydia's mood shot skyward. She was a sucker for compliments.

"I could stay at Mom's, only she makes everybody get up at five to work outdoors. I don't mind hard work, but before dawn…" Shannon shuddered. "And Dad's, with pregnant girls everywhere you look, it's like this never-ending reminder that I'm not making something of my life."

"Having babies is not 'making something of your life.'"

"Those girls don't raise their babies, but still—"

"Any fool female can procreate. Cows have babies every spring, but cows can't publish a book or plant a garden or sit in a porch swing and admire the sunset. That's making something of your life. Having babies is like going to the bathroom. Sure, it's natural, but it's not worth bragging about."

Shannon felt better than she had since Tanner told her her pussy smelled. "You know why living with you would be so healthy, Grandma? Because you are so incredibly wrong that you clarify what is right. Being around you sweeps away the confusion."

"I'll take that as a compliment." Lydia turned to go into the house. "And stay as long as you like. You can live vicariously through me."

———

Supper was spinach manicotti and sourdough bread with hand-cranked huckleberry ice cream for dessert. Angel Byron stayed in her cabin, claiming nausea, but the other three girls at the dinner table were the whiniest group Roger had ever been trapped in a room with.

"Too hot."

"Too dry."

"Dirty."

"Hicksville."

They are okay taken one at a time, but pregnant girls were never meant to bunch up. Roger escaped by offering to run a dish of ice cream down to Angel. She answered her door wearing a maraschino cherry red fleece bathrobe, and when Roger offered the ice cream she said she couldn't eat a bite. She took the dish from him anyway and invited him inside, where she proceeded to wolf the ice cream so quickly Roger got a headache just watching her. Angel had eggshell white skin and black eyes. Her hair was cut shorter than Roger's, which as a general rule, he didn't care for, but on Angel it worked.

She said, "Don't tell anyone you saw me eat this."

"Okay."

"I have a reputation."

When Angel handed the dish back to Roger, she touched his wrist and said, "If I came to your cabin, would you send me away?"

"No."

"Would you ever come to me first?"

"I brought you ice cream."

"You know what I mean. Would you come to my cabin if I didn't come to yours?"

"No."

"That's fair. I like it when I understand the rules."

———

Back in his cabin, Roger poured himself a juice glass of brandy and put Chet Baker's *Young Chet* on the CD player. He pulled his boots off on the bootjack and dug under the bed behind his photo album for a pair of woolly slippers Gilia had given him for Christmas. They were red with monkey-head toes. He kept them hidden whenever he had company, but they were the ideal slippers for an evening of brandy, jazz, and a book.

The book was the part of the equation he had been avoiding. *Disappearance* sat on the end table stump, next to his rocking chair, which was in front of the unlit woodstove. Roger propped his slippered feet on the oven door and rocked and sipped brandy. He wasn't ready to touch the book quite yet. First, he had to formulate hopes. It seemed important to know what he was looking for before going off in search of it. The book had to be about terrible things—child abuse and kidnapping and violent behavior—or else no one would have published it. They don't print novels about happy people.

Roger finished off his brandy and set the glass on the stump. He picked up the book and gently turned it in his hands. There was fear the book would change his life, and equal fear it wouldn't. The temptation was to read the ending first, but he knew the boy disappeared and wasn't found or Lydia would not have seen him in the story.

Eden Rae O'Connor opened the door and came in. She was wearing a long, oversize T-shirt with a panda bear on the front and, from what Roger could see, nothing else. She was crying. Tears tracked makeup down her cheeks and quivered on the end of her chin. The top of her shirt was wet from tears. Her hands cupped her huge belly, as if to keep that one part of her together while the rest fell apart.

"Did you scrog with Angel Byron?" she asked.

"I took her ice cream."

"You better be nice to me. I'm more pregnant than she is. You can go at it like rabbits after I'm gone, but right now I can't share."

Roger set *Disappearance* back on the stump. "Come in and let me rub your shoulders. I'll make you feel better."

Eden walked into the cabin. She said, "I'm under a lot of stress."

———

"I came to an important realization last night," I said. "Guess what it is?"

My mother looked up from the sugar swirling in her iced tea. One of her favorite pastimes was to dump two heaping spoonfuls of sugar into a glass of iced tea, then stir like hell and watch as the crystals went from real to imagined.

She said, "You realized that questions like 'Guess what I'm thinking?' make your friends and loved ones gag."

"I realized that no matter how long I live, I shall never sleep with Linda Ronstadt."

Lydia licked her spoon dry. "Sam, sometimes the inanity of your conversation astounds me. Do you sit in the bathtub at night and make lists of stupid remarks?"

"It's an acceptance-of-age thing. Haven't you ever had to accept that you aren't going to do something that you always, in the back of your mind, thought you would one day do, if only you lived long enough?"

"No."

A white-capped sparrow sat on the windowsill, looking in at us. Lydia dipped her fingertips in tea and flipped a spray of drops on the window, directly at the bird. The bird did not flinch.

Lydia said, "So I am to infer that in the back of your mind you always thought you would sleep with Linda Ronstadt."

"When I was young I thought sooner or later I would sleep with everyone. And now I know I'm not."

"We must notify Linda."

"It isn't simply because I'm monogamous with Gilia. I've been monogamous before, lots of times. But back then I assumed eventually the women would leave me and I'd be single again."

"Monogamy doesn't count if you assume it's temporary."

"But now, as I've grown old, I see that everything you choose to do means giving up a bunch of other things you thought you might do later. Monogamy with Gilia means never sleeping with Linda Ronstadt."

"I hope to hell you don't try to pass this off as deep thought."

We were having this discussion in the end booth of Dot's Dine Out, which was no longer owned by Dot. She sold the diner to a stock analyst named Garth, who thought feeding rural types was the equivalent of the simple life. No one expected him to last a year. Meanwhile, Dot bought a condo in Mesquite, Nevada, to be near her son who was in a halfway house for cult refugees.

"Dot would never leave customers sitting out here for an eternity," Lydia said. "She knew the meaning of the word *service*."

"Garth likes to get things right."

"Garth is going to get me right over to the Dairy Queen. I have to pick up potting soil at the hardware store before they close."

"That's hours from now."

"Yes, but there might be a run on potting soil." Lydia drained her tea in a single long draw. "I always thought I would be an Olympic swimmer."

"You don't swim."

Lydia gave me a look.

"I mean, I've never seen you swim."

"I was quite the mermaid back in junior high, before I had a baby."

"Another career you sacrificed for me. How many does that make?"

"I still might pick up swimming someday, when I find the time. That's the difference between you and I."

"You and me."

"You've given up on Linda Ronstadt, but I haven't given up on swimming in the Olympics. You have accepted the aging process."

"I act what I am, and you don't."

"You act older than that fossil out at Haven House. He's still plotting to run away to Greece with his girlfriend." Her voice rose in a shriek. "*How long can it take to cook a cheeseburger, for God's sake!*"

"Mom, calm down."

"I'll calm down when you bury me."

———

I had been having a lot of trouble with sanity of late. It started with waking up in the morning to a tidal wave of formless grief, as if getting up was the most difficult and useless thing a human could do. Then I would be okay through coffee and a bagel, sometimes I pulled off the morning till lunch with Gilia, but early afternoon brought the full range of ennui sliding into malaise and across to overwhelming fatigue.

It embarrassed me no end that others seemed to go along in the day-by-day sameness of routine without screaming or rending their flesh. I didn't scream in public, or anywhere else, for that matter, and I wasn't totally certain what rending of flesh entailed, exactly. Yet I was often overcome with an almost but not quite irresistible urge to poke out the eyes of perfectly nice people.

I lived then, and I still live now, by a strict personal code. When an acquaintance, or even a good friend, stops you on the street and says, "How you doing?" the man holding up his end of civilization lies. He says, "Terrific! And you?" to which the acquaintance or friend replies, "Never been better." Small talk—lies—holds society together. Without it, everyone would act like they lived in New York.

I had a wife I loved and two children. I had enough money to live where I wanted to live and do what I wanted to do. I was insuranced. I did good for the world, in the form of my home for unwed mothers, and I had a creative outlet, in the novels. I even had a poem accepted by the *Kansas Quarterly*, although the editor who liked it died, and the new editor sent me a contributor's copy but never published the poem. So what was the matter? Why did I need to poke eyes out simply because people acted as if I were invisible?

I had heard of a disease where the sick person cannot help but shout *Cocksucker* in inappropriate situations. When I was younger, I felt this disease was awfully convenient and could probably be cured with a buzzer. But now, I was starting to understand. I was dangerously close to bad behavior in public myself; I just hadn't decided what form it should take.

No one knew I was walking the tightrope, or at least I thought no one knew. Maybe they all knew. I imagined Gilia and Maurey talking about me when I wasn't around. "He's been hanging on by a thread for years," Maurey says. Gilia says, "He likes it that way." Then they would go back to comparing *Star Wars* to *The Empire Strikes Back*.

Recently, I had been trying to come up with a socially acceptable way to explode. I didn't want to hurt anybody, especially Gilia, so running off with a woman twenty years younger than me was out of the question. I had long since given up on the sport screw. And I didn't want to retreat into drugs and alcohol. I had too much experience to think knocking yourself stupid avoided depression. Suicide was not an alternative. Life may be hell, but at least it was interesting. It might get better. From what I could see, death rarely gets better. I was looking for a form of pragmatic insanity. A way to be taken seriously without breaking anything that can't be fixed.

An hour after our lunch at Dot's, Lydia gave a lesson in how it's done.

———

What happened was Lydia walked down to Zion Hardware for her potting soil. She spent a few minutes comparing nutrients on the various bags, then explained to Corinthia Knudsson the best way to clean pine tar off overalls, not that Lydia had ever cleaned pine tar off overalls, but Corinthia looked so pitiful standing there in the aisle, lost among the choices of cleaning products, that Lydia felt the poor woman needed help.

Lydia said, "Lighter fluid and ashes—woodstove ashes work better than cigarette, but use what you have."

Corinthia thanked her and bought lighter fluid. Lydia told

Dave Peters if his dog crapped in her yard one more time, she would castrate it. Dave promised his dog would not crap in her yard again, and Lydia said, "See that he doesn't."

She arrived at the checkout stand feeling pretty good about the whole thing. She was part of her community. People knew her and paid attention when she spoke. It beat the heck out of lock-up.

Levi Mohr had spent one semester at BYU and now was working in his father's hardware store while he waited to go on his mission. He had no idea who Lydia was or what she represented.

"Three dollars, fifteen cents," he said. As Lydia dug though her purse for correct change, Levi added, "I gave you the senior discount."

Lydia leaned across the potting soil and pulled the cash register off the counter. It missed Levi's foot, which was the only good luck he had that day. Instead the cash register hit the floor with an awesome crash. Lydia swept aside a glass cookie jar filled with donations for the Class of '93 Senior Trip, then she toppled the blank-key rack, sending hundreds of keys over the key-cutter machine and across the floor.

Levi jumped her from behind, pinning her arms. She screamed, stomped his instep, and gave him an elbow in the balls that pretty much took the fight out of the boy. Lydia lit into an aisle of Coleman lanterns, stoves, and camping paraphernalia, then she turned to the power tools. Drills rained like hail in May.

At that point, Lydia stopped screaming and concentrated on destruction. A silent crowd stayed out of her way as she worked through gardening and automotive. On aisle two, she picked up a hickory ax handle that made the glass doors on the socket set display a piece of cake. The sheriff's department arrived between kitchens and dinette sets. There were three of them. The two rookies were at a total loss, and if the situation had been left to them, eventually they would have shot her, but Mangum Potter, who had been around GroVont longer than even Lydia, knew what to do.

He said, "Lydia, you've made your point."

Lydia stopped in mid-backswing and looked over at Mangum, then back at her swath of destruction. Her posture went wimbly, and she sobbed once. As the law closed in, Lydia threw the ax handle through eight settings of Fiestaware. Then she gave up.

———

Three years earlier, Lydia Callahan and Hank Elkrunner had been living in a converted sheep wagon in the bowels of Canyon de Chelly, a couple miles beyond the White House ruins. Lydia drove their cherry red Ford F-1 pickup truck into Chinle to the post office to pick up her contributor's copy of *Harper's Bazaar*. She complimented the girl at the window on her turquoise bracelet and the girl burst into tears. Some fugitives would have been tipped off by this show of emotion, but Lydia was busy checking to see if *Harper's* spelled her name right and didn't notice the four agents until one of them said, "Lydia Callahan."

Lydia screamed, "*Rape!*" and ran into the women's room. One agent came out with a cat scratch across his nose, and another pulled his weapon for the first time in a thirty-year career. The Navajo postal workers and patrons formed a silent double line from the women's room door to the waiting FBI Chrysler. Fearing an insurrection, the FBI called the Park Service for backup, but in the end, Lydia was taken without incident. There was a photo run by the Reuters news service of Lydia standing in the harsh New Mexico sunlight wearing shorts and a halter top, her hair in braids and one fist raised to the sky in defiance.

Lydia was quoted as saying, "I will flee no more forever."

Her article in *Harper's Bazaar* was entitled "Ageism in the Feminist Movement." It was written in response to the new president of NOW, who'd called Lydia a *fringe dinosaur*. The FBI got hold of the magazine and gave it some high-tech radium bath, followed it through four safe mailboxes, and was waiting when Lydia arrived at the post office on that March morning of 1990.

Most of Lydia's family, and that included me, Maurey, and Shannon, believed quite firmly that if Lydia had kept her mouth shut, the FBI and Secret Service would not have even been looking for her. But she made herself such a high-profile fugitive that they had to track her down and prosecute. It wasn't just *Harper's*. Lydia wrote scores of "Nonnie, nonnie, can't-catch-me" articles. She wrote so many letters to the editor that they were collected into a book called *Notes from the Underground*. It wasn't a bestseller, but every review used the term *cult following*. Lydia always did want a cult following.

———

Gilia answered the phone on the third ring. She held the receiver so Esther could hear the conversation, but Esther was more interested in eating an earring.

Gilia said, "What?"

She listened a few moments and became just distracted enough for Esther to hook a finger in the earring and pull. "Ouch!" Gilia yelped. She said into the phone, "No, not you. My ear."

She listened a few more moments, then hung up.

She found me in the library with Eden Rae and Honor, where we were going over Eden's release documents. I was explaining blind adoptions.

"These papers say I can't tell you where the baby goes, and when he or she gets old enough to come looking, I can't tell him or her who you are."

Eden didn't comment. The process depressed her no end.

"Of course," I went on, "laws change. What's right and legal now may not be right and legal in twenty years. There's always the chance of this child showing up on your door, so I would advise against keeping secrets from your future husband."

Eden said, "Future husband, my ass."

Gilia interrupted from the doorway. "The sheriff called. Your mother trashed Zion Hardware."

I looked up from the papers. "Trashed?"

"Mangum says a bomb would have been more delicate."

"Jesus," Eden said. "You come from a violent family."

Gilia said, "He wants you down there right away. Says he'll have to stun gun her if she doesn't mellow out."

Rather than bolting down to the sheriff's office to save my mom from the stun gun, I made a side trip to Zion Hardware, in hopes of saving her from far worse. Owen Mohr and I discussed inventory and Levi's long-term trauma. Owen inflated prices a bit, but considering the state of his store, he was decent about the matter; Owen took pride in being a good businessman, not a gouger. He arrived at a number, I wrote a check, and we shook hands, all without lawyers. Things like that still happen in small towns.

I found Lydia in the women's holding cell. She sat folded on the floor with her back against the wall, her knees up under her chin and her arms around her legs. Brandy Epstein was lowering the parole-officer boom. "I hope you enjoyed your little tantrum, Mrs. Elkrunner, because it is going to cost you two years."

Lydia had shut down. She gave no sign of knowing where she was, much less who was talking and what was being threatened. She had disappeared into the zone known only by those who have served time. Her face was gone.

Brandy turned on me. "I have to revoke her."

I said, "Owen Mohr isn't pressing charges."

Brandy stared hard at me for longer than I was comfortable being stared at by a parole officer. "How much did it cost you?"

I met her eyes straight on. "Eleven thousand."

She blinked. She turned back to look down at Lydia on the floor. Lydia gave no indication she had heard the exchange.

"Okay," Brandy said, "but the party segment of our relationship is over. I want her in my office every Monday, eight a.m. If she's two minutes late, she goes on report."

"She'll be there."

"And no more goldbricking the community service. She owes me five hundred hours, and so far she's given me four. From now on, if that old man craps, I want her there to change his diaper."

"Why are you taking this so personally?" I asked. "She made a mistake. The only one she's hurting is herself."

Brandy walked over to Lydia and stood closer than she should have. "Too many kids come through my office who can't buy their way out of trouble. It pisses me off when someone can."

Brandy walked out of the cell. I crossed over and touched Lydia's shoulder. "Let's go home, Mom."

9

MAUREY PIERCE LAY ON HER BELLY WITH HER RIGHT EYE screwed up against the spotting scope. Beside her, on the blanket, she had arranged a pair of Bausch & Lomb binoculars, a Peterson's *Field Guide to Western Birds*, and a silver thermos of black coffee.

She spoke slowly, scanning a marshy pond at the bottom of the slope. "Cinnamon teal, a ring-necked, a couple types of goldeneyes. There's a heron in that aspen by the inlet."

Roger tugged his bandanna low over his eyebrows. "Busy little pond."

"Springtime in the Rockies." Maurey cupped her left hand over her left eye, trying to ease the squint pressure. "We had a pair of trumpeters nest in here last year. I was hoping they'd come back." She swiveled the scope to the right. "There's a coyote on the ridge."

"Where?"

Maurey pointed out what looked to Roger like a tan rock. He picked up the binoculars and focused in on the coyote.

Maurey said, "Every female down there is either about to or has dropped in the last few days. In the wild, copulation stops once the female gets pregnant."

"I didn't know copulation stops."

"There's no point if she's already knocked up." She glanced over to see if Roger caught the drift, but he was busy pulling a book from his day pack.

He said, "You ever read this?"

Maurey checked out the cover. "I tried once. The man wrote it used to live on Ditch Creek."

"Did you know him?"

Maurey returned her attention to the spotting scope. "I pulled him out of a snowbank when he got stuck. As I recall, he wasn't much of a winter driver."

"What'd you think of the book?"

"Jesus, what is that in the reeds? All these female ducks look the same." She adjusted the focus again. "It was one of those books spends three hundred pages making you love a person, then the writer kills him and you're supposed to cry and think the book was wonderful. I saw where it was headed and bailed out."

"The baby disappears in the end. He doesn't die."

"His mama does. Sam told me the ending. He thinks this Loren Paul was hot stuff before he went off to Hollywood. Sam took it as a personal insult the guy would rather be rich than sensitive."

Roger unscrewed the thermos and poured an inch of coffee into the lid. "Lydia thinks the book is about me."

Maurey kind of froze in position, like she was holding her breath, even though she wasn't.

"She thinks I'm the kid—Buggie or Fred or whatever his name is."

Maurey turned her head toward Roger. He sipped coffee, not looking at her, pretending to be casual. Maurey said, "Did Lydia explain why she thinks you're a boy in a novel?"

"She says it's a memoir, which is a novel, only true. And she thinks the pieces fit, so it could be me." Roger sneaked a look at Maurey. She seemed okay, not threatened or anything. If his more or less adoptive son was nosing around for birth parents, it would make him nervous, but Maurey seemed untroubled. "Tell me about the woman who brought me to the ranch."

Maurey took the thermos lid from Roger, drained the coffee, then gave him back the lid. "I met Mary Beth in Amarillo, a long time ago. She was living in a hippie commune in Oklahoma, with a drug-abusing hard dick called himself Freedom."

Roger returned his attention to the coyote. "There's a drug-abusing hard dick in the book called Freedom."

"Maybe every drug abuser silly enough to name himself Freedom was a hard dick back then."

As Roger watched, the coyote arched its back and leaped—like a ballerina—and came up with a ground squirrel in its teeth. The coyote swallowed the ground squirrel in one mighty gulp.

Maurey dropped back into the prone spotting scope position. "All those commune kids had silly nicknames. Mary Beth was Critter. Freedom had a son whose name was Brad, but they called him Hawk, if you can believe that. The minute he got off the commune, the kid changed back to Brad."

"The Freedom in the book was Ann's boyfriend, before she got pregnant. He's only mentioned in a couple of paragraphs."

"And Ann is?"

"Buggie's mother. Buggie's father was killed in the hospital parking lot the day Buggie was born, and Lydia's theory is that Freedom did it. Then, five years later, Buggie disappeared from a campground on Jackson Lake. Freedom could have snatched him, and if it's the same Freedom, Mary Beth might have ended up with the boy."

"You got a lot of big ifs there, son." Maurey studied Roger to see how much he wanted to believe the idea. He seemed dead serious, but then, Roger always had seemed dead serious.

"Mary Beth told me Freedom got himself killed in a drug deal, and a couple of his friends dumped you on her. She was working in a dental office in Boulder and just getting out of all that hippie jive, and she was too poor to keep you herself. I was taking in an assortment of lost souls back then, so she drove you up."

Maurey pulled herself to her knees She resented like hell the old age *push* it took to get her off the ground. "You had a little suitcase about the size of an overnight bag, and in the bottom was a picture postcard of the Tetons. I think that's why she first thought of me."

Maurey stood. "Let's go over by the springs. I need to check on an American redstart Pud swears is nesting in a willow patch."

Roger shook out the blanket. "Lydia says I have to track down the author. She says I have a responsibility to discover what happened during the missing years."

Maurey unscrewed the scope off its tripod. "What do you think?"

"I think she's a nosy bitch. What good can come from me knowing stuff that had to be so lousy I stopped talking?"

Maurey stalled for time by writing the date and place next to the drawing of a ring-necked duck in her Petersen's Field Guide. Ring-necked ducks have a ring on their bill. She'd never understood why they weren't called ring bills instead of ring necks, but even more important, this seemed one of those moments when she was supposed to come through like family. Maurey had always known Roger would go searching for his past someday. Her maternal instincts cried out for her to protect the boy, but she knew from bitter experience that once the kids are out of high school maternal instincts are often wrong.

"You remember that time when you and Auburn got into a fight in the school cafeteria?"

"That was no fight. Auburn punched me out and left me lying on the linoleum floor."

"Do you know why he hit you?"

"One of those jock friends of his was calling me a pussy, and when I wouldn't stand up to the jerk, Auburn pushed his friend out of the way and hit me in the face. I guess he was embarrassed to have a brother who was chicken."

"I talked to Auburn that night, and he didn't think you were chicken. It was the opposite."

Roger snorted a laugh. "He didn't punch me for being brave."

"He said you showed nothing. No fear. No shame. You weren't even angry. He couldn't stand it that you could be called a pussy in front of the whole school and not feel anything."

Roger tried to remember what he had felt. In times of attack, his automatic reflex was withdrawal. Something inside would shrivel into a hard little ball surrounded by a cushion of not caring. The Tar Baby syndrome.

Maurey went on. "Auburn said he wanted you to feel something, even if it was only blood in your nose."

Maurey reached across and touched Roger's arm. "What I'm saying is, it's not healthy for a boy your age to hide in a cabin off by himself, insulated from any possibility of pain. Feelings have to be exercised, like muscles, or they rot."

"I feel." Roger carefully wrapped the blanket around the coffee thermos and placed them both in his leather day pack. "Sometimes."

"It's your decision. Do what you want, but I think if there's any chance this writer is your stepfather, and he can tell you what happened to make you like this, it might be a good idea to hear what he has to say."

"You think so?"

"You started talking again, Roger. Now it's time to wake up."

———

Lydia telephoned the federal penitentiary outside Lompoc, California.

Hello, to whom am I speaking? Ivan Belle, I need to speak to a client there...an inmate...His name is Hank Elkrunner, he's located in minimum security, and I am certain you will have no trouble locating him...I am his wife, Lydia Elkrunner...Yes, Ivan, I know visiting hours start at 8:30 a.m. every day but Tuesday and Wednesday; the problem is, I'm in Wyoming and unable to come to California at this time, and I really, really need to talk to Hank...It's an emergency...I am quite aware of that, but those rules are meant for real criminals; Hank couldn't hurt a kitten. He never even broke a law that I am aware of until he helped me evade persecution, and I don't see how you can condemn a man for defending his wife...Look at it this way. If a close family member had died, would you bring him to the phone?... No, I don't want you to tell Hank a close family member has died, I'm simply trying to ascertain the depth of emergency that would motivate you to behave like a human being...No, Ivan, nobody died. Do not tell Hank somebody died. Just go get him and bring him to the telephone...I hear you, Ivan, your lot in life must be difficult, being a bureaucrat who doesn't make the rules but only enforces them... Exercise your imagination and feel what I am feeling. Can't you drum up an iota of compassion...I need to talk to Hank! Don't give me that policy bullshit—you could bring him to the phone if you wanted to. You could if you had an ounce of decency. Ivan, don't hang up on me, you motherfucking slime sucker!

Lydia smacked the telephone against the table edge with such force that the earpiece broke off and flew across the room.

———

Eden Rae's water broke while she was changing Willa Potter's colostomy bag. There was a sound, like a puppy sigh, that either came from her or Willa, then liquid running down her thighs.

Willa held the bed rail with both hands and peeked over at the mix of water, mucous, and streaks of blood spreading across the tile. "Did I do that?"

"No, Mrs. Potter. It came out of me."

Willa stared hard at the floor. "You better go find your people."

"I don't have any people."

Willa watched Eden's hands pull away the soiled plastic bag. The hands moved quickly, stripping the tubes, replacing the bag gasket, taping the tube to Willa's leg. Willa thought Eden had the hands of a child.

"You better let me be, and go find the folks you're staying with. They'll know what to do. They've seen this before."

"You think it could happen right now, any second?"

"Not any second. You have some time yet."

"How long do I have? There's things I wanted to do before it came."

Willa let go of her hold on the rail and settled back onto the bed. "I've had six and lost one," she said, "and each one was different, but my guess is you ought to settle in where you're going to be sometime soon."

The wall-mount TV came on suddenly, loud, showing a man who could clean gravy stains out of trousers. The man shouted, *"Have you ever seen anything this amazing!"* and the studio audience cheered like he'd scored a touchdown.

"Raise up," Eden said.

Willa arched as high as she could while Eden felt under her back until she located the TV remote control jammed against Willa's bony shoulder blade. She pushed the Off button, and the man disappeared.

She said, "I'm sorry. About the one you lost."

Willa said, "Me too." With her right hand, Willa cradled the cool plastic bag against her thigh, while Eden coiled the spare tubing and Zip-locked away the old bag. As she turned to leave the room, Willa raised her head and said, "You find you some people."

———

Eden trickled water down the hall to the duty station, where she told Penny, the night nurse, she had to go home. She didn't say why, and Penny didn't ask. Penny had all the stress she could endure taking care of geriatric invalids; she didn't want anyone's problems she wasn't being paid to deal with.

She said, "Make sure you clock out."

———

Pink light soaked in from the east as Eden Rae walked across the parking lot and unlocked the Madonnaville van. A silver moon sliver hung over the chairlift docking tower on the mountain south of town. Pine siskins and finches took defensive positions on bird feeders over by the fake Japanese garden, with its handicapped-access pathways. Even though it had been explained to her over and over, Eden had no idea what was happening in her body. She'd never paid attention to the details, which meant the first contraction, coming as she drove past the airport turnoff, scared the beJesus out of her. The second, ten miles and fifteen minutes later, was quicker, sharper, even more unbelievable. It made her hands jerk down, causing the steering wheel to twist, and both right tires dropped momentarily off the asphalt into loose gravel.

Gilia and I were asleep when Eden pried off her shoes in the doorway and slid into our bed. She lay between us, on top of the covers, holding her belly and staring at the ceiling, waiting.

Gilia's eyes flickered. She rolled to her side and dropped her arm across what she thought were my shoulders, but knew immediately weren't.

"Eden?"

Eden concentrated on her next breath. Nothing that came before or could come after mattered as much as her next breath.

"Is anything the matter?"

"No."

Gilia propped on her elbows and looked down at the girl's face. Across from her, I went from deep sleep to total alertness in a single heartbeat.

"Are you having the baby?" I asked.

"I think so."

No matter how many births I've been in on, I hyperventilate. The thing is, I cannot fathom a person springing alive from between the legs of another person. The miracle floors me. Chemicals surge through my brain, and neurons fire like Fourth of July. Over the years, I have turned into a birth junkie. I need the buzz. The hyperventilation is so predictable that I keep a bag—originally designed for those throwing up on Delta Airlines—in the top drawer of my bureau.

I dived out of bed and ran for the bag.

"Have you had contractions?" Gilia asked.

Eden nodded.

"Let's wake up Honor and see where we stand." This last was meant for me, but I missed it. I stood there against the wall, puffing into my Delta Airlines barf bag and staring at the pregnant girl on my bed. To me, women in labor are the most beautiful objects on Earth, an opinion not shared by most women in labor. The couple of times I've commented on their incredible radiance, women in the midst of a contraction have snapped fairly brutal comebacks.

"Sam," Gilia said. "Wake up Honor. But don't wake up Baby Esther."

"I can handle that."

———

Honor Edmonson, the home nurse-practitioner, measured dilation and timed contractions and announced that everyone could eat breakfast, but lunch would be at the hospital, if at all. I offered to help Eden back to her own room, but she wasn't disposed to leave our bed. In my experience, even a mild, low-maintenance woman becomes willful in labor, until in the last few moments before birth, reason and docility fly right out the window. And Eden had never been known as low maintenance. She wanted a Dr Pepper in a plastic cup with no ice, then she wanted a stuffed Pooh bear she'd brought out from Pasadena, then she wanted every pain pill in the compound.

I phoned Dr. Hazen, who was on the fifth tee at Teton Pines golf course. Dr. Hazen talked to Honor and decided he had time to finish the nine holes, but Honor told him if he wasn't at the hospital when we arrived, she would stick his putter up his crack, headfirst. Honor was willful in her own way.

Soon, I pulled the van up to the front door, and Gilia and Honor brought Eden outside. Eden held the Pooh bear in the crook of her left arm. She shaded her eyes with her right hand and peered into the back of the van.

"Where's Roger?"

Gilia answered, "Up in his cabin, I guess. I heard him earlier in the shower."

"Roger has to be with me."

"Sam and Honor will be here. They'll take care of you."

"I'm not doing this without Roger."

Honor said, "Eden, the baby's going to come when it comes, and I'd be a lot happier if that was the hospital instead of out here in the yard."

Eden balked. "I'm not going without Roger."

I found Roger in his cabin, plucking bass to a Stan Getz

CD. He had *Zuleika Dobson* perched on the music stand. Roger turned his page without missing a beat.

I picked his jacket off the floor and held it out to him. "Eden Rae refuses to have her baby unless you're there."

Roger stopped mid-note. "Why me?"

"My guess is she has you mixed up with the father."

"I'm not the father. She was pregnant when she came here."

"Yeah, but you've been diddling her. Come on."

Roger leaned the bass against his desk and slipped on the tennis shoe with the broken lace. "Diddling?"

"I imagine in Eden's mind, one diddler is the same as another."

Roger wondered why he ever thought his actions might be secret. You live way the hell up a dirt road in the mountains, and the whole state knows if you so much as spit upwind. People in huge cities have more privacy than hermits. "I've never been at a birth before."

"It'll make you a better man."

I drove with Honor and Roger on each side of Eden in the middle seat. Eden held Roger's hand so tightly it hurt. During a contraction, she called him *Jimmy*—"Jimmy, you lied like a dog."

"How's that?" Roger asked.

"Told me you're sterile."

Honor checked her watch. "Six minutes and going down. We're cutting this closer than I had in mind."

I said, "She should have gone straight to the hospital from Haven House. Saved herself a drive up and down the mountain."

Eden yelled, "*Don't criticize me, you prick.*"

I shut up and drove.

———

At the hospital, the anesthesiologist gave Eden an epidural. Dr. Hazen strode through the delivery room, still wearing his golf shoes. Honor gave him a dirty look, but like doctors everywhere, he deflected it without missing a step.

"How's our little trooper doing today?" he asked.

Eden hissed, like a cat.

The doctor chuckled as if she'd said something utterly charming. He said, "Don't start without me." Then he left the room to wash up and change.

Eden's eyes left the ceiling and searched out Roger at her side. "Who was that cocksucker?"

———

I hyperventilated into a Johnny Horizon litter bag. Roger stood beside Eden, his wrist crushed in her iron grip. Honor stood between Roger and Dr. Hazen, who sat on a stool at the end of the bed, looking into Eden's cervix.

"When I say *Push*, you push for all you're worth."

Eden said, "Stick it up your ass."

"Okay, push."

Eden's face was fascinating. Sweat sheen, eyes, the tips of her teeth, purple vein throbbing in her neck, every facet of Eden's life had come down to the word *Push*.

Dr. Hazen placed his hands like a quarterback awaiting the snap from center. "That's it. Harder now."

Eden's fingers clawed blood from Roger's wrist.

Dr. Hazen said, "Bo Bo needs a bigger door."

Honor handed him a pair of scissors—long handles, short blades—and to Roger's horror, the doctor scissored Eden Rae open.

Eden Rae's eyes rolled behind the eyelids, and her breasts sucked in on themselves. I don't think she noticed the pain of being sliced, not on top of the pain the baby was causing.

Dr. Hazen said, "Now's the time."

She drew a sharp breath and tore her head from side to

side. She hissed through her teeth. Her face glistened like a garden slug. Something soaked and candle waxy and bruise colored appeared between Eden's legs. And flesh, of a sort. It didn't look like anything I'd seen before, and I've seen a lot of births.

Eden's chest buzzed. She growled, "Get that out of me."

Dr. Hazen held the baby's head in his palm. It had a blond stream of hair, and its eyes were closed. He said, "Push it out yourself."

Honor leaned over, blocking Roger's view. "Show the prick how tough you are."

"*JesusChristmotherfuckshit!*"

Events overlapped. I had trouble following the order, and Roger, who'd never been at one of these things, was totally whacked-out. Dr. Hazen was saying the head was out, and Honor was saying *Push* in a voice without panic but close enough to it that everyone knew there was something out of the ordinary, and over it all, Eden was screaming. Blood and fluid spurted onto the doctor's forearms, spreading onto Eden's hospital gown. His hand was inside Eden up to the wrist, and I couldn't see how the baby's head and the doctor's hand fit in the same gap, but they did, and Eden was hurting from it.

Dr. Hazen said, "Push her knees up under her armpits."

When Roger and I didn't jump to his order, Honor yelled, "*Now.*"

We each took a thigh—me, with two hands, Roger with the free one—and pushed toward Eden's head, way beyond what I would have thought possible.

"Is this right?" Roger said, but no one answered.

Roger needed to know this was normal, it happened every day. He looked across at me for reassurance and didn't get it. I was swallowing vomit.

Dr. Hazen said, "Take her suprapubic," and Honor shoved

Roger hard, pushing him toward Eden's head. Roger said, "What?" but Honor was already up on the bed, with both her hands planted on Eden's belly and her knees on Eden's ribs, giving Eden her weight and saying, "Come on, Eden, push it. *Push it!*"

"The arm's caught up behind his head. Wedged in good," Dr. Hazen said. He rotated his wrist into the baby's face, sending Eden into a higher pitch of screaming.

I said, "Cesarean?"

Honor gasped between pumps on Eden's belly. "Too late."

The blood and noise were nothing like births I'd seen before, and nothing like the births I'd seen in movies or read about in books. It went beyond my imagination, and I knew I was seeing a human come to life, or die, or maybe both at once. I knew whatever this was mattered. Life is important.

Dr. Hazen had both hands on the baby, one supporting the head, the other up inside Eden Rae. He twisted the baby clear around, till the eyes faced downward. I could see the nape of the baby's neck. It looked like wax paper.

Dr. Hazen said, "Now."

Honor shoved all her weight into Eden Rae's belly and the baby squirted out so quickly Dr. Hazen almost missed the catch.

It was over. Eden fell back, sucking air but no longer trembling from pain. Roger and I lowered her thighs. Honor calmly came off the bed. I reached for my breathing bag. The delivery turned matter-of-fact.

Dr. Hazen cradled the baby in his left arm and clamped and clipped the cord. He said, "We avoided breaking his clavicle. That's a plus."

Honor rubbed the baby roughly with a towel, as if scrubbing out an ink stain, as the skin tone went from blue to pink. The baby started to cry.

"What happened?" Roger was crying also.

I said, "Eden had a baby."

Eden released her hold on Roger's arm, leaving finger indentations and orb-shaped blood lines where the nails had dug in. She turned her head to the side, away from Roger, staring at the gray wall. Her eyes were open.

After a bit, Honor said, "It's a boy."

Eden blinked, once.

Honor said, "Do you want to see him?"

Eden said, "Get it away from me."

Honor turned and walked out of the room with the baby. The vein pulsed in Eden's throat, beating like the baby's heart. Roger reached across the pillow and touched the pulsing vein.

Eden said, "I want to go home."

Roger drew his hand away from her neck. He made his decision.

10

THE ROBBERS ME AND BILL KILLED WERE NAMED HENRY AND HANK MILLER, and from what Shadrach told me, we'd done worse things than put an end to those two. They went out of Butte, Montana, where they'd been strikebreakers during the copper wars. Their method of stopping a strike was to shoot the leaders until more cooperative leaders took control. Their mistake was in trying to blackmail the copper kings for ordering the crimes. The kings owned the judges, they didn't care who knew they ordered a bunch of union killings.

That got the Millers run out of Butte. Then they turned to saloon robbing, which led naturally enough into bank robbing. They picked Shadrach up at a sporting club in Virginia City, where his job was general grunt for a pack of high-strung women. Shad didn't mind where the Millers took him, so long as it was out of Virginia City. Up till our little bank, Shadrach had been made to stay outside with the horses. Ours was a shakedown run for one of the bigger banks in Billings where they had real money.

"I flunked the test," Shad said.

"You're alive, and the Millers are dead." I said. "They're the ones flunked."

Life didn't swap out in a single breath the way it had during the quake or when the boiler blew. This time took longer, even though it was just as certain. At first, things went even better than before. There was an element of townfolk looked up to killers of bank robbers. Young boys pointed me out in the street as someone to admire. Mr. Cox gave me a ten-dollar bonus. Frank Lesley quit being so snooty. Agatha's sparking level took on a new interest. Whenever she talked about me killing Hank Miller, her skin colored and her breath grew quick. She saw me as dangerous and desirable.

Shadrach moved into my place there out by the Great Northern track. I'd missed having company in the evenings since Dad got smashed into, and it was a pleasure having him around, even though he had to get up at dawn every morning and run up to the Coxes to do Bill's bidding.

In my estimation, Bill took advantage of the situation with Shadrach. Bill figured he had himself a slave. He made Shadrach jog two miles for soda pop and wash his long johns and dry down his horse. I never heard Shad complain, but when he came in at night, he was worn through.

Things could have gone along in that vein for a good while, and I wouldn't have minded. Of course they didn't. We'd killed two Miller brothers, but as fate had it, there was four of them.

———

Billings had an underground bowling alley. People nowdays think there weren't bowling alleys and skating barns and even telephones before the Great War, but we had all those in Montana. It was an interesting time to be young and live in a town, ever month some new marvel arrived. Anyway, me and Agatha and another couple was at the bowling alley, and I rolled a hundred ten. Agatha rolled higher, on account of the pinboy was sweet on her and set her pins tighter than mine. You could see them bunched up so close if you so much as blew on the number one, all the rest collapsed.

I forget what the other couple rolled. The boy was lanky, I remember that. The girl laughed at the wrong places. She could of rolled higher than her boy too, but she was feminine enough to throw a few frames so he wouldn't be outshone by a woman. Agatha would never lose a game on purpose to make a man feel superior, and I admired her for that.

I bought Agatha a strawberry ice but not one for myself because I was still saving money, and we came outside. The bright sunlight made vision difficult for a moment, when all of a sudden, I heard three *pops*, and the glass window behind exploded, cutting the boy we was with across the eyebrow. I hit dirt and pulled Agatha under a Brush Runabout. Agatha was upset no end. She'd fallen on the strawberry ice, and for a moment, I thought she was shot. That was an awful moment. I thought ever'one I cared for was going to die violently and I'd best not care for anyone again. It couldn't have been two seconds before I knew Agatha wasn't dying, but that's how fast my mind worked.

A police came running and asked me what happened and I said I didn't know. Then the volunteer fire wagon swept past, headed north toward the Great Northern depot. I saw smoke and concluded that the shack Dad bought for thirty dollars was afire. I ran up, but nothing could be saved, including the money I had hid under the floor.

Shadrach was there. He said Roy and Ephir Miller started the fire. I said, "Who?" and he said the dead robbers' brothers, and we'd best leave town in a rush. We went to find Bill, who was hiding in the basement of the Bluebeard. Two hard cases had come to the Cox house and inquired after him and me. He told them we were not home. At first, they didn't believe him, so he told them where I lived.

"You got my home burned," I said.

"What else was I supposed to do? They'd have killed me if I hadn't told them something."

It was agreed we should evacuate Billings. My first impulse was to buy a train ticket the opposite direction as Bill and Shadrach proposed to go, but I had no money. Bill loaned me a mare of no-count named Molly Maguire, and that put me in his debt. We gathered our belongings, which in the case of me and Shad was nothing much, and prepared to flee.

Agatha cried. She said I was running off when she needed me.

"Those men won't bother you after we're gone," I said.

"But I'm old enough now to marry."

This brought me up short. I touched a tear as it crossed the freckles on her cheek. "We'll marry soon as I come back. The Millers'll get on to something else quick enough."

"No, they won't. They'll follow you. I'm not going to be a widow, Oly Pedersen."

"Let's worry about making you a widow after we're married."

Bill called for me to get on my damn horse. I kissed Agatha on the mouth, then mounted, and the three of us rode south.

———

My idea as to why people in modern days think the West before the war was bleak and without improvements is because the only ones writing books back then was the sons and daughters of homesteaders. Farms and ranches is all you hear about, 'cause cowboys are more interesting than fellas who work in the bank. Birthing calves and surviving hailstorms is entertainment—if you ain't doing it—whereas skating barns is entertainment to do, but not to read about. The truth is, folks in Billings had more in common with those in New York City, or maybe even Paris France than they did with ranchers forty miles south of town. Down along where the Big Horn crosses the Wyoming border, there weren't indoor toilets and telephones. No bowling alleys. Dropping into that part of Wyoming was like stepping back twenty years.

Shadrach took us to his family's line camp up above Horseshoe Bend on Medicine Mountain there. Bert Pierce, his father, trapped fur along with Shad's brother Meshach. If you're wondering about Abednego, he died in birth. Took his mama with him. Bert Pierce didn't turn to opium as my dad did, but he gave up ranching and personal hygiene. Two bachelors who skin animals for a living make for a rank household. Those two had also been around one another long enough they'd dispensed with the use of words. Bert still spoke, when he had to, but Meshach had reduced communication to five or six animal sounds which covered ever'thing from "Pass the buttermilk" to "Get out of my way or I will kill you." We stayed at their place a week, and I never did hear Meshach say a word in English.

An old man name of Silas Crombie owned the former Pierce ranch, along with most all the other former-home ranches in the area. Rumor had it Silas Crombie wasn't above giving a nudge to some of those ranches teetering on the brink of calamity. I wouldn't doubt it. He was mean as a badger with bad teeth.

Shad got us hired at the Crombie Ranch, him and Bill as cowboys, me as common labor. Crombie hinted that I was a charity case, but he sure didn't work me like he was doing favors. While Bill and Shad hardly ever got off their horses in the course of a day, I rarely got on one.

They started me in irrigation. Now it is over and done, I admit that I came to enjoy irrigation. There is a satisfaction to be gained in moving water. You clear the ditch, remount the head gate, learn to read flat ground. It was gravity flooding we did. Water flows downhill, and there's nothing in God's plan you can do to bring it back uphill but wait for rain. The cattle stayed in the mountains all summer while I grew grass. Buffalo grass is best, but don't ask me why, buffalo grass pretty much disappeared with the buffalo. Mostly what was left was sweet flag and bottlebrush, some timothy. Early fall, me and a couple others—not Bill or Shad—cut hay, then the cowboys moved the cattle onto my meadows, where they grazed till winter, when the hay came back into the picture.

It wasn't banking, but I was alone most of the day, outdoors, and that was nice. Nightfall in the bunkhouse was spent with dime Western novels and poker. Poker brings out the worst in a man. Bill won on a regular basis throughout July and the bulk of August, until one night I caught up with him out by the horse trough.

"What you think them poker boys would do if they caught a man cheating?" I asked Bill.

He stuck his head under the water, then pulled out and shook himself like a dog. "Shoot him, maybe. Beat him within an inch of his life and get his ass fired, for certain."

"There's thumb cuts in the face cards. I didn't put them there."

He placed his hat on his wet hair and faced me. "You got an idea of who did?"

"Nope. But before the next new deck, I recommend you trim your nails."

After that, Bill's winnings evened up. General belief in the bunkhouse was he'd had a run of luck and it played out. The superstitious blamed an owl Bill shot. I kept to myself.

———

Soon as irrigating was done, Crombie decided to replace the buck fences with barbed wire. Stringing wire isn't near as satisfying as moving water. Crombie had seen pictures of the latest posthole digger in the *Police Gazette*, but he was too stingy to buy the real thing.

He said, "Nothing but two shovels clamped face-to-face. We can do that."

I got blisters on blisters from digging holes with his two shovels.

Crombie chose a Ross Four-Point wire, which you may not be aware is the most vicious damn wire ever made. Had barbs could skin a pig. This was before modern stretchers and staples, when your wire was as liable to snap free and whip across your face as not. My entire autumn was spent stanching blood flow. To this day, I get a tic in my left eye when I see a barbed-wire fence.

And, add to the natural pains of fencing, we had a late-year thunderstorm. I was stretching wire across Alkali Creek, when lightning struck fence a good half-mile up the ridge. The charge traveled down wire and caught me so hard I was blown clean out of my boots. When I told them jokers at the bunkhouse, nobody believed me. I showed the burns from my Levi grommets, but they still called me a liar. I'd of quit, but the next day, the rain turned to snow. Only a fool quits a job going into wintertime.

———

Agatha Ann wrote me a love letter every Sunday afternoon after church. I'd bought her a jar of red ink on her last birthday, and she had wonderful penmanship. People used to put stock in penmanship. Now, nobody gives a hoot. You want something wrote nice now, you hire it out.

She'd started Billings Polytechnic, where she was learning literature. She wanted to write poetry and set it to music. Her poetry was melodious. She used words such as *soul* and *heart* and *blackness* in every poem. She wanted us to be wed soon so she could have babies. She said babies would make her a higher-quality poetess. Her plan was for me to work in daylight for Mr. Cox and come home at night and help her make babies, and the next morning she would write a poem about her soul.

The letters generally took a week and a half to reach the ranch, sometimes much longer. Once, I got three in a single day. Bill teased me about mail from a girl, but I knew he wanted love letters himself, if only for the chance to show off. It irked him no end the girl writing me was his sister. To his dying day, Bill maintained Agatha was homely and my only interest was their father's bank.

I do not possess any of Agatha's red-ink letters. To save them from Bill's mockery, I memorized each one, then burned them in the cookstove. However, at this time, I will recite you one.

This letter came between Christmas and New Year's 1914.

My Dearest Oleander,

I hope you are staying warm and indoors since the winter thus far has been brutal in Yellowstone County. I trust it is not so loathsome in Wyoming. Frank Lesley escorted Jerusalem Snider and I to the moving pictures yesterday evening. They played a Theda Bara picture named The Galley Slave. *Jerusalem and I agree Theda Bara is the ideal of womanhood. If you do not return home soon and make an honest woman of me, I believe I shall go to California and become an actress. Ha!*

Your loving betrothed,
Agatha Ann Cox

I asked Bill who Theda Bara was. He said she was a sex maniac. He'd heard she had relations with Douglas Fairbanks and Dorothy Gish at the same time. I didn't tell Bill his sister wished to emulate her.

Bill was not the one to talk about sex maniacs. He himself was of an age where hardly a thing in the world mattered more than the rut. Except maybe talking about the rut. Bill claimed to have taken hundreds of women. To hear him, you'd think every fallen angel between the South Canadian River in Oklahoma and the

Milk in Montana fell before his unquenchable appetite. He acted like he'd done something the rest of us should envy, but all them women Bill had, he paid for. Don't take skill to seduce a whore. Takes five dollars, tops.

The one hardship Bill saw to life as a cowboy on the Crombie Ranch was the three-day ride to the nearest professional.

"I can't concentrate on my work if I'm filled up with pressure," he complained.

Shad told him to relieve his pressure on a yearling. Shad had worked in a bad house, and he said those women have no pity. "You'll gain more satisfaction from a calf," he said. "Calf won't go down to the kitchen after and make fun of your whanger."

I personally never witnessed Shadrach having his way with a bovine. He may have been pulling my leg, I do not know. All I know is, more than once I heard him say your average maverick is sweeter than your average whore, and it could be the truth that he knew first-hand. I wouldn't have doubted it, coming from his brother Meshach, so maybe Shad was raised that way. He was still my friend. I've never judged folks by their inclinations.

Come January, Bill located a whore not ten miles from the ranch. I have no idea how he found her. I think Bill could sniff out a willing woman like one of them French hogs on a mushroom. Saturday he rode off to the east, and Sunday he came back with a smile.

He said, "She told me I'm the most forceful man in her experience."

Shadrach said, "They're supposed to say that. It's part of the job."

"But this fair flower is sincere," Bill said. "I've been around, and I can tell when they lie."

Her name was Swamp Fox. At least, that is what the cowboys wound up calling her. She was of Kiowa-Crow mix, with maybe some Irish thrown in, and she lived in a sheep wagon up the head of Burnt Wagon Draw. Every cowboy in the bunkhouse took his turn at riding up the draw. Even Shad went the once. When he came back, I asked him how she was and he said about the way you'd expect for a woman named Swamp.

But the others swore she was as capable a whore as any you could find in Cheyenne. They'd gather round the dining board and draw straws for the privilege of riding out there next. I guess poker only goes so far. Nowdays, whores in winter have been replaced by satellite TV.

One evening, it came to Bill that I never took part in the straw drawing. Right there at the mess table, in front of everyone, he called my manhood into question.

"Oly Pedersen, you are a virgin," Bill said.

I lied. "Like hell I am." Had she heard, my words would have pierced Agatha to the heart.

"We all know you're a virgin," Bill said. "We can tell by the way you pass water." The six or so men around the table nodded knowingly, as if what Bill said made a lick of sense.

He went on in this vein. "Real man's water flows up in an arc like a rainbow. You piss straight down in the dirt."

"What are you doing, watching me pee?"

"Proves you're a virgin," Bill said.

The final throwdown of all this talk is I went to rut on some woman I had no desire to rut on. I know damn well I shouldn't have. I knew at the time I was playing the fool. But it is a sad fact of human nature that an enemy's scorn can cause you to betray those you love.

The wind was whipping and popping, and the snow made that *squeak* sound under Molly Maguire's hooves which is a sure sign of below zero. I rode the ten miles out to Swamp Fox's sheep wagon, wondering what in hell I was doing. I mean, Billings had blocks of ill repute where naked women leaned out the windowsills of their cribs, calling to any male who went by. I'd even been in the Lucky Diamond one Christmas, for a drink. The Lucky Diamond was as palatial as any house in Egypt. It was so high class if the girls had been dressed, you'd think you was in an embassy, maybe, or a normal school back east. But I hadn't gone upstairs. Not a once. I was saving my money and myself for Agatha. She was saving herself for me. It only seemed fair that I should approach our union as unblemished as herself.

Besides, Agatha told me if I ever went upstairs she would cut off my tallywhacker with pinking shears. Say what you might about Agatha Ann Cox, she was spunky. She even showed me the shears.

A quarter mile this side of the wagon, I met a young cowboy name of Wisconsin John coming my way.

"Going in for leftovers?" he asked.

"I'm just out for a ride," I said.

He slapped his thigh with his hat and whooped into the wind. The whoop was carried off almost before it left his mouth. He leaned toward me in the saddle. "Wear spurs when you mount her," he shouted. "Without purchase, you're liable to fall in." Whisky John thought that was about the funniest thing he'd ever heard. I rode on.

The sheep wagon set at the head of a long meadow in what appeared to be the loneliest place on Earth. There was no trees, no hills, no nothing but white snow, white sky, white canvas on the wagon with a black pipe drifting smoke the same color as the sky and snow. A mule was tied to the corral poles. Somebody had stacked hay underneath the wagon, but not enough to insulate proper. I'd of probably turned back if it wasn't so cold and such a long ways home. I should have. I knew it at the time, but I didn't. Instead I tied Molly next to the mule and knocked on the wagon door. There's no one to blame but myself.

Inside was warm from the firebox and a lantern there. Swamp Fox was propped on a shelf bed at the far end, eating a baked yam dribbled with honey. She licked her fingers and said, "Three dollars."

"I was told two."

"Three."

"I ain't got but two."

She pondered calling my bluff. Nobody who had three dollars was going to ride way out here in frozen hell, then turn around and go back without spending it.

"Show me," she said.

I turned out my pockets—two dollars. I wasn't lying.

"Two, then, but don't expect feed for the horse."

She wasn't ugly by any means—a mite fat, and she smelled like you would expect a person would who'd been rutted on a few times between baths. But her hair was shiny black, and her posture wasn't slovenly or nothing. I've seen lots worse in the Billings' cribs.

She had a wooden bench by a pull-down table where she must of fixed meals when it was too cold to go out. Sheep wagons look like nothing from outside, but once inside, you'd be impressed at how the herders use the room. Swamp Fox must have had twenty hinges affixed to things for swinging down and up and out. It's like being in a closet, only a big closet. Ever'thing you'd expect to find in a shack twice the size is there. The bench even had a built-in bootjack, for the convenience of customers.

As I bent to pull my right boot off the jack, I heard a rustle like a mouse in a paper poke, and I looked under the bed into a pair of brown eyes.

"Somebody's under there," I said.

Swamp Fox made a *grunt* sound. It was one of those guttural noises that can be taken for *yes* or *no* or *so what*. An all-purpose kind of *huh*.

"It's a little girl," I said.

"My daughter."

What I saw of the little girl was all eyes and cheekbones and scrawny neck. I don't believe she was as full-blood as Swamp Fox. Her eyes never blinked a once.

"What's she doing down there?" I asked.

"Sleeping, if she knows what's good for her."

I leaned in to take a better look. She had on a potato-sack dress and was lying on a ratty blanket. She had an old book in there with her, but I couldn't read the title or tell you what language it was.

"If you and me together break the bed, we'll crush her."

"Been a lot bigger men than you on this bed, and it's not broke yet."

"But what if it breaks under us?"

Swamp Fox gave it a moment's thought. The girl drew back a bit, as if she was afraid I might reach in and touch her. Swamp Fox said, "Evie can sit on the bench till you're through with me."

"I cain't do it with her watching."

"Then she can stay where she is."

"I cain't do it with her listening. How old is she, anyway? Ten? Twelve?"

Swamp Fox spoke in Crow, and the girl scooted out from under the bad, past me, and to the door.

"Wait a minute," I said. "Where you going?"

The girl looked from me to her mother and back to me. Swamp Fox made the Plains Indians sound for *Go!* The girl went.

"Is she going over to the neighbor's to wait?" I asked. Swamp Fox laid back on the bunk and dangled her hands over her head. I said, "I know she is not, 'cause there ain't no neighbors. Not for five miles. You got her waiting outside in the cold, don't you?"

"You didn't want her here."

"But I don't want her freezing outside whilst I wallow in her mama."

"Be quick then."

TIM SANDLIN

I put my boot back on and left. The wind caught me right off and took my hat twenty yards south. When I chased it down and went to my horse, the little girl was crawling out from under the sheep wagon. Turned out she could speak English after all.

She grabbed hold of my sleeve and said, "Mother will blame me if you go. She'll say she can't make money with me underfoot."

"She can't. Not with Christian customers, anyway."

"Please, Mister. She'll get rid of me if she can't work."

I looked down at the little girl, crying, barefoot, wearing nothing but a potato sack. The twin muscles that ran from her nostrils to her upper lip stood out farther than other people's. I noticed that right off.

I dug into my pocket. "Here. I'll pay her for taking up her time. Then she won't blame you for lost income."

The girl stayed next to my horse, trying to stand out of the wind. "Mama's a whore. Whores don't take money for not working." I was to find later in France that this was a complete untruth. I sailed through the whole war paying whores for not working, then pretending that they had. Whores don't care if you use them or not, so long as you pay the price. It was just my luck for my first whore to have pride in her profession.

I said, "Hell." The girl was pleading with her eyes and quivering like a rabbit caught in a snare and about to be snuffed from life. "Come on back in," I said. "It's better to have you in there watching than out here freezing. If them's the only choices."

I doubt if a young man ever lost his innocence under more unpleasant circumstances. The girl sat on the bench across from the firebox and drew pictures on the table top with a coal chunk while I mounted her mother. Swamp Fox spread her fat legs and grabbed hold of me and put me in. I tried to look away from the girl, to concentrate on the folds of Swamp Fox's neck, but it could not be done. Not by me, anyway. Ever time I snuck glances

146

at the girl, she was staring, unblinking, at me. If there was any blessing at all, it was that it soon ended.

———

Four weeks later, I was cleaning ditches up on the Musselshell and had me a lunch of biscuits with cold gravy and coffee. There'd been a Chinook, and the aspens were going into a false bud like they sometimes do when it gets warm too soon. After my coffee, I went to water a juniper, and when the flow come, it brought a sharp pain like ground glass in my willy. I knew right then that I had been cursed.

———

Shadrach said Meshach knew a cure he learned from the Crow chief White Man Runs Him. White Man Runs Him had been a scout with Custer in '76 and gone on to elder statesman of his tribe. According to Shadrach, the old Indian'd had many cases brought on by his tastes in white women, and he'd worked out a surefire, failure-proof cure. So Shad rode up Medicine Mountain to find Meshach while the rest of us suffered in various levels of silence. There was seven of us had it, including Bill and Shad, and I only remember one who screamed when he made water. Name of Ernie; not a day over fourteen. Ernie cried himself to sleep and swore to God Almighty he would never stick his pecker in a hole again. Ever'body else just looked grim.

Shad came back with a poultice made of ground thistles, alum, balsamroot, and a secret ingredient Meshach said would one day be the Crow's revenge against the whites. When the entire male population of North America had a case, the Crow would cure themselves and let everyone else piss thorns.

Whatever was the secret ingredient, it stunk to high heaven. Shad stirred the mix into a twenty-inch Dutch oven filled with spring water and horse urine, and he boiled the results on the woodstove for sixteen hours. Bill said he wasn't about to drink horse piss, but Ernie said he'd do anything it took to put out the fire in his dick. I went along with the deal, on the theory that Meshach might be half coyote, but he wouldn't poison his own brother. After an hour or so, Bill had to pass water, and when he came back inside, he allowed how he'd drink the stuff after all.

Bill was reading a *Police Gazette* his father had sent down. The front page concerned the war between the Allies and Axis in Europe. I had more important things on my mind, but Bill read every article on the subject and pored over the photographs, some of which was gory. There was also maps and lists of which divisions were doing what.

Bill said, "We're missing all the fun."

I gave no response. Smelling the potion we were fixing to drink made Bill's statement somewhat obvious.

He went on as if somebody was listening. "Here we are, wasting our time on cows in Wyoming, when there's thousands of boys no tougher than us fighting in Belgium."

"What's Belgium?" asked Ernie. He was getting more and more nervous, pacing the wall like a trapped barn cat.

"The stretch between France and Germany," Bill said. "Men are dying there for the cause of freedom and justice for all. We should be in on it."

I said, "Not me. I'm not going clear to another continent to fight a war against people I don't even know."

"Then you are a coward," Bill said.

I bristled up. "I don't mind fighting people I do know, such as you if you don't shut your trap."

"You can stay here and shovel horse manure if you want, but Shad and I are going to enlist."

An older cowboy named Joe spoke up. He was twenty-five

and had more experience than the rest of us. "Enlist in what? The United States ain't even in the war."

Bill shook his periodical. "Canada is. Says here they'll take American boys in the Canadian army if we volunteer to fight the Jerries."

Shad came through the door, carrying a load of river rocks. "What's a Jerry?" he asked.

Bill said, "The bastards you and me are going to kill when we go to war."

Shad carried the rocks to the stove and dropped them into the pot of bile, or whatever it was. "Are they Indians?" he asked. "I ain't killing Indians."

"They're European."

I walked over to the stove and looked in at the bubbling glop. "You're cooking rocks," I said.

"Heating them."

"Heating them for what?"

Shad didn't look too happy about his answer. "The cure has two parts. The medicine is only the first part."

"What's the second part?"

I'll tell you what the second part was. The second part was clamping a scalding-hot rock up against your testicles. To this day, I have not decided if that was a legitimate piece of the Crow curing or if that Meshach was a vengeful bastard. I've asked doctors and all they do is laugh.

Shad thickened the broth to about the consistency of heifer scat, and we drunk it, then we each of us used a pair of socks as oven mitts to lift a rock from the pot and hold it to our privates. Shad said if we didn't press hard, the cure wouldn't take and we'd be forced to run through it again.

That bunkhouse was a picture Charlie Russell would have loved to paint—seven cowboys, sitting on their bunks, pushing red-hot rocks into their nut sacks. You may not believe me when

I describe this occasion, but I have the scar for proof, and should you doubt my word, I will be happy to show you.

Lydia said "No."
Oly smiled.

Thirty minutes later, the potion kicked in and we stampeded for the outhouse. Let me tell you the truth, given a choice between Shad's potion and a hot rock on my scrotum, I'll take the hot rock.

11

No matter what you may have heard in the song, folks who live here do not swoon at springtime in the Rockies. It's high water and mud. Rain for weeks at a time, snow into mid-June. The pretty part of spring with blue skies, green grass, and tolerable temperatures only lasts two or three days, and some years it don't happen at all. The West is superior to ever'where else the rest of the year, but come spring, most natives take a vacation.

I myself am different. I was never much bothered by muck. I do enjoy the rise of sap in willows and aspen. Calves and colts appear all of a sudden like a magic show. Porcupines drop out of trees; you see birds with more color than ravens and sparrows. The yellow flowers bloom first, then the blue and violet. A man don't have to get fully dressed to visit the tippy-toe. I began to think maybe I could sneak back up to Billings and rejoin my life with Agatha.

Since its onset, our courtship had been conducted by the highest moral standards. We held hands; we kissed when no one was around to see. Regular kisses, not the spitty kind. She cooked me cakes and pies, biscuits and the like. Courtship in those days had more to do with food than sex.

But then, as spring came to bear that year, Agatha's letters took on a boldness she had not shown evidence of in the past.

She discovered the worded simile as a way to express what we would be doing with each other soon as we were married, and she hinted it might not have to wait that long. Her poems changed from *soul* and *blackness* to *passion* and *unbridled heat*. She wrote me this long poem she called "I Sing the Body Electric" that consisted of a list of body parts.

Lydia couldn't stand it. "Wait a minute. Walt Whitman wrote that poem."

Oly stopped. He swallowed, his Adam's apple rising and falling like a kiwi in his neck. He slowly turned to Lydia, as if he'd forgotten she was there behind the microphone.

Lydia said, "Your true love stole the poem."

"I am relating the story of my life here."

"That may be true, or you might be making the whole thing up, but either way, 'I Sing the Body Electric' is by Walt Whitman."

"He must of lifted the words from Agatha."

"Whitman lived back in Civil War times."

Oly blinked real slow, the kind of blink that makes spectators hold their breath. "There wasn't no electricity in Civil War times. That proves you are a fiend."

"Fiend?"

"Now, turn the machine back on and don't interrupt no more. I can't remember when you're interrupting."

The first day the ground cleared, Shadrach took his pallet and moved out of the bunkhouse. He said he needed to sleep where he could see stars, that all those cowboys made him feel clogged up. My belief is he wanted to get away from Bill a few hours at night. Bill had been taking advantage of the debt to the point where the others were wondering what was what. I heard a kid named Jimmy ask Shad about it once.

"How come when he says 'Frog,' you jump?" Jimmy asked.

"He's my bud," Shad said.

"Nobody treats their bud like a slave."

"I owe him."

Jimmy spit in the horse trough. "If I owed a man as much as you must owe Bill, I'd shoot him in the back."

There must have been the temptation for Shadrach, and it says good of his character that he didn't yield to it. Or he could of mounted his horse and rode. Gone to Texas or Bolivia or some such. But Shad stayed put, and Bill used him for all he was worth.

Whatever was the reason Shad started sleeping in the sage, it soon saved my neck. For life was set to change yet again. Like the earthquake and boiler explosion, this change came while I was abed, unaware that when I awoke, a new chapter would be begun. I was dreaming about Mama and her fiddle. In my dream, she played a good deal better than she did in real life, but she still wasn't smiling—even a dream couldn't bring that—when someone tapped my foot, and I woke up to see Shadrach kneeling next to my bunk.

He whispered, "The Millers are out there."

I came to right quick.

"Ephir's covering the front from the barn," Shad said, "and Roy has the back door from them bushes by the outhouse. They can't neither one see that window." He pointed to a four-pane window on the north wall. "Gather up and meet me at the creek."

Then he was off to awaken Bill. I didn't have any idea what to do except what Shad said. I didn't even own a pistol. Bill and Shadrach did, in case they came upon a cow with broke legs, but I didn't, 'cause I was nothing but common labor. I figured Bill would want to fight it out, but from the sound of whispers coming from his side of the room, he didn't put up much of an argument to that effect. Bill never was one for shooting at men who could shoot back. Shad disappeared out the window as I dressed in the dark. I dug my saddlebags from under the cot and packed what few belongings I had, including a book by Rudyard Kipling, the red harmonica I couldn't play, and a brush set sent to me by Mrs. Cox.

Boots in one hand and saddlebags in the other, I eased out the window ahead of Bill and dropped to the earth. As I crouched along the wall there, expecting a bullet at any moment, I couldn't help but think of the life I might have lived if only I hadn't killed anybody and offended their kinfolk. I thought about Delphi, Greece, which is a place I always wanted to go but never did, not yet, anyway, and Delaware. And I thought about Agatha's freckles, how sweet they made her aspect.

Of course I didn't get shot, or I wouldn't be rotting in a Home for the Elderly, but thinking I might helped me to realize that Agatha mattered and crawling around in the mud at night with her brother didn't. I made a deal with God that if he would let me survive till morning, I would ride to Billings and beg Agatha's forgiveness for Swamp Fox.

We crept this way and that, using whatever cover there was to avoid the Millers. Ephir wasn't much of a problem, unless he moved, but there was a good thirty feet where being discovered by Roy was a definite possibility. A dog barked once, and I thought I heard movement from over there by the outhouse, but I was afraid to look. We snuck around back of the Crombie main house and dropped down to the meadow where Shad waited with the horses. He'd saddled mine and Bill's, but Shad himself planned to go bareback. We led the horses downstream a quarter mile, not saying a word. Along about first light, a pair of shots rang from back at the ranch, and we mounted quick and took off. To this day, I am unaware as to whether our predicament caused the death of innocent cowboys. I was always afraid to find out.

Shadrach led us along an animal trail down into the Big Horn Canyon, across the river, and back up the other side. I don't think anyone not raised there could have made it—at least not in high water. Somewhere near the state line, we stopped to let the horses blow while Shad climbed a rock to check our back trail for Millers. I'd been thinking about this deal I struck with God, and I decided God wanted out. My purpose at the time was to make Agatha happy, not hurt her, and telling her about Swamp Fox was not the way to make her happy. There didn't seem to be any call to cause my little flower pain without reason. Add to that, Agatha was not a girl to forgive, much less forget. Telling her about the whore would be tantamount to kissing my future with her good-bye, not to mention them pinking shears, which as I said earlier, I did not take as a bluff.

No, God wanted me to keep my mouth shut. The deal may have been submitted by me, but I was certain God rejected the proposal. Which left the question of what I was planning to do instead.

Shad came off the rock and said, "Nobody's behind us. At least, nobody in a hurry."

"They're probably scared to follow," Bill said.

I didn't say squat to that. Those Millers weren't scared of us, and if they weren't following now, they soon would be.

"Where we going from here?" Shad asked.

I said, "France."

The both of them looked at me like I'd swallowed cactus buttons. I said, "The Millers won't follow us into a war."

"That's using your brain," Bill said. "We'll go to Canada and sign up and be on the battlefield in no time flat."

A battlefield in France didn't sound a whole bunch safer than getting chased all over the West by Millers, but anything beat waiting around to get shot. In France, at least we wouldn't have to wait.

"How far away is France?" Shad asked.

I said, "'Bout halfway between Chicago and China. You don't have to go if you'd rather not."

"Like hell," Bill said. "Shad goes where I tell him."

I said, "Not this time. Going to war has to be done of free will."

Shad looked up canyon, where an osprey was hovering over the river, waiting for fish to surface. A squirrel took the opportunity to chew us out. The Millers weren't after Shad, not that we knew of, anyway. He could of pulled out right then and gone about his business.

"Who would we be fighting?" he asked.

I looked to Bill for an answer. He'd read up on it more than me. He said, "Germans, and Turks. Maybe Bulgarians."

Shad mounted his horse and looked down on us. He said, "I got nothing better to do."

———

I got a room in the Cattle Baron Hotel, which was the name of the old Shamrock after it was rebuilt. They offered me the very room we were in when Mama was killed and Dad ruined, but I said No. I had no interest in that sort of thing. We were only staying in Billings the one night, to sell the horses and make our farewells to the Coxes. The next morning we planned to board a sleeper for Williston, North Dakota, at which point we could catch another train to Calgary, where most of the Montana boys went to sign up. Bill told me there was a whole troop of us—Americans in Canadian uniforms. He said after the war the Americans who stayed home would be ashamed that we protected them from the Kaiser while they was too weak chinned to protect themselves. I think most of the Montana boys just wanted to fight; they weren't particular who they fought against. Or like us, they was running from a fight somewheres else.

Me and Agatha took our supper in the hotel dining room. She wore a blue dress with a pattern of white clover on it. Her golden hair was pulled back in a tortoise-shell clasp. She was so beautiful I couldn't pay attention to my beefsteak and potatoes, and afterward I had no recollection of the taste. We walked up Twenty-eighth past the Polytechnic to the Great Northern tracks and back. We walked by my old shack, which had been rebuilt with railroad ties and packing crates and was housing a family of boys from Norway.

Agatha's emotions wavered from loving to angry to sad and back again.

"I wouldn't have picked you if I'd known you are so inconsistent," she said.

I said, "You can choose somebody else if I've disappointed you." I felt I had to say that to be honorable, but I surely hoped she wouldn't take me up on the offer. I was straight crazy about the girl and had no desire to lose her.

"Maybe we should get married tonight," she said. "If you are set on getting killed, we can at least say were married first."

Why didn't I marry Agatha Ann that night? We could of run off to Huntley and woke up a judge and forced him to marry us, but we never did. Near as I can see it, the long and short is neither of us had the impetus needed to commit such a rash act. Her father would have thrown a hissy fit. I might be dead soon, and she would be looked on by other men as tainted goods. I don't know. There were lots of excuses, but not a good reason. If I live to be a hundred, I'll never know for sure why we didn't or if it would have made a difference if we had.

Instead we ended up back at my room in the hotel. Agatha laid on the bed and cried a little, not much, and I laid beside her to give comfort. I could of took her that night; she wanted me to, I know, and some days I regret not doing so. Other days I know I would have regretted it if I had. There's situations you find yourself in where you know damn well you're going to live to regret whatever you do.

———

We lay on the bed all night, embracing, not sleeping, not talking. We each felt what the other was feeling till the sadness grew so thick if the night had lasted another hour, I think we'd of both stopped movement forever. The next morning we drank coffee but didn't eat breakfast. She walked to the depot with me, where we met Bill and Shad and Mr. and Mrs. Cox. Mr. Cox's eyes went funny when he saw us together, hand in hand, but he didn't ask questions. Maybe those came later. Shad was wearing a new shirt. Bill had his boots shined so they glittered when he stepped up into the train. Mrs. Cox cried, but Agatha did not. She kissed me and walked off before the train pulled out. Then the good-bye was over. We were on a train heading toward a war.

12

IMMEDIATELY AFTER EDEN RAE REJECTED HER CHILD, ROGER Pierce took the Madonnaville van without my permission. He drove up the GroVont Highway, past the Dairy Queen and the town triangle, and on to Lydia's house. The house where I spent the impressionable years from thirteen to seventeen. The house where Maurey Pierce and I practiced our rites of passage. He parked on the front yard, clomped up the steps, and knocked on the door.

No answer.

He knocked again, and as people will, he looked up and down the street for clues. Lydia's antique BMW was nowhere in sight, which meant she had probably driven off in spite of legal ramifications. The catty-corner neighbor's vertical blinds twitched. Lydia claimed an agoraphobic peeping Tom lived over there, glued to her binoculars and police band radio. According to Lydia, the woman no one ever saw knew more of what happened in GroVont than the postmaster. Roger waved to the blinds, then he turned and opened the door. GroVont is a modern Western town. That means people lock cars and trucks, but not houses.

Roger called, "Anyone home?"

"I'm in the kitchen." It was Shannon, not Lydia. Roger

started back out in hopes she hadn't recognized the voice. But then he saw the flash of blue terry-cloth bathrobe crossing left to right in the gap of a half-open kitchen door. He caught a glimpse of auburn hair hanging down in a loose ponytail, and his feet stopped functioning.

Shannon said, "What?"

"I'm looking for Mrs. Callahan."

"Gilia's up at Madonnaville, far as I know."

"The other Mrs. Callahan. Sam's mom."

The kitchen door opened farther, and Shannon appeared, rubber spatula in one hand, coffee mug in the other. The mug had an artist's rendition of Funshine the Care Bear on the side. A spot of whole-wheat flour dusted Shannon's right ear, above the dangling turquoise earring.

"I never think of Grandma when people say *Mrs. Callahan*," Shannon said. "I guess the fear of Lydia's wrath has me by the short and curlies."

Roger looked quickly at the pine flooring in the living room, trying his best not to imagine Shannon's short and curlies.

"I'm making pecan pancakes," Shannon said. "There's plenty enough for two."

"I'd better go find Lydia."

"Don't make me eat them all. I'll gain five pounds and wind up blaming you. We wouldn't want that."

Roger remembered he hadn't eaten yet today and he was starving. "We wouldn't want that," he repeated, then he mentally kicked himself in the butt for sounding like a moron. He tried to come up with something pithy or at least intelligent to say. He said, "No, we wouldn't. Or I wouldn't. Nobody would. I mean, five pounds wouldn't change you any, so probably you're the one who would. Wouldn't."

Shannon nodded, looking at him, processing the rap. She said, "You sound like a man could use coffee."

Roger liked it that she had called him a man. It was a positive start.

———

Roger sat at the breakfast nook, cradling coffee and watching Shannon move to the stove, to the refrigerator, to the sink full of dirty dishes. Above the sink, legal pad–colored sunlight swept through the curtainless window and flowed across the kitchen to create tiny explosions in Shannon's hair. Roger pretended he could smell the auburn sparkles. In times of spiritual stress, Callahan women may put on weight, but they never fall so low as to be seen with dirty hair.

Shannon was rattling. "Lydia said I can live with her until I collect my wits, which got scattered all to hell and back down in Carolina. In Greensboro, my loose strings got tied up all at once, so there was no call to stay put. No job, no boyfriend— although those were intertwined. Somewhat."

She turned toward Roger and did this thing with her eyebrows where they draw down over the lids, as if calling her own bluff. Roger had seen the same look on Maurey.

"The strings didn't tie up so much as they got snipped. All of a sudden there was no reason to get out of bed. I'm the sort of person who if there's no reason to get up, I won't. I'm not that enthusiastic about shopping."

Roger was willing to say whatever it took to keep her talking. "Do you have a reason to get up here?"

Shannon balanced six pecan pancakes on a spatula. "Lydia kicks my butt out of bed. She forces me to brush my teeth at sunrise, because in prison they make the inmates rise and shine at something like 6:30, and she hasn't gotten out of the habit. From what Dad says, before she went to the pen Lydia never rolled out of the sack in her life earlier than she had to pee."

When Shannon brought the pancakes to Roger, she leaned

toward his plate, and her bathrobe slipped open. Roger saw cleavage. Just the smallest of swells, like an ocean wave on a nice day. His girls had always been in late-stage pregnancy, which meant Roger was accustomed to swollen breasts laced by blue veins and mauve splotches. He'd never seen a normal breast with smooth skin tone. Roger sat stunned.

"You mind taking off the handkerchief thing while we eat."

Roger touched the tie-dye bandanna. He'd had it on so long he usually forgot it was there. "Sure." He took it off and, leaning forward, stuffed it in his back pocket.

"I'd rather look at you than your hippie colors." Shannon two-finger nudged the plate toward Roger. "Eat 'em up, Tiger."

"What's that?"

"Dig in."

Roger pushed his fork through a stack of pecan chunks floating in sourdough. "Why call me Tiger?"

Shannon laughed as she turned to her plate, which held the same number of cakes as Roger's. "It's a Southernism. I fall back on the Southern belle deal when I'm not in the South. I would never call a boy Tiger in Carolina."

Inwardly, Roger groaned. He'd gone from man to boy in her eyes in less than a minute. "I don't mind. It's okay, only nobody ever called me Tiger before, to my face. I thought maybe you'd heard something I hadn't."

The butter was real, from a stick, as opposed to the tub of yellow gunk they had at the Home that was supposed to be good for your heart. Shannon seemed to have a system for slathering that involved measuring out the same-sized pat between each two cakes.

She said, "In Greensboro Day School, kids' nicknames were the opposite of who they were. The star halfback was called Sleepy. The prom queen was Beer Bottle Betty."

"So Tiger is?"

Shannon glanced from her melting butter to Roger. "I couldn't very well call you pussycat."

He chewed and swallowed, thinking this over. "So you see me as a pussycat?"

Shannon administered syrup. "You're sweet."

Roger thought, *I'm dead. I wish I was dead. I wish I was in a coma. I should never have started talking.*

What he said was, "The only nickname I ever had was Auburn used to call me shit-for-balls."

Shannon cocked her head in the smallest of tilts. "I don't see the metaphor."

"He didn't mean it as a metaphor."

When Shannon bit off her first piece, she closed her eyes. Roger stared, waiting for her to swallow so he could see the movement in her throat.

It was worth the wait. "I can't believe that big ox is my half brother," Shannon said. "Auburn has no imagination. No sense of humor. I'll bet a hundred dollars he grows up to be a Republican."

Shannon opened her eyes and caught Roger staring at her. They sank into an eye lock.

"You're a half brother too, in some way."

"Your mother sort of adopted me."

"Sort of?"

"It's more spiritual than legal."

Shannon nodded and looked down at her cakes to cut another bite. "Then we aren't really half brother and sister, except by spiritual adoption."

"I guess that sums it up."

She raised her eyes again and smiled. "I'm glad."

Roger had no idea how to take that.

—

Roger discovered Lydia Callahan in the Haven House solarium, standing rigidly, her arms crossed over her breasts, staring out the plate-glass window at the Teton Mountains shimmering in the distance. Oly sat in his wheelchair, hunched farther forward than looked safe, probing his right ear with a Q-tip. As Roger entered, Oly withdrew the Q-tip from his earhole, inspected whatever off-yellow waxy substance encased the cotton dab, then he popped the tip into his mouth and twirled it, like a child on a Dum Dum Pop.

Without looking at Oly, Lydia shuddered.

She said, "In all those years of exile, I never dreamed coming home would be like this."

"Beats feeding horses." Roger compared any difficult task to throwing bales off the back of a wagon at below-zero temperatures. It gave him perspective.

Lydia turned her laser eyes on Roger. "It's you."

"Who did you expect?"

"A mad woman of a certain age whose dream is to elope to Greece with Mr. Pedersen there." Lydia nodded to Oly, who pulled his hearing aid from his other ear and commenced mining for a snack. He gave no sign of hearing or comprehending the conversation. "The crone absolutely believes I am out to usurp her position in his affections. She barges in every five minutes dead set on stopping me before I seduce this wretched excuse for sentient meat."

On the words *wretched excuse for sentient meat*, Lydia's voice rose to a bitter growl.

Roger watched Oly dig. The old man used a counterclockwise drilling action combined with a short, thrusting pump. Stiff ear hair bushed around the cardboard stick. His lobe dangled, big as a soupspoon.

Roger said, "I hope I'm in as good a shape as Oly, when I reach a hundred."

Lydia's upper lip drew back in a way not usually seen on a woman. Her forehead stretched tight, line-less. "I have no intention of ever reaching one hundred." She paused for emphasis. "Or any age in which I feast on my own bodily fluids."

Her focus went from Oly to Roger. "Did my son send you here to drive me home? I want you to go back and tell Sam I am perfectly capable of operating a vehicle. The local police understand the upshot of crossing me, so my only concern is the highway patrol, and I can avoid them."

Roger gathered his courage and crossed the line from which there was no way back. "I came to tell you I want in."

Lydia smiled, insincerely. "Isn't that nice. In what?"

"I'm ready to find out what happened to me, who my mother is—was. How I came to be here."

For the first time in several days, Lydia felt vindicated. It was one of her favorite emotions—vindication. Quite often, she offered correction to Shannon or me or anyone else in her path, but we rarely appreciated, much less acted on, her advice. Lydia was forced to fall back on *I told you so*. *I-told-you-so*s, while uplifting, were simply not as satisfying as having the object of her comments adjust his behavior accordingly.

She said, "What are you talking about?"

Roger hadn't been around Lydia enough to recognize her affected vagueness. And he didn't know at what age older people start to forget. For all he could tell, Lydia had blacked out their conversation in the A&W.

"You said you'd figured out who my father is—was. Stepfather." He tried to place himself in the book. "You said you know the man who wrote the novel, and the novel might be about me."

Lydia turned her attention to her Radio Shack recording equipment. "I never met Loren Paul personally while he lived in this area. I did have a run-in with his wife once, at Browse and Buy, but as I recall, she was a snob, unlike myself."

Roger knew *myself* was wrong, but he didn't say so. Lydia knew he knew and wasn't saying so, which irked her almost as much as if he'd corrected her grammar. She realized it was unfair for her to be irked either way, but that didn't faze her.

"You said he'd moved to Hollywood to write movies," Roger said. "I've decided to call him, on the phone."

"And what will that prove?" Lydia unplugged the thumb-sized microphone from the tape machine. "He's not going to know if you're the lost boy over the telephone. At best, Loren Paul might confirm there actually was a boy and he didn't make the story up. We already assume that much."

"I don't."

"Even if he denies the boy's existence, how can we believe him? After all, he's in the movie business." She wound the cord around her finger, wondering where she'd left the twisty that was supposed to hold the cord together. "The only way to know whether or not you are the child Fred is to confront Loren Paul. We must show up on his doorstep. Unannounced."

"We?"

"You don't think I would let you go to Santa Barbara alone. What kind of woman do you think I am?"

"Wait a minute." Roger had so many qualms he didn't know where to begin. The decision to delve into his past had been spur-of-the-moment, when Eden told the nurse to get her baby away from her, or maybe earlier, when the nurse crawled on top of Eden to pound on her belly. Whenever the decision had been made, it had been impulsive. Lydia had obviously thought this out in more detail than he had.

"You said Hollywood. Hollywood isn't Santa Barbara."

"Loren Paul and his wife reside in Santa Barbara. It's where successful screenwriters go to age gracefully. The desperate ones stay in Tarzana."

"How would you know that?"

Lydia'd made it up based on reading a *People* she found in her parole officer's waiting room is how she knew that. She wasn't about to admit this to Roger. "I did the research." She opened the box the setup had come in and began to fit pieces into pre-formed plastic slots. "It doesn't take a genius."

Lydia paused to admire her fingernails against the black recorder case. Her nails were recovering from prison, slowly but inevitably. Lydia saw them as symbolic.

"Although my innate intelligence did make it simpler for me than it would have been for the average male," she said. "I called the Writers Guild of America and asked for his address."

"And they gave it to you."

"Why not? I'm no stalker."

Roger's impulse was to stall. He'd never been one for impulsive changes, himself, and he hated it even more when someone else tried changing him before he was ready. Roger made decisions gradually as he went about stringing fence or fixing a generator. Plucking his bass with John Coltrane. Reading. Back in high school English lit, he'd been the only kid in his class who didn't think Hamlet was a total pansy. Choices evolved for Roger, and it took something as extreme as Eden Rae screaming a baby out of her body for him to make a quick one. Lydia's decisiveness had thrown off his own.

"I'll need time to work on my truck."

"We leave the Friday afternoon of Memorial Day weekend. That's my window—three days without a command performance for the Nazi parole officer."

"She won't make it to California without new brakes, and I can't put them in that soon. Sam won't let me off to work on my truck."

"Sam will let you off when I tell him to let you off." Lydia dropped her brush into her purse and clicked the latch.

"Besides, we are taking my BMW, so it is no concern whether your truck has brakes or not."

"Your car needs a brake job too."

"Not if one downshifts properly." Lydia paused for dramatic effect. "Roger." She went for eye contact. She often went for eye contact when it was least expected. "Don't go wimbly on me. It's eleven hundred miles to Santa Barbara, which we can drive in eighteen hours, easily. Add another four hours for side trips and round it off to one full day there and one full day back. That leaves twenty-four hours to complete our business in time for me to report to the bureaucratic bitch Tuesday morning."

Roger met her gaze head on. "What side trips?"

"Something always comes up." Lydia broke the eye contact, somewhat unnerved that Roger had matched her, intensity for intensity. "We must plan for every mishap."

Roger crossed his arms and stared at Lydia. He was old enough to know when someone was working an angle on him. He just couldn't see it. He knew she would be in serious trouble if they were caught out of state, and she wasn't the type to do good deeds without a return. "I'd still rather take my own truck. I don't like driving other people's cars. Not that far, straight through. Your plan doesn't allow for me sleeping, coming or going."

"I shall drive while you take naps."

"You don't have a license."

Oly's throat rattled and he spoke, sounding like an Old Testament God with a head cold. "I can drive an automobile."

Lydia's heart gave a little jump. "I always forget he's not dead."

Oly swiveled his tortoise head in Lydia's direction. "I will take my fair turn behind the wheel."

Lydia continued speaking to Roger, as if they were alone in a room full of plastic plants and sunlight. "Ignore that sound."

"Why should I do that?" Roger asked.

"If you listen to senior citizens, it only encourages them."

Oly burst into song. He sang, "*I will be by your side,*" to the tune of the last phrase of "Sidewalks of New York." This, he repeated several times.

Lydia suddenly flung her attention toward Oly. She called, as if calling to someone in a high wind. "The tape machine is put away, Oly. You don't have to be awake."

Oly chewed his lower lip, which can be done if you've stretched it daily for nearly a century. His head bobbed a bit, then he came out with, "I am stapled to your backside, so far as California is concerned."

Lydia turned back to Roger. "What is the coot talking about? I can't make out a word he says."

"He says he's going to Santa Barbara with us," Roger said.

Lydia dropped into denial. "Do you know what *No way, Jose* means, old man? Is that a term bandied about by you dough-boys back in the Great War?"

Oly sat up, almost straight in his chair. His body had the posture of a whitebark pine, way off alone on a ridgeline. "You are unable to travel without Oly Pedersen."

Lydia said, "Watch me."

Oly's goiter bobbed in counterpoint to his Adam's apple. It made for a disquieting effect. He said, "If you leave Oly behind he shall tell the woman who comes to visit wearing green trousers. Has a mustache here." He gestured where Brandy Epstein's mustache was. "Walks like she has a dowel rod up her patootie."

Roger said, "What's a patootie?"

"My parole officer's a-hole," Lydia said. "What's a dowel rod?"

"A stick."

Oly plowed on. "The woman told me. She said if you do anything I don't want or don't do anything I do want, I should telephone her right away and she would clap you back in the hoosegow."

Lydia sat down hard. "I cannot believe I'm in the presence of a being who just said *hoosegow*." She shouted directly at Oly, "Hopalong Cassidy is dead, Gabby! It's your turn now!"

Oly stuck the hearing aid back in. "No need to raise your voice. I can hear fine. You're the one misses half of what any given person says."

Roger said, "He's got a point."

"I don't care what he's got. We can't take a hundred-year-old satchel of bones and blood on a road trip."

"Why not?" Roger said.

"What he said," Oly said.

Lydia couldn't understand why Roger was taking Oly's side. Why would any man take the side of another man against her? That atrocity had never happened before prison. Three years of being out of circulation seemed to have changed the rules—tipped the balance in a way she didn't care for.

"For one thing," she said, "we only have three days to reach the coast, discover your roots, and return home. He'll be forcing potty stops every ten miles."

"I can hold my water as long as you can, little lady."

"I'll drive myself alone," Roger said. "Sam will loan me the van."

"You'll do no such thing." Lydia sat with her purse on her lap, strumming the fingers of both hands across the clasp. To the casual eye, she looked uncertain—the classic female stuck between two distasteful choices, refusing both. Her gaze wandered from the floor to the mountains to Oly. In reality, she had already accepted the hard facts and was now quickly working out a new implementation.

She said, "Do you have any concept of how long that frowzy bureaucrat will put me back inside if you were to die on this trip?"

Oly snorted, bull-like. "I shall outlive you, missy."

First *little lady* and now *missy*. Even Roger knew Oly was flirting with violence. At the rate he was offending Lydia, there was a decent chance he wouldn't survive till lunch.

"How am I supposed to spirit you out of Heaven House?" Lydia asked.

"Haven House," Roger said.

"I was making an ironic point."

Roger shrugged. He didn't see the point of mispronouncing words on purpose, ironically or any other way.

"Someone will object," Lydia said. "That bodyguard girlfriend of yours will dial 911."

Oly clenched both handrails of his chair with whatever grip he had left. "I am with you till we complete the mission."

"It can't be done."

If Oly had had a chin, he would have stuck it out. As it was, he stuck out his turkey neck. "You are a sharp cookie. Make a scheme."

———

Roger found me in the former tack room turned office, fighting with my first computer, a brand-new Macintosh Centris. What I couldn't figure out was why when I hit Return at the end of a line, it returned twice. And why I couldn't make the tab come out right or start a new page at the end of the one I was typing. Whatever is simple on a typewriter is complicated on a computer. And vice versa.

Roger stood at my shoulder, watching. "What are you doing, Sam?"

"I make the arrow go side to side with this mouse goober,

but when I reach the edge of the pad, the arrow stops. I can't make it go on farther."

"Pick the mouse up."

"What?"

"Lift the mouse off the pad."

"Won't that make the arrow disappear?"

"No, it won't. Lift the mouse."

I lifted the mouse. The arrow didn't disappear.

"Put it down in the center of the pad."

I did.

"Now move the mouse."

Problem solved.

———

Roger gave me the lowdown on the *Disappearance* book and Lydia's theory—Santa Barbara, Freedom, Fred, Oly's part in the scenario.

"Loren Paul had great potential as a novelist. He could have been a literary lion," I said. "The last I heard he was writing a daytime television serial mostly set in the powder room at Caesar's Palace, the one in Vegas. Some sort of trash about bonus baby women and their personal assistants, locked in for a month."

"I haven't seen TV in a while," Roger said.

"He's making a billion dollars on it," I said. "Too bad. He once published a novel called *Yeast Infection* that was revolutionary."

"You think Loren could be my stepfather?"

I hit the Save key—I knew that much—and moved to my coffee-making station. "I went looking for my dad once," I said. "It turned out badly. I wreaked havoc on a bunch of innocent folks. You want a cup?"

Roger nodded. The one trait I'd passed on to him was the coffee habit. "You think me showing up might hurt this guy and his wife?"

"Anytime you change the past, there are consequences."

Roger trailed across the tack room after me. "The past is done with. The facts can't be changed."

"How people see the past is what matters. Facts themselves are irrelevant. This trip may or may not screw up Loren and his wife in Santa Barbara, but it's almost bound to change you." I poured water from my liter bottle into the Hot Shot. "You sure you want to change?"

Roger opened my dorm-sized refrigerator and pulled out a can of milk. "I'd like to know what happened before I came to Wyoming." He opened the can with what in my youth was called a church key. I don't know what the thing is called now.

"I'm happy enough." His mouth pursed, like he was tasting the statement for accuracy. "I'm okay, anyway, except for the suicide beyond my control thing."

"There is that."

"It feels like I'm a kid, content to play in the sandbox, only a Dempsey Dumpster is hanging over my head. It's hard to get on with life, knowing it might fall on me at any moment. I can't relax."

"So it's better to make the Dumpster fall on your head than to wait for it to crash of its own accord. Symbolically speaking."

"Lydia says it's not healthy for me to hang around you and a bunch of miserable pregnant teenagers. She told me this story about Jim Bridger and the arrowhead."

Actually, I told the story to Lydia first, but she's long since forgotten her source. This is it: An Indian zings an arrow into Jim Bridger's back, but it doesn't kill him. Jim goes about his mountain man business for twenty years with an arrowhead embedded just below the shoulder blade. It bothers him quite a bit, but he can live with the discomfort. Then, a preacher comes along who claims he can Bowie knife the arrowhead out of Jim. The operation hurts like holy hell, but afterward Bridger is out of pain for the first time since the Indian nailed him.

"It's Lydia's seminal story," I said.

"Seminal?"

"She defines herself by it. She used to tell it to Shannon in the crib."

"Maybe that's why Shannon grew up so peculiar."

"My daughter is not peculiar. She's the picture of mental health, in her own way. Have you considered why Lydia wants the two of you to go off on this adventure?"

"Three, now Oly's coming with us."

I poured boiling water over the grounds. "What's in it for Lydia?"

Roger gave the question some thought while I pushed the screen through the liquid and onto the soggy grounds—cowboy coffee you don't chew. Neither one of us believed my mother was capable of committing an act of goodness, for the sake of itself. Roger was young and I'm idealistic, but he wasn't that young and I'm not that idealistic.

"Perverse curiosity," Roger said. "She read the book in prison when she had time on her hands, and she thinks she's figured out the unsolved mystery. She wants to see if she's right."

I poured the coffee into two mugs I got free for contributing to public radio. "That's possible, but Lydia is not a basket you want to put all your eggs in."

Roger dribbled milk into both mugs. "I don't think of Lydia as an egg basket."

"She's as likely to ditch you at a rest stop as not. She did it to me once when I was little. She claimed she thought I was asleep in the backseat."

Roger lifted his cup and sipped. "You don't trust your mother."

"Not for a second."

DAWN FOUND LEROY FOLDED INSIDE A CARDBOARD KITCHENAID refrigerator box under a boulevard overpass on the south fringe of Trinidad, Colorado. He slid from the box and walked barefoot across gravel and glass to a Speed Limit 35 sign, where he unzipped and peed, leaning his forehead against the post, scratching a Z-shaped scar over his liver. A vehicle bigger than a station wagon but smaller than a bread truck rolled down the four-lane street. Some newfangled rig that had come out while he was in Bogotá. The car—or whatever it was—lights swept across Leroy as it pulled into a Zippy Mart parking lot. A man in a hard hat and a down vest got out and went inside.

Leroy stepped out of the shorts. Naked, he sniffed the crotch, then turned them inside out and put them back on with the pockets flapping on his thighs like wing pouches. He spit a substance solid enough to bounce. He stuck a finger back where his upper molars used to be, and dug a food morsel from between his gums and cheek. The hard hat came from the Zippy Mart, slapping a pack of Tareytons against his forearm, got back into his boxy vehicle, and drove away. It was bright enough now the man didn't turn his headlights back on.

Leroy needed coffee. He'd learned to live without what most others considered necessities if he had to, but he'd never come to terms with a morning without coffee.

———

An electronic beeper buzzed when Leroy entered the Zippy Mart. It was empty except for an underweight girl with cropped neon hair and a roofing nail in her cheek, sitting behind the counter, reading a Silver Surfer comic. Leroy had seen the weird hair and body spikes in Venice Beach, but he hadn't realized the style had reached Colorado.

She glanced up at him and snapped her bubble gum. "No shirt, no shoes, no service."

"What's that mean?" Leroy crossed to a coffee urn and poured coffee into a huge cup. Must have held a quart.

The girl bobbed her nail at a sign next to the smokeless-tobacco display cutout of a cowboy. NO SHIRT, NO SHOES, NO SERVICE. Another sign read: WE RESERVE THE RIGHT TO REFUSE SERVICE TO PREMENSTRUAL WOMEN.

"Normally, I wouldn't go anal on you, but my boss will be along soon, to get the night deposit, and he'll fire my butt if you're hanging out in here like that."

Leroy chugged a fair portion of coffee, then he refilled his cup.

The girl said, "I like your tattoo."

Leroy picked up a packet of buffalo jerky, aerosol deodorant, and a box of Red Hots and walked to the cash register.

The girl seemed mesmerized by his flaming-babies tattoo. She said, "Why are your shorts on inside out?"

"Other side is dirty."

She nodded and said, "Oh." She was wearing acid-washed Levi's with silver pocket studs and a Zippy Mart uniform shirt that was pale pink with thin red stripes. A card pinned to her breast read Z.

"What's Z?" Leroy asked.

"Zelda. They screwed up my name tag, and now I'm Z. Listen, Mister, you can keep the coffee 'cause you already drank it, but I can't sell you the other stuff."

Leroy looked from the jerky to Zelda's eyes, swollen that pink puffiness you see on people who work night shifts. She had an acne rash around the spike and what might have been a hickey on her neck, over the tonsils. She looked like a dropout.

"Give me your shirt," Leroy said.

"Are you squirrelly?"

He enunciated each word, leaning into her face. "Take your shirt off and give it to me."

Zelda blinked. Twice. "What about the shoe rule?"

"I'll take them too."

Zelda popped her gum thoughtfully, while Leroy waited. He had become an accomplished waiter, the last few years. Before Bogotá, he would have taken what he wanted, walked out, and risked her calling the cops.

Zelda fingered her top button. "I don't know what my boss will say. He's Church of Christ."

"He will thank you for following the law." Leroy leaned farther over the counter to check her shoes—low-rider tennies without laces. No doubt too small. When he looked back up, Zelda stood there with her shirt wadded in her hand. She wore a red lacy bra that covered her nipples and the undermoon of her breasts.

"Do you live in Las Animas County?" she asked.

The shirt stretched across Leroy's back, but so long as he didn't bother with buttons, it was functional.

When he didn't answer, Zelda went on, "I just wondered if you're from here. I get off soon. We could go to my place and smoke weed. My mom and dad will have gone to work by the time I come home."

Leroy tipped his Styrofoam cup and drank till black liquid dribbled off his chin. "Not me." He set the jerky, deodorant, coffee, and Red Hots on the counter, then he pulled a bag of Planters nuts from a wire rack next to a magnet display with sayings like BORN TO FISH and HONK IF YOU'RE HORNY. "Get me a pack of Lucky Strikes."

When Zelda turned to find the cigarettes, Leroy swiped a lighter. "That'll be eight fifty-three," she said.

He dug into the pocket, which was awkward, it being on the outside *his shorts, and drew out the filthy fiver he'd been holding on to since California. "This is close as I can come."*

She looked him in the eye and gave a twitch of a wink. "Maybe we could trade up for the rest."

"Maybe you could bag my stuff and call it even." He stuck the five in his outside back pocket, behind the lighter. "What was that you said about a night deposit?"

13

LYDIA TORE OPEN THE PACKAGING ON AN ALCOHOL-PREP gauze strip and threw both the packaging and the alcohol strip into the garbage. She unscrewed the top of her plastic cup, entered the one and only stall, turned, and dropped her jeans and panties. Brandy Esptein had explained in graphic detail the secrets of the clean catch, as if Lydia had never been to a doctor in her life, never peed in a cup.

"Wipe the area thoroughly with the sterile pad, then urinate for two seconds, stop, hold the cup in its position, and resume your urination."

Lydia said, "Yeah, right."

Lydia had no intention of giving a clean catch. In her experience, a clean catch only applied to the urine in the cup. There was nothing clean about the urine on her fingers, her thighs, the toilet lid. What kind of person lets go for two seconds, then stops? A desperately ill person, maybe, searching for solace in a medical test. Not a convicted felon pissing for the amusement of her rabid parole officer.

So Lydia skipped the start, stop, start again. She splattered anyway, and the cup came dangerously close to overflowing. She'd been late leaving the house after lunch, and the fear Brandy would write her up for lack of punctuality made her hurry when she should have used the can. She exited the stall, balancing the cup carefully, and crossed to the sink to wash her hands. Before screwing the lid on the plastic cup full of wheat-colored liquid, she spit in it.

She said, "Analyze that."

Back in Brandy's office, Lydia found Brandy typing away on a computer the size of a small car. Lydia resisted the terrible temptation to spill on the computer or Brandy's lap or both. She needed cooperation today, and a spillage wasn't the way to get it.

Lydia set the urine cup on the edge of Brandy's desk. "Did you ever stop to think this is a sick way to make a living?" Lydia said. "The essence of your existence is other people's wee-wee."

Brandy glanced up from her computer. She was wearing a home-knit sweater—no doubt a gift from a relative with too much time on her hands—and chewing gum. "Did you happen to look around during your visit to the powder room?"

"Your facilities need a good cleaning, if that's what you mean."

"Did you take note of the video camera? Should you bring in substitute urine or add foreign liquid to the collection cup, I will know."

"You not only get your jollies playing with my number one, you also watch me do it?"

Brandy stopped typing and focused her attention on Lydia. "Let me assure you, nothing in our relationship gives me jollies." Brandy swiveled in her chair, opened a two-drawer file cabinet, and pulled out, presumably, Lydia's paperwork.

"How did we get from GroVont to Jackson today?" Brandy asked.

"My son drove me in the company van. I don't know how you got here."

Brandy squinted at the paper. "You only have the one son?"

"Sam's sitting outside, or he's probably gone over to that

new coffee place on the square. Sam loves yuppie coffeehouses. Makes him feel like he's somewhere else."

Brandy clicked her pen open and wrote in the file. "There's a rumor going around that you've been seen driving."

"You're new here, *Brandy*, so maybe you don't know. Rumors in this valley are all lies. You wouldn't believe what I've had said about me to my face. One shudders to think of the wild accusations locals make behind my back."

Brandy touched the tip of her pen to her ear, which was encircled by a whorl of new penny-colored hair, sprayed stiff against the Wyoming wind. To Lydia's astute eye, Brandy seemed to be choosing her battles.

She chose to pass on this one. "Just keep in mind, you have no license."

"How could I forget when you remind me twice a week?"

Brandy pretended to ignore Lydia while she entered information into Lydia's paperwork. It must have been quite a bit of information, because the scratchy-pen silence stretched out past Lydia's comfort zone. Even though she knew Brandy was faking distraction, Lydia could not tolerate being ignored on any terms.

"Aren't you going to ask how many bombs I purchased recently?" Lydia asked.

Brandy didn't look up. "How many bombs have you purchased?"

"None," Lydia said. "I did, however, file a discarded toothbrush into a serviceable shiv. I learned a lot about the making of shivs, in the big house. You can manufacture one out of practically anything. I had a cellmate who turned a tampon tube into such a weapon she could have skewered an entire Brownie troop, like shish-kebabbed onions."

Lydia leaned forward, trying to catch Brandy's eye but failing. "She would have too. Shish-kebabbed a Brownie troop. If they were white. The woman hated with an intensity you don't normally find in the general population. The two of you would have made the greatest of friends, had you but known one another."

Brandy sniffed. Lydia tugged a Kleenex from the box on the desk between the computer and her clean catch. She passed the Kleenex across to Brandy, who blew into it, making a sound not unlike a kazoo with a mute on the tip hole, and said, "How much progress have we made with the oral history?"

"That's what I want to talk to you about."

Brandy finally looked up at Lydia across the Kleenex wad. "Don't even dream you can wriggle your way out of this."

"Of course not."

"Just so you understand reality."

Lydia took that a couple different ways before she went on. "I know your heart is hardened where I am concerned. We got off to a bad start."

"My heart hasn't softened since then," Brandy said.

Lydia oozed a low sigh. "I am resigned to completing the oral history, but the challenge is doing it by Oly Pedersen Day." She stared at the crease in Brandy's forehead. Lydia had been lying for over fifty years, and she was good at it. She knew intense eye contact is met with as much suspicion as none at all. You have to fake eye contact in order to gain trust. Focus should be on the eyebrows, only Brandy's eyebrows had been plucked to oblivion, so instead Lydia made contact with the vertical fold running through Brandy's third eye.

"Oly hasn't left out a detail since birth. We're stuck in the Great War, and at this rate, by August, when Oly celebrates his happy hundredth, he and I shall be mired in the Depression."

Brandy's eyelids narrowed and flattened—the sign of doubt. "I'm not going to tell him to skip decades, not for your convenience."

"I wouldn't hear of it." Lydia smiled, which only increased the doubt. "Oly's life has been a fascinating journey. We must record every pothole in the road, for posterity." Lydia saw she was spreading it a bit thick. She'd have to flash cynicism or Brandy would never buy the bottom line.

"Let's face the ugly facts," Lydia said. "The troll may flatline at any moment, and you, being a sadistic government flunky, would make me start over on some new codger."

Brandy blinked. Lydia came off as so much more truthful when she insulted than when she talked posterity. "What's your point, Mrs. Elkrunner?"

Lydia didn't rise to the Elkrunner bait. "My point is, we should concentrate the sessions. With your permission, I want to take Mr. Pedersen out of Haven House over Memorial Day weekend. I want to bring him into my home, install him in my son's old bedroom. In three days of taping, we could finish this odious chore and I could get on with my rehabilitation before the turning of the millennium."

Lydia stood up, for emphasis. She nested her fingers on both sides of the urine cup. "I want to become a Goddamn model citizen, and it'll never happen at two hours a Goddamn week."

Lydia sat back down with a *plop*. She said, "So to speak."

Brandy didn't budge.

Lydia said, "As it were."

Brandy tapped her government-issue pen on the desktop.

Lydia said, "In point of fact."

———

"That woman embodies every cliché circulated about people from Philadelphia."

I fidgeted with the tiny spoon that came on a tiny saucer with my cappuccino. It was similar to a coke spoon owned by my distant first wife, way back in another world. Once every year or so, I wondered what had become of her.

"Is Brandy from Philadelphia?"

"How should I know? My point is that she embodies the clichés, not that she ever lived there. As a matter of course, I heard her people came out of Delaware or Vermont or someplace. One of those minute Yankee states that would fit in Yellowstone Park."

Wanda was my other wife's name. It took a moment to come up with it. "I'm not certain Vermont fits in Yellowstone. Maybe you're thinking of Connecticut."

"We are not discussing small states, Sam. I'm telling you what a tight twat Brandy Epstein is."

"That must be a cliché I missed. The one about women from Philadelphia having tight...you-knows."

"*Twat*, Sam. It's a perfectly good word. Far more specific than *you knows*."

My mother and I were drinking fancy coffees on the deck of a new place called Cowpoke Grinders. Outdoor dining was new for Jackson, Wyoming, where snow covers the ground seven months of the year and it's too cold to eat outside four of the other five.

The moment Lydia had seen the place, she'd ripped the name. "*Cow poke* is obscene, Sam. The mental picture it conjures is horrendous. And matched with *Grinders*? I shudder to think what nightmares I shall have tonight."

Then she ripped the latte I bought her.

"What is this?"

"Latte. They're popular these days."

She sniffed the lip of the cup. "It smells like a concoction the Navajos brewed down in Canyon de Chelly."

"I've heard Native Americans invented the latte," I said, not meaning it.

"My friends didn't drink the stuff. They poured it in cracks to kill spiders. And Indians hate the term *Native American*. They would go apoplectic around any tourist who dared use it."

"Writers like me call that reverse political correctness."

"Red Mesa High School is the home of the Redskins. How's that for reverse political correctness?"

Before I could react, Lydia went on to rip Brandy Epstein—the Philadelphia-cliché thing. So now we're back where we started.

"She's an idiot, in the bad sense of the word."

Typical of Lydia to think *idiot* came in more than one sense. "Did she give the okay to take Oly Pedersen?"

Lydia sipped latte and pressed her lips primly together. She seemed to enjoy the drink, in spite of comparing it to spider poison. "*Fi*nally." She blew air on the first syllable. "But only after I stuck my tongue up her fat side."

The mental picture was disturbing, far worse than *cow poke*. "Is that literal?"

Lydia cocked her head to look at me, as if in a new light. "Sam. You have multiple flaws, as we know, but in my opinion, the greatest flaw of them all is this tendency to fake stupidity."

"Sometimes I'm not faking."

"See. You're still doing it." Finished with sizing me up, she looked back down at her hands on her latte. "Brandy said only the hours the microphone is turned on and Oly is speaking count as community service. She said I'm not being paid to baby-sit."

Lydia dropped into silent moodiness while I played with my tiny spoon. I knew she'd get on with what she had to say soon. She didn't need leading questions from me. What I wondered about was the weather. We generally suffer through thirty days of rain and snow, either in May or June, and so far May had been sparkling blue, which didn't bode well for June. One thing I'd learned about weather—and therefore life itself—when the times are good, you'd best brace yourself. Soon, it will all go tits up.

Lydia sighed, a sound not unlike a door closing on *Star Trek*. "This is such an odious task. I cannot abide being nice just so people will give me what I want. It's an awful position to be in."

"I can't help but wonder about the motivation here."

Lydia went on, as if she hadn't heard me, "I know what you are thinking. You think I'm nice naturally, so it shouldn't irritate me to be nice for a purpose."

"That's not what I'm thinking."

"I simply don't like civility forced on me. It should be graciously given. Not dragged out against one's will."

I tapped the spoon on the edge of my cappuccino cup like a toastmaster asking for attention. "Here's the part I'm not catching, Lydia. This road trip with Oly and Roger is high risk. You could lose your freedom, and I don't see the point."

"Must there always be a point?"

I considered this fairly. "If you're taking a chance on going back to prison, I would say yes."

Lydia reached into her purse, which today was a velvet bag that originally came on a bottle of Crown Royal, and pulled out a file. To me, Lydia filing her nails in the middle of a conversation was one of those tells, like poker players use on each other. We were about to enter the realm of faulty rationalization.

Lydia filed, right hand on left forefinger. "Roger needs me, poor boy."

"I'm your son. I know how you feel about being needed."

Lydia's attention went to her middle finger. "I'm making an exception for Roger. He must find his past in order to complete his future. How would you feel if you didn't know who your parents were?"

Unresolved issues crept into my mind. "I don't. Not both of them, anyway."

"We're not talking about you. We're talking about Roger

and the horrendous events that brought him to Jackson Hole. He deserves the truth."

I drained my cappuccino. "Speaking of telling Roger the truth, I dug out my Chevron USA map and discovered Santa Barbara is forty miles from the Lompoc Federal Correctional Facility."

"That has nothing to do with me."

I watched Lydia's face. She appeared calm yet alert, like a deer that suspects the next clearing contains a blind. It occurred to me that my mom was more comfortable talking to people she'd just met than she was talking to those of us who knew her.

"When are you planning to tell Roger?" I asked.

"Tell Roger what?"

"That the reason for this trip has more to do with Hank Elkrunner than Loren Paul."

Lydia blinked, the once, but other than that, the tight-skinned look didn't change. I'd say her reaction was concentration on no reaction.

"This trip is for Roger's benefit. Hank's whereabouts are not material to Roger's history."

I wanted to touch her—her wrist or the back of her hand—to reassure her that I wasn't condemning her for selfishness. But I didn't. Lydia was not a person who encouraged spontaneous touch.

"Lydia," I said. "While we're helping each other learn our flaws, I've noticed you lie when you don't need to. Lying for a reason is one thing, but you lie just because you can."

She started to protest but dropped it in mid-righteousness. There wasn't much use. Instead she gave up on her fingernails. She set the file beside her latte cup and looked me more or less in the eyes. I took this as a sign we were done dancing with the truth. Time for the crux.

"I must speak to Hank, face-to-face," Lydia said. "My survival depends on it."

"That's a tad melodramatic."

She bit the edge of her lower lip, pondering, deciding how much of herself she could expose. "My life is stuck. I cannot go on, and I cannot go back. I am unable to live in the present, under these circumstances. My position is intolerable, and I must see Hank before that can change."

Lydia's attention rotated inward. Even though her eyes still appeared to be on me, I knew better. I knew if I turned blue and gagged right now, Lydia would not notice.

She said, "Hank is the only person I've ever chosen to love."

"Thanks, Mom."

Her eyelids flickered irritation. "Don't make everything about you, Sam. You are my closest relative. You and Shannon. I am obliged to love the two of you, but I chose Hank when I didn't have to."

"What about Grandpa?"

"Who?"

"Did you love your father because you were obliged to?"

Lydia hesitated a moment too long. "That's complicated and none of your business."

I didn't know what to say. She was revealing inner feelings, which Lydia only did once every twenty years, so she deserved encouragement, and yet she was hiding the inner feelings I thought mattered. It wouldn't do to press her on my interests, once she'd started on her own.

After reviewing all my choices for an answer, I chose to say, "Oh."

Lydia tapped her newly filed index finger on the glass tabletop. "Part of the reason Hank is in prison in the first place is because of me."

"All the reason Hank is in prison is because of you. You committed the crime. The only thing Hank did wrong was to protect his wife," I said and then added for emphasis, "You."

"Me." Her fingers went into a rolling drumbeat. "And now

I'm free and Hank isn't." She slapped her hand, palm down, on the table. "I cannot accept the guilt behind that fact."

"You never would accept guilt."

"I refuse guilt." Her eyes flashed, and the Lydia fire from my youth shone through. "Hank must hear the truth—I refuse guilt."

"Hank knows you better than anyone. He knows you aren't feeling remorse over him being in and you being out."

Lydia's hands flew to her face, over her eyes, but with gaps between the fingers. Her voice was a muffled moan. "But I am."

I said, "Holy Christ."

"It's worse than guilt. It's shame." When she moved her hands off her face, she looked ten years older than she'd ever looked before. The tanning-booth tan was long gone, replaced by a jaundice tint. "I am ashamed every day and every night, and I can't stand it. I could bear prison. I can't bear this." Her eyes bore down on me. "I must tell him."

"He'll be out in three years or so," I said. "You can tell him then."

Lydia wailed, "*No!*" Her voice broke like a child's. "In three years, I'll be sixty. I will have lost every single snippet of what makes me unique."

Her face was mottled rose and pink. Her lips arched, showing gold fillings in her teeth. She didn't care, and I was amazed.

Here's the thing: when I was a teenager, Lydia said she could never respect any girl who went out with me, because no girl who had a moral compass would go out with a boy like me. Ever since that day, I've hoped to see Lydia showing genuine regret over hurting someone. Anyone. I'd rehearsed it over and over in my daydreams, how she would cry and I would stand over her and crow, "Now you know how it feels."

But now, it wasn't that satisfying to see Mom miserable. It

was like someone had hit an innocent dog, even though Lydia was far from innocent. I didn't like the feeling. For maybe the hundredth time in my life, I realized satisfaction hardly ever makes you happy.

———

I have lived in or near small towns much of my life, and studied small towns both as a hobby I take seriously and research for novels I don't. Here is what I discovered that runs contrary to the prevailing cliché. Five hundred people may be in on a secret, and it still remains a secret from the ones who might be affected.

For instance, when Maurey's cousin Delores drove off the pass, practically everyone in town knew she'd been drunk as a sorority sister at homecoming, and a few of us even knew she did it on purpose, and yet to this day, fifteen years later, her parents don't know. No one ever told them their daughter killed herself dead drunk, and no one ever will tell. That is how small towns in America work.

By the Monday night before Memorial Day weekend, all of GroVont and most of Jackson knew Lydia was planning to spring Oly Pedersen from assisted living and run off to California, but I wasn't worried about Brandy Epstein or anyone in charge out at Haven House finding out. Locals might gossip maliciously to just about anyone about misdemeanors such as driving without a license, but they'd keep their mouths shut for felonies. Certain people, such as local parole officers, live in a Ziploc sandwich bag, so far as communication is concerned.

I was put in charge of getting Lydia's BMW ready for the road. Even though the car was twenty years old, it only had one hundred and ten thousand miles on it, because Lydia had been out of town much of its existence. I bought her new tires and had the clutch repaired. Without telling her, I had the brake lights fixed. The cigarette-lighter fuse had to be replaced so she could plug in her microphone for on-the-road recording of the oral history. Years ago, Lydia had made Hank pull both it and the turn-signal fuse. She said it wasn't anybody's business whether she was going to turn or in what direction.

Meanwhile, she and the minimum-security unit in Lompoc exchanged a flurry of forms and phone calls, getting her cleared for a visit. I wasn't let in on the details. Normally, that wouldn't stop me from creating them in my imagination, for the sake of our story, but it doesn't seem to matter so much, so I won't. I do know the Lompoc authorities were unaware of Lydia's paroled-felon status. She and Hank had been married on the Ahtahkakoop First Nation Reserve in Saskatchewan, and the Cree aren't big on sharing information with American prison officials.

Roger did something on his old school computer and came up with five movies written by Loren Paul, but we only found one at Video Maniacs—a Showtime adaptation of *Yeast Infection*. We watched it together Thursday night, while he did his laundry. It was interesting, but I couldn't understand why the Georgia peanut farmer had an Australian accent. Far as I could tell, the budget must have come in right at twelve dollars.

LEROY WAS BEGINNING TO REGRET LETTING ZELDA ATTACH *herself to his mission. He hadn't been with a girl he didn't pay for in years, and at the moment of decision, the rewards seemed worth the bother. And she did offer to steal her brother Gordo's Chevrolet Monza 2+2.*

But then the bitch opened her yap. She didn't shut it the entire length of Colorado. Pueblo, Colorado Springs, Denver, Fort Collins—Zelda twisted the nail in her cheek and blinked more than Leroy thought was usual, even in high-strung women, as she compared Depeche Mode to the Bangles. The Bangles came up short. In her opinion, Ace of Base was rad, but 10,000 Maniacs sucked big-time. Leroy hadn't caught on that she was talking about musical groups until north of Colorado Springs, up by the Air Force Academy, when she went off on the Grateful Dead.

Leroy said, "The Dead haven't been worth shit since Pigpen died."

Zelda said, "Who?"

After that, he concentrated on driving the interstate, while she babbled and twitched. Leroy hadn't driven a busy highway like this in a long time, and it was entertaining to think about gunning down the other drivers.

Near midnight, just past Virginia Dale on the Wyoming–Colorado border, the Monza ran out of gas.

"I told you we should fill up back there in Denver when we stopped to shoplift dinner," Zelda said. "You're one of those guys who can't even hear when a chick talks."

"Grab any stuff you might want later and get out."

"You want to smoke a doobie first? I've found doobies make the dark clouds lighter."

"Get your tail out of the car."

Zelda pulled her pink suitcase and matching vanity bag out of the backseat and stood off on the shoulder, smoking pot.

"What are you planning to do, Charley?" she asked. As a test, Leroy had told Zelda his name was Charles Manson. She'd never heard of the original, which meant she had flunked. To Leroy, this meant the girl was so stupid she deserved whatever he did to or with her. Leroy rationalized many of his actions by that standard—stupid people have it coming.

"We're going on," Leroy said. He flipped open Gordo's elk-gutting knife and stabbed the passenger seat. He cut a long gash in the seat cover, then he pulled out the stuffing.

Zelda said, "You think anyone will come by? I need to whiz, and I don't want headlights catching my bum."

Leroy swore to himself as he dug around the backseat floor for the bag of goods he's stolen from the Zippy Mart. No amount of chi-chi was worth putting up with this much stupidity. If they ever got around to screwing, he'd have to duct tape her mouth shut.

She called, "Yell if you see any lights."

Leroy flicked the cigarette lighter till he had a steady flame; then he used the aerosol deodorant as a blowtorch. Soon, the passenger seat was ablaze.

"What are you doing to Gordo's car?" Zelda asked from the bar ditch, where she squatted, Levi's at her ankles, joint clenched between her teeth.

Leroy didn't answer. He gathered his few belongings, got out, and walked over to Zelda.

She stood up and buttoned. "Gordo's car is afire."

He took the joint from her mouth. "I hadn't noticed."

"Yes, you had." Zelda took a couple of steps toward the car, as if she had an impulse to put the fire out. Then she came back to Leroy. She held her hand out for the joint. "You set Gordo's car on fire."

Leroy ignored her hand while he smoked the joint and watched the fire. Leroy enjoyed fires.

"You think we should move back?" Zelda said. "In movies, burning cars explode."

"No gas in that piece of junk," Leroy said. "She won't explode."

Flames filled the interior of the Monza. A window shattered from the heat, and the fire popped up in intensity at the sudden rush of oxygen.

Zelda said, "Gordo worked all summer to buy that car. He paid six hundred dollars."

"Gordo got hosed."

"But why should we burn it?"

Leroy flipped the roach into the darkness. "Look at us, you filthy slit. You think somebody driving by is going to stop for you and me if we stick out our thumb?"

Zelda took a good look at herself and Leroy, whose name she thought was Charley, and she had to admit, very few people would feel comfortable confronting them at midnight on a deserted mountain pass. She came across as okay in her acid-washed jeans, T-shirt, and 4-H jacket, but even with an unbuttoned ZIPPY MART shirt covering his scarred back, Charley's appearance instilled fear. He looked like a killer of random strangers. That was what had drawn her to him when they first met. Life in Trinidad was so boring, even the risk of death felt like an improvement, and she relished the look on her father's face when he found them together. Charley was almost bound to catch her daddy's attention.

"I wish you wouldn't call me that word," she said. "It's not gentlemanly."

"What word?" Leroy said.

A pair of headlights flickered in and out down the mountain, winding up from Colorado. "There they are," Leroy said. "When they pull up, don't you talk."

The pickup truck coming over the pass contained Barnett Cutt and Rowdy Talbot, heading home from a rodeo in Boise City, Oklahoma, where they'd both lost. Barnett was a calf roper in his mid-twenties, Rowdy, a bull rider fresh out of high school. Of course, Leroy didn't know their names. I do, because I spoke to Rowdy the next winter at a snowmobile hill climb in Jackson.

When I talked to him about that night, Rowdy was drinking a beer—Blue Ribbon in a bottle. He had his wrist in a cast, on account of being stepped on by a bull. He said, "That was the single most peculiar event of my life, thus far."

"I would imagine so," I said. "What are you, eighteen?"

"Nineteen."

"I would hope running into Leroy is a once in a lifetime event."

"We came over a little rise, and there was this car, in flames, dead center of our lane. I could see right off it was a Monza. They have an aluminum block I've been told will melt in a fire, so I was all for stopping to see if it's true, but Barnett was hesitant. He doesn't like unforeseen experience. Besides, he was in a rush to make Laramie to water his horse.

"I said, 'A person might be in that car. We ought to check it out,' and Barnett said, 'Anyone in there's dead. I'm not up to finding no dead bodies tonight. My ass is whipped already.'

"But then we saw the girl off on the shoulder there and Barnett hit the brakes. It's a known fact calf ropers are weak brained when it comes to women in a mess.

"Barnett pulled up behind the burning car and we got out and the girl started in." Rowdy switched to a high, what he thought of as girlish, voice. "'Are you for-real cowboys? I never met an honest-to-God cowboy, just the drugstore kind and some truck drivers in boots. I'll give you some dynamite boo for a ride into town.'

"I drifted over to the Monza, while Barnett drifted to the girl, which is the difference between calf ropers and bull riders. The fire was mainly smoke by then, but there was a holy load of smoke. A tire blew, which made me jump. I couldn't see the block to tell if it was melted or not.

"Barnett said, 'How'd the car come to catch fire?'

"She said, 'Charley lit it so people would help us. He didn't think y'all would stop this time of night. Had it been my choice, I'd of at least tried for a while. It's not like we were fixing to die.'

"Barnett stared off in the dark behind the girl. I reckon he knew something bad was up."

I couldn't help myself. I said, "You reckon?"

Rowdy eyed me suspiciously and hit the beer before he went on. "Barnett said, 'Where's Charley now?' and the girl said, 'In your truck there.'

"We both of us turned to see the ugliest one human imaginable—looked like a thing slid out of slime—and he had the .280 Remington from Barnett's gun rack in his hands, cracked open to see that it was loaded. He snapped the bolt to and more or less pointed the rifle Barnett's direction. His voice was so quiet, I had to strain to make out the words.

"'Join the other gentleman at the fire.'

"Barnett looked from the ugly man to me, then at the Monza on fire, then back to the ugly man.

"The girl talked fast. 'Charley, I want you to do me a favor. I want you to refrain from killing these nice cowboys who stopped to help us.'

"I didn't like the sound of that.

"The Charley character said, 'I do not grant favors.'

"She said, 'But they're cowboys. You can't go around killing cowboys. It'll attract attention we don't want yet. You kill strangers and you won't get time to kill the folks you set out for. We don't want that, now do we, Charley?'

"Barnett moved over by me. Charley said, 'Take off your boots.' I said, 'Why?' and he said, 'You don't want your feet in them when I start shooting.' So me and Barnett hopped around to take our boots off, and as we finished, Charley hung each boot over the barrel and pulled the trigger. Those shots echoed off the mountains like rolling thunder. He blew our boots so far away, we never even bothered looking for them.

"*Meanwhile the girl carried a big bag and a little bag to the truck, and she got in the driver's side, then scooted over and sat there, looking out at us. She had extremely short hair, for a girl. What there was of it was this exploded orange like a Nehi.*"

I started to say, Nehi? The sardonic way, like I'd said Reckon? but the kid wasn't stupid. He would know I was mocking him. Catching condescension is a rare trait in bull riders.

Rowdy said, "*After he'd disabled our boots, the ugly guy went into the dark and came back carrying a plastic grocery sack. I was scared Barnett might try something heroic and get us massacred, but Barnett just stood there. I guess he was like me, hoping this would end with us alive. Charley didn't seem to care either way. He got in the truck and started it.*

"*Barnett showed his bit of gumption. 'You don't need my horse,' he said. 'It'd only take a minute to unhook the trailer.'*

"*The guy acted like he didn't hear. He wrestled with the stick shift—it was tricky, and even trickier when you were holding a .280 on the rightful owner. Finally he got her in first.*

"*The girl looked straight at me and winked. She seemed real happy.*"

Rowdy stopped the story and finished the beer while I waited for more. When I realized no more was forthcoming, I asked, "So what happened?"

"*We walked all night in our socks, that's what happened. No one else was stupid enough to stop till the highway patrol picked us up at dawn.*"

14

THE GREAT WAR CHANGED IT ALL. NOT IN THE PERSONAL HEARTBEAT LIKE THE earthquake, boiler explosion, or the Miller brothers, but it came out just as sure and complete. I went into that war such an American—such a Westerner, if you know what that means. Us Westerners believe in the sanctity of goodness—honesty, beauty, hard work, a man's word, a well-broke horse. There was right and there was wrong, and the two stayed on their own sides of the fence.

A code of being died in those trenches, not just for me, but for all of Europe. The difference between right and wrong died. Christmas died. America was affected, but not transformed. Americans were too far away and came in too late for their code to be demolished beyond recognition. But after the war, Europe was not one bit like it was before the war, and neither was I. I went in a Westerner and came out a puff of air above a street grate.

The deal began as a lark. Me, Bill, and Oly worked our way up to Calgary and joined the Canadian Expeditionary Force. Those folks didn't give a hoot that we weren't Canadian. They wanted men willing to fight, which was us. Mostly the American boys were from Montana. It's a historical fact that Montana has lost a greater percentage of her youth than any other state in ever' single war in the twentieth century. There could be two reasons: either (1) Montana boys love a fight, or (2) we're not good enough at it to avoid death. I suspect number one.

They put us with a bunch of other states' boys in tents out east of town, in the flats along the river there. We marched in ranks and learned how to affix bayonets on rifles. Most of us already knew shooting, except me. I never did catch on to the shooting.

To start, I'd say it was posturing. The boys bragged a good deal. At night, around the fires, they'd say they hoped the war would last long enough so they could get there to kill the Boche. *Boche* is what they called Germans. I never heard anybody say Jerries after Bill did that one time in the bunkhouse. Bill was the worst for bragging, of course. He was always going on about killing men and loving women. He looked forward to French women the way most men look forward to baseball season. Bill firmly believed all French women want it all the time and all French men don't know the proper method of giving it to them. I wonder to this day on what information Bill based that opinion.

Then, in April, we got word of the Germans gassing the First Canadian Division at Ypres, and the casual braggadocio crashed overnight. You take a country with a population small as Canada's, and you wipe out fifty thousand of her boys in a day, and almost every family will feel the grief. We were told of a yellow cloud that drifted across the mud and killed or prostrated the entire army, and how Germans in special masks came through the forest bayoneting our boys as they writhed helpless and blind on the ground.

It must sound silly now, but in those days, men believed there was an honorable way to conduct a war. You fought fair when you killed the enemy. Imagine that. We were raised to respect the other guys as humans who just happened not to be on our team. We treated them the way we expected them to treat us.

Gas put an end to that ideal. Then, later on in the next war, after the atomic bomb, even civilians stopped believing in that nobility of the warrior bunk.

But in 1915, us boys in training were deeply offended by the foulness of killing people with poison gas. Suddenly, the Canadian army was frothing for vengeance. Before Ypres, most of the boys in my troop couldn't have told you why they were fighting on one side as opposed to the other. We backed the English because they talked more or less like us. Beyond that, no one had much of a notion as to the politics involved.

After Ypres, the bragging turned mean.

———

The second fire combusted when our division was camped by Halifax about to ship out for England, and we got news of the *Lusitania*. Personally, the idea that Germans could float up and sink a boatload of humanity made me more nauseous than incensed. I'd never been aboard a boat would hold over four passengers, and from Nova Scotia, the Atlantic Ocean appeared to go on forever, with no place to run to or hide in. I stood on this windblown bluff top, looking over the gray water, feeling smaller than I ever felt in Montana or Wyoming. I'd seen the ocean before, in San Francisco, but I hadn't been about to cross it amongst enemies with torpedoes. The troop ship seemed tiny and helpless in comparison to the Atlantic Ocean. A toy in a bathtub. A lot of boys used the *Lusitania* to whip themselves into another frenzy of *Kill, Kill, Kill!* But all I felt was shriveled.

Being on the boat itself proved even worse than thinking about being on the boat. Now that I'm old and wise, I see throwing up saltine crackers for three weeks as a blessing. I realize at the time I felt so God-awful, my mind wasn't free to fret over our exposed position. Drowning would have come as blessed relief.

Bill and Shad weren't the least bit ill. They made sport of me—or Bill made sport, and Shad smiled my direction, which was almost worse—and I hated the both of them for the entire voyage. Bill got caught cheating at faro, and I figure those boys would have thrown him overboard if Shad hadn't produced a knife. I didn't feel an ounce of sorry. Had I been able to shout, I'd of shouted, *Go ahead. Toss the bastard!* Some of the sick ones improved after a few days, but I never. In a life of highs and lows, that ocean crossing must be listed as a low.

———

We stayed in England for two months, only I don't recall many details, so that nation must not have been impressive. It was cold, for summer—I remember that—and the food was boiled. We marched and packed our kits and unpacked our kits and cleaned our rifles. My dream was a dry firing pin. I don't recall attaining my dream.

I wrote Agatha Ann a letter every evening, no matter how bushed I was. She wrote me. My interest in the mail exceeded my interest in reality on a day-to-day basis.

———

My awareness of immediate surroundings returned in earnest when we arrived in France. A man can't live solely for the postal system in a place where you're likely to be shot. Or blown up. I'd have to say more boys were blown up than shot, although it was fairly even.

All that comes later. First we had to march down a long road with poplars on either side. The land was domesticated and pretty at the same time. The locals were supportive without being chummy. I guess they knew better than to get close to men on that road.

Troops going to war sang as they marched back then. That's

one of the many habits the Great War put an end to—singing soldiers. The French were especially likely to burst into what I took as a show tune as they walked along in their coal blue jackets, red trousers, and black boots. This was before the Army made them cut off their hair, on account of lice, so they looked individual and dashing, marching along, singing. When they were ordered to get haircuts, a bunch of French battalions mutinied, which wouldn't have happened in the Canadian Army, but that's neither here nor there. I'm not about to judge a soldier by his vanity.

———

We spent the night outside this town that had been bombed to tatters, in what I guess you would call huts. They weren't canvas, more like slapped-together clapboard. A stiff breeze would of blown them and whatever was in them into the river. Soon as we got settled, Bill left, looking for French women, and Shad went off for food. I was too worn-out to do much but write Agatha. I told her about the quaint pony carts and hunched-over people we'd passed. I left out the bombed farmhouses. I fell asleep with my boots on.

Shad woke me up an hour later. He'd found turnips, I guess. Some Europe version of turnips, anyway. We didn't have salt, so they weren't worth waking up over. Bill showed up around two in the morning and said he'd found two sporting houses. The one with a blue light out front was for officers only, and the one with a red light was for enlisted men. Bill said the red-light house had too long a line outside the door, so he snuck in the window of the blue-light house. He said the blue-light hussies were more enthusiastic than the red lights. I don't see how he knew this for a comparison. He hadn't been in a red light, and for all I knew, he was lying about having been in the other. Bill lied so much, you couldn't tell when he was telling the truth.

Next day we marched for many hours. It was sunny and pleasant, so I didn't mind. I was young then. Late afternoon, with the sun behind our backs, we walked down a ramp into the communication trench. It stopped being pleasant from there to the first line. We must of walked six miles in the trenches. Some places it was wide enough to pass men carrying equipment, and some places it wasn't. Wires were strung crossways, so you had to pay attention or risk a bad fall. Being from the Western U.S., where folks rarely spend time in a ditch, I didn't care for the closeness of it. Felt like a long grave to me. It smelled of rot. A multitude of rats fed on things I didn't want to look at.

The big guns boomed all day, both ahead and behind. I couldn't tell ours from theirs, but every so often there'd be a whistle a different pitch—I only learned later—and the sergeant escorting us hurled himself face flat into the dirt, and a moment later we hurled ourselves, and somewhere close the earth exploded. The sergeant would stand up, look at us in disgust, and mutter, "Skoda 75" or "Whizbang." I still don't know how he could tell which was which.

I wasn't scared so much as I should have been. We'd been told most of us would be dead in a couple of months, and those who weren't dead would be wounded or crazed, but I didn't believe that. I thought about Agatha and her freckles and what we'd do after we married—where we might live, how I would make a career, names for the boy and girl children. I thought about the surviving Miller brothers and the likelihood of their forgetting me and going on with their own lives. I didn't put much trust in that. I wondered if being in the war would make me such a hard case I could go back and shoot both Millers. As a rule, I wasn't one to pretend I might shoot people. Not like Bill. But if Roy and Ephir Miller were sworn to keep after me, it would be self-defense to shoot them any way possible, even if I didn't call them out in a fair gunfight. Nobody had fair gunfights anymore. I'm not certain they ever did. That whole fast-draw, face-off-in-the-street story might have been made up by dime novelists. They made up so much malarkey. Ninety percent of the Indian lore that was agreed to by all writers wasn't true. The odds figured to hold up for gunfighters also. I'd be better off using my Army time learning how to bushwhack.

———

We had us a Scotch Presbyterian sergeant named Dell McDell who was a son of a bitch. He didn't like me, on account of I wasn't Presbyterian or a true Canadian of Scotch descent. Hardly any in the company were, but that didn't matter none to McDell. He took offense to me on sight.

The sergeant met his end at Somme, only a week before I endured my wound. Mostly when fellows get killed, all hard feelings are off, and it shows how hard my feelings were that to this day I cannot speak with respect of the man.

That first night on the line, after we'd marched fourteen hours hauling fifty-pound kits, he says, "Private Pedersen, sentry duty." We'd been folded into a depleted company, so it's not as if he didn't have rested choices. He just didn't know who among the new bunch to hate, so he fell back on me.

And he stuck me at number nine, which was up the trench, at a dead-end closer to the German line than our own billet. I had no notion what to expect. When I said good-bye to Shad and Bill, I figured the odds of seeing them again at even.

I scooted bent over through all the posts and clutter that accumulates in a trench, until I finally made number nine, where the sentry on duty, who was from Halifax and had an accent I could barely fathom, said, "The Boche, they're too quiet tonight."

I said, "I thought we wanted quiet."

He shook his head. "They stop firing when they have patrols out, for fear of hitting their own men. Likely as not, they'll come over and cut your throat while you're taking a piss."

I resolved not to take any pisses. He watched as I affixed my bayonet and clicked off my safety. He said, "This is your first day."

I said, "How did you know?"

He laughed, but not in a funny way. "Don't attract attention to your post." Then he was gone.

I don't mind saying, eighty-four years after the fact, that I was more frightened alone there in the middle of France in the blackest darkness than I have been since—not even later, when we went over the top with little chance of survival. Especially not then. By the time we got around to doing something stupidly dangerous I was to the point where being dead was nothing special. It doesn't take long in a trench to reach that conclusion.

But that night on sentry duty, I still hadn't lost the cloak of civilization. I was more human than animal, and as such, I didn't want to get hurt.

I crawled up on the firing platform and peeked over for my first look into no-man's-land. It was so dark I couldn't tell where the German parapets started, even though they were less than a hundred yards out. I could see ghostly forms kind of waving. I shot one of them. Maybe I missed, or not, because my bullet had no effect. I fired again, and suddenly the land between me and the Boche line was lit by a flare and *bang*, something cracked into the sandbag beside my head. In the light of the flare, I saw the waving stakes that supported our wire, then another *crack* hit, and I pitched backwards into the trench.

I didn't look back over for six hours. They could of walked up and shot me in the trench, for all the guarding I did.

———

The night was long and miserable, and I was never so glad as soon after dawn when Jacob Wibberley scooted up the trench in my relief. Jacob came out of Kamloops, British Columbia. I'd known him since our first camp and even met his mother and fiancée when they traveled over to see us off on the train when we left Calgary. He was a tall, slim boy whose goal was to be a schoolteacher. His fiancée was not as pretty as Agatha.

Jacob slapped me on the shoulder and said, "How goes the show?"

I said, "Quiet," not letting on I'd been frightened to pieces all night and might have run back to Billings if he hadn't shown up when he did.

"Kill any Boche?" he asked.

"No, but I gunned down a couple of wire stakes."

He chuckled at my funny and crawled up on the firing platform to take a peek. A moment later, his foot slipped, and he fell back, bouncing off the earthen wall.

I laughed aloud and said, "Same thing happened to me first time I looked over."

Then I saw his leg was twisted up under him. That wasn't the way a man should land after a short fall. I leaned down and turned Jacob on his side. He had a hole in his forehead. His eyes were already clouds.

I jumped away as if from an electric shock. I'd seen killed men before—remember Henry and Hank Miller—but this was different. This was an eighteen-year-old boy with a family. I'd played cards with Jacob. I'd spoken briefly to his loved ones, who would soon be engulfed by a wave of grief. His fiancée didn't know her beloved was dead. She was still going on with her life, not aware of the pain she would soon be subjected to.

I looked down at the body of Jacob Wibberley and I made a vow: I swore no matter how awful conditions got in that war, I wasn't going to die. I swore I would never put Agatha through the torment Jacob's sweetheart was about to feel. My purpose from that moment forward would be to spare Agatha.

Jacob Wibberley was the first death I witnessed on the front. After him came hundreds and probably thousands. I couldn't of counted the number of boys died before my eyes. The worst consequence of war—to my mind, worse even than ruined families—is how cheap life becomes. This is particularly true in trench warfare. If what had happened to Jacob had happened two months later, I would have gone back to headquarters and reported his death and then proceeded on to breakfast with no more than a *happy it wasn't me.*

Death became casual. Death should never be casual, whether in a trench or in a nursing home or anywheres. There's nothing casual about a person expiring, any more than there is about a person being born.

Every so often an arm or a leg would show up, sticking out the side of a dirt pile or along the mud in the track. The men made jokes about it. Constant death inevitably brings out the wags. They'd say, "Give Tommy a hand," or "Let Tommy take sentry duty. He's got nothing else on." Unidentified body parts were always named Tommy. A leg at one trench intersection was used as a turnstile for several days, until rats finally reduced it.

I can't read stories or watch movies these days, because the storytellers kill side characters with such abandon. Sometimes even major people pass on for no reason. They made us sit through a movie in the recreation hall last month—*Rambo.* Irene Dukakis enjoyed it, but I never. If I'd been allowed my way, whenever that Rambo killed, he would have had to write down the name of the person he killed and make a list of all those who loved him. If everyone—real or story—was required to do that there'd be a lot less casual killing in this world.

———

The only thing kept me from falling into the abyss was once every week or so when the call came over—*All out for mail.*

We'd rush out of our tents or the mess hall or wherever we were and line up for the precious lifeblood that flowed between us and our former selves. Agatha wrote every day. The letters piled up so sometimes I got ten at once. Bill was jealous no end. She sent him one letter a week, if that.

He'd stand too close to me and my mail and sneer. "Dad will never turn our fortune over to you. You'd best forget noodling my sister. She doesn't care for you one bit. She told me the truth."

I knew he was lying, but it shook me anyway. Some men received letters from their sweethearts saying they'd stopped waiting. Afterward, those men didn't have much life expectancy. I used to hide Agatha's letters and only read one a day, in the order in which she'd written them. When I was reading a letter from Agatha it felt as if she was right there next to me. I could see her lips moving as she wrote and her eyes roving back and forth across the page. Sometimes I concentrated on her fingers. She had slim, long fingers with perfect nails. Agatha was proud of her nails. I knew each one better than I knew my own.

I cannot fathom how Shad got along without mail. He never received a letter the whole war. Not a one. He didn't seem to mind, although I couldn't tell what Shad minded and what he didn't. He kept taking care of Bill's needs—heating his coffee, cleaning his boots—even when the other boys teased. He didn't tell why, and neither did I. Bill liked to believe Shad served him out of loyalty. I never could set him straight.

———

Winter in the trenches had to be the worst home place on the planet, what with mud and cold and rats so hungry they wouldn't always wait for a man to turn corpse before starting in to eat him. You'd think we looked forward to spring, but if so, you'd think wrong. Spring brought offensives. Bored generals who'd spent the winter in Paris or some such decided it was warm enough to sacrifice ten thousand humans to gain fifty yards of territory.

Lorry teams of shells and batteries came slogging up the mud ruts. New divisions arrived. They swapped our useless tin helmets for steel, and in doing so, saved a number of lives. Ladders came pouring into the lines for climbing quickly out when the whistle blew. Engineers had us dig pits for our gas shells. It's true. A year back, we'd thought gas was the coward's way, and now we were setting them up ourselves.

Our company dropped back a couple of miles, to catch up on sleep and fix broken equipment. That's how we knew we were chosen as first across. They liked cannon fodder to have momentum going before we popped over the top.

Then one night—I think it was a Friday—they formed us up and we advanced in half platoons, back through the communication trench. I remember looking about at the faces—Shad, Bill, some who had been with us in Calgary, many who hadn't—and wondering what in blazes those boys were thinking. No one seemed nerve racked or bloodthirsty. Jaws weren't set like before a football game. They joked a bit more than usual. Otherwise we could have been young men starting off to our daily work in Billings, Montana.

As we reached the front, our artillery commenced to lob a wall of fireballs in the Boche first line. I thought I'd witnessed barrages before, but I'd never seen anything to compare with the flaming hell that rained down on their trench.

Shad stood next to me on the line to watch.

He said, "Nobody could survive that."

I made a joke. "They'll be no greeting committee when we arrive."

"I don't like the wind," Shad said.

"What wind?"

"That's what I mean."

And here's where I learned all I needed to know about the British. They'd planned to lay down gas at dawn on a certain morning, and by God, they were going to lay down gas at dawn on that morning. They didn't give a bloody damn that there wasn't no breeze carrying from us to them. They fired the shells anyway.

The canisters hit this side of the German trench, and the gas just sat there like a lime green fog.

"I'm not passing through that," Bill said.

Our captain heard him and pulled out his handgun. "I have orders to shoot any soldier refuses to leave our trench."

"You wouldn't shoot your own men," I said.

He licked his lower lip and cut his eyes up and down the assembled troops. He raised his voice for all to hear. "Those are the orders and they'll execute me if I don't obey, so don't test me."

"Bill here was only joshing," I said. "When the time comes, he will answer the call."

Bill himself didn't look so certain.

Down the line, a whistle blew, then another up line, and over we went.

The artillery barrage stopped all of a sudden. We could see beyond the gas fires licking whatever was left over there. I tried to crouch and run, but over the winter no-man's-land had been chewed to bits. Running through the mud was like dancing over melted tires.

Our wire-cutter patrols had been out all night snipping trails for us. We passed a couple of their bodies, hung on wire like clothes on a clothesline. Nobody screamed their wrath the way they do in motion pictures. Other than machine-gun fire and artillery off a ways, it was practically quiet. Or maybe my ears were clogged by fear. I don't know. I remember that morning's advance as quiet.

They hadn't let us carry gas masks, and ours were no good anyway, so we held our breath as best we could and ran through the fog and jumped into the German first line. A couple of boys got sick and crawled along, but most of us made it into the line. I couldn't see anyone or thing alive. Not even a rat. Lots of bodies in mangled positions. Lots of abandoned equipment. Our artillery had wiped the enemy out.

Bill wanted to collect souvenirs. I was too superstitious to steal from dead people, and Shad didn't care. Shad found a dugout. We couldn't tell if it held Boche or not, and we weren't of a mind to waltz down and see, so we each popped a grenade down the hole and moved along. I don't know if I killed anyone or I didn't.

The captain who'd threatened Bill earlier told us to push on to their second line.

"The artillery hasn't softened them yet," I said.

"It'll strike before we get there. Don't concern yourself."

And sure enough, the inferno started up again, a couple hundred yards on farther east.

"Let's move," the captain said.

"What about the whistle?" I asked.

"*Move.*"

So we jumped over the top. Again.

Now, there were bodies everywhere and craters so deep a horse could break legs falling in one. Some craters contained live Germans who wanted to surrender, and some, live Germans who wanted to fight. Gunfire broke out up and down the line along with screams of passion and pain. In noise terms, this push was opposite of the earlier one. A machine gun opened up on us. I don't know how many fell. When you're running across open ground, you have no idea what's happening five yards to either side or behind. You keep moving.

The wall of fire we were running toward started moving toward us. Someone in artillery must have decided they were firing long and they should back it up. I didn't notice at first, till I felt Shad's hand pull me up short. I looked at him and he nodded toward the exploding bombs marching our direction. Slow and sure as a summer squall in Montana, the wall of flames came more quickly than a man could run.

Shad signaled me and Bill to jump into a crater off to our right. The crater must have been the result of a good-sized bomb, because it was three feet deep and more or less circular. There were four Germans already in it. Two dead—one of them dead for days, by his looks, the other fresh—and two live. The live Germans tried to surrender, but Bill shot them.

I said, "Did you have to do that?"

Bill said, "You're next." His eyes glittered and snapped like a horse stuck on barbwire. I don't think Bill knew who I was and he might have shot me if Shad hadn't started throwing up a breastwork of corpses. Bill didn't help, but his attention left me. He sat against the far ledge, staring at his hands, both front and back.

The firewall boomed toward us, the smoke so black you couldn't see five feet any direction. All you could do was hear raining bombs. Those seven-nines was called Jack Johnsons, after the Negro boxer, on account of how black a smoke they put out. A huge blast sounded off and a body came flying over, missing my head by the width of a nose and hitting Bill full-on. The body was burnt black and naked, so you couldn't tell what army it had belonged in. It doesn't matter.

Bill lay there with the naked, burnt cadaver on him, and he started to whimper.

"Are you hurt?" I shouted over the din.

Bill didn't answer. He just kept making frightened hound dog sounds.

Shad changed his mind about building a wall of bodies and pulled them back into the crater. Me and Shad each took two dead Germans and pitched them over our bodies like a pup tent or a blanket, while Bill whimpered under his. They weren't worth anything in a direct hit, but they could absorb spent shrapnel if it fell down on us. Which it did.

Bill was weeping and Shad and I yelling nonsense syllables at each other and God. If anything, the bombardment picked up a notch. It was too loud and continuous to hear individual bombs, unless they landed close. I'm not ashamed to say I wet myself. Bill soiled himself even worse. Amongst all the noise and smoke I couldn't help but feel rage that it was our own artillery pounding us. There's a certain raw nobility in being killed by the enemy, but getting blown to smithereens by your own side is nothing but stupid.

That's the moment—through the smoke and fire and chaos—I saw Agatha. She stood on the lip of our crater, young and fresh as the day the boiler blew me onto her daddy's porch. I could see her and see through her, like looking into running water. Her face was lit by a little smile, the smile she kept only for me, and she was pointing.

She said, "Come out this side."

Shad yelled, "We can't stay put." He tried to move Bill, but Bill would have none of it. He'd stopped the weeping and turned to stone. Shad hit him in the face with his rifle, but Bill didn't so much as flinch.

Shad shouted, "Come on, you filthy bastard."

"I'm going," I yelled. I threw off the dead Germans, grabbed my rifle, and jumped the direction Agatha pointed. I ran ten or fifteen steps toward the first line, when a bomb exploded at my back. The concussion blew me some yards in the air before I came down on my face. Amazingly enough, I still had my rifle.

I figured then that Shad and Bill were dead, but I must be

truthful in saying I didn't much care. I expected the same for me. All I felt was disappointment that I wasn't going to keep my vow to Agatha.

I belly-crawled a ways, then made it to my feet and started walking. Just then, Shad passed me by. He had his rifle in his left hand and Bill thrown over this right shoulder. I took Bill for dead, but he wasn't. He wasn't even scratched.

Our barrage line ended fairly soon, and we emerged from the fire not fifty yards from the German first line, now occupied by our boys. Possibly the most unlikely piece of luck we had that whole day was no one from our side shot us when we walked out of the smoke. Agatha stayed beside me all the way to the trench.

Looking back now, I realize it wasn't truly Agatha, not even in the spiritual sense. It was my mind saving me the only way it knew how, by going insane.

———

That night, the Cameronians relieved us, and we dropped back behind the lines. Over the decades, there's been vicious talk about the British throwing Canadians, Australians, Irish, and other non-British troops into first waves. I'm not certain if these complaints are true or whining, but I do know the Cameronians died in greater droves than the rest of us. Almost every push began with a Cameronian slaughter, so it was a surprise for them to relieve us instead of the other way round.

When what little was left of our company gathered in a bombed-out village, I decided the time had come to tell Bill what I thought.

"Shad's debt is paid," I said. "He no longer has to wipe your bottom."

Bill was heating coffee water over a campfire he'd made from scrap lumber and books. He had recovered his composure—by that I mean he'd reverted to the shallow braggart of his youth.

"There wasn't no terms of calling off the debt," he said. "Shad knows the rules."

I looked over to Shad, who sat with his legs out and his back against the wall of a house. I think it was a house. The wall was all was left.

"Don't you consider that you've paid the debt?" I asked.

Shad shrugged. He was too worn to talk. I was still operating at a heightened sense of alarm. It takes me longer to come down off a battle than it did others.

"He saved your hide out there," I said to Bill. "Can't you show appreciation?"

"One has nothing to do with the other," Bill said.

"You won't think that next time you've froze up in a crater."

Bill's laugh was semi-hysterical. "There's never going to be a next time—not for me."

"How you plan to manage that?" I asked.

Shad spoke with closed eyes. I think he was more beat down by the experience than we'd supposed. "We did not die this time. There will always be a next time, until we do."

"Not for me." Bill stirred coffee into boiling water, cowboy-style. "A man would be crazy to go over the top into that firestorm. I'm no coward, but neither am I crazy."

Shad and I considered this statement. Of course you had to be suicidal to go over, but enlisted men had no choice. If we obeyed orders, the Boche killed us, and if we didn't obey orders, our own army killed us. There was no middle ground.

"How you planning to decline the next attack?" I asked.

Shad opened his eyes to look at Bill in the firelight. I think he was genuinely curious to hear the answer. If a man could choose to no longer go into battle, we both were interested in how it was pulled off.

"I don't know the answer yet," Bill said. "I only know I'm done with charging hell."

Just then, a little bowlegged lieutenant from Toronto showed up and gave me a letter. "This came right before the push. I had no time to find you. Figured now would be soon enough if you survived."

I recognized the handwriting. "It's from my Agatha."

"She ain't your Agatha," Bill said. "She's my sister."

I tore open the letter and read by firelight the words which I will now recite from memory:

Oleander—You must be expecting this letter, so here it is. You know how disappointed I am that you would rather run off to France than be with me. You have broken my heart by your callousness. I can no longer plan my future around us. I must pick up the pieces of my life.

Thusly, I have married Frank Lesley. He is in training to assume the presidency of Daddy's bank. You were my first choice but you abandoned me and I cannot forgive you that. I trust you will have the good manners never to return to Billings. Agatha Ann Lesley.

There was a P.S.

P.S. Bill informed me of your dalliance with the red woman of ill repute. You can go back to her when you tire of your European vacation.

I screamed like an animal. "You told her about Swamp Fox."

Bill was all innocence. "Told who?"

"Agatha." Blinded by tears and rage, I felt for my rifle. "You told her, after making me go to that woman."

"Of course I told her," Bill said. "She's my sister. I can't hide from my sister that her fiancé wallowed with a syphilitic whore."

I found the rifle, with its bayonet still attached, leaning

against the wall there next to Shad. I spoke quietly. "You don't have call to interfere."

Shad looked from the bayonet to me. "I owe you, same as I owe him."

"Don't forget that."

During this exchange, my vision cleared enough to see Bill on the far side of the fire. He was sipping coffee from a tin cup. He must of seen me go for the rifle, but unlike in the crater, he showed no signs of terror.

He grinned. "Nobody made you do anything."

I roared and charged around the fire.

Bill simply stood his ground, cup in hand, stupid grin on his face. I think my attack paralyzed him. Maybe. Or maybe he knew I'd never bayonet an unarmed man, no matter what a foul enemy he was. Whatever the cause, Bill did not flinch.

I stopped, my bayonet tip against his windpipe.

He stared, unblinking, into my eyes. "You are not strong enough to kill me."

I stared back into his eyes, watching the fire flicker across his pupils. I prayed for the strength of purpose to stick him, knowing already I didn't have it. If I hadn't spoken to Shad, or if I hadn't had to run around the fire instead of taking him head on—I don't know. All I know is, once I hesitated, it was too late.

Bill said, "You don't deserve Agatha."

I flung my rifle away. He was right.

———

I shut down from that time till well after the Armistice. It wasn't that I turned suicidal soldier like others who received a letter saying their sweetheart had married a coward. I stopped feeling. Too much death, too much gore, gas, lice, and rats feeding on cadavers—without Agatha to connect me to civilization, I stopped being human. Wasn't any grand trick. It's easier not to be human in those conditions. The rest of the war was going through the motions.

Bill got himself advanced to sergeant and transferred twenty miles behind the line, where he groomed General Currie's horse. Bill didn't mind leaving his slave, Shad, for the duration. He figured they would start where they left off soon as the carnage ended.

I didn't die, of course. No suspense in that. I did take a cush wound during the Courcelette show. A splinter of iron from a sausage bomb tore up my thigh and into the hip bone. It wasn't drastic enough to quit me of the war, but it got infected, and I spent a year in a convalescent hospital—a former Catholic abbey—in Ireland. My time there would have been soft if I hadn't been located in a huge hall full of moaning, screaming, dying, or bored-stupid military men.

Except for the occasional leave, Shad lived through the entire war on the front lines. He's the only one I know of from our original Second Division who didn't die, transfer back, or save themselves by a wound. No one from First Division made it beginning to end.

I got back to the front December 1917, about when the Americans started showing up, two years after the *Lusitania*. The Yanks came along lately, but if they hadn't, Lord knows how long the politicians would have let that war go. Those villains could have ended it anytime, only both sides were so blown up with patriotism and bloodlust, they never considered stopping. By 1918, no one was left who recalled why the war commenced. The trench troops hated the general staff and the politicians a lot more than they hated Germans.

They kept us fighting and killing right up through the morning of the last day, long after the final lines had been drawn. I fought in World War II also—

"Hold on, Hoss," Lydia said. "Are you going to drag me through another war?"

Oly closed his one eye and focused the other on Lydia until she calmed down, then he continued:

> I fought in World War II also, and the two wars had no point in common. Men came back from the second knowing they'd accomplished something important. Those who survived the Great War were bitter, on account of being used. The boys that died died for no reason.

"That's a harsh way of wording it," Lydia said.

Oly said, "No reason."

15

LYDIA MADE A MAINTENANCE CHECKLIST FOR SHANNON. SHE was only going for three days, mere weeks after a ten-year absence, but you'd think Lydia was embarking on an expedition to the South Pole.

"The asparagus fern will need twelve ounces of filtered water on Saturday, and the philodendron gets four ounces and a sprinkling of the blue fertilizer Sunday morning. Do you know what I mean by a sprinkling?"

Without looking up from her book, Shannon made a right-handed sprinkling motion. She was lying on the old couch, leftover from the time when I lived there, under her favorite pink blanket, reading *Even Cowgirls Get the Blues*, and occasionally sampling a store-bought cupcake or homemade iced tea from the end table beyond her propped-sideways couch cushion.

"If I feel dampness on my star cactus when I come home, you're grounded for the summer," Lydia said.

"Don't worry," Shannon said. "I'm good at not watering plants."

"I will telephone from Salt Lake and Las Vegas, on the off chance Brandy Epstein may come sniffing around."

Shannon finally looked up. "I'm supposed to wait by the phone?"

"Roger, that ingenious boy, taught me how to check messages from afar on my answering machine. If by some miracle you should leave the house in the next three days, record any vital information there. I will retrieve it and call Brandy, pretending to be up at Sam's ranch. What is that hideous garment you have on?"

Shannon lifted the blanket to look down at the Denver Broncos jersey—number 7, several sizes too big, holes in both armpits—that hung on her body. She seemed to be seeing it for the first time.

"I found it in Hank's closet."

Lydia blinked against the idea of Shannon in Hank's clothes. Torn between despair and anger, she chose anger.

"Hank did not give you permission to wear his shirt. And why are you lying under a blanket, eating bonbons in the middle of the day? You're not Marie Antoinette."

Shannon held out a cupcake as an offering. "This isn't a bonbon. It's Dolly Madison."

Lydia more or less exploded. "The sun is shining. Flowers are blooming. And you are stretched out like a beached otter. A pregnant beached otter. They sleep on warm rocks on their backs with their tits to the sky. Totally useless beasts. And you're one of them."

As a matter of fact, sleeping on a warm rock with her tits to the sky sounded pretty good to Shannon. She had been satisfied on the couch, under her special blankie, with food and a book. She hadn't felt satisfied that often of late, and she wasn't in any hurry to throw away her peace of mind.

"That's me," she said. "The useless beast."

Lydia snatched the blanket off Shannon, like a magician snatching a tablecloth out from under a full set of dinnerware.

"*Hey*," Shannon squealed.

"Don't you pull that self-pity bunk on me." Lydia literally kicked the couch.

"I was lying here perfectly content," Shannon said. "There's no self-pity in being content."

"There is for you. You're content because you think you have no hope, so you may as well eat and read your life away."

Shannon was surprised at Lydia's insight. For all her raving and criticizing, every now and then Lydia nailed one. Contentment through lack of hope was exactly what Shannon was thinking at the store when she bought the Dolly Madisons.

"I want you up, off your ass," Lydia said, using more force than usual.

"You mean right now or in general?" Shannon said.

"Right now."

Shannon dutifully shuffled to her feet. Lydia's snatching away the blanket had exposed the men's boxer shorts Shannon was wearing along with the football jersey. The boxer shorts had been inherited from a boyfriend who left in a hurry a couple of years ago, and Shannon only wore them when there wasn't much chance of being seen.

"Do you have the faintest idea how I feel when I look at you?" Lydia said.

Shannon's posture wasn't up to snuff, but otherwise she felt like a recruit being verbally reamed by a drill sergeant.

"You're not yet thirty," Lydia barked. "Healthy, financially secure, fairly beautiful, in your own idiosyncratic way. You have advantages the rest of the world's women are willing to die for, and you are wasting them on self-pity and mood eating." Lydia looked Shannon up and down like she was sweatpants on the sale rack. "You've got everything I once had and lost."

"I don't think that's my fault."

Lydia's hands formed fists. Shannon thought her grandmother might strike her. Instead Lydia visibly pulled herself together. "Listen carefully, Shannon."

Shannon nodded but did not speak.

"When you reach a certain age, you are going to look back at the past, and you are going to think, *If I'd only known then what I know now.*"

"I already think that."

"I shall now give you the benefit of the wisdom coming from someone who does know now what you should have known then, which is now." Lydia placed her hands on Shannon's shoulders. "The time has come for you to take action."

Shannon nodded again. It's not as if she disagreed. "Like what?"

"*What* does not matter one whit. Do you understand? Find a hobby, take a lover. Ride a motorcycle naked. I've found public nudity almost always jump-starts the vaporous spirit."

As Shannon nodded one last time, her lower lip began to quiver. Her greatest fear was weeping in front of Lydia. The fear of weeping was about to make her weep.

"What if I do the wrong thing?" Shannon said.

"The wrong choice beats the holy hell out of no choice. Look at me. No, Shannon, not at the wall. At me."

Shannon looked at her.

"All my choices have been wrong. Sending Reagan's dog a poisoned chew toy was wrong, but I had to do something about that leather dick, and it was less wrong than shooting a random bureaucrat or setting myself on fire in front of a TV camera."

"Those were your choices?"

Lydia released Shannon's shoulders. "They were all I could see in the heat of the moment. Here's the deal: 90 percent of the time, whatever you do will turn out to be a mistake, but that's still better than doing nothing, which is always a mistake. You get one life, Shannon. Don't waste it on the couch."

Shannon knew everything Lydia was saying was true, even if she did word it in a way that came out sounding ridiculous. Shannon was fortunate. She did have potential. She could do anything she wanted, only so far, whatever she'd tried doing had ended in ugly, public disaster. Sometimes she thought *potential* meant having the opportunity to fail at an unlimited number of dreams.

Life was a disappointment. Shannon's eyes went slick, and the tears started to leak. "I don't know what I'm supposed to do."

"Of course you don't know. You never *know* anything. You *think*. You *feel*. You *believe* it *probable*. You hedge every bet. Shannon, you're never going to live until you cut off all the options but one. You can't obsess on two things at the same time."

"I feel like I can't obsess at all."

"There. You *feel like*. You don't *know* squat."

Shannon reached down and picked up her pink blankie. It'd been the blanket she couldn't sleep without from the age of one and a half to six. She'd found it in my remembrance drawer recently and reverted to her toddler needs. "When I meet a new guy I'm absolutely certain I can't live without him, but after a while, he proves me wrong."

"That's not obsession. That's addiction."

"You think I should join a love addicts support group?"

"I think you should stop thinking and attack. Pick a man, if that's what you want so much, and chase him down like a wolf after a moose. A wolf will chase a moose for days—weeks even, then, when she sees the chance, she zips in and *rips* out its Achilles tendon. With the moose crippled, the wolf tears out its throat and eats its liver while the moose is still alive."

Shannon was aghast. "That's what love is to you?"

"That's what life is. If you don't have the enthusiasm and nerve to chase down what you want and rip its throat out with your teeth, you might as well call it quits, put yourself to sleep like a beloved dog who's so old his quality of life isn't worth the pain."

Shannon clutched the pink blankie to her chest. With effort, she brought her breathing and tear ducts back under control. "I want to do what you say, Lydia. I want to badly. I just don't know how to go about the first step."

"Like I said, you can start by getting off your ass."

Shannon glanced down at the couch. "I did that."

"Then you must decide what you care about. Something must be important enough for you to go on. If you don't find a good reason to go on, you will live a miserable, fat life."

Shannon held the blanket to her nose and inhaled the smell of her childhood. "So, what's important?"

Lydia sighed. "Figure it out, Shannon. I have to go pick up my fossil friend."

———

Irene Dukakis almost nipped the expedition in the bud before it even began. Irene was one of those assisted-living lawyers you hear about, not a real lawyer, but after being institutionalized, she'd spent so much time researching her rights that she knew the senior-citizen statutes better than any licensed lawyer in the county. Ever since she'd heard Oly was spending the weekend with Lydia, Irene had been working the books, and when Lydia and Roger came to pick up the old guy, Irene was ready.

She caught them out by the BMW—Lydia, Roger, Oly, and Ellis Gill. Roger was restacking the luggage in the trunk, making room for Oly's chair. He wished they'd picked Oly up before loading the car. Not that either of them was taking more than an overnight bag—with a leather day pack for him and the fake saddle purse for her—but still, it looked odd to have suitcases in the trunk of a car that wasn't supposed to leave town.

Ellis was giving Lydia the medication rundown. "The pink one in the morning with a full glass of water, these two at one thirty before his nap. A tablespoon of this—are you listening, Mrs. Elkrunner?"

Lydia said, "What?"

That's when Irene came flapping out of the double front doors. Her dress was four or five shades of shimmery rayon green, and she wore white gloves. She had on paper overshoes, the kind nurses' aides wear in intensive care units, over what appeared to be tennies. Her hand was raised in the air, waving a spiral notebook.

Irene started in from twenty yards away. "You can't take him. If you do, I'll sue your trousers off, Ellis Gill. I can shut this holding tank down in a heartbeat. You'll wish you were on the *Titanic*, where it's safer."

Ellis's face dropped a few shades of pink. Lawsuits were his greatest fear as an administrator. He wouldn't even hire any woman named *Sue* because he was superstitious, like people who are afraid to say *cancer*.

Irene came to a halt, right in front of Oly's wheelchair. She was panting from the charge across the lawn. "There are protections against your sort in this state," she said to Lydia in that New Orleans accent that comes across as *Brooklyn meets cracker*.

"What sort is that?" Lydia asked.

Irene turned on Ellis. "This person was in prison not three weeks past. God only knows what deviance she practiced in that hole of hell. You cannot turn my Oleander over to a convict."

"This is her community service. She's doing this instead of prison." Ellis stammered on the *th*'s, which didn't endear him to Lydia.

Roger stood between Irene and the suitcases tucked way up in the trunk. He said, "I'll take care of Oly. Don't you worry about Lydia molesting your boyfriend."

"Molest, hell," said Lydia. "Two million dollars would not entice me consort with that Gila monster."

Irene shook the notebook before Ellis's eyes. "You cannot take an involuntary commitment off Haven House property without signed permission from his next of kin."

Ellis said, "Mr. Pedersen has no next of kin."

Throughout the uproar, Oly maintained his hibernating-turtle personality. He sat in the chair, staring in the general direction of an aspen across the street. Lydia had come to realize the upright-catatonic act was a convenient sham. Pretending he was deaf, dumb, and paralyzed got Oly through most social situations.

"I'm the closest Oly has to a relative," Irene said. "You must have my say-so, and I won't give it."

Lydia's attention left Oly for Irene. "What makes you related to him?"

Irene drew herself up to her full four feet nine inches of height. "I was the last woman he was with, intimately."

Lydia said, "I don't want to know that."

Roger said, "Oly, you are my role model," and playfully socked Oly on the shoulder. Oly started to go over sideways, before Roger caught him.

"How long ago? Lydia asked. "Because if it was before the end of World War I, the old boy has been holding out on the oral history."

"Twenty-two years. Fourth of July," Irene said.

Lydia immediately thought about herself, as she was prone to do, wondering how old she would be the last time she had sex, wondering if maybe she had already had her last time and didn't know it. Would it be better to know the last time was the last time, or let it sneak past, always assuming there would be more, until it was too late?

"You haven't been with a man in twenty-two years?"

Irene gave Lydia a look of exasperation. "Oly hasn't been with a gal since then. I didn't say a word about me."

Meanwhile Roger had been doing the math. "That would mean Oly was seventy-eight when you guys did it."

Irene said, "Seventy-seven."

"Either way is impressive," Roger said.

Irene propped her free hand, the hand not holding the notebook, on Oly's bald head. "It was nothing to brag about. Oly started something he couldn't finish."

Lydia said, "Thank you for sharing."

Ellis scratched his head above the ear, making his comb-over swirl like a tumbleweed. "That still doesn't make you next of kin."

Irene rubbed a glove across Oly's head affectionately. "Wyoming had common-law marriage back then. Legally speaking, we were man and wife, at least for a day, and he hasn't been man and wife with anybody since, so I'm the closest he's got to kin."

"Let me look at this law." Ellis took the notebook from Irene. He studied it, while the others waited in various levels of patience.

"I don't see anything about common-law marriage here."

"Everyone knows common law." Irene snatched the notebook back. "I simply researched the statutes that say she can't take him without a relative's permission. Even if I'm not next of kin, you'll have to find someone who is."

Lydia pulled the keys from her pocket and jingled them in Roger's direction. "This is a farce. Roger, put Mr. Pedersen in the car and his chair in the trunk."

Roger moved to lift Oly by the shoulders.

Irene said, "I'll sue if you do."

Lydia swung around on Ellis, who was wishing he hadn't gotten out of bed today. "Ellis," she said, "are you going to let yourself be bullied by this woman?"

Ellis was smart enough to know whatever he did, he was letting himself be bullied by a woman, so he chose to cover his butt. "When it comes to lawsuits, I strongly feel it is better to err on the side of caution."

"You are cautious as a mouse," Lydia said.

Oly's head moved side to side in small jerks. Remember that scene in *Wizard of Oz* where the Tin Man comes to after the oil fix. That's what it was. An awakening of rusted joints.

He spoke. "Irene."

Irene said, "Don't bother yourself, Oly. I will protect you from this vixen."

Oly said, "I haven't been off this plot of land in six years."

He kind of lost the drift of his thoughts then, watching a pair of ravens fight over a diaper they'd pulled from the Haven House Dumpster.

Lydia said, "And?"

Oly's focus returned. "When they brought me to this place, I was told I would never leave till the day I died. Do you know what that feels like, to walk into a building, knowing it's the last one? You may never leave."

"I had a cell mate with that problem," Lydia said.

Irene put the tips of her white-gloved fingers together. "I don't know how it feels, Oly. They allow me to attend church on Sundays with my niece."

"They don't let me go off anywhere, until now," Oly said.

He lifted himself from the chair and walked, bent but steady, to the car. Roger opened the backseat door. Oly ignored the boy. He opened the front-passenger door, turned around, and lowered himself into the seat with his legs still outside, his feet on the driveway pavement.

"I'll be back Monday," Oly said.

"Are you certain that is what you want?" Irene asked.

Oly used both hands to haul his legs into the car. Then he turned, face forward, staring out the windshield, back in the passive mode.

Irene latched on to Lydia's rotator cuff. "You'd best bring him back in the same condition you took him."

Lydia pried Irene's fingers loose. "My God, Irene, he's not a rug shampooer."

"Just you bring my Oly back. Alive."

16

After Armistice, I had nowhere to go and no reason to do anything or not do anything else, so I volunteered to invade Russia. Most Americans don't have a notion about that war. When I tell them, they say I'm making up a tall tale, but the fact is Americans, British—with Canadians and Australians—and a few French went in through Finland, while more Canadians, Americans, and Japanese landed in Siberia. Our purpose was to save the royalist white Russians from the Bolsheviks. The hitch: after the horrible deprivations during the war to end all wars, nobody had the enthusiasm to jump right into another one. The politicians couldn't drum up support from a worn-down populace, and the soldiers didn't have the spine for defending one bunch of Russians from another bunch of Russians. President Wilson hated the Tsar and backed up Lenin, till Lenin started winning. Now, it was the other way round. Our soldiers didn't buy it.

So, a year later, the North Russian Expedition gave up, but meanwhile me and Shad decided to go see the Baltic. At the last moment, before the train pulled out for Finland, Bill yanked some strings and came with us. Bill always had a talent for yanking strings. He said he wanted a crack at Bolo girls. My belief is Bill couldn't handle the thought of losing Shad.

You'd assume I spit in Bill's eye and shunned his presence, after all he'd done, but by the end of the Great War, I was too hollowed out. I didn't have the juice to maintain hatred. I'd had time to think in the convalescent hospital in Ireland, and I'd come to the conclusion that Agatha would have written that letter even if Bill hadn't told her about Swamp Fox. The thing Agatha loathed most was boredom, and the thing she wanted most was romance, as evidenced by her pleasure in poetry. I don't know if poetry bred romance or romance bred poetry. All I know for certain is that Agatha was not a girl to sit in her daddy's house in Billings, Montana, waiting for a man. The one virtue she never displayed was patience.

And besides, I had wallowed with a syphilitic whore. Bill did too, and his motive for telling on me was selfish, but that didn't change the facts. I wallowed. The consequences were mine, not Bill's. So, while I didn't cozy up with Bill Cox in North Russia, neither did I punch him in the face. Compare it to playing on a baseball team where the pitcher is a heel. You still play with him. You just don't tell him secrets.

As to the incursion, there's not much worth relating, except that guff about *it's the humidity, not the temperature* is true. Thirty below on the Archangel Railroad is more miserable than thirty below at the Jackson Hole Ski Area. Mostly, our job was to cover British retreats and wave good-bye to white Russian deserters.

Years later, when Bill was a person of note in the Mountain West, he used to tell anyone would listen that him, me, and Shad walked from Finland to Moscow and back. I even read the story in a newspaper or two and heard it told at Armistice Day banquets. There was no truth to the claim, but when I gave people the real story, no one wanted to hear. Folks like to believe the far-fetched and bizarre. That's why I don't exaggerate in this oral history.

Lydia said, "Is that supposed to be a joke?"

Oly said, "You're here to record, not give up opinions."

Lydia said, "Let's skip Russia and jump to 1980."

Oly said, "Slim chance."

Spring of 1920 found us in Le Havre, France, where Bill and Shad boarded a ship bound for New York. I stood on the pier and watched them go. The United States of America held no allure for me. At Agatha's demand, I'd sworn to God never to return to Montana or Wyoming. California seemed interesting, but I remembered how sick I'd been crossing the Atlantic the first time. I would need one heck of a good reason to cross again, and at that point, I had no good reason to rise from bed in the morning, much less cross the Atlantic.

I do admit, though, it felt eerie seeing those two pass from my life. One of the few pieces of wisdom my father gave me before he dropped into the opium fog was this: *if you're raised on crap, you'll take a hankering to it*. I'd been raised on Shad and Bill, and while I hadn't exactly taken a hankering to them, I had grown accustomed to their habits. Shad especially gave me solid ground on which to stand in bad times. Him and the Army kept me from going completely to hell.

———

Once they pulled out and I was no longer in the Army, I'm ashamed to say I did just that—went completely to hell. I no doubt would have followed Dad into the fog, had opium been readily available. Instead I turned drunk. I drifted into what was the capital of the drinking world at that time—Paris.

There is no way to overstate the river of alcohol that flowed through Paris in the early 1920s. Every poet, painter, and debauched man and woman gravitated to Paris, where they were met by open arms and an aperitif.

I myself used my mustering-out check from the Canadian Army to pay twelve francs rent on an unheated carriage garage full of nineteenth-century furniture, wall hangings, and knick-knacks in the garden of a run-down house in Montparnasse owned by two elderly sisters whose husbands and sons had perished in the conflict. The old girls were closet drunks themselves. After that first month, I earned my keep by running grocery, cheese, and wine errands for the sisters, who never left that house for weeks at a time. The both of them sat in the dark front parlor, rocking their chairs and sipping Vin de Fruits rouge I bought them by what in America was called a half gallon. I don't know what they called it, other than *big bottle*.

I wasn't one to drink myself stupid all alone in a dark garage full of spiders and mice, not when the biggest free-for-all of the twentieth century was busting loose a hundred yards down the butte. That particular century—this particular century—is known for decadence, especially toward the '60s and '70s, when the pill and penicillin made sex harmless and the children rediscovered dope, but no times come close to the unfettered wildness of Paris in the summer of 1921. Unless maybe it's Paris in the summers of '22 and '23.

My booze of choice was a liqueur called marc, something of a cross between beer and wine with the kick of whiskey—loads of sugar, more loads of alcohol content. Since mostly I didn't have money of my own and most of my drinks were cadged, I drank whatever was offered, whenever and with whoever offered it, but the few times I bought for myself, marc always came first.

Marc was introduced to me by a Polish poet named Josef. Josef said he was a poet, anyway. Thousands of people back then said they were poets. Josef sniffed ether and spoke English, after a fashion. He'd fought in Russia, although I never pinned him down as to which side he was on. He maintained the Western Front was a walk in the woods compared to Russia.

"Ask any German soldier which front they preferred for comfort and a chance at survival, they shall say France. The Western Front was for pampered namby boys."

I would have hit him, but he was my only friend, if you want to call it that, and by then, I was hitting everyone else. I got in so many fistfights that summer, I was actually 86ed from some bars, which was practically impossible in that age of drunkenness. More than the once, I've laid down on the public sidewalk and slept next to writers and painters who are known to this day.

Most of 1921, and a good part of 1922, is only a smoky blur in my memory. Two nights stick out—three. The third changed my life in a heartbeat. The first was a riot between Dadaists and surrealists in the Théâtre Antoine. I don't know what sparked it off, but hundreds of men and some women were so infuriated when creative types didn't agree with their system of thought that they fought all through the theater, into the lobby, and out on the street. I was in hog heaven. First I jumped in with the Dadaists, then, when the surrealists needed help, I switched. For the most part, the cubists stood on the curb and picked their noses. My dream would be to see gangs of poets, writers, painters, actors, and sculptors battling each other over artistic theory in America. We would be the better for it.

The second night to remember came in the Caméléon. The Caméléon was a cross between a nightclub and a university. Drunken brawls were interspersed by lectures. This rainy night in early July—July 4, which meant something in Montana, but not Paris—they showed paintings at the Caméléon, and for some reason, maybe out of patriotism, I acted like an American. That is to say, I loudly denounced art that I didn't understand. The paintings were bright colors broke into shards like shattered glass glued back together all wrong.

That's what I told Josef. "A monkey could do this," I said loud enough for all to hear.

Josef tried to shush me, but I was on a roll.

"I'll wager you whatever money I've got on me"—none, by the way—"a monkey did this by throwing a tantrum, and they've posted it as a joke to fool the idiot critics."

A little Spaniard in a black suit, funny hat, and a cocaine rock visibly perched along the inner rim of his nostril took offense. I know he was Spanish, because he spewed the language at me for a minute before he said in perfect English, "Are you calling me a monkey?"

"Are you calling yourself an artist?"

He spit out a Spanish insult. With insults like that, you don't have to know the language to know what you've been called.

I admit, I threw the first punch. He turned just as I struck, so all he got was a glancing blow to the shoulder—nothing you would think worthy of the upshot, which was his friends and hangers-on pummeling me. A huge, smelly man in coveralls got my left arm, while a dandy in a top hat and spats got my right, and a screaming delirious woman with a harelip and a walking stick beat me. I recall that harelip. And she was mean as a copperhead. She called me all kinds of nasty names, most of which I didn't understand.

When men wade into a person, their intent is to incapacitate their opponent, knock him out, stomp him in the scrotum—whatever it takes to make the victim stop fighting. Women, on the other hand, fight to spoil your looks. They scratch your face. Bloody your nose. Box your ears. To a woman, being ugly is worse than being unconscious, so their goal is to make their opponents ugly.

That woman did as much damage as she could to my face before she wore out, then three or four of the men lifted me off the floor, carried me to the door, and hurled me over the sidewalk and into the street. Just before I was heaved through the door, I got a look at the Spaniard. His arm was snaked around the harelip like she was his darling. She was lighting his cheroot. His eyes met mine, and he smirked, as if to say, *Look at what I am, and look at what you are. See the difference and suffer.*

My psychological take, now that I'm firmly implanted in senior citizenship, is this: I craved punishment. Because I had betrayed Agatha and rutted on Swamp Fox, I thought I deserved the stuffing beat out of me every day and every night. I didn't think in those terms then, but I certainly behaved as if that was my intent.

Josef came outside in the rain to pull me back to the sidewalk so I wouldn't get run over. I was all for charging back in to wipe the smirk off the Spaniard's weasel face, but Josef pinned my arms to my sides and wouldn't let go.

"Fool, that was Picasso you attacked," he said.

I'd heard the name. You'd have to be a deaf-mute to live in Paris and not have heard of Picasso. "I don't care if he's Napoleon, only a coward lets other folks fight his fights."

"Picasso is the wealthiest artist in the world. His minions do battle for him."

I stopped the struggle. "Wealthy artist?" I'd met a large number of artists in the bars and cafes of Paris, but never one who was rich. Mostly, artists at that time starved. I didn't think there was such a thing as *wealthy artist.*

"The work you said was painted by monkeys will sell for a hundred thousand francs."

He took his hands off me. I tucked my shirttail in one side of my pants but forgot the other, on account of I was drunk. "That painting was simple. I could draw that with crayons and scissors."

He leaned out to pick up my hat, which was brim down in an oily puddle. "Many say they can, but only Picasso does."

I walked to the window and looked in at the crowd of people drinking, dancing, and carrying on as if there'd never been a war. The room was full of smoke and laughter. A group stood semi-circle around the Spanish whelp, entranced by his pontification. The woman had a hand on his chest. On the wall, the paintings hung like smashed stained-glass windows.

I said, "You say people pay for that?"

"Everyone wants a Picasso."

I spent the last of my mustering money, that had been hid in saddlebags beneath my soiled clothes, on paint and brushes, and I became a Bohemian artist. Canvas was expensive, so I cut up black velvet draperies that were lying around my carriage-house storeroom. I found the colors stood out better on velvet than they did on canvas. I'm surprised da Vinci and Rembrandt and all those old guys didn't think to work on velvet.

It didn't take but one walk along the banks of the river to see dozens were copying Picasso, Modigliani, and the few who actually made a living. They'd paint at home, all but the last two strokes, then set up their easels across from Notre Dame and wait for the tourists who were starting to discover Paris again after all those years when travel was ill-advised. As the tourists passed by, the artists would apply the finishing touches and offer to sell the painting, cheap.

The problem was there were too many artists, and by hanging around eavesdropping on would-be buyers who spoke English, it was evident that bunch didn't cotton to Cubism, Dadaism, surrealism, or any other postwar modernism. American tourists wanted something that looked like itself, only French.

By the hundreds, they said, "I don't know anything about art, but I know what I like."

Then, on a blistering-hot afternoon, while contemplating where my next drink was coming from, in the Tuileries Gardens, I found a *Western Story Magazine* on a park bench. Lord knows who left it there. The stories themselves were god-awful cowboy myth junk—black hat, white hat, *yep, nope, smile when you call me that, pardner*—but the picture on the front cover was a Charlie Russell painting. I always did enjoy Charlie Russell, even back in Billings, and I got to wondering how he would fare up against the Parisians, or how they would fare at his subject matter, and inspiration slapped me upside the head. Okay, I had an absinthe hangover, but that doesn't make the inspiration any less real.

The next day was free Friday at the government museums all over town, and I spent the day studying Renoir, Lautrec, and Matisse. I looked at van Gogh and Gauguin too, but they weren't right for my needs. What I needed was a way to paint cowboys and Indians and Western landscapes seen from afar by someone who needed glasses but wasn't wearing them.

That night, by lantern light, I painted a grizzly bear treeing a mountain man; only instead of Russell, I pretended I was Renoir. It looked good to me.

Thirty minutes on the quay the next morning and a tourist from Chicago bought that griz for forty francs. I was in. I had me a product that looked French but was familiar to Americans with money.

Renoir, Lautrec, and Matisse were big in Paris thirty, forty years back, but the artists along the river and up on top of Montmarte considered them ancient. I was the only artist on the Left Bank with velvet Impressionist pictures of cavalry officers on parade and worn-out Indian braves in a blizzard. Americans snapped up my output fast as I could put it out. The galleries wouldn't touch me. I hand-sold every painting. And the artists drawing flower pots from six different directions at once, so you couldn't tell what you were looking at, were jealous no end. Half my profits went into buying drinks and meals for the competition, or I'm certain they would have dry-gulched me and knifed my velvets. Even so, there was enough for me to stay drunk as a skunk, which was the extent of my needs at the time.

I was an artist.

———

One night at the carriage house I showed Josef a new painting I'd done of a Cheyenne maiden washing authentic Indian leggings in a mountain stream. I had cottonwoods and willows and a beaver paddling around a beaver lodge. It was the last scene I hadn't yet copied from the *Western Story Magazine*, and I was fretting over getting hold of another magazine with Russells inside. They didn't sell them at every corner newsstand in Montparnasse.

I was explaining my situation to Josef as he perused my piece, when he said something that caught my attention.

He said, "I have seen this woman."

I said, "I made her up. Or Charlie Russell found her in Montana, and I adapted him, pretending to be Lautrec. How could you know her?"

"There are a band of people like her living in a field out north of Clignancourt."

"What people like her?"

"Red savages. They rode in a wild west show, I think."

I studied the girl in the painting. There was no way Josef could know that exact girl. For one, the convenient fact that made me happy to copy Lautrec was, sometimes he used a smudge of paint for a face. Impressionism was the best style if you couldn't draw faces any better than I could. But my maiden was noticeably Indian, with furs, an Indian dress, and moccasins. To a Polish poet, all Cheyenne girls looked alike.

He went on. "The owners of the show abandoned the cast at a circus ground. They are trapped by circumstance. You should visit their camp. I would think you could find a model for your paintings."

"I don't use live models. I use magazine pictures."

"Models often sleep with the artists, I think. At least, Picasso's do. And Man Ray's. He takes the photographs of women and they couple with him. You cannot couple with a magazine."

I considered the options. The last thing I needed was another faithless woman, but then it might be interesting to be amongst people I had a common background with. That hadn't happened in a while.

"I think you should go see these people," Josef said. "They might need your help."

———

I walked all the way to Clignancourt, which in 1922, was a whole different town away from Paris. You went off around Montmarte, up through flea markets that are beyond belief to regular Americans. Imagine a city built from its own dump. History lesson: the flea market was invented in Clignancourt— first in the world—and it was so called because all the clothes and bedding and practically everything sold there were infested. To my mind, it should have been called a lice market, but I suppose fleas sound romantic.

My route took me by a number of bars. On a muggy day, I had to rest often, and it didn't feel polite to take advantage of the hospitality without tasting their libations.

Tell the truth, I needed a nip before meeting folks from home. Looking back years later, I think I had a premonition of change. It had been five years of emptiness since Agatha's letter. Despair gets tedious if it lasts long enough. My velvet creations had been a child's step back to life, even though I didn't admit it, and while part of me knew it was time to take a second step, most of me would rather get sodden and avoid expectation. By the time I found the circus grounds way out the far side of Clignancourt, I fear I wasn't in the best shape for a social call.

The grounds were dried ruts and mostly empty. A set of tipi poles stuck up from the petrified slop—a four-pole base, so they must have been a mountain tribe as opposed to plains—but there wasn't a cover. There were two wall tents and an old French Army truck type ambulance set up on bricks. They had an outside fire ring for cooking.

Two decrepit women sat on upturned buckets at the fire ring, which was smoking from the ash but not giving any heat. Very old Indian women look older than very old white women. I don't mean this as prejudice, I mean it as fact. Indian women spend more time out in the weather, be it sun or rain. White women get out of the sun and rain soon as they feel discomfort.

I lurched, drunk, up to the women and said, "Is there an appropriate place for a man to pass water?"

They looked at one another and talked a language I wasn't familiar with, then they looked at me and talked overlapping, so quick and bird-like I wouldn't have picked up their meaning even if I knew the language. They both were short a high portion of teeth. One had a nose you could hang a nightshirt on. The other's face was wide, round, and flat as a hubcap.

The long-nosed woman raised a claw of a hand and pointed toward the ambulance. I should have known she hadn't understood the question, but in my inebrious and pained state, I took her to mean, *Potty's in there.*

I walked across the ruts in that bent fashion a man adopts when the need to go is paramount, took the single step, ducked, and burst through the door in on a girl giving a man older than the two women a haircut.

The ambulance had four bunks—two lower, two upper—on each side and a three-legged stool for the old man smack center. The girl stood behind him, facing me, with a comb in one hand and scissors in the other.

I said, "Excuse me, Miss."

A light sparked in her eyes like she recognized me. She lifted the scissors off the man's scalp and said, "Good day."

I admit her saying, *Good day,* instead of, *What the hell are you doing?* charmed me. The girl was nineteen, maybe, or younger, not a full-blood and possibly not even half. Over time, I've found women of more than one racial background tend to be striking in appearance, which this girl was. Her eyes were deep, dark brown, yet not so Oriental as full Indian. Her mouth was small, with a strongly delineated upper lip. The neck is where you cull the beautiful from the merely pretty, and this girl had a long, smooth neck the color of bourbon. Her hair was in braids wrapped in fur, and she wore dangling earrings of silver and turquoise.

I stared at her as long as it just took me to tell you what she looked like. In spite of my staring, she didn't seem uncomfortable.

"May I assist in some way?" she asked.

"Toilet."

She pointed with the comb. "We have a closet behind the tent, over there. You are welcome to it."

The old Indian on his stool hadn't so much as twitched when I came in. I learned later he was deaf as a post, but at the time, I took him as stoic.

I turned and started out, then I stopped. "Will you still be here when I come back?"

The girl shrugged—lips flat, eyes into and out of a quick squint, shoulders lifted, hands palm out—in what seemed both a comment on and an evasion of my question. It was a vastly feminine gesture. "Where else would I go?"

———

Her name was Evangeline, and the Indian in her was Crow. The Bradley Brothers Wild West and Equine Extravaganza had come to ground in Austria for the war years. By Armistice, they'd eaten the horses, and those performers who could slip away had slipped. Still, the Bradleys held the troupe together for a tour of Italy, Switzerland, and some of France, but in Paris, they went belly up. The brothers—who weren't brothers any more than they were Bradleys—took what money and equipment was left and absconded. All but Evangeline, two old Flathead sisters, the deaf Navajo whose hair she'd been cutting, and two Cossacks the Indians didn't care for had filtered off—some back to the States, others absorbed into Europe.

The Cossacks were over in Paris, looking for work. They'd said they'd be back soon, but they took their saddles, so Evangeline didn't expect to see them again.

She did not take it as a loss. "The Russians had bad habits. Drink. And Samuel says they fornicated with horses."

"Samuel?"

She nodded toward the old man. "They tried to fornicate with me, but I threatened to cut them. I hope you aren't looking for fornication too. Most men are."

I assured her fornication was the last thing on my mind, although it wasn't. "Speaking of drink, would you be interested in going out for one?"

She stared at me in infinite disappointment. "No. Thank you."

I should have figured. In Paris, in the '20s, those who weren't drunk didn't drink. It was all-or-nothing, and the ones who drank nothing looked down on us who drank all. Evangeline made motions like I'd overstayed my welcome. She put away her barbering implements and brushed past me, going outside. I followed, like a puppy. She was so pleasing to the eye, compared to the flappers, hookers, and dope addicts

I was used to, that I wanted to put off the moment of being away from her.

I caught up at the fire ring. "Is there anything I can do to help you out?" I asked.

Her eyes flashed anger and her upper lip drew up in a snarl. "You can feed me."

The suddenness of emotion startled me, but then her eyes and face kind of closed off, not wanting to appear needful.

I said, "Okay." I know it's not fair getting a date by offering food to a famished woman, but the whys of her coming with me didn't matter so much. If all courtship has to be fair, there wouldn't be any courtship.

———

When Evangeline was ready to go off on our date, I discovered the old Flatheads and the Navajo were coming with us.

"This is France," I said. "We don't need chaperones."

She slipped on a pair of moccasins. I didn't mention earlier she'd been barefoot and wearing her wild west show Indian princess costume up to that point. I got so wrapped up in her face, hair, and neck, I forgot to tell about her on down below.

She said, "The old ones are hungry."

I could tell if I didn't take the lot, Evangeline wasn't going to come, so I fell back on graciousness. "Sure. I meant for all of us to go together all along."

———

I treated the bunch to a brasserie, which is a cross between a café and a restaurant. Those are two separate businesses in France, not like here, where you can name an eating place anything you please. The brasserie served *croques*—sandwiches made from French toast—and a meat pie and some sort of Brunswick stew concoction. It also sold marc. That's where my interest lay.

The Flathead sisters buzzed to themselves over the stew that they ate with spoons, while Samuel shoveled down a blood sausage big as an artillery shell. Evangeline ate a remarkable number of eggs scrambled with bacon and smelly cheese. I drank my lunch.

Evangeline said, "You are unhappy."

"Not that I know of."

She touched a napkin to her lips, blotting the tiniest bit of egg yolk. "Alcohol hides misery, first. Soon, it causes it."

"How old are you?"

She gave the shrug I'd seen earlier, which meant *I don't answer questions if they are meaningless.* "Old enough to know what drink does to ambition."

"Odd word choice there." I watched her over my marc glass. In her pigtails and earrings, she could of passed for a child dressed for Halloween.

I said, "Every man was in the war is either dead or unhappy. I'm amongst the lucky ones."

For emphasis, I set my drink on the table with a firm *click*, only I hit the ash tin and my marc spilled. It annoyed me no end. I've always been known as a careful drunkard, at least with the alcohol itself. I may break furniture, but I rarely spill a drop of what counts. Evangeline sopped up my mess with her cloth napkin while I flagged down the waitress for another round. The waitress pretended not to see me. Then she pretended not to understand my French. I had to stand in front of her, waving my glass, before she agreed to meet my needs.

Finally, when we were back where we started, Evangeline said, "You do not behave like a lucky one."

"You should see the fellows who drew the alternative."

"They died many years ago. I think there is more to your unhappiness than the killing." Her brown eyes were on me like a hawk on a prairie dog. It dawned on me that this was a point in my life where I could either lie like usual and go on the way I'd been going on, or tell the truth and let the results fall where they might.

"There is more."

She nodded—she'd known all along—and suddenly, I discovered myself telling her about Agatha. I told how we met and our lengthy engagement and what I did to ruin it. The night before I left for the war. All those letters coming and going both ways, then the last letter and how it turned me into a ghost who hadn't died yet.

I hadn't told anyone in Paris the Agatha story, not even Josef at my drunkest. I hadn't uttered the name Agatha in front of Bill or Shad, not after the letter and my failed attempt to bayonet Bill. Something came over me in the brasserie. It must of been the time and place to let go. And Evangeline must have been the person.

I finally wound down. She sipped her coffee and asked, "How long ago?"

"Five years." I searched the brasserie walls for a calendar, but there was none. "A couple months ago."

She stared at me with pity in those big eyes. Normally, I don't want pity from others. Being so full of it for myself, it seemed anti-cowboy to accept it from a female. But right then, I was more than open to pity from that girl.

She said, "This Agatha must be stupid. Only a selfish slattern would send that letter to a man in the middle of a battlefield."

Affecting a tragic demeanor, I downed more marc. I wasn't sure what *slattern* meant, and it intrigued me to wonder where this young Indian girl would have picked it up. "Agatha was selfish, all right, as the next girl, but she wasn't stupid. It was my own fault what she did, for patronizing the crazy whore in the sheep wagon."

Evangeline carefully, delicately, placed her fork across the top of the little china plate her eggs had come on. She folded her hands, one across the other, on the tablecloth. She looked from her hands to me. "How do you think the prostitute felt?"

That stopped me short. I'd spent my energy working out how I felt and how Agatha might feel. I never considered Swamp Fox.

"I was one of dozens," I said. "I doubt if she felt an iota when it came to me."

The room was falling into a clockwise spin. I concentrated on Evangeline's eyes at the hub of the turning wheel. Her eyes stayed upright and even, not rotating like the ceiling or the walls. If she'd blinked, I would have been sick.

She said, "All women feel. Even those who give their bodies for money."

"Yes, well, I spoiled my future prospects over that diseased degenerate. I can't claim to care much what became of her. She caused me no end of pain, and it's my wish that she died and went to hell."

Evangeline grew calm. Her fingers stopped moving. Her eyes closed. It was as if her body folded in on itself. Nothing but a tiny pulse in the throat showed she was alive. The old Flatheads and the Navajo stopped chewing to look at her, no doubt wondering what was up. They knew her and I didn't, so they may have seen her turn placid before. I had no idea what to think, except I needed her eyes open to keep me from whirling off in the air.

Then her eyes opened, gazing into mine. She said, "I'm thinking you deserve Agatha."

I leaped to my feet and sent my chair smashing to the floor. I wasn't so drunken not to catch her meaning. She'd shown nothing but scorn for Agatha before, and now saying I deserved Agatha, meant Evangeline felt the same scorn for me. I'd opened my deepest secrets to this girl, and she'd responded with an insult. What did it matter to her that I thought more of me than the whore that brought my ruin? I was the put-upon, tragic figure in my story. Who was this girl to say I deserved Agatha?

"I'm buying food for you and your starving tribe. You got no call to—"

Here, I leaned forward to get close to her face, only I kept going, leaning on through the plates and silver and the table itself. There was a terrible crash.

———

One of three things happened next: I either knocked myself out or I passed out or I blacked out. I never was told which. I suppose it doesn't matter, except the first two are bad and the last is awful. In any event, I cannot record the immediate aftermath.

———

I came to my wits on a cot under a blanket, but not between sheets, in one of the wall tents I mentioned earlier. Right off, I noticed my nakedness followed by the discovery of my clothes in a folded pile on a chair by the door. Evangeline sat at a low table before a mirror, brushing her hair and humming what I took as a show tune—"Swanee," maybe, but she was so quiet, it was hard to tell. She'd changed out of her Indian princess costume into a pair of breeches and a white blouse. Her long dark brown hair was the most beautiful sight I'd seen since before the war.

She saw me gazing at her in the mirror, and she smiled at me, which came as a surprise. I remembered all that had preceded my dive through the table. My behavior hadn't been what any woman would consider endearing.

She said, "You soiled your clothing. Flower and Moccasin Woman washed them for you."

I didn't say much, just wondering who had undressed me

naked. I figured Flower and Moccasin Woman as the Flathead sisters. Didn't take a genius to make that leap.

I sat up on the cot, pulling the blanket with me to hide my bare chest. "Evangeline," I said. "I guess I'm in love with you."

She stopped brushing. "I know."

"How would you know such a thing?"

Her eyes met mine by way of the mirror. She seemed calm, serious, and interested all at the same time. "You were in my heart."

You would cause less of an impression by whacking me with a sledgehammer than Evangeline caused with that statement. "Is having a person in your heart some sort of Crow spirit thing?" I asked.

She gave that shrug I described earlier, the sign you'd ask a question she wasn't interested in answering. Seventy-some odd years have gone by, but I can close my eyes and see Evangeline's shrug. I think that gesture was what made me fall in love with her.

"We should get married right away," I said.

She stared, big-eyed, the picture of a detached woman.

I glanced at my clothes. This would have been the moment to drop on one knee, but somehow, considering my state, that didn't seem proper.

"What I meant to say is, will you marry me, Evangeline? We can make a fine life together."

Evangeline resumed brushing her hair. That wasn't what I had in mind. I'd hoped she might dance into my arms, but I suppose I'd given her something to think about, and brushing was more conducive to thought than jumping in bed with me.

She said, "Why right away?"

"I haven't had much luck with long engagements."

"What does that matter now?"

"I've come to believe when it's time to move, people should move, and it's time for you and me to move."

She placed the brush on the table, took one last appraisal of herself in the mirror, then swiveled around to face me head on. "I have two conditions."

I could scarcely believe her words. My luck had gone from empty to overflowing in a single gasp. "Does that mean you're saying *Yes*?"

"Only if you meet my conditions."

"I'll meet them. Whatever they are, you can count on Oly Pedersen. You are the sun in my sky."

She smiled again. Those smiles of Evangeline's were rare, but I already looked forward to them. "First," she said, "you must stop drinking alcohol. I will not be the wife of a drunken fool."

"Done. I was fixing to stop that anyway. With or without you, my time as a sot is over."

"Second," she said. "I want to go home. I will be your bride if you promise to take me to Wyoming."

That one made me drop my blanket. I'd planned to live the rest of my days and die in Paris, France. At the very least, Europe. The American West had been one long humiliation, and I'd sworn to God Himself never to return. The notion of going back to that land and way of life brought on nausea, not to mention the spinning whirlies.

Evangeline waited while I worked out the various elements of the proposition. She was patient, I had to give her that. Agatha would have sat still for all of three seconds, then cut me dead for my lack of resolve. Evangeline seemed to understand how I had to weigh doing what I wanted most against doing what I wanted least.

Through all the confusion of thoughts flying this way and that, I did find one truth: I had to stop comparing Evangeline to Agatha.

"Will you stay with me, once I take you there?" I asked.

"I will be your wife until you no longer want me or I am

dead," Evangeline said. She did that thing with her hands again, I'd seen earlier in the brasserie, where she retreated into herself and found a quiet place where no one could touch her. Right then, I saw I could marry this girl, and I could love her while she loved me; I could spend my remaining years with her—Evangeline was my fate—but I could never know her.

I said, "Okay, then. Let's go home."

17

SHANNON PACED. SHE DRANK GREEN TEA, THEN SHE DRANK chocolate schnapps, because that was all she could find under Lydia's sink. She washed her hair, and after that, she turned off the bathroom light and bathed in the dark, which didn't calm her anxiety one bit.

She saw the men from her past, in the dark. Ten men in ten years—not so out of line for a single woman on the loose, but Shannon had been deeply involved with each of them. Engaged to four. Cohabitating with seven. The beginnings had been self-consuming passion, and the endings horrific. Six months after love at practically first sight, she would realize she didn't feel the way people are supposed to feel, and she'd break for the door. I'd rather her be that way than to try and make it work for years after hope was lost like so many couples.

Yet, in spite of the importance and drama, in the black of Lydia's bathroom, Shannon could not lift one man, in her memory, over the pack. She could recall traits and physical quirks—the beautiful one, the basketball freak, the poet, the rich, the poor, the obsessed with Duran Duran—but emotionally, the men in her past were interchangeable.

Perhaps, she would have been more at ease that night if Lydia hadn't come home from prison and thrown out her

TV. Or if she'd had something better to drink than chocolate schnapps. The truth is Shannon was not adept at being alone. Comfortable solitude is a skill that must be learned. It doesn't come easily for some people.

My theory, as Shannon's father, is that this inability to sit still by herself at night was the reason for the boyfriend parade. Even though she would never say it out loud, least of all to me, Shannon was one of those Southern girls who think a compromise of a mate is better than no mate. You get the best you can at the time, because being alone is proof of failure.

Or maybe I'm way the hell and back off base. How many men know what their daughters think of the other men in their lives?

Whatever the reason, Friday night before Memorial Day, the day Lydia ripped into Shannon and left town, Shannon found herself with no TV and no one to talk to, and she didn't like it.

She walked outside barefoot, wearing a cotton nightgown, and stared at the sky. The moon was past full, on its way to waning. She saw about three times more stars than she'd seen when she went outside at night in North Carolina. She thought she heard a coyote howling at the moon, but then she decided it was the neighbors arguing over money.

Roger's hulk of a truck was parked in the yard, where he'd left it after he came into town to pick up Lydia. He'd given Shannon the keys.

"She's hard to shift gears on, and the brakes are freaky, but you're welcome to give her a try," Roger said. *"Can't have you stuck with no wheels."*

Which was nice of him to say, and she might have given it a try, if there were anywhere to go in the middle of the night in GroVont, Wyoming. The stores were closed, and she didn't know anyone well enough to drop in after midnight. She could run into Jackson, to the Cowboy Bar, only that felt like taking advantage of Roger's goodwill. Besides, she'd have to hurry to make last call, and the men you meet walking sober into last call weren't the sort who would help Shannon feel better.

What she felt most like doing right then was howling at the moon. She probably should have, because howling helps, but she didn't. Instead she walked back into the kitchen and rummaged through the drawers for a sheet of legal pad paper and a giveaway pen from Haven House. She drew a line down the middle of the page and, at the top of the page, wrote REASONS LIFE IS GOOD to the left of the line and REASONS LIFE STINKS, to the right.

Then she sat on a straight-back chair at the kitchen table, clicking the pen in and out and staring at the page for three hours. Shannon was stuck in place, frozen by her options. A couple of times she almost wrote on one side of the page or the other, but in the end, she couldn't motivate herself to move.

By now, it was four in the morning, and she had to whiz. I could have told her, had I but been there to help: whenever life grinds you to a halt, wait awhile, and you'll have to use the bathroom, and that will get you moving again. That's how I deal with depression.

So Shannon made a wad out of the paper and threw it toward the trash can. She walked down the hallway past Lydia's bedroom and into the bathroom, where she lifted her nightgown, dropped her panties, sat on the toilet, and wept.

———

I've seen Shannon's mother cry on the toilet too, and a number of pregnant girls. Women must feel safe with crying on the can, as if they're multitasking fluid disposal. I don't know that I've ever seen a man sob while sitting on a commode, but then, after careful thought, I'm not certain I've ever seen a man other than me sitting on a commode.

After she'd cried herself out, Shannon sat slumped forward, elbows propped on thighs, staring at her crumpled panties on the floor, waiting for morning. She'd left the bathroom door ajar, so there was enough light diffusing in from the hallway that she could make out eyeball whorls in the pine slats. By not quite focusing, she recognized owl eyes—the right one slightly lazy—in the wood. Or fox eyes. Some type of animal eyes. Another slat had a wing-of-moth effect.

Coming to a halt while sitting on the can more or less negates my prescription for dealing with depression by killing time till you have to go. You're already there. Where before, when she was stuck in the kitchen, her brain had been racing this way and that, as if it was avoiding a fire, now her head felt emptied. She felt emptied. Life had not only come down to no reason to get out of bed, now there was no reason to get off the pot.

The toilet freeze didn't last as long as the kitchen table freeze had lasted. The sun came up. Shannon noticed that, without her being aware of the change, the bathroom had taken on a warm glow. Hair on Lydia's brush was visible, over by the sink. And the drawing Esther had made of a stegosaurus eating nachos on the wall.

Shannon thought of her half sister Esther and said aloud, "This will not do."

———

The truck gears were manageable, barely, if your father taught you the lost art of double-clutching. The brakes weren't. Shannon left town in a Don't-care-if-I-live-or-die mood, but the first careen around a blind corner over a drop-off down a cliff into the river unmasked her true feelings about dying today. She didn't want to.

So Shannon wrestled the stick into first and proceeded to creep up the mountain road. Spring run-off was pretty much at its peak. The river was a churning brown, waving the willows like the wind was blowing when it wasn't. The aspen were leafed out on the edge of GroVont, but still budding in the canyon. She passed three dead porcupines on the shoulder, a sure sign of coming summer.

Shannon eased past her mother Maurey's TM Ranch, because she knew if she stopped, they would put her to work, what with it being dawn and all. Instead she drove clear up to Madonnaville, where she expected to wake me up. Shannon wasn't looking for work; she needed comfort and direction. My specialties.

———

Instead of asleep, where I should have been, Shannon found me standing on the Madonnaville van's front bumper, my head deep under the hood, trying to force a metric socket onto a non-metric nut.

"Why aren't you in bed at this time of morning?" Shannon asked as she approached. "I was counting on bringing you breakfast on a tray."

"God, that sounds wonderful. Give me ten minutes to get inside and back between the sheets."

"Too late." Shannon stepped up beside me on the bumper. "Wouldn't count if I did it now."

The wrench slipped, barking my knuckles, which is about what you'd expect with me and tools. "I can't believe Roger abandoned us just when we needed him most."

"There's never a time you don't need Roger most." Shannon peered under the hood. The van was a big, old Suburban. The engine looked like the city of Oz, seen from afar. "What is that thing there?"

"Air cleaner, and don't touch it. You look too nice to get greasy." Shannon did look nice too. Shannon always looks nice.

Her hair was clean. She wore this blouse with a new moon curved neckline and a hint of puff in the sleeves. I couldn't see her lower half, but the part I could see was an inspiration.

She said, "You have to take that thing off to work on the other thing."

"The carburetor."

"Yeah."

I decided to give it a five-minute break. I backed out from under the hood, stepped to the ground, and wiped my hands on a dish towel. Shannon followed. Sure enough, her lower half was as nice as the top—old Wranglers and red cowboy boots. As a fashion rule, Shannon wore sandals at this time of year, so that meant she'd put some thought into her look before coming up the river.

"You didn't drive Roger's death trap out here, did you?"

The answer was obvious, what with Roger's truck parked in the Home turnaround between the van and a Lincoln Town Car with rental plates. Instead she said, "You haven't answered my question."

I walked around to the driver's side, popped the door open, and reached in for my Minit Stop coffee mug. "I need to deliver a baby. The new parents are chomping at the bit down at the Best Western in Jackson, and I'm afraid if I don't show up on time, they'll come charging out here. I could take Gilia's Subaru, only I hate leaving her and Baby Esther with no way out."

"Champing at the bit."

"Are you sure?"

"Not chomping."

I considered challenging her, because *champing* made no sense, but it wouldn't matter if I was right or wrong. I've yet to win an argument with a female. "The birth mom's leaving this morning. Normally, she'd be long gone by now, but there were complications from a torn labia."

"That hurts to think about."

"And her parents were in Trinidad and Tobago till yesterday. Eden Rae delivered early, and they weren't of a mind to rush back and resume parenting. She's a bit of a handful."

"Hence the pregnancy."

"Hence." I nodded toward the Town Car. "Her father flew in this morning, real early."

Shannon took the cup from my hand. It was the kind with a top with two holes, one for drinking and one for air. She rotated the cup around till the other hole, the one I hadn't been using, faced her, and then she drank my coffee. She's like that.

She said, "I thought birth moms and adoptive moms met these days. The buddy method."

"Not this birth mom. Eden Rae's a bit frank for comfort."

"*Frank* is an odd word."

"There's no telling what's going to come out of her mouth."

Shannon's attention drifted away in other directions. She was facing the sun, with her chin slightly upturned to catch the morning rays. She looked so much like Maurey had at thirteen, when I loved and lost her, that my eyes flushed and I couldn't speak. For something to do, I tried taking advantage of her distraction to gently retrieve my coffee.

Shannon jerked the mug away. She said, "I am in crisis."

I'd known as much. That's why I stopped going on about Eden Rae, to let Shannon have the silence it takes to broach a subject that matters, as opposed to the trifles we talk about most of the time. I may be oblivious, but I'm also her father. I knew she hadn't put on boots and risked crashing into the river to find me for a chitchat.

"What crisis is that?" I asked.

She turned her face to me, searching for any hint of patronization. "I knew something was wrong before," she said. "Then yesterday Lydia told me life is short and I'm wasting mine.

Pretty soon I'll be old and then I'll be dead and they can write a big *So What?* on my tombstone."

Nobody can tolerate thinking of their child as dead, even from old age. I offered up denial. "Lydia tells me the same thing all the time. Weekly. You can't let my mother's criticism control your mood. You'll go nuts."

"But this time Lydia is right."

"That's not good."

"It's awful."

Shannon went back to seemingly studying clouds over east, toward Bacon Ridge. Her eyes had the shine of heightened emotion that can make a woman so beautiful yet so frightening. "I want my existence to mean something," she said.

"Your life means something if someone loves you and you love someone. We've got each other covered on the *meaning* issue."

"I need more than that." She blinked several times in succession. "I want passion. I want to wake up caring what happens today. Lydia thinks I should get a hobby. Or take a lover."

"I'd prefer the hobby option. You don't want the thing that matters enough for you to go on to be something you can lose."

"I've had lovers. They don't matter."

"Have you had a serious hobby?"

Her face flashed anger. "Are you kidding? I'd rather be miserable than think the world revolves around whatever I knit. Or collect. Or whatever."

"In a depressed pinch, I fall back on family."

Shannon hit the coffee. It was Kenya AA. Good coffee if you need to absorb complex concepts.

"Family isn't enough," she said. "You and Mom matter to me, but I don't see basing my future actions on making you guys proud. I need more."

I almost said, *You'll find the answer,* as an autoresponse, but luckily I caught myself. In these blessed talks where your child lets down the defenses and tells you how she feels, it's crucial to avoid easy lies. Only a moron parent says, *Everything is going to be okay. You'll figure it out, honey. Buck up and smile.* Things don't always turn out okay, you can't always figure it out, and sometimes smiling makes you come off as a clown. Kids know that. From preschool graduation on, a kid knows, *Everything will turn out for the best* is a crock.

Instead I said, "Maybe you could write a book. That helps me. It doesn't take cooperation from anyone outside yourself, and if you're terrible at it, you won't know for years. The trouble with knitting is if you stink, you find out right away."

Shannon laughed, which is about the most you can hope for when giving advice to your child.

"You're no help at all, Daddy," she said.

"Yes, but I'm here."

That's when the lodge door slammed and Eden Rae's father came striding out across the yard. A second later, the door re-opened and Eden Rae appeared, dragging a Josie and the Pussycats suitcase on wheels with a matching overnight bag draped on the handle. She carried the Pooh bear by his red T-shirt.

I do love running the Home for Unwed Mothers, and I do love the girls. There is only one hitch, or at least, one hitch of any substance. Parents. Even the good parents irritate me, and to be blunt, the good ones are in the minority. Being the mother or father of a pregnant teenager is difficult, I understand. What I don't understand is why so many of them botch the gig.

For one thing, this isn't Faulkner's time or place, where the violated female hides in her bedroom for nine months and then buries the baby under the spreading sycamore tree.

Many mother-to-be teenagers don't even stop going to school nowadays. I like to think Maurey Pierce and I pioneered the screw-public-opinion gestation back in 1963. We stayed right here in GroVont, in front of God, the mayor, and the PTA, throughout pregnancy and beyond. Nobody lynched us. In modern times, parents who ship their daughter off to an unwed home tend toward the type more concerned with social standing than daughter sanity. That doesn't rub well with me.

Eden Rae's father was named Dan. Dan had a burr haircut and tuck-in shirt. He coached American Legion baseball. Was a member of Pasadena Rotary. If Eden Rae's mother hadn't threatened divorce, Dan would have banished Eden Rae to live on the streets in some inner city, dependent on the goodwill of pimps and dope fiends.

The afternoon Dan brought Eden Rae to Madonnaville, after he told me about American Legion baseball and Rotary, he said—in front of his daughter—*Eden Rae made her bed. She can lie in it.*

I got the idea those words had become a mantra around their house.

Dan came striding across the Madonnaville front lawn, ignoring the flagstone walkway, leaving his daughter to lug her own bags. He said, "We are leaving. I will take care of the charges now."

I looked from Dan and his jutting jaw back to Eden Rae. She'd morphed into the anti-Eden, a shadow of the girl I knew who would just as soon spit in your eye as brush her teeth. Before giving birth, she'd been on fire. I don't know if the change was post-partum or her father's presence, but I blame the father.

I said, "My wife, Gilia, can itemize the bill and mail it to you. There's no call to worry about money this morning."

Dan ran his hand over his head, front to back. If the rod had been any higher up his butt, he'd have had to stand tiptoe. "That is not acceptable. A legitimate business would have the invoice prepared since you know I have a plane to catch."

Shannon said, "Is Eden Rae flying with you?"

Dan glanced at Shannon, no doubt thinking she condoned pregnancy in teenagers. "Of course, Eden Rae is flying with me."

"Then you should have said, '*We* have a plane to catch.' You might as well bite the bullet and acknowledge her."

I jumped in before things turned ugly, not that I'm averse to things turning ugly. I just thought Eden Rae deserved a better send-off. She'd been family for five months. She couldn't help it if her father was a dick.

"Gilia is with the new baby this morning," I said.

"You advertised a nurse on-site for that task. A bookkeeper should keep books, and a nurse should nurse. I see no reason for the jobs to overlap."

"Gilia is my wife, not my bookkeeper. And the nurse has weekends off, unless one of the girls is about to pop."

Dan blinked at the word *pop*. "That is not an excuse for disorder in your business. I am certain there is someone who can tend"—he hesitated, trying to think of what to call it—"the child."

Shannon was watching to see how I would handle the irate father. Unwed-Mother-Home interactions always fascinated her, the way some people enjoy horror movies and car wrecks. Eden Rae had gone passive. She wouldn't have reacted if you stuck a tack in her foot.

I said, "You can wait in the office while I relieve Gilia." I knew better than to offer to let him see the baby.

Dan said, "Let's keep it short."

—·—

It's been interesting, watching myself grow old. The novelist in me likes to sit across the room in the recliner and observe as the years pass and my way of coping evolves. The interesting trait I've noticed lately is this: I can often tell what's going to happen in any given situation, because I have been in so many situations. I am far more accurate predicting tomorrow than I am remembering yesterday.

I knew walking back into the lodge that leaving Shannon and Eden Rae outside together would lead to trouble. I could have saved everyone a truckload of grief by refusing to leave or dragging Shannon in with me, I even had a ready-made excuse, what with the need for a baby-sitter. And yet, I walked away. Sometimes the novelist would rather make things colorful more than safe. It's a bad habit, fine in fictional characters, but not at all healthy in real people.

Eden Rae tipped her chin toward the to-go cup in Shannon's hand. "You got any more of that? Daddy came in too early for me to caffeine up, and he's sure as shitting not going to let me have any at the airport."

Eden Rae had lost maybe twelve pounds since giving birth, but the weight had shifted. Now, she looked more in line with a chubby teenager than what she'd been two weeks ago. The weight was mostly thighs and butt, although when she moved toward Shannon, she still wobbled a bit like a pregnant walker.

She went on, "He thinks coffee makes me feel grown-up, and feeling grown-up makes me preggers."

"It's Dad's coffee," Shannon said. "You can finish it, if you're not afraid of cooties."

Eden Rae reached for the cup. "I've risked more than cooties in my life." She took a drink, the third person to work on that one cup of coffee. "So, who's your daddy?"

"Sam." Shannon nodded toward the lodge. "Sam Callahan."

Eden Rae whistled through her teeth. "Jesus. He must be one trip of a father."

"*Trip* is a nice way to put it."

"He's got to be better than mine." Eden Rae studied Shannon's face like looking at a mug shot. "You're the old nag Roger's all strung out and bleeding over."

Shannon's reaction was physical. She lurched against the van and steadied herself by holding on to the mirror.

"You're her." Eden Rae stared hard at Shannon. "None of us would sleep with that boy if it wasn't for you. You keep him safe."

Shannon didn't know where to start. "The girls here—they sleep with Roger?"

"Not all of them. Angel Byron is about to pee herself from waiting for me to leave so she can get her turn. She knows about you too."

Shannon's mind raced from one new piece of information to the next. It was as if the sun had come up blue instead of yellow; everything took on a different light. "What is it about me that you and Angel know, exactly?"

Eden Rae finished the coffee in one long chug. "That Roger's so pussified by you, there's no chance of his turning into a complication for us. Last thing a girl here wants is a complication, but the first thing I wanted, anyway, was a good scrog."

For a moment, Shannon was so lost she didn't recall what *scrog* meant. *Scrog* wasn't the word used by her generation. They'd said *bonk* or *diddle*. Sometimes *hump*.

"You knocked-up girls scrog Roger?"

"I already told you that."

"Does my dad know?"

Eden Rae considered the question. She'd never wondered who knew and who didn't. "Not officially, he doesn't, I guess. But he must have a clue."

"You're overestimating Sam if you expect him to pick up on clues."

"I've run into him or Gilia when I was coming down from Roger's cabin in the night."

Shannon looked up the Miner Creek draw behind the lodge and the circle of guest quarters. Roger's cabin was up there in the woods. She'd seen it from the compound but never had the urge to walk up the hill to look inside. Roger had always been a vague curiosity to her, his mysterious past, his quiet way of moving. The only time she'd been around him for more than a couple of days was back when Gilia and I got married. Roger had been fourteen or so, and she still thought of him that way.

Shannon said, "I don't see how this can be."

Eden Rae handed the empty cup back to Shannon. "Which part don't you see? Roger's the only boy within miles, and I'm not about to buy a vibrator, not on my allowance."

"I think you're mistaken about him being pussified." Shannon wasn't even certain what Eden Rae meant by *pussified*. Was it *in love* for people who won't use the word *love*, or more like sexual obsession? Or something else? "You know. With me. I'm five years older than Roger."

"Eight. He told me."

"Eight? Are you sure?"

"Why would he lie to make it sound even more bizarre than it is? You're ancient."

The lodge door opened, and Dan appeared, followed by Gilia. I was inside with the baby.

"Go up to his cabin if you don't believe me. Check out that picture album he keeps on the stump table. Or better, look in his closet. That one's a doozie," Eden Rae said. "Roger's out of town somewhere. He won't know."

"He left with my grandmother."

"Angel's going nuts. Roger's never been gone overnight before, and she's ripe enough to gaz on sight."

Dan stalked up, in an even fouler state than he'd been in when he came out the first time. Now, he not only had the humiliation of an unwed mother for a daughter, he'd also had to pay through the nose for the privilege. He'd been such a jerk, Gilia'd reamed him on the bill. Rates are discretionary at our Home.

He said, "Get in the car, Eden Rae."

Her eyes dampened at the thought of leaving the only family she'd had for five months. At least, that's what I like to think. It could have been hay fever.

"Can I say good-bye to Gilia?"

"I told you. Get in the car."

Eden Rae and Gilia shared a few moments of meaningful eye contact in which Gilia let Eden Rae know how she felt and Eden Rae thanked Gilia for feeling that way. Then Eden Rae pulled the handle out on her suitcase and rolled it to the Town Car.

"Good luck, Eden Rae," Gilia said. "I hope you have a happy life."

Eden Rae said, "Yeah, right."

———

My Gilia and Shannon stood in the parking turnaround and watched as the rental Lincoln carrying Eden Rae and her father turned on to the river road, headed back down to the airport.

Gilia said, "It's always sad to see them go."

Shannon said, "Wouldn't surprise me if that one came back next year."

Gilia picked a pinecone off the ground and knocked on it. The cone was a spruce and the nearest spruce tree was a hundred yards off. Gilia looked at the cone in her hand, wondering how it had traveled from over there to over here.

She asked, "What were you two talking so earnestly about?"

"She thinks Sam must be a trip as a father."

"Eden Rae usually isn't that gracious." Gilia underhand tossed the cone back toward the mother tree. "At least you can't call Sam a controlling creep like Dan the Man. It makes me nauseous turning her over to that wad. Did she seem okay to you?"

"She was fine. I think I'll take a walk, back up the creek."

I'd told Gilia about Shannon's arrival and crisis when I relieved her from baby duty, before she went to figure the bill, so Gilia was aware of the volatility of Shannon's mood. "You want me to go with you? Sam can handle the baby."

Shannon opened the van door and put the coffee cup back in its holder. Then she shut the door with a slam. "No, thanks. I'd like to walk alone."

———

Shannon crossed the creek on a plank footbridge. She stepped around a large piece of fiberboard flat on the ground beside a pile of dirt and rocks. Next to the rock pile, she saw a small mound of earth with a cross at one end like a child would make burying a hamster. Shannon didn't think Roger was the sort of boy to own a pet hamster. Ranch kids hardly ever own pets that can't be worked or eaten.

The cabin itself was the urban romantic's dream of what a mountain cabin should be. Shannon saw that Roger had faced it toward the best view possible—the Tetons. A couple of bleached skulls hung above the side window, but Shannon couldn't tell what animal they'd come from. One was long and thin with large sinus sockets and a bullet hole through the third eye. A horse, maybe, or a moose. The other had a flat face— probably an elk. She was certain they were both grass eaters, but not cows. That narrowed the choices to four or five possibilities.

Roger's porch had a pile of split firewood stacked on the right and unsplit firewood stacked on the left, making a sort of walkway to the screen door, which had a horseshoe handle. Shannon's boots clomped as she crossed the porch. She wasn't about to sneak up on anyone. Roger was gone, but she didn't know him well enough to know if he'd have someone staying there while he went to Santa Barbara. The renowned Angel Byron might have moved in, in Roger's absence.

She knocked, waited, knocked again. She looked down the rise to the compound below. Roger's porch was visible from the picnic barbecue area and the second floor of the lodge, but not from any of the girls' cabins. If what Eden Rae said was true, about the girls sneaking out at night to bonk with Roger, Shannon could just imagine the intrigues they went through to spy on each other going up and down.

Shannon pulled the screen door and pushed the front door. She eased herself in.

What she noticed first was how cool the cabin was compared to outside. Three windows made it lighter than she had expected. She'd been in the girls' cabins down below, and they felt dark and smelled like mouse turds, but Roger's cabin smelled slightly of woodsmoke and a hint of maleness. The logs were waxed gold instead of flat brown.

Roger's room was neat and organized as a toolbox. Woodstove, freestanding food closet, built-in clothes closet, chest of drawers, kitchen area—chair, table, hot plate, and coffeemaker. A Dutch oven and two pans hung from the wall. There was a floor lamp beside a rocking chair and a stump table. Shannon checked out the book on the stump—*Sirens of Titan* by Kurt Vonnegut.

The bed was a double mattress on a stripped pole frame, covered by a quilt Shannon recognized from her childhood. It had been on her mother's bed. She immediately pictured

Roger in the bed, under the spread with Eden Rae, then with a dozen other girls, all young, beautiful, and third trimester. Homemade shelves over the bed held Roger's books, CDs, and CD player.

On the floor next to the stump, partially under the bed, Shannon found the evidence she'd come hoping to find. Or hoping not to find. She found it before she made up her mind what she was hoping for. The photo album had a green, fake-leather spine with a leaf pattern. Shannon moved *Sirens of Titan* and sat on the edge of the stump, fingering the corners of the album. As she opened the cover, her greatest hope was that the photos would not be pornographic.

The album held maybe thirty plastic sheets that could be folded over to protect the contents, but only four of the sheets were in use. All four were full-page photographs of her.

Page 1—Shannon in a gray tube top on a beach, probably Ocracoke, laughing at someone or something out of frame. Her right hand is extended as if she has just tossed a Frisbee. Her teeth show, and Shannon abhorred any photo in which her teeth show. Nipple pooches poke from her shirt. She didn't know who had taken the picture or how Roger got hold of it.

Page 2—Shannon in her bridesmaid outfit the day Gilia and I were married. The dress is yellow and without frills. Gilia chose it. In my opinion, it was far more tasteful than those neon purple prom monstrosities you see on so many bridesmaids. Shannon's skin is translucent, the color of eggnog. To me. Roger might have seen something else. I know she looks wholly alive in the picture. Gilia and I have a copy in our bedroom.

Page 3—Shannon mounted on a dappled horse on a ridge-line in the mountains. Her hair is in pigtail braids, and she stares down at the photographer from a superior position. Her posture makes cynicism moot.

Page 4—An extreme close-up of Shannon's face. She is beautiful beyond words, and of course, Shannon hated the picture. From her point of view, bags hang from her eyes. Her nostrils are too big, and her nose too small. She looks like her mother.

But then, when Shannon opened the closet and pulled out the oil painting leaning against the wall next to Roger's bass guitar, her amused detachment flew out the window. In the framed by barn-wood painting she sits straddling the downhill end of a teeter-totter, looking up at the artist. Her hands are on a bar in front of her lap. A malamute nuzzles her ear. Shannon recognized the dog—Rocky. Rocky had died a couple of years ago, so the Shannon in the painting was at least that much younger than the Shannon looking at her.

The piece itself could have been painted by an early, unformed Gaugin trying to emulate a late, fully formed Gaugin. The colors—dark green, gray, yellow, some blue—were harsh. The brushstrokes, violent. It was quite good. But what struck Shannon like a brick to the belly was the complexity of the expression on the face. The face glowed with an inner happiness verging on seductive, yet the eyes gave away something more. The eyes held a sadness Shannon didn't know was in her. The painted Shannon had emotional depths the real Shannon dreamed of. If Roger saw her that way, maybe he saw the true Shannon. The painting wasn't faked. It wasn't accidental. This was the Shannon Shannon wanted to be.

She drew the painting closer and squinted to read the signature in the lower right-hand corner—*Roger Talbot* in left-hand–slanted cursive.

Shannon said, "I didn't know the prick could paint.

———

You pick up a baby person and you hand her to her new parents. Or his. Can you imagine such a thing? Of all the non-traditional chores my job entails, this is the most tangible. I admit I'm a birth junkie, and they are life shifting, but at the births, I'm a spectator. At the Gotcha moment, I am the womb itself. So to speak.

Passing a child to its parents is a marker moment, right up there with marriages, births of your own children, or the death of a parent, actually well above one of my marriages, and since I hadn't experienced death of a parent, I wasn't certain how it felt, even though the novelist in me had played pretend many times. Passing a baby mattered more than losing virginity, I can tell you that.

There is a breath of an instant when the child leaves your hands and goes to the arms of the mother or father, where time falls out of whack. The new parents are so high on giddiness, terror, and relief that you can see their heads crackling. The baby suddenly has possibilities. It's like surfing the birth canal.

My would-be parents gave up on the Best Western. I knew they would. I was inside, on the phone with a nice woman at AAA, trying to get them to come do whatever it took to make my van go. Gilia was changing the baby for the third time since breakfast, because it's bad form to pass on a soiled baby. As soon as I heard the iron clapper being rapped at the door, I knew who it was.

"Send the truck this afternoon," I told the AAA woman, and I hung up before she had time to read me the Rules of Agreement.

They were Eli and Carolyne Wilcox from Indian Mound, Tennessee. Eli sold high-end shoes. Carolyne owned an Amway franchise. Normally I like to have a formal handing-over ceremony where I place the baby in the mother's arms and say, *Mr. and Mrs. Whomever, you have a new daughter.* Or son. Whichever.

But Carolyne blew past me and into the changing room before I had time to say, *Pleased to see you again.*

Carolyne took the baby from Gilia like a pushy shopper. Gilia told me later Carolyne gave her a hip shot. Eli stood back away from the group, pale and twitchy. It was a snap to read who'd been the driving force in this adoption.

Carolyne said, "We only use cloth diapers."

Gilia said, "Do you have any on you?"

"Of course." Carolyne popped open her bag and pulled out a genuine cloth diaper.

Eli nodded vaguely outside. "What makes the rocks out there red?"

That's when Shannon stuck her head in the door. She said, "I'm leaving. You'll have to water Lydia's plants."

I said, "What?"

"Don't screw it up. Lydia will kill us both if the right plants don't get the right amount of water and plant food."

Eli was watching Shannon instead of the baby.

I said, "What if I don't know which plants to water?"

"Use your imagination," Shannon said. "We all know you have one."

Then she left.

Eli looked at me. I said, "That's my daughter."

Carolyne said, "Get over here, Eli. You're in charge of the camera."

———

Shannon telephoned Lydia's house from the Jackson Hole airport.

"You have not reached Lydia Callahan and Oothoon Press. If you have anything to say that I might give one whit about, wait for the message and leave a beep."

BEEP.

"Hi, Lydia. It's me. Shannon. Shannon Callahan. I'm flying

into Las Vegas this afternoon, and I need you to pick me up. I'm on Delta. The plane gets in at 4:10 p.m., which should leave you plenty of time to swing by and—"

BEEP.

"You have not reached Lydia Callahan and Oothoon Press. If you have anything to say that I might give one whit about, wait for the message and leave a beep."

BEEP.

"Get me. If I miss you guys, I'll fly on to Santa Barbara and leave a message on your phone as to when I'll be there. If I miss you in Santa Barbara, I'll go on to that writer's house. I'm sure I can track down anyone famous as Loren Paul."

BEEP.

"You have not reached Lydia Callahan and Oothoon Press. If you have anything to say that I might give one whit about, wait for the message and leave a beep."

BEEP.

"Don't let Roger get away."

THERE'S NOTHING SO IRRITATING AS HAVING ONE OF YOUR parents' nags come true. Maurey's mother—before she mixed the wrong chemicals and jumped off the Snake River Bridge—had this jingly aphorism that used to irritate Maurey no end.

"I just pray that someday your children will treat you as badly as you've treated me."

What kind of curse is that to wish on your kid? From my under-standing, it's fairly universal, but still, just because everyone says a thing doesn't make it moral.

Anyway, Maurey got hers from Auburn the night he told her he was spending the summer in Puerto Vallarta.

Maurey said, "We were expecting your help on the ranch. You could make enough working for us to go back to UW next fall."

"If you won't pay for school, I'm not going."

Maurey resisted the impulse to nail the TV remote through Auburn's neck.

Auburn continued, oblivious, "I'm only going to college for you. If I have to pay for it myself by irrigating out here in the middle of nowhere, I won't go. I can make more on the oil rigs than I'll ever bring in with a phys-ed degree."

Auburn was majoring in physical education. His ambition, before this conversation, had been to coach high school football.

Maurey held herself steady and breathed in and out through her nose three times, slowly. "If your plan is to roughneck the rest of your life, why are you spending the summer in Puerto Vallarta? I wasn't aware they had rigs in Puerto Vallarta."

"I'm young." Auburn propped his feet on the coffee table. He had a microwave burrito balanced in his lap and a Coors Light in his left hand. His attention was centered on an ESPN strong man competition—two hulking men pulling tractors across a tennis court—and he wasn't paying attention to Maurey's dismay. Breaking it to his mother that he was dropping out of college was no big deal to Auburn. "I deserve some fun before I settle into the grind."

"And a job would be the grind?"

Auburn glanced toward Maurey, then back at the large-screen television. "You don't want me to end up like you and Dad, do you?"

Auburn's dad, Dothan, sold RVs in Fresno, California. He was on his fifth wife and second bypass.

"No," Maurey said. "I don't want you to end up like me."

Sarcasm flew right over Auburn's head. To him, she'd just conceded to the wisdom of driving to Puerto Vallarta for a three-month drunk.

Maurey did what she always did when life made her want to scream. She escaped into the horse pasture and mingled with the uncomplicated loved ones before ending up in the barn, where she went to oil her saddle.

That's where she found Leroy.

He was asleep on a horse blanket he'd pulled off a stall rail. Mouth open, gums bleeding, filthy cutoffs, feet black from neglect—your basic nightmare come to Earth. Maurey recognized him immediately.

She stepped into the tack room and came back with an old three-tine J. C. Penney pitchfork her father had bought her mother on their first wedding anniversary. That should tell you all you need to know about Maurey's parents' relationship. She stood poised to spear, watching Leroy's chest pump in and out under the disgusting tattoo. The question was whether or not he remembered her. They'd only been around each other a few minutes twenty years ago, and Leroy—Freedom, back then—had been looped on pharmaceuticals. It was hard to see how he could remember, but then, the parting had been less than civil, and if he didn't remember her, what was he doing here?

She poked a tine into the sole of his foot. "Get up."

His eyes flew open, but he didn't move. "Don't do that again."

Maurey poked him again. "Get up, or I'll run this point up your cock."

Truth be known, Maurey was trembling in fear. She had a sociopath in her barn, and Pud was off fixing a ranch satellite-TV system, and there was no else around except Auburn, who wouldn't be much use, even if she wanted him to jump in. The important rule when dealing with lunatics is never show weakness. She had to act the opposite of how she felt.

"In Wyoming, it's legal to waste trespassers," Maurey said. "I could kill you dead and not even have to fill out paperwork."

Leroy gathered his legs under him and sat up. "Where's the boy?"

Maurey didn't pretend ignorance as to what boy. She'd been thinking about Freedom ever since Roger showed her the Disappearance *book. As Maurey went back over the day Critter had appeared at the ranch and abandoned the child, odd pieces had started to fit. As unlikely as the book's version of Roger's past felt, it was the only version she'd come up with that seemed even vaguely possible. That meant this freak at the end of her daddy's fork was a murderer and a kidnapper of little boys.*

She said, "That kid Critter dumped on me only stayed a week before I had Social Services take him off. I heard they put him up for blind adoption."

Leroy said, "His mother owes me a life."

"She's dead. I read the book." Which was sort of true. She'd heard the story from Roger, even if she hadn't actually read the words.

Leroy's eyes brightened like headlights flashing to high beam. "What book is this?"

"There's a book about that boy."

"Fred."

"His stepfather wrote it after you stole him."

Leroy jerked to his feet. Maurey braced the pitchfork, right hand back, left hand forward, figuring Leroy was set to charge. Leroy's eyes stayed on the points of the tines aimed at his chest. He didn't look at Maurey.

"I never stole no one. I took what was mine. That woman knew she owed me a son and she kept him from his fate. She threw the balance off. The universe itself is out of line until I'm repaid that life."

Maurey took the thought process as insane. She said, "He'd be too old now, even if you found him. He wouldn't act like a long-lost son all of a sudden."

"I'm not out for a son. I'm out to bring nature back into balance. I'm out to kill me someone close to that boy. Or kill the boy himself— I'll decide which when I catch him."

Leroy smiled at Maurey—a toothless, gruesome, jack-o'-lantern grin, void of humanity. "That Social Services story is bullshit. Tell me where the boy went, and you and your loved ones will be safe."

Maurey eased the pitchfork closer to Leroy's tattoo. "I am safe. You're the one likely to end up skewered."

Leroy scratched his balls under the cutoffs and regarded Maurey with all the fear of a teenager deciding whether to drown a kitten. "Let's try this the easy way. Where is he?"

"In your craziest dreams, do you think I would tell you, even if I knew? Which I don't."

"All right. That leaves the hard way."

Maurey tightened her grip. "Test me, pal."

The Dutch door behind Maurey swung open and she heard a girl's whine. "Charley, where'd you get to? I can't wait in the truck no more."

Maurey said, "Charley?"

Leroy, who Maurey knew as Freedom, and Zelda knew as Charley, said, "Ignorant slit, I told you to wait. I'll be there soon as I have the information."

The girl said, "I got the information already. While you were down here playing hard dick, I smoked a pipe with the nice boy in the house, and he told me all you need. Why's that woman pointing a fork at you?"

Maurey desperately wanted to turn to see what kind of a tramp had plied Auburn with marijuana. Any mother would want to know, only she was afraid to take her eyes off Freedom for fear he would make his lunge. But then, not looking meant the girl could walk up and hit her in the head with a rock.

Maurey chose to keep her attention on Freedom. He had to be the more dangerous of the two. The girl sounded too stoned and stupid to find a rock.

The girl's voice was irritating. "Your son's name is Roger. He's a geek. Listens to queer music. Doesn't know sports. The kid in the house says he don't even smoke boo. He says Roger is useless."

This would have all been fascinating had Maurey not been in a survival situation. Maurey's in AA, although maybe I'm not supposed to say that. It's supposed to be anonymous. She hates it when Auburn drinks Coors Light, and she hates it even more when vixens give him dope. She was naturally tempted to whirl and spindle the girl, but that would leave Freedom free. She had to be practical.

Leroy said, "Let's go up and reason with the kid in the house. Find out where my bastard is now."

"I know where he is now. He went off with an old lady in search of his father."

Maurey heard the girl come into the barn, crossing toward the horse stalls.

The girl said, "You told me you're his father, Charley. This Roger sounds like a mess to me. Don't even know who he's related to and who he's not."

"The kid tell you the old lady's name?"

"Of course he told me the old lady's name. He gave me a beer too. I left him a joint for being so sweet."

"Jesus Christ." Leroy started around Maurey but stopped when she thrust the pitchfork his direction. Leroy spit on the floor.

"I know damn well you can't stick me unless I am about to hurt you or yours, and that is not the plan for universal balance. Not yet, anyways. So stop being such a cowgirl."

Maurey swiveled the pitchfork as Leroy circled her, until the girl came into view over by the tack rack. She was a pitiful teenager with awful skin. Her hair looked like road kill. Maurey couldn't see why Auburn had let her in the house.

Leroy knew. He stopped and closed one eye to focus the other one on Maurey. He said, "You ought to kick that kid's ass. That's what I'd do if any son of mine did drugs with this twat."

Then he walked out.

18

I WOUND UP BRINGING ALL FOUR WANDERING INDIANS HOME, OF COURSE. Evangeline wasn't about to abandon the old folks to the Clignancourt circus grounds. The trip cost a fair amount of money, which I made on Impressionist paintings of Evangeline in her buckskin dress. I used all the black velvet in the carriage house and even ended up buying some at the flea market. It didn't take as long to earn the fares as you'd think, because a Paris artist who stops drinking can save cash quickly.

I must of created a hundred works of art in two months. Tiger Lily from *Peter and Wendy* was all the rage then, so I hid Tinker Bell in many of my scenes. I'm certain you can, to this day, discover paintings of Evangeline—big eyed and fair skinned—in the better art collections of Europe and America.

When I broke the news that I was leaving to the old Montparnasse ladies, I gave them a going-away gift of a painting of Evangeline on a pinto horse, wading a mountain lake. The both of them wept, although I fear it was more from losing their wine-and-cheese runner than out of sentiment. Or maybe they were moved to tears by my painting. They perked right up when I told them Josef would be along to discuss the rental.

Evangeline and me were married on the ocean liner *Olympus* on New Year's Eve 1922. The captain married us in the ship chapel, with only Samuel, Moccasin Woman, and Flower in attendance. Later, at the New Year's party in the ballroom—where I didn't drink a swallow—we were toasted by the multitudes. They called us Picasso and Hiawatha. I should have kicked some fannies for that, but I was too happy, sober, and nauseous, so I skipped the violence.

I know what you are wondering, and it's true. I was just as sick for my second trip across the Atlantic as I'd been on the first. Sicker, if that's possible. My honeymoon was spent knees down in the WC. At Evangeline's insistence, we hadn't consummated our love until we married, and we hadn't married till we were on the boat. Worse came to worst, as it usually will, and we never finalized the marriage contract for two weeks after the wedding. We were sailing under the armpit of the Statue of Liberty before I was able to lie with her without the room turning upside down.

You're no doubt cynical about the sincerity of my marriage bonds. You think Evangeline married to get out of a bad spot and she withheld the matrimonial chore till she knew I couldn't beg off the bargain. I thought along those same lines myself, especially the weeks in Paris while I supported her and the old ones and she said the marriage and the other would have to wait.

But you and me would both be wrong. Evangeline turned out sweet as any wife ever was for a man. The entire time on the voyage while I was sick as a poisoned cat, she took care of my needs. She patted my brow with a damp cloth. She sang me lullabies through the oceanic heaves. She didn't have to do that. I would have married her and taken her home even if I'd known I was nothing to her but a taxicab.

Evangeline grew even more affectionate in her actions toward me after we were married than she'd been before. How many men can say that of purely white wives?

And in New York City, where we stayed in the Iroquois Hotel—next door to the Algonquin—our lovemaking was tender. She came to me without restraint. It was as if there was the whole world of people way over on the horizon where we could see them gathered but not hear or smell them, and over here, by ourselves, was me and Evangeline. We mattered, and everybody else didn't.

———

By New York, the Flathead sisters weren't chirping at each other any longer. Moccasin Woman, who was the bigger of the two, cut the crown off Flower's favorite hat. Flower retaliated by filling Moccasin Woman's moccasins with oatmeal that set hard as concrete. After more than seventy years of inseparability, they'd fallen out over a male, i.e., Samuel the deaf Navajo. Old women will carry on that way. I myself have witnessed it in the purgatory they call a nursing home. Hell, men will too, only men tend to die before the schism turns long-term ugly.

Samuel himself didn't seem to notice. When the old biddies got to screaming at one another over his affections, he closed up like a possum on a telegraph line.

"I wondered where you learned that trick," Lydia said from the driver's seat.

"I know not of what you speak."

"You go catatonic in social situations."

"That is a damnable lie. I am known for my outgoing ways. Ask the crones at the home. Ask What's-her-Name Dukakis. I am as alert as an antelope in hunting season. Where was I?"

"New York."

Samuel ditched the party on the train ride west. In Marion, Ohio, we were seated in the Union Station lobby, awaiting the Northern Pacific, when Samuel stood up, pronounced a short speech in Navajo, and gave me the silver-and-turquoise collar corners he'd been wearing since the day we met. Then, with grand dignity, he walked off, out the double station doors.

I held the corners in the palm of my hand. "What'd he do that for?"

Evangeline took them and leaned in to clip them on to my collar points. With her up close like that, I felt her sage breath lightly on my face, and I could smell the natural fragrance of her body. It made me heady.

She said, "Samuel wished to pay his debt to you. For bringing him back to his home nation."

I looked across Evangeline's hair to where he'd disappeared through the doorways. "Where's he going?"

She moved back to admire my shirt and me. "New Mexico, I imagine. Or Arizona. Samuel probably doesn't know the name of the state his tribe calls home."

The Flathead girls broke into wails you could hear clean across the lobby. They were singing their native death chants, and most tribes, when they're dying, sing loud. Only white folks die with a whimper. People setting nearby gave us a wide berth and pretended we were invisible. Those far away stared at us. I pleaded the sudden urge to vacate my bowels—even though I didn't have such an urge—and made tracks across the lobby, away from my traveling companions.

Marriage to one woman can be a joy beyond abandon, but I advise against taking on her people.

———

I hadn't realized when we bought the cross-country tickets that the train stopped in Billings, Montana. I should have known. There's no other way across to the Flathead rez, except the Union Pacific through Salt Lake and up, but that's way out of the way.

We had a sleeping berth and I stayed in it with the curtain pulled the whole eight hours. While I'd never promised Agatha I wouldn't come to Billings, she had assumed as much. My great fear was running into her. She no doubt had babies by now. And a car. Probably a large house with a veranda.

Evangeline knew I was hiding from Agatha. She said, "You don't want your former beloved one to see me."

"I don't want her to see me."

"You are ashamed. You wish to hide your Indian wife from your friends and family."

"Honey, I got no friends or family."

"Then why do you conceal yourself when we are in a town where you might be recognized?"

Evangeline was disappointed in me. I loved her so much it upset me no end to disappoint her, but still I stayed in my berth. I was proud of Evangeline. She was sweeter than Agatha could ever have been. I just didn't want the two of them meeting and comparing notes.

———

After we dropped off the sisters, I got a job rangering in Yellowstone Park. Dropping off the sisters was no simple task, in its ownself, but we pulled it off, so I won't delve into that saga, other than to point out there'd been a reason they left the Flathead Reservation for the Wild West Show in the first place, and there were individuals on the res who remembered that reason and didn't want the old girls back. Evangeline finally found a grandson of one of them—Flower, maybe—who was willing to take them if they'd work his farm, for the Flatheads were farming back then. I later heard they lasted a month before jumping a train for Arizona.

Enough with those two. I'd thought when Evangeline asked me to take her home, she had a specific location and family in mind—wherever she came from, for example. But Evangeline wasn't homesick for family. She missed the high mountains—the flowing of waters, the radiant light, the silence of the Rockies. She didn't care where we lived, so long as no one lived upstream, and Lord knows, I didn't yearn for a Western metropolis like Billings or Denver. When I heard they were hiring rangers in Yellowstone, I jumped for it.

The only qualification was you had to be able to ride a Harley-Davidson motorbike, which I couldn't. I told the Park superintendent I'd been a messenger in the war, and he didn't ask what I'd been up to since. He sent me to the motorcycle barn, where I would have been unmasked as a fraud, except Snuffy Bowlin, the man in charge of the motorcycle rangers, had been an American volunteer in the Canadian Expeditionary Force like me. Those men kept each other's backs for years after the war, primarily from a sense of superiority over the American veterans who came to France three years late. I was never out of a job, so long as any of my comrades were alive and hiring.

First time I set a motorcycle, Snuffy showed me how to kick the starter and pop the clutch. She reared up and left my ass in the dirt, which turned out for the best, when she sailed full throttle into a limber pine.

Second time, I crashed in the creek, and third, I hit a horse. Snuffy stayed with me until soon enough I was a genuine national park motorcycle ranger.

In the main, that meant traffic control. The speed limit was twenty-five on the flats and twelve on the hills and curves. The major cause for citations was drivers not honking their horns before going around a curve. They don't ticket for that now. Most, but not all, Yellowstone roads went one way part of the day and then back the other way the other part, except us on motorcycles could go either direction, so long as we dismounted and leaned our machines against the inside wall when we met cars on the passes.

Yellowstone had a tame buffalo herd and a wild buffalo herd, and it behooved a ranger to remember which he was dealing with. Our job was to haze the tame herd past visiting dignitaries that swarmed on the park that summer. We also hazed elk, antelope, and bear for tourists' entertainment. Try hazing antelope by motorcycle sometime. It's a richly rewarding pastime.

President Harding came through the end of June, on his way to Alaska. We paraded every form of wildlife imaginable past the presidential entourage. A bear that took food from his hand made the Secret Service antsy. Little did they know, Warren Harding would be dead a month later while still on the same vacation where I saw him. Most of us rangers, as well as the journalists traveling with the president, figured Harding's wife poisoned him for rampant adultery. He did die after a bout of food poisoning, and he was the only one in the party who got it, and Mrs. Harding did refuse to allow an autopsy, but that doesn't prove a woman got away with killing the president. Other presidents—most presidents, so far as I can tell—practice rampant adultery, but you don't see their wives poisoning them. Seems a harsh punishment, even for a Republican.

The only serious crime we investigated was elk-tooth poaching. Elk ivory cuff links were coveted by members of a national organization called the Elks Lodge. The ivories are the eyeteeth of an elk, like elephant ivories, only smaller. Poachers killed the elk, ripped out their eyeteeth, and then left the carcass for scavenger animals. It was awful to come upon. All those who weren't elk tooth poachers hated those that were. In the West, there's a public-relations gap between meat poachers and trophy poachers. You won't find much sympathy for trophy poachers.

The Park Service placed me and Evangeline in a little cabin behind the Fountain Ranger Station, along the rim of the geyser basin there. I know when people tell their oral histories, the most boring part corresponds to the happiest part, because that's the way stories work. Good times are interesting to live, but worthless to tell about. Suffice it to say, there was a summer in my hundred years on Earth when life was worth the trouble.

Evangeline and I lived by the Firehole River in a snug cabin with a woodstove for cooking and a double bed for creating love. She'd learned to cook in Austria, before the food ran out, so we ate in a more exotic fashion than your typical park ranger. In the evenings, after dessert and coffee, me and Evangeline would walk arm in arm about the geyser basin. The level of beauty with the forest bathed by alpenglow as seen through the mists of hot springs would take my breath way.

Elk appeared on the banks of the Firehole to drink and the birds chose that time of day to sing for the joy of singing. Evangeline pointed out the various small mammals that crossed the flats, and she knew the names of all the waterfowl. The sun seemed to hang on forever that summer, before finally setting in a carnival of pink and orange. We walked back to our cabin in the faltering darkness and lay in each other's grasp, so peaceful neither of us wanted to sleep, for fear of missing a moment together.

———

Of course I knew the days of being all right would end, and sure enough, they did. The difference between this and other times of somewhat fun was that in the other times, I fretted so much over losing what I had that I never enjoyed having it. With Evangeline, I didn't dread the oncoming disaster. I simply went about each day, living as full as I might, without thinking about the next. I recommend that attitude, should you ever find yourself happy.

Still and all, I do wish the peaceful times of summer could have lasted a bit longer.

The sole rangering duty I didn't relish was predator control. In those days, Yellowstone's upper-level bureaucrats ordered us employees to trap, poison, or plain old shoot every coyote and wolf in the park. In 1923, we killed eight wolves and almost three hundred coyotes, which may not sound like a lot of wolves, but there were only nine to start. The Bechler Station ranger got the ninth in 1924.

When I say *we killed*, I mean *them*. I'd had my fill of violent death in France, and I wasn't about to continue the pattern back home in the Rockies. Evangeline used to tease me, on account of I wouldn't trap mice in the cabin. I said they had as much right to keep going as I did. So I never shot a coyote or wolf, and whenever it was required that I set out a trap or poison bait, I urinated on it.

Which brings us to late August, when Snuffy sent me up past Gibbon Meadows to check a trap line.

The day was warmish and clear blue, with a hint of autumn. The air was almost too sparkling for summer. Birds and plants had a shimmer of anticipation you don't see during the hot days of July. I rode up an old wagon track from God knows when. Maybe a prospector cut it, or the Army back in the '80s. In 1923, the Park didn't have rules concerning where a man could drive a motorcycle.

I rolled through a stand of lodgepole pine down into aspen that gave way to willows along a soggy creek bottom and turned into a pretty meadow where I came up on two men on horseback roped to a grizzly sow. A yearling cub huffed to and fro in a nervous fit off to one side while the mother grizzly charged one horse and then wheeled on the other. The men—Bill Cox and Shadrach Pierce, by God—whooped and hollered and flailed hats at their horses, making a mess of the peaceful afternoon.

Any fool who's ever roped so much as a fence post knows it takes three men, three ropes, and three well-trained mounts to subdue a full-grown grizzly bear. You triangulate—offer resistance from two sides when she makes a run at the third. There's no sense in two men alone attempting the stunt. Even if you choose a sickly bear and your horses are powerful, what are you going to use for an exit plan?

The grizzly reared up on her hind legs and paused a moment to gather her wits, then she dropped, bounced off her front feet, and charged Shad. Bill's noose had her by the right hind-foot, while Shad's was cinched around her neck. The sow was dark brown with a dusty gray hump and a flat face. One ear had been notched in a fight or by a bullet. Dragging Bill's horse with her, she made ragged progress on Shad, whose appaloosa shied sidewise, snorting and circling to avoid those awful claws. Shad dug at his scabbard, but she was coming so quick he had to reel in rope with both hands, like playing a really big trout, or she would shake off his necktie and be clear to finish him without restraint.

Bill screamed profane words at his horse whose eyes bulged in panic. The bay bucked and spun, causing Bill to hang up on the rope looped around his pommel. The cub was bleating like a castrated sheep and the mama roared. She'd straightened out her confusion. Now, she was single-mindedly set on killing Shad.

I said something along the lines of "I knew it would be those two." Something like that. What I meant was I'd been braced for months, waiting for the event that would explode my life, and I'd always suspected when that event arrived, Shad and Bill would be close by.

Then I shouted, *"Holy shit!"* or *"Hellfire!"*—I can't recall which—gunned the beJesus out of my motorcycle, popped the clutch, and charged the bear. I spun dirt clear across the meadow, making as much noise as possible on a Harley-Davidson. Which is a lot of noise.

The bear glanced at me but kept after Shad. I suppose she'd decided to tear him apart first, then deal with the rest of us one at a time. I passed so close to her I could have kicked her backside, and only swerved at the last moment to keep from flipping over Bill's rope.

I came in for a second pass, but she ignored that one too. Shad's horse was circling so fast I was about to get my neck wrung. So, instead of making another run at the mother, I turned to the cub.

As I said before, this was a yearling cub, so he wasn't cuddly as a Teddy bear. He was big enough to cause damage in his own right if he got angry, only so far, the cub was more frightened than dangerous. He stood on two legs, looking altogether like a hunchbacked teenager, while I spun a 360-degree, dirt-kicking slide around him there. He couldn't swivel quick enough to face me clear around. He just stood there, bleating, disoriented by so much sound.

You want to get a female grizzly bear's attention, go after her cub. Only once you've got her diverted, I'd advise moving away with haste. The bear left off Shad and came across the clearing like a freight train jumping the tracks. She yanked Bill backwards from his saddle and the saddle frontward from the horse. The bear ran, dragging the saddle twenty feet to the rear. Shad's horse ran with her, the alternative being broke legs.

I saw Shad and Bill were safe for the moment and the time had come to clear out, but it was too late. Grizzlies can outrun any horse, and believe me, this one could catch a motorcycle spinning in dirt. She came up fast and big and swatted me off the motorcycle, tearing my shoulder. I flipped in midair and landed on my back, and she was on me like a dog on a bone. There was this moment of me looking up into that grizzly's eyes. It was a moment I'll remember long after I'm dead.

"Wait a minute," Lydia said.

"You face down an enraged grizzly and tell me I'm wrong," Oly said. "Till then, I don't want to hear another word."

"That works for me."

Her mouth opened. I saw drips of spittle hanging off her teeth. Smelled the stench of her breath. I thought then about Evangeline, how sweet she was and how short our time together had been. I thought dying here was better than dying in the trenches, because I'd known her, and dying before I met Evangeline would have meant my life was wasted, whereas dying now meant I'd amounted to something. You'd be amazed and awestruck to know how much a man can think in the heartbeat before oblivion. Time stretches. That's how I figure it. You can have three minutes worth of thought process in a single second.

A nickel-sized hole appeared in the bear's forehead and blood gurgled out. I heard the loudest shot I'd ever heard, louder than the shell that wounded me in France. Another hole appeared in the roof of her mouth. She made a sound like gargling salt water, then she collapsed.

LEROY PUNCHED OUT THE BOTTOM RIGHT PANE ON LYDIA'S
back door. He reached through the glass shards, opened the door, and
entered her utility room. He moved past the washer and dryer, into the
kitchen, where he crossed to the refrigerator and drank his fill of vanilla
soy milk straight from the bottle, until milk ran down his chin and
dribbled onto the floor.

He set the milk on the counter next to the telephone and left the
kitchen for the living room, where he found Zelda standing by the open
front door.

"It wasn't locked," she said.

"Shut it."

"What?"

"The neighbors know the old lady is out of town. We don't want them
seeing the door open and calling the pigs, now do we, you dumb twat?"

"Okay." Zelda closed the door. "I'm going to find some new
clothes. These I've got on are starting to smell like you."

Leroy ignored her. He went into Lydia's office, which had once
been my bedroom, and rummaged through the desk. He found piles of
unopened bills, a pint bottle of Jim Beam Shannon had missed when
she took her turn at snooping, and a manuscript entitled We Don't
Need No Stinking Balls. The name on the title page was Sylvia
Dupree, who had for years been one of Lydia's authors before Oothoon

Press shut down when Lydia went underground. Sylvia's treatise was based on the systematic elimination of men. She claimed spermless procreation is now scientifically possible, and therefore, the unnecessary gender should be phased out.

Interestingly enough, I later tracked down Sylvia Dupree and discovered she is an animal-control officer in Forty Five, South Carolina, named Ralph Singleton. He'd written the Oothoon books as satire, but when they blossomed into hits, he kept his true feelings under wraps.

Leroy threw the manuscript in the trash.

Zelda's voice came from Lydia's room. "There's some men's clothes in here. You want a change?"

"Get me a belt."

"Don't you want clean underwear?"

"A belt."

Leroy drained the Jim Beam, then he went back in the living room and knocked over a Tiffany-style lamp, on general principle.

Zelda stood in Lydia's doorway, holding Hank's old concha belt from his rodeo days. "What'd you do that for?"

"Because I could."

"They're going to know we was in here."

"So?"

"And for your information, Mr. Big Shot, no one's called cops pigs since Woodstock ended. Even I know that much."

Zelda moved on to Shannon's room to rifle the closet, in hopes of finding something she could wear in public. Lydia's closet had been a washout. Leroy walked back into the kitchen and opened the refrigerator again. He found nothing but an empty jar of Grey Poupon, two artichokes, and some leftover salmon loaf. He tasted the salmon loaf and, in disgust, threw it through the soy milk he'd left on the counter.

As soy milk splattered on the wall and phone, Leroy saw the blinking light on the answering machine.

He poked Play.

BEEP.

"Hi, Lydia. It's me. Shannon. Shannon Callahan. I'm flying into Las Vegas this afternoon and I need you to pick me up. I'm on Delta. The plane gets in at 4:10 p.m., which should leave you plenty of time to swing by and"

BEEP.

"Get me. If I miss you guys, I'll fly on to Santa Barbara and leave a message on your phone as to when I'll be there. If I miss you in Santa Barbara, I'll go on to that writer's house. I'm sure I can track down anyone famous as Loren Paul."

BEEP.

"Don't let Roger get away."

Leroy called out, "Time to move your ass."

"I'm not through making my choices."

"Anyone not in the truck in forty seconds gets left in this hole."

Zelda came into the kitchen wearing Shannon's ex-boyfriend's UNCG SPARTANS basketball jersey. "What do you think, Charley? Does this make me look fat?"

19

BY THE TIME HER FLIGHT LANDED IN LAS VEGAS, SHANNON had worked herself into such a state of nerves that the red welt of a hive popped up on the fleshy side of her arm, in the elbow crook. She was sitting next to a talker, of course. Airlines always sat Shannon beside talkers. She imagined they had a computer file of people who wouldn't complain if they were treated shabbily, and she was on it. This talker was a chamber-of-commerce type in a sports jacket he bought on sale in a pro shop at a West Jordan golf course. He tried to sell her a time-share on the Salton Sea in California.

"The Salton Sea is the new playground of the stars," he shouted at her, even though his mouth was close enough for her to smell Altoids. "America's next Riviera."

Shannon said, "What's a time-share?" and spent the next hour staring out the window while the man answered her question.

So, in Las Vegas, when she came through Baggage Claim and found Lydia, standing beside a stainless-steel water fountain, her arms crossed over her chest and her lips puckered in annoyance, Shannon was ready for her turn at talking.

"I need to find a store. I was in such a hurry, for fear I might miss the next plane and be stuck waiting, that I drove straight from Dad's place to the airport. I don't have a toothbrush or fresh panties, and I need Benadryl cream. How's your trip, so far?

Lydia wasn't about to let Shannon get away with idle chatter. She said, "This better be good. We've lost two hours for you."

Shannon fought the urge to scratch her hive welt. It was a losing battle. She never had been adept at not scratching itches. "I'm here to rip the moose's Achilles tendon with my bare teeth. Like you said. Aren't you thrilled I'm taking your advice?"

"I am far from thrilled. This journey is on a tight schedule and we have no time for your personal dramatics." Lydia raised her chin in righteous indignation. "Who is your moose?"

Shannon said, "Roger."

Lydia fell back a step. She steadied herself with one hand on the drinking fountain. "You chose Roger Pierce as your reason to face tomorrow?"

Shannon covered her nerves with glibness. It's a family tradition. "Why not? Roger is there. He's a moose. I'm a wolf."

"A cradle-robbing wolf."

Shannon gave up the fight and scratched. "I can't believe that would bother you."

Lydia bit the edge of her lower lip as she studied Shannon. In spite of what appeared to be a case of fleas, her granddaughter certainly looked more alert than she had yesterday on the couch. The stunned-cow flatness had left her eyes, replaced by a crystal light, like a person with a high fever. Her posture had gone from braced-for-a-blow to hopeful.

"Actually, I'm impressed you had the imagination to choose him," Lydia said. "I wouldn't have thought you capable of originality." She frowned. "Aren't you two related, in some bizarre fashion?"

"I'm trying not to let community standards affect my actions. You and Mom are my role models in that way."

Shannon looked down past the various carrels. "Where is the boy? I need to get started."

Lydia marched off toward the escalator. Shannon followed, a step to the side and a bit behind. Even though the airport was packed by tourists, gamblers, and families trailing packs of small children, the hordes parted for Lydia. Shannon, who was used to pushing her way through crowds, couldn't help but wonder what about this woman made people instinctively get out of her way.

As they were passing an Orange Julius stand, Lydia turned on Shannon. "You just be careful he's not a passing fancy. Roger's going through an emotional firestorm on this trip. He doesn't need a female using him to pull herself out of a funk."

Shannon looked down at Lydia. She'd never before realized she was at least an inch taller than her grandmother. Lydia had always been such a huge presence that she made Shannon feel small by comparison.

Shannon said, "How comfortable are you giving lectures against using men?"

Lydia almost smiled. Instead she sniffed. "I have extremely high standards in loved ones. You'd do well not to give me cause for shame."

———

They found Oly and Roger down by the car rentals, feeding nickels into a slot machine. To be precise, Oly was feeding nickels into a slot machine and Roger was feeding nickels to Oly.

Lydia said, "I told you not to give him money."

Roger glanced at Shannon, then looked away and smiled. The smile and the look didn't match up, as if he wanted to acknowledge Shannon's entrance without seeming to see her; or to admit he'd seen her without looking at her; or maybe as a way to say he was happy she was there, while stressing his neutrality on the subject. To Shannon, it was a remarkably complicated way of not saying hello.

Roger said, "He's up twenty-two dollars."

Oly, by comparison, actually didn't see or acknowledge or look at Shannon. His concentration was absolute—nickel to slot, wait for the *bing*, nickel to slot, wait for the *bing*, no pause, even when he hit and a stream of nickels clattered into the steel bowl for Roger to collect. It was a slot machine specially built for gamblers in wheelchairs, with a hole underneath for legs and a button you pushed instead of a lever you pulled. A person can be quadriplegic and still play slots in the Las Vegas Airport.

Lydia said, "We can use the cash for gas." She tapped Oly's shoulder. "Come on, Mr. Fossil. Time to hit the highway."

Without pausing his slot-feeding rhythm, Oly dropped his left hand and set the wheelchair brake.

Lydia leaned forward and popped the brake back off. "I know you're not deaf, old man. Let's roll."

Oly was wearing painter overalls over a very old and very dirty T-shirt. He had flip-flops on his feet, and the toenails were thick as butter pats. His skin was the color of peed-on snow. Shannon hadn't seen him since the summer before she started high school. She'd been with some local girls at the Jackson pool, sunbathing and watching boys, when one of her friends pointed out Oly, who was being lowered by mechanical chair into the therapeutic hot tub. In his bathing suit, he seemed, to Shannon, like the world's oldest human back then, fifteen years ago. Now, he came across more as an animal than a person. An amphibian. Or maybe a newborn manatee.

Oly swiveled his head to Lydia. "I haven't had so much entertainment in seventy-one years. I see no call to limit my pleasure."

Roger said, "What happened seventy-one years ago?"

Oly didn't move his head, but his eyes cut from Lydia to Roger. "The decent portion of my days ended."

"That would be pertinent as hell if we gave a damn," Lydia said. "But we don't, and neither does anyone else in Nevada. So let's move west. Do you need a potty before we load up?"

Oly's mouth turned down into what Shannon saw as the nastiest face the nasty-looking man was capable of. He glared at Lydia.

Naturally, she deflected the glare. "Well, do you?"

Shannon said, "I do."

The interstate west out of Las Vegas toward California is surreal, by any standards, but it's surreal more in the lines of Dr. Seuss than Salvador Dali. It has all the charm of a rhinestone necklace on a camel. Depending on the time of day and day of the week, one direction will be bumper-to-bumper, jam-packed, while the other direction is a ghost road. The Saturday of Memorial Day weekend, eastbound traffic coming from Los Angeles was a blood clot—stop-and-go way the heck out an hour from the nearest exit ramp, wrecks every twenty miles, overheated breakdowns cluttering the shoulder—while the westbound lanes were nearly empty of cars and light on trucks.

The landscape is second-rate. I've driven I-15 twice over the years and found the desert lacking both times. There are no trees, which normally I would find interesting, but that stretch of road isn't raw enough or flat enough or even empty enough to evoke awe, not like Death Valley to the north or the Mojave to the south. It feels like a huge vacant lot. Common practice in the West is to change a baby in the backseat of a traveling car, then throw the soiled diaper out the window. Nevada should proclaim the dirty disposable diaper as its state flower.

A hundred yards out there, past the human trash and disruption, the landscape turns movie set. You expect to see a column of cavalry topping the mesa or a crusty prospector with an overloaded burro named Betsy.

Roger had driven all Friday night, to Mesquite on the Nevada border, while Lydia curled in the backseat and Oly fell into an old-age trance with his mouth open like a dying bird. In Mesquite, Lydia loaded up on coffee and took over while Roger dozed. Oly spread a Chevron map of the Western United States open on his lap. He seemed to be following their progress, but it was hard to tell. He may have been using it as a blanket.

After Vegas, Shannon joined Roger in the backseat. Roger, on the passenger side, twisted his key ring between his fingers and stared off at the desert. Roger had an amazing key ring. There must have been twenty-five keys strung on a leather thong. Lord knows what locks they went to.

Shannon, behind Lydia, stared at the back of the driver's seat, waiting for the last suburbs of Vegas to die out before lighting into Roger. Shannon had the highest hopes that a new chapter of her life was about to begin. She was sick and disgusted with the old chapter. The approach she decided to take was to put Roger on the defensive and then to sweep in for the maiming.

She said, "You had relations with Eden Rae."

It wasn't a question, so Roger didn't answer. He looked from the diaper-littered desert to Shannon. He'd spent so much of his time imagining her, seeing the actual Shannon felt dreamlike. There was a separation between Roger and himself.

"I spoke to Eden Rae this morning," Shannon said. "Her father came to get her, and we talked before she left."

Roger tried moving the conversation away from relations. "She claims her father is the biggest pinhead on the planet."

"I don't know about biggest on the planet, but he's top ten, anyway. The jerk managed to insult Dad and Gilia and everyone else."

Roger twisted the key ring into a figure eight, then turned it inside out. He didn't know what to say. He could tell Shannon expected a reaction, but he didn't know what. He would gladly have told her what she wanted to hear, if only he knew what that was.

Shannon said, "Eden Rae told me all about you."

Roger forced himself out of the dream state. If he didn't treat this conversation as real, it might end badly. "She doesn't know all about me. By next week, she'll forget my name."

"What makes you so certain?"

"The girls say they'll stay in touch, but no one ever has."

Shannon's eyes bored into Roger's. She was going for the tendon. "Eden Rae told me you have sexual relations with every girl at the Home for Unwed Mothers."

The front seat had grown silent, more silent than before, when neither Lydia nor Oly had been talking. It was as if both were holding their breaths. Even Oly seemed alert.

Roger said, "That's not true."

Shannon said, "Which part?"

"I don't sleep with all of them."

"How many pregnant girls have you slept with?"

Roger pulled his bandanna low over his eyes. Whenever he looked straight into Shannon's eyes, he lost concentration. This didn't feel like the proper time to lose concentration.

Shannon said, "I've noticed whenever you're uncomfortable, you hide behind that bandanna. Give it to me."

"What?"

"Give me the bandanna so we may continue this conversation."

Sheepishly, Roger pulled the bandanna forward, off his head. He hadn't been in public without it in quite a while, and handing it to Shannon made him even more exposed than he already was.

Shannon rolled her window down and threw the bandanna out. Roger twisted to watch it flap along the highway.

"Why did you do that?"

She rolled the window back up. "So we can visit without distraction. Now, tell me how many pregnant girls have you slept with."

Roger watched in horror as the bandanna blew into the ditch, where it lay looking more like a diaper with blood on it than tie-dyed headgear.

Shannon said, "Roger."

He turned back to her. "I've always thought it was bad manners to count."

Shannon nodded. That statement put him in a class above most of her former lovers. Hell, it put him in a class above her. She knew exactly how many men she'd slept with. "Would you say you've had sex with half the girls who came to the Home since you started living there?"

Roger thought. It was difficult without the familiar pressure on his forehead. He felt disoriented. "I wouldn't say that, no."

"Thirty percent?"

Roger did some quick math. "Twenty-five, maybe. But I wouldn't normally say it out loud, even if it's true."

"Twenty-five percent or twenty-five girls?"

"You were asking about percents. I don't count girls."

"But you do count percents."

"I don't count percents. You asked me for an estimate, and I told you. It seemed more honest than not counting and acting like I didn't know."

Shannon broke away from staring at Roger and looked off the side of the highway. They were coming to the Nevada–California border. Buffalo Bill's and Whiskey Pete's appeared on either side of the interstate like hallucinations in the desert. A roller coaster swept between the buildings. She could see children with their arms raised, screaming.

"Eden Rae said the girls weren't afraid of sleeping with you, because you're in love with me."

Roger felt a wave of nausea. He disguised it well. He had years of training in disguising fear-induced nausea.

Shannon plowed on. "She said it made you safe. The girls had been sexually active before pregnancy, and they didn't want to stop. They chose you because you wouldn't get attached and become a messy entanglement, because of me."

Roger considered this line of logic as Lydia drove along the banks of a dry lake. There wasn't a blade of grass out there. All he saw were a couple of what looked like sailboats made out of soapbox derby carts on spidery wheels. None of the girls had ever said why they came to him. They just came.

"I don't think many of them thought it out like that," he said. "They wanted fun, and I was the only boy around."

The conversation wasn't going the way she'd planned on the airplane. Roger was supposed to be embarrassed by his promiscuity. If he truly loved her, he should feel guilt for betraying her, or at least he should be flustered at getting caught.

She decided to go at him from a new angle. "I went inside your cabin."

"Why would you do such a thing?"

"I saw your photo album." She waited for him to recoil in shame, and when he didn't, she added, "And the painting in the closet."

Roger's brow wrinkled. He was so young that it took a good deal of brow furrowing to bring about a decent wrinkle. Shannon used the time to compare their ages at various rites of passage—*When I'm thirty-nine, he'll be thirty-one. When I'm forty-nine, he'll be forty-one.* She ran clear through the sixties before Roger answered.

"Are you supposed to do that?"

"If you didn't want me going into your cabin, you would have locked it. Not locking it was a subconscious slip. You wanted me to see your hidden objects."

"You've never been anywhere near the cabin before. How was I subconsciously to know you'd drop by while I wasn't home? My door doesn't even have a lock that locks."

"That means when you built it, you wanted me to discover your secret."

Roger realized she was probably right. He ran a bluff, anyway. "I didn't realize I had a secret."

"A person looking at the photographs in the album and the painting in the closet would assume you have an obsessive interest in me."

"What person would assume that?"

"Well, me." Shannon wondered if maybe she had been wrong. What if the flight to Las Vegas has been based on bad information? She tried to recall the four photos and the oil painting. Would a normal, uninvolved person interpret them as obsessive interest? Eden Rae had, and Eden Rae was normal, sort of.

She asked, "Do you have an obsessive interest in me?"

Lydia could no longer stand it. "Jesus, Shannon, what part of *No, duh,* don't you understand?"

Shannon said, "I'm having a private conversation back here, Lydia. I'd just as soon you butt out."

"You want a private conversation, wait till you have privacy."

"Turn on the radio."

Oly leaned forward and turned on the radio. Lydia held her right arm out to save him from tossing forward into the floorboard. A talk show from Hesperia came on—a right-wing zealot raving against gun control who wouldn't let the woman who'd called in talk.

"Find another station," Shannon said.

Lydia twirled the radio tuner. "Not many choices out here in the wilderness." On the far-left end of the dial, she found a Christian rock band singing about basking in the golden light of

Jesus. It sounded as if they'd put new words to "I Am Woman, Hear Me Roar," by Helen Reddy.

"Turn it up," Shannon said.

"I'd rather hear the gun nut. He was making an interesting point," Lydia said.

"Turn it up."

Oly leaned forward, again, and cranked the music up to the point of buzzing the speakers. Lydia stiff-armed him back into position, again.

Shannon touched Roger on the back of his wrist. She shouted over the religious rock, "So, are you in love with me, or what?"

Roger stared at her fingers on his wrist. He'd imagined her touch a thousand times, at least. He'd rehearsed the moment, dreamed about the moment, masturbated about the moment, and, now, it felt just like he'd imagined.

He shouted, "Yes. Do you mind?"

Shannon smiled at him. "That's what I'm here to find out."

———

In Baker, the giant two-hundred-foot thermometer between the town and the interstate read 101 degrees. One hundred and one in May hit Shannon like a slap in the face.

"Can't you turn up the air conditioner?" she asked.

Lydia said, "In your dreams."

In Victorville, they passed the exit to Roy Rogers Boulevard, and Oly went off on a Roy Rogers movie he'd acted in—*Son of Paleface*. "It was 1952," he said. "They had me falling off horses all summer."

"Do you think anyone anywhere believes that?" Lydia said.

Roger said, "I do."

"Look at this husk of a man," Lydia said. "If he fell off a horse, his bones would crumble into dust."

"He was young in 1952," said Roger.

"Oly was never young."

As they came up on the Apple Valley exit, Oly started making odd, sheep-grunt noises and pushing the Chevron map of the Western United States toward Lydia, who pushed it back.

"Keep still," she said. "I'm listening to this." Christian rock on the radio had been replaced by a minister who sang his sermon like a Navajo storyteller. He ranted in iambic meter about the prostitutes of Los Angeles, although he substituted Gomorrah sometimes instead of saying Los Angeles. The singsong preacher claimed that millions of prostitutes walked the streets of Los Angeles, more prostitutes than the combined populations of Barstow, Bakersfield, and Victorville all put together.

"Are you not happy they turned Sodom into the sex act instead of Gomorrah," Lydia said. "I'd hate to know I'd been Gomorrahcized."

Oly thrust the map at her again.

Roger and Shannon held hands. If you were in a truck passing the BMW, you wouldn't think the two people in the backseat knew each other. They both stared out their respective windows in stony silence. Only by zooming in on the eighteen inches between them could you see his left hand was intertwined with her right hand, and a tremendous amount of communication was passing back and forth through that touch. An entire courtship was flowing between their hands. A year of approach-and-flee dating had been experienced and put behind. Birthdays, Christmases, Valentine's Days, their first break-up and make-up—Roger and Shannon were shooting through their relationship like the Starship Enterprise blasting into warp speed.

While on the exterior, nothing moved.

Oly said, "Turn."

Lydia said, "Give me a reason."

Oly thrust the map before Lydia's eyes, blocking her view of the interstate. She one-hand tore the map free in time to swerve left to miss an orange barrel set there to divide the highway from the exit. A semi-truck passing her swerved left, and the driver hit his triple-tone air horn—sounded like a train coming through a crossing.

"Don't do that," Lydia said.

Oly said, "Turn."

Lydia pulled onto the shoulder and stopped. "Hand over the map."

She studied the map while more trucks whooshed by, shaking the BMW from side to side. She said, "Okay," and backed a couple hundred yards to the exit onto State Highway 18. She said, "We'll go this way."

———

California State Highway 18 is an asphalt strip no wider than a bicycle path. It feels like a straight shot into the void. Lydia had spent much of her adult life in Wyoming, with time set aside for being a fugitive on various reservations, so even though she'd been in prison up by Oakland, she still pictured California the way an outsider would. She saw the state as one continuous overdevelopment stretching from San Diego to San Francisco, with patches of forest going on up to the Oregon border. Or Washington. She never could remember which of those two was on top and which on bottom.

It was Lydia's preconception that a person in California was never out of sight of a Starbucks, so it came as a mild shock to see miles and miles of nothing much. She'd taken inordinate pride in the miles of nothing much in Wyoming. It was weird to find a similar yet vastly different nothing in California. And the sky was an unsettling hue of blue, closer to Carolina blue than mountain blue, but the total lack of humidity made it feel farther up there, like the blue started halfway to the moon. The ridges off in the distance looked the way they would as seen through binoculars.

This prejudgment of California caused Lydia to make a mistake she would never have made in the Rocky Mountain Time Zone. She drove past the last gas station. She had assumed stations came along every ten miles or so, and she was wrong. Our gang pulled into Pearblossom running on fumes and prayer.

All of which is a roundabout way of explaining why they stopped at the scary gas station. The collapsing establishment had no sign—just two old-fashioned pumps with fish bowl tops perched out by the highway. The store hadn't been painted since the Dust Bowl. There were mattresses and blown-out lawn furniture out front and what appeared to be a graveyard for vehicles that died in the desert out back. A torn-apart motor-cycle on the front porch was being worked on by a Mexican who didn't look up when they pulled in, even though a pack of dogs materialized out of air and raised a true cacophony of noise.

"You think they're more likely to sell gas or rape us?" Lydia said.

"I don't care, so long as they have food," Shannon said.

Lydia said, "Go inside and if no one murders you, buy us lunch. And pick up some Evian in case we break down out on the third ring of hell."

Roger opened his door and showed the dogs how nonthreat-ening he was by letting them sniff his fingernails. "This looks like a place where they take pride in not selling Evian."

Oly said, "Make mine jerky. Buffalo jerky if you can, but I'll eat beef. Heavy on the nitrates." His mouth made chewing motions. "I do enjoy my nitrates."

As Shannon and Roger crossed the porch past the guy working on the motorcycle, the screen door slapped open, and another Mexican came out. This one was tall, and the sleeves had been cut off his flannel shirt to reveal a dark blue buzzard tattoo on his left shoulder. He waited for Shannon and Roger to pass by; then he went out to the pumps, where Lydia was unscrewing her gas cap.

His voice was a bit of a mumble. "Fill 'er up?"

Lydia blinked at him without comprehension. "I am sorry, but you have me at a disadvantage. I do not speak nor understand Spanish."

He frowned. "Would you like your automobile filled with gasoline?"

Lydia glanced in the open car window at Oly to see if he was catching the pathos of the conversation. He stared straight ahead, waiting for jerky.

Lydia said, "Isn't that charming? I haven't seen a station that serviced the customer since"—she pretended to think long and hard—"since I don't know when."

"Do you or not?" the tall Mexican said.

"What?"

"Want me to fill the tank?"

"Why, yes. That would be gentlemanly. My friend Roger should have done it, but he's enamored by my"—she hesitated, glancing again at Oly—"daughter. They went into your store. She needs a toothbrush."

Without a word, the man pulled a socket wrench from his pocket, twisted a knob on the pump, and flipped a lever, making the flap dials reset to zero. Lydia noticed L-O-V-E in blue ink on the knuckles of his left hand and H-A-T-E on the knuckles of his right. He had a series of blue-black teardrops etched on the inside of his left arm, below the buzzard.

"I see you've been inside too," Lydia said.

He stared at her with flat eyes. "Too?"

You have to understand, Lydia was dressed like a Malibu real estate agent out to cocktails. She hadn't been certain of the timing for her visit to Hank, so she dressed as if there would be no chance to change—Donna Karan skirt and shirt, Cole Haan shoes. She'd slept in the outfit, in the car, but still, she didn't look the part of an ex-con on the run.

"I was in Dublin Women's. Federal. Outside of Oakland. Where were you, if I may be so bold as to ask?"

He grunted. "Solano."

Lydia nodded knowingly. "I've heard state pens are sewage on a plate compared to federal." She gave him her most charming smile. "Do you find that true?"

The man looked off across the desert and snorted his contempt. Most people would have picked up on the anger behind the snort, but Lydia was so intent on winning him over that she missed it. To her, being in prison gave them a past in common.

"Dublin was horrid, but I'll tell you one thing." Lydia flipped her hair as if she were seventeen. "It's the only pen in America where inmates have keys to their own cells. What do you think of that?"

The screen door banged, and Shannon appeared. "They're not set up for credit cards, Grandma," she said. "The girl told me you can't take a credit card if you don't have a phone. Did you know that?"

Lydia said, "Yes, I knew that."

"Can I borrow twenty dollars? I didn't think I'd be needing cash when I drove to Dad's this morning."

Lydia opened her purse and turned away from the Mexican while she dug for her billfold. After Shannon said, "Thanks a bunch," and went back inside, Lydia continued where she'd left off.

"The screws have keys, of course. Can't lock out the law, but we could lock our cells when we left or while we slept. Isn't that convenient?"

Oly opened his door and spoke. "*Ingnore a la mujer loca.*"

The Mexican said, "*¿Ella está demente o es una cabrona?*"

Oly said, "*Ella es una cabrona demente. En la noche, ella me quema con cigarrillos. Ella es una mujer violenta.*"

The Mexican clucked sympathetically and then turned to glare at Lydia.

Lydia said, "Since when do you know Spanish?"

"Since 1939," Oly said. "You'll hear the story before we're through on the tape machine."

"Well, what did you say? What did he say? Is your buddy here a friend or foe?"

"I told him you are a powerful woman and he must treat you with respect or the Highway Patrol will come and cause him no end of pain."

Lydia considered this from several angles. "I suppose that is true, when you think about it."

Shannon and Roger emerged for the store. Roger had a six-pack of Guava Jarritos and a tube of Pringles. Shannon carried a brown paper sack. She said, "Have you tried Lucky Star toothpaste? It looks like Spanish Crest."

20

Shad's boots came into view, and I looked up to see him standing against the sun, a carbine tucked in the crook of his arm. I couldn't swear to this, but I believe he was wearing the same civilian clothes as last I saw him in Le Havre. Looked like a lumberjack in a cowboy hat.

He said, "That's a nice motorcycle." He pronounced it to rhyme with *fickle*.

I craned around, searching for the Harley-Davidson, but being pinned beneath the grizzly bear, I couldn't locate my machine. "Does it look damaged?"

Shad spit tobacco juice. "Nope."

"We had her under control till you butted in." That was Bill coming over after picking himself out of the dirt. "Ever since you were too little to get a boner, you've been forcing your way into situations that are none of your affair. Seems like you'd be embarrassed by your behavior, eventually."

Bill's hair was to his shoulders, and he wore calfskin—shirt and breeches—and a necklace strung with elk ivories. Wormy mustache. He looked like General Custer in his seedier days.

"What happened to the cub?" I asked.

"He took off." Shad nudged the mama with the toe of his boot, I suppose confirming her mortality. "He's big enough. He might survive."

"Not if he comes up against me," Bill said.

My left shoulder was feeling the sting, and breath came as a struggle. I said, "You fellas mind lifting his mother? She's too heavy for me to push."

———

They tied me to Shad's appaloosa in case I passed out, which I wasn't about to do in front of Bill—it's a proven fact hate will keep you awake longer than love—and Shad rode my motorcycle into the hospital in old Fort Yellowstone at the park headquarters. It was a nice four-bed hospital with all the accoutrements needed for medical service, except most of the time we had no doctor. The afternoon Shad and Bill hauled me there, the person in charge was the park's horse veterinarian. It didn't matter since all I needed was a sew job. Sewing men and sewing horses isn't all that different.

He gave me an injection of something that made me woozy, then another injection that numbed my shoulder and upper back. They let me hold a hand mirror in front and look into a wall mirror in back so I could watch him wiggle the needle back and forth through my skin—not painful, but raspy, like fingernails on a blackboard. The needle was big enough to sew canvas, and the thread looked like fishing line. I imagine it was.

The sleepy shot made me talkative. That's my excuse. If I'd had my head, I would not have released information in front of Bill.

I said, "Evangeline's not going to be happy if I'm a couple hours late to supper."

"More like a couple days," said the horse doctor. "We'll need to watch for infection. Only the good Lord knows what foulness a grizzly has in its claws."

I said, "Tarnation." That's how people under the influence of medication spoke in the West. We didn't have the potty talk you hear these days.

"Tell me where you live, and I'll ride your cycle over and tell her you're alive. If she wants, I could bring her back to see you," Shad said.

I glanced over toward Bill, who was sitting on a bench reading a *Police Gazette* magazine. One foot was propped on the other knee to expose his boot that was stitched and made from an exotic animal. I don't know what, but it wasn't cow.

"She won't want that," I said. "Just tell my wife I'm fine and I'll be along soon as I can get there."

Bill looked up from the magazine. He blew the word out as an exhalation. "*Wife?*" He broke into a grin. "You fast-moving old panty sniffer, I knew you weren't broke to pieces over my sister. Wait till I tell her."

I knew right then I'd made an error in judgment. I just didn't know the repercussions.

———

I lay prone in a meadow with my hip jammed tight into a sagebrush and a bouquet of lupine fluttering at my ear. The bear sat on its haunches, six feet or so to the side, snuffling at the dirt. A raven flapped down and landed on my boot. Behind him, a pair of coyotes paced in hopes the bear would wander off somewhere so they could have at me. It felt as if a line of red ants was crawling across my neck, under my armpit and back of my shoulder, where they commenced to bite.

Craning my neck forward, I strained to see the grizzly. What I saw was my torn-open gut and my intestine snaked across the meadow grasses to where the bear had dragged it. He was leaned forward like a dog at its food bowl, slurping me up.

I screamed. The raven flew. I awoke soaked in sweat with a terrible pain in my shoulder.

———

The room was painted bone white and had four narrow beds, but the other three were empty. There was a sink and a closed cabinet. My clothes were folded on a wooden stool. Curtains you wouldn't usually find in a hospital blew in the window, and I heard a motorcycle revved up beyond where park personnel normally revved. I figure the motorcycle woke me up. Or the ache in my shoulder. It was a deep ache, not simply a surface wound. It felt as if my muscles had gone under a hammer.

You can call it intuition or premonition or the spiritual side of morphine, but something felt out of place. I swung my legs to the side, and holding my arm tight to my breasts, I stood in my underclothing. Vertigo spun me ass over head, but after I stayed still a minute, the room settled, and I was capable of walking to the window and looking out.

The hospital room was on the third floor of the former fort. I could see down into a park-like grassy area, where Shad was circling my bike and Bill and Evangeline were engrossed in conversation by the horse rings. I couldn't hear their words. From the posture of their bodies, they appeared at the height of tension. Bill faced away, but Evangeline's mouth was a hard line and her eyes blazed. Bill reached across to grab Evangeline's wrist. She flung his hand off and spit out an angry oath. Then she walked quickly away and into the door beneath my window.

Bill turned to watch her go. His face showed a smile that made me sick to my stomach. He glanced up at my window only I jerked back before he saw me. I think.

By the time Evangeline came up the stairs and through the door, I was in bed, pretending to sleep. I heard her footsteps crossing the room and her touch at my brow. I opened my eyes slowly to look at her above me there. Her color was up, kind of a reddish brown like varnished mahogany.

I said, "You look nice."

She said, "Do you hurt?"

"Not so much. There wasn't cause for you to come all the way up here."

"Yes, there was."

We gazed at each other over a space of time. I thought then, and still think, Evangeline was the most beautiful aspect I ever beheld. To this day, I can close my eyes and picture her in the headquarters hospital room, staring down at me.

I said, "Are you troubled?"

She blinked a couple of times. "I was concerned about you. The man said you'd been attacked by a bear, but he didn't tell me more. I didn't know why he had your motorcycle, and then he drove fast coming over the pass and made me nervous. I've never ridden a motorcycle before today."

This was the lengthiest speech Evangeline had made in our eight months of matrimony. I knew it was the result of more than anxiety over my welfare.

She leaned in to study what she could see of my stitches. "Has the doctor said when you can go home?"

I sat up. "We'll leave soon as you bring my clothes from over there."

She walked across to the stool. "The shirt is torn."

"It'll be okay. You can sew it, back at the cabin."

I didn't get infected, but what I did get was tired. I slept for most of the next three days, propped up by pillows at the head of the bed so my shoulder stayed somewhat upright. Evangeline spoon-fed me a medicinal soup she claimed came from her heritage, but I didn't believe her. The central ingredient tasted like geyser runoff—sulfur with traces of iron and orange algae. The sulfur didn't do my tear any harm, and it possibly did some good since, like I said, no infection set in, but it did have a powerful affect on my stomach. I put out farts could have knocked down a buffalo.

Friday evening, one of my farts blew so strong it woke me up. Evangeline sat on the side of the bed, a damp rag in her hand, a slight smile playing across her lips. A Mona Lisa smile. I'd been a Paris artist, and I'd seen the actual Mona Lisa, so I knew that smile, even if it wasn't on velvet. That smile meant *I am amused by the smell of your fart*. Look at her and you'll agree.

Evangeline comforted me by dabbing the damp, warm cloth to my forehead. "Your friends came calling while you slept."

The cloth felt nice, but her words chilled me to the core. "What friends is that?"

"The men from the hospital. Mr. Cox and Mr. Pierce. They told me the story of your injury."

I moved Evangeline's hand away and tried to command her attention through contact between the eyes. She would have none of it.

"Those two are no friends of mine," I said. "Or maybe Shad is. I can't say. If he's such a fine fella, why's he been dragging along after Bill Cox all these years? He may be tainted too."

She glanced my direction, then away. "You do not approve of Mr. Cox?"

"No more than I approve of a rattlesnake in my blankets."

"And yet he saved your life."

I found myself nonplussed. And confused. Which one of them was she talking about? "Bill told you he saved my life?"

She nodded. "Twice in France and then with the bear."

That brought me off my pillows. "Those are absolute lies. Shad saved me from the bear, after I was done saving him. Bill never saved nobody—not in Yellowstone and not in France. I don't know how much conversation you've had with the man, but he is to be shunned by all right-minded people."

Evangeline got up and carried the rag to our wash pan on the woodstove. She stuck the rag in the water, then wrung it out and hung it on a peg to dry, all before she looked back my way.

"He's coming to supper tomorrow evening. The both of them are."

It may sound far-fetched to say I gasped, but that's what I did. I gasped. "Why, for God's sake."

She stared down at the pine flooring and came to the crux of what bothered her. "Are you so ashamed to have an Indian as your wife that you would hide me from your people?"

There it was again. I have no notion where she got the idea that a white man married to an Indian would feel embarrassment. Maybe she was raised by parents who thought that way since Evangeline wasn't full blood herself. Or maybe she learned it in Europe. To my death, I will deny she got it from me.

"I got no people, Evangeline. And of course I'm not ashamed. If I had people, I'd introduce you and be joyful in it, but I don't. All I have is you. You're all I need."

Her eyes came off the floor, and she gave me a look of defiance. "They are coming to supper. I want you to act civil." She took my pants off a nail and tossed them across the room, where they landed on my lap. "And out of bed."

In Paris, when Evangeline fixed a Stroganoff, she employed veined beef and sour cream. Compare that to Fountain Ranger Station, where she made it out of elk Snuffy gave us and sweet cream I bought from the Hamilton Store at headquarters. The elk was tough, being as Snuffy gave us the cuts his wife refused, and the cream changed the flavor, but the meal was still far better than what Bill or Shad deserved. No matter what gossips whispered about Evangeline's native ways, no one ever said she wasn't a first-class cook.

She seemed worrisome all day, as if she wasn't looking forward to visitors any more than I was. Early afternoon, she chased me out of the cabin—told me to take a bath. This I did by mixing one of the less-hot hot springs with river water. Most of those springs were so close to boiling, you couldn't fetch a bucketful without risk of a burn, but a few were only scalding and could be buffed down. While I tub bathed, I managed a soap lather sufficient for shaving. I also cleaned out my wound best I could and rewrapped the bandage.

Bill and Shad arrived in later afternoon, driving a four-door Model T Ford touring car with no windshield. Not a new Ford either, this automobile was one of the originals. Bill stepped out wearing a driving scarf, goggles, and fringed gloves like he was a European tourist. Shad looked same as ever. They'd brought a bottle they said was port, although I doubted if either knew what that meant. They weren't sophisticated about liquor, having never lived in Paris.

Bill got huffy when I turned down a taste. "You too uppity to drink with your childhood friends?" he said.

Evangeline cut her eyes my way while I took up the bottle and peered through it. Bottles didn't have labels that year, on account of prohibition. As a ranger, I could have arrested Bill on the spot.

"I'm law enforcement now," I said. "You shouldn't flaunt your ways in my face."

Bill laughed and poured himself a jarful of the golden liquid, reaffirming my opinion of his alcohol savvy. I never saw any golden port in all my days of drunkenness.

"You wouldn't turn in your oldest and dearest friend." He turned his attention to Evangeline, who was setting out every dish and piece of cutlery we owned. She'd put on a calico dress I'd bought her in New York City. To me, it showed her figure nicely and was much too good for company.

Bill said, "Did Oleander tell you how the three of us met?"

We sat at an outside table I'd drug over from the public picnic area. While Evangeline served the repast, Bill told the Miller brothers bank-robbing story. He'd forgot me and him met Fourth of July when he offered to shoot me. He also got the robbery wrong. He made himself the hero who faced down the outlaws, while I cowered behind the teller cage. He had Shad fire off a dozen shots, then Bill disarmed him because he could tell Shad was a good boy led astray and not fodder for killing. Shad knew it was all a tale, but he never contradicted a word. I have thought about Shad Pierce for many years now, and I still can't come to terms with why he put up with Bill's nonsense. It couldn't be that promise of servitude given in his youth. I don't imagine. No one signs away their whole life unless they want to.

Bill told about the other Miller boys shooting at me and Agatha when we came out of the underground bowling emporium. He made me cowardly in that story too.

"Oly dived under an automobile and left my sister to fend alone. He wouldn't come out till I'd chased Roy and Ephir Miller to the town limit," he said.

"Agatha must have been proud of you," Evangeline said. In all the time spent with her, I never learned to separate sarcasm from sincerity. That strikes me as important skill in a marriage.

"I just did what any good citizen would do," Bill said.

Rather than tell the true story, I asked about a subject close to my heart. Besides expecting to run into Bill and Shad ever since we came west, I'd secondly been waiting for the Roy and Ephir to surface on my doorstep.

"You ever hear what happened to the surviving set of Millers?" I asked.

Shad stopped with a fork full of Stroganoff at his lips. "They was hung."

"Hung dead?"

Bill spoke with what I call a smirk. "Not two months after we last saw those boys, they got caught rustling beef steers in Lincoln County. Folks down there are quick with a rope. There

321

weren't weight-bearing trees close by, so they hung the both of them from a telegraph pole. I saw a picture in a *Billings Gazette*."

I stared off across the basin as a moose came from the forest and picked his way between the fumaroles, working his way to the river. He was majestic as can be, wending through the steam.

"When did you see this *Billings Gazette*?" I asked.

Bill pretended to shoot the moose. From the space of his arms, I'd guess he was firing an invisible Lee-Enfield. "Mom sent me a packet of newspapers every week while we were in training camp."

My voice got quiet. Evangeline and Shad heard the menace, but Bill didn't. "You mean you knew they were dead before we left Calgary? Why didn't you tell me?"

He glanced from the moose to me. "You never asked."

"Those two were why we went to France. Our years in the Great War were wasted time."

"I wouldn't say that," Bill said.

"We fought for nothing."

Bill affected a look of wonder. "That's hardly true. You wouldn't have met this lovely lady and found joy through wedlock if I hadn't led you to France. How can you think you fought for nothing?"

This is a philosophical stance that has bothered me for at least eighty years and maybe longer, maybe all the way back to Mama's violent death and those Congregationalist women saying it was God's will. If Mama hadn't died, I wouldn't have met Agatha and if I hadn't met Agatha, I wouldn't have met Bill or killed Millers and so forth through the Great War until Evangeline. Does that mean my mother's demise and the millions dead in the war was to my personal benefit? That's a stretch I'm not willing to admit.

You hear it regular in nursing homes: *If I hadn't been raped by that cur, I'd never have given birth to my darling daughter*—and here the speaker makes the leap I don't follow—*therefore, the rape was a blessing.* I do not believe a bad experience leading to good results makes the bad experience worthwhile. That's just me. The war was not a good deal simply on account of without it, I wouldn't have found happiness. Sometimes the price is too high.

Bill, naturally, thought the Great War was a lark. At least he did looking through six years of hindsight. He spent the next hour regaling Evangeline with our grand adventures in the trenches. His memory of war was as far from mine as the sun is from Jupiter. Even Shad snorted disbelief at a few stories involving camaraderie and high jinks.

Evangeline listened to Bill's malarkey with concentration in her eyes, as if she bought it. She asked the pertinent questions—"Weren't you frightened?"—and gave the expected comments—"You boys should have been court-marshaled for that trick." Bill told her about battles and drinking contests and fistfights with Australians, as if they were all of equal value. He gave his version of nights in houses of ill repute, including me in the tales, which wasn't necessary. He never knew I paid those women not to perform.

He told one about stealing a Mark I tank and driving to Marseilles that I know he made up whole cloth. Maybe someone heard about someone else doing it and Bill adopted the story as his own. Evangeline laughed appreciably more than once, which was rare for her. Evangeline loved life and enjoyed a good joke, in her own way, but she was never much for out-loud giggles.

For dessert, she brought out a huckleberry pie made from berries she'd picked in the near vicinity. It steamed straight from the woodstove and smelled like my belief in heaven. Along with the pie, she served up the last of the heavy cream she hadn't put in the Stroganoff. I never tasted anything so good, before or since.

As Bill poured cream over his pie, he said, "This brings to mind the fresh strawberry tart my sister's chef bakes whenever I go to visit."

I couldn't help myself. I bit. "Agatha has a paid chef?"

He grinned that gum-exposing grin of his across the huckleberries. "You don't expect her to cook for herself, what with three young ones and another on the way." He made a show of looking around the cabin, assessing my financial worth. "You should be thankful Agatha threw you over. She's made Frank Lesley buy her a mansion of a house and a new automobile. And jewels. If you'd married her, she'd have run you ragged supporting all those babies."

I chuckled. Evangeline gave me a look.

Bill turned snide. "Or maybe you wouldn't. I see you and your Missus don't have offspring. A person might expect you would, by now."

I said, "We'd rather wait and enjoy each other for a bit before we start a family."

Evangeline set her coffee cup down by her plate and did that thing I'd seen in Paris the night we met, the thing where she goes placid. It's as if she shuts her being down. Folds into herself so nothing of her spirit shows. I guess she didn't like me saying *start a family* as if the two of us weren't one already. Or maybe she did dream of a child and resented that I hadn't give her the opportunity yet. To tell the truth, we'd never talked babies. I'd assumed sometime in the future, but I hadn't put any serious thought to the matter. I don't know what Evangeline assumed. I imagine now that I should of asked.

Bill shoveled a wad of huckleberries down his gullet. He swallowed and looked at Evangeline while speaking to me. "I'm happy to hear you are barren by choice," he said. "I was afraid that disease you picked up from the Indian whore left you with an unloaded gun."

Without a word, Evangeline rose and walked into the cabin.

———

No more was said of babies for another six or eight weeks. My shoulder healed to the extent I could work, which in September and October meant patrolling the south border. For some reason I never caught on to, men from Wyoming think they have a God-given right to kill big game in Yellowstone National Park. They have no more scruples over poaching than Robin Hood in Sherwood Forest, especially when it concerns moose. Wyomingites pretty much wiped out the moose population along the Upper Snake River there; then they blamed the wolves and demanded we exterminate them, and of course, we did—with the exception being me.

So, I was away from home sometimes three, four days and nights. Upon my return, Evangeline always expressed singular delight at my arrival. Neither Bill nor Shad nor any unpleasantness from their visit was mentioned, even though I knew they were living in Gardiner, Montana, only eight miles north of headquarters. It is somewhat an amazement we hadn't crossed paths with them earlier than we did.

On the evening of which I speak, I'd been in West Thumb a few days and just come back. Evangeline cooked a knockwurst and potato dish she learned in Austria. It was mighty good, although she herself didn't eat but a taste.

Together, we took our evening promenade about the basin. Tourists don't know this, but October is the fairest month in Yellowstone Park. It snows a bit in September, just to clear the pine pollen and riffraff from the auto camps. Then the air turns to a clean sparkle like nowhere else I've ever been. The mixture of low humidity, cold nights, and bracing days makes for a wondrous quality of light.

We wandered quietly, with Evangeline's fingers touching my arm, along a path we preferred between the hot pots and pools. As if a sign, over in the middle distance a geyser erupted to a height of ten feet or more. You could glimpse the water column when the wind blew the steam aside, like watching a beautiful sight through fluttering curtains.

"You remember what Mr. Cox said after supper," Evangeline began.

Bill said a lot, but I didn't ask *what*, on account of he only said the one thing that wounded.

"Yes, I do."

She went on a few steps by my side. Have I ever told you of Evangeline's physical carriage? She moved like a trained dancer. Even though she was inches shorter than me, she didn't seem so when we walked.

"Would you rather become a father or remain as we have been?"

My stomach gave a flop. My knees buckled, and if she hadn't been steadying my arm, I might have staggered.

"Are we discussing the planning stage or the done deal?" I asked.

"Would it matter?"

"I suppose not." It's funny how you can crave a thing you never even knew you wanted. At that moment, I realized I'd been wanting a child—boy or girl—for many years, at least since those nights in the trenches when I felt without connection.

"I've dreamed of someday being someone's father. I lost my own." In my mind, I saw Dad in San Francisco, the day he carried me on his shoulders while we watched the Chinese funeral. "I have resolved to do a better job of parenthood than he did."

Evangeline continued the walk. From the relaxed musculature of her face, I could see relief. Whenever a woman breaks news of this sort, she can never assume how the man will take it.

Evangeline said, "The time has arrived for you to practice your resolution."

We stopped, intertwined hands, and turned to gaze at one

another. I knew right there on the spot that no matter how long I stayed alive, or what became of me, things would never get better than now.

I needed confirmation. "Then, it is true?"

Evangeline smiled and nodded. "Have I made you happy?"

I looked into her eyes and felt her skin against my hand. This woman was all I ever wanted and more than I deserved.

I said, "I am happy. There is no doubt."

———

Every joke has its punch line, and I got mine.

The glee I felt over impending parenthood was impossible to suppress. The next morning, up at headquarters, Snuffy saw it all over my countenance.

"Who bit you in the butt?" he asked.

I beamed. That's what I did. "What do you mean?"

We were walking from the motorcycle barn over to the dining hall at the Mammoth Hotel. It's a short stroll across cut grass we walked most days I was posted at headquarters.

"You look like you swallowed a toad."

The sky was a brilliant blue, the pine needles a rich green. Elk scat steamed. It would be hard to imagine a day more deeply itself.

I couldn't keep the news to myself. "My bride is with child."

He kind of chuckled and cut his eyes my way. "And you no doubt think this is a positive development." Snuffy had seven offspring himself—five before the war and two after. He always said he joined up as an excuse to get out of the house.

"I do indeed," I said.

"Well, to each his own."

Inside, we ran into Bill and Shad hunched over coffee and beefsteak. Bill was dressed in his buckskin outfit, which had gone out of fashion when Wild Bill Hickok was gunned down in 1876. You don't see no one but drug pushers and lawyers dressed like that nowdays. He'd grown the worm mustache into a looper since we last met, and I couldn't help but count more elk ivories on that necklace of his. Oldest friend or not, if I caught the son of a bitch wasting an elk for two teeth, I would throw his tail into a small room with no windows.

Shad nodded in my direction. He ate steak with a toothpick lodged in the corner of his mouth. I'm not sure how—or why—he did that.

Bill said, "What's with him?" meaning me. That's how visually excited I was. Anybody in the world who saw me that day would have immediately known I was walking on air.

Snuffy grinned real big. He'd gotten to know Shad and Bill since the day Shad brought my Harley into the barn. He considered them funny folks.

"His wife has a bun in the oven." Snuffy chortled. That's the proper word for what he did—chortled.

Shad was okay with it. "Congratulations," he said. "There but for the grace of God, go I." Pregnancy brings out the card in even the most taciturn of men. Something about admitting you did what had to be done to make a woman that way and now you're facing the consequences strikes the male gender as hilarious.

But Bill frowned. I could sense he didn't like being proved wrong about the unloaded-gun crack. He didn't so much as look my way while Snuffy and I proceeded across the dining hall over to our usual table.

I ordered a Salisbury steak that was tough as a baseball mitt and coffee, and as I sawed away on the meat, I watched Bill stew. He was working out a method to get back at me. I could see it plain as the cloud on his face. I regretted telling Snuffy. I regretted us coming to dinner. I regretted me coming to park headquarters. I should of stayed at the cabin and been with

Evangeline. We could have locked the door, pulled the curtains, and played cards. She enjoyed a game called hearts.

When they rose to leave, Bill tossed money on the table, then he walked to the counter and dug a toothpick out of the dish there. Shad, who already had his pick, disappeared out the door. I thought they were gone and I was safe, but then Bill nodded to himself, and he turned and worked his way across the hall, coming through the mostly empty tables.

I steeled myself for whatever nasty remark he might choose to make. In my mind, I knew he couldn't touch me. I was loved by Evangeline and on the cusp of an expanded family, and he wasn't either one.

Bill slid up to our table and leaned in, propped on the knuckles of his right hand. Snuffy regarded him with curiosity, not knowing our history. I kept my eyes glued to the saltcellar.

"Here's what I'd like to ask the squaw," Bill said. "What I'm mighty interested in." He leaned lower toward me. "Ask her which of us is the natural father of that baby."

21

LYDIA AND ROGER SWAPPED DUTIES IN SANTA CLARITA, ON the theory that a driver with a license would be better when passing through the outskirts of Los Angeles. For a boy who lived up a dirt road, the intersection of 405 with the San Fernando Valley Freeway was truly terrifying. A pickup load of teenagers flipped Roger off on the merge. He had no idea why.

Shannon saw signs to Santa Monica and wanted to go there. "We have time for a detour. I want to see a movie star."

Oly had refused to give up the front seat or the map, which put Lydia in back with Shannon. "This isn't a pleasure trip," she said. "We have no time for movie stars."

Shannon looked out the window at the sparkling city to the south. The sun had gone down, and lights streamed out across the valley and up the mountains. The brightness gave the illusion of going on for eternity. "I've never been to LA. It seems kind of pitiful to come this far and miss it."

"You are in no position to curry favors. It's because of you we are behind schedule." Lydia was in a foul mood. She'd lavished all her charm on the gas-station attendant, and he had been impervious. Twenty years ago, he would have been panting like a hound in summer, simply begging to be graced with a smile. Hell, ten years ago, he wouldn't have charged her for the gas. What made it so bad was that her power hadn't dissipated slowly, a bit at a time over the years. She could have dealt with that, maybe. But she'd gone into prison as a force to be reckoned with and come out a tiny shred of the aged mass. Strangers dismissed her as irrelevant. Hatred, she could fight; being dismissed was intolerable.

Lydia ground her teeth in an unladylike fashion. She said, "And don't pretend I didn't hear you refer to me as *Grandma* in front of two males."

———

Roger thought it was around 11:30 when they reached the first Santa Barbara exit. He didn't wear a watch and the BMW dash clock was broken, but Roger had a ranch boy's innate body clock. He was seldom wrong by more than two minutes.

He asked Lydia, anyway, in case California had thrown off his inner timepiece.

She said, "Ten thirty. You have somewhere you need to be?"

Roger tipped the rearview mirror to look back at her. "I could have sworn it was later."

"We're in a new time zone," Lydia said. "We picked up an hour back in Mesquite."

"I forgot." Roger hadn't been out of his home zone in years. It felt weird that hours could jump back and forth. "Do they have Daylight Savings out here?"

Lydia said, "Everybody has Daylight Savings."

"Arizona don't," Oly said.

Shannon awoke with a start. She'd been dreaming about soaking in a hot tub with Eugene, her first boyfriend from years gone by. In the dream, Eugene's penis looked and felt like a wine cork. She held it in her hand, saying, *What am I supposed to do with this?* when she suddenly came to in a car.

"Where are we now?"

Roger said, "Santa Barbara. We've reached where we're going."

Shannon turned to Lydia, whose face was the color of parchment in the interstate highway lights. "Do you know how to find Loren Paul's house?"

Lydia's eyebrows stretched out tightly—a negative sign. "It's too late to go knocking on a stranger's door tonight." Her voice took on that overly casual tone that her loved ones knew disguised prevarication. "We'll head up the coast a ways and find a motel. Roger needs to shower before he meets his step-father tomorrow."

"You don't know he's my step-father," Roger said.

"You don't know he's not. We must assume he is, until proven otherwise."

"Why?" Shannon asked. She had caught the disinformation tone. In spite of her generally droopiness of spirit, or maybe even because of it, Shannon was sensitive to mood shifts in others. After all, she is my daughter and I am a novelist. Recognizing moods is my life. "Why are we taking for granted this man was married to Roger's mother?"

"Because we're Goddamned optimists, that's why," Lydia said.

Shannon wondered if she was supposed to take that as a joke or irony, or maybe Lydia believed she was an optimist. Lydia's self-image had always struck Shannon as a mysterious and constantly morphing blob, not unlike ectoplasm with warts.

Roger had more specific doubts. "Why should I drive up the coast? They have motels in Santa Barbara."

Lydia touched her hair, above her ear. It was her Katharine Hepburn gesture. "It'll be cheaper if we go north a bit. Santa Barbara is the most expensive city in America, and I'm paying for the trip. The rest of you are along for the ride."

"We're here so Roger can talk to Loren Paul in person," Shannon said. "He's the reason for the ride. I don't see how you can say Roger is just along."

"You know perfectly well what I mean. Don't twist my words." Lydia leaned forward to tap Roger on the shoulder. "Keep going. We'll pick a town forty miles or so up the coast, somewhere between here and Santa Cruz."

A light came on in Shannon's brain—the moment of *Aha*. "Isn't Hank up in here? I remember Dad telling me he flew into Santa Cruz when he came out to a parole hearing."

Lydia didn't slap herself in the forehead in amazement, but her voice jumped. "I completely forgot about that. Hank is in Lompoc. I wonder how far away we are from Lompoc."

Oly raised his head from the map, stretching his turkey neck nearly tight. "Forty miles, and it's where you meant to go all along."

They dropped into mutual silence. Lydia's eyes went to Roger's, watching her through the rearview mirror. From his expression, she couldn't tell how surprised he was. Mostly he showed resigned disappointment.

She said, "That statement is such an exaggeration, it falls into the category of falsehood."

Oly hmphed, a sound that irritated Lydia no end.

Shannon said, "You mean it's true? You dragged Roger all this way as an excuse to see Hank?"

Lydia broke the eye lock with Roger. "We drove—all this way—to find where Roger comes from and what caused him to stop talking. I only recently put it together that Hank is nearby. I think if I'm going to such trouble and risk to help Roger, the least I should be allowed is two hours for my own needs."

"That's a twisted way to word it," Shannon said. She looked toward the driver's seat, at Roger. "Did you know you were being exploited?"

Roger's eyes went forward, checking traffic, then back at Lydia again. "Sam said there was more to the deal than Lydia

was letting on. I figured she would tell us when she was ready."
He glanced over at Oly. "How did you know?"

A line of drool dripped down the corner of Oly's face like a
teardrop, only shiny instead of salty. He said, "I may be senile,
but I'm not stupid."

"I could have sworn it was the other way around,"
Lydia said.

"The entire population of Haven House knows where her
Indian lover is in prison. All you had to do was look at a map
to divine the true call for our journey."

No one spoke for five miles. Lydia studied her nails.
Shannon worried at a loose thread in the seat cover. Roger
drove with both hands on the wheel, working out whether
he should feel screwed or not. Like Lydia said, he was getting
what he wanted, or what she had convinced him he wanted.
He wondered if seeing Hank had been the only drive in her
encouraging him to seek out his history, right from the beginning, and if so, should he resent her pretending an interest
in him.

He decided he had a right to feel screwed, but even so, he
didn't. Whatever Lydia's reasons, without her needling, he
probably would not have worked up the energy it takes to dive
into the past. Roger considered his choices and chose not to
condemn Lydia.

Shannon, however, looked at the facts from a different
perspective. She said, "Shame on you, Lydia."

Shannon expected curses, rage, and possibly even a slap. No
one got away with criticizing Lydia. Lydia criticized others; she
did not accept it herself.

Neither vile nor violence erupted. Lydia just sat there, twisting
her wedding ring around her finger and staring at the back of the
driver's seat. A chill skipped its way up Shannon's spinal column.
Lydia's silence was more frightening than her wrath.

Oly said, "Before the hotel, I must visit a liquor store, if you please."

———

Lydia insisted on separate rooms for girls and boys. She said, "Do what you must after lights-out, but Maurey Pierce would rip my hide if I set her kids up to share a bed." So Roger was stuck with Oly, who as soon as they let themselves through the Comfort Inn door, rummaged his suitcase for a plastic sandwich bag containing a child's soft-bristled toothbrush and a travel tube of Pepsodent.

Roger sat on the end of a queen-size bed, flipping channels on the TV and listening to Oly brush his gums. Roger hadn't known people without teeth needed to brush. It wasn't something he'd thought about. Oly was the noisiest of brushers too. Sounded like a horse drinking from a stock pond.

Like almost everyone who prides themselves on not owning a TV, when Roger found himself someplace with television, he watched too much of it. We used to have satellite TV at the Home for Unwed Mothers, before Roger came there, because Maurey's husband, Pud, is a satellite-system installer. That's where they make their money. Raising horses is just a way to pour cash down a hole. Pud set us up with satellite, but the girls argued so much about what to watch—the dish brought in over three hundred channels back then—that I pulled the plug. Believe me on this: there's nothing more irritating than a covey of pregnant girls carping at each other. Teenagers think being with child makes their personal desires into imperatives.

The Comfort Inn TV carried thirty-two channels, but Roger didn't find a one worth spending time on. There was a show where a man wrestled a crocodile that was okay until the first commercial. Another channel played nothing but weather reports. Roger couldn't fathom why anyone would watch weather reports for more than two minutes, which is how long it took to find out the forecast. Two stations broadcast sports. Roger had no interest in team sports. His brother Auburn had been a jock. As a reaction against him, Roger discovered jazz and books.

He mostly flipped channels for the sake of flipping channels. The road trip so far had him too confused to settle on one show. He'd expected a case of nerves over meeting Loren Paul, who might or might not know the secrets of his past. That was intense enough, but then Shannon dropped out of the sky, and she was a big deal too. The two big deals canceled each other out. He couldn't focus on either one.

Shannon seemed to be taking something for granted, and she assumed he was taking the same thing for granted, but he didn't know exactly what it was. Were they going steady all of a sudden? It felt like they were, although they hadn't talked and hadn't touched beyond holding hands. He'd missed the courtship segment. Or was this the courtship segment? Was he supposed to marry her now, or what?

He heard a flush, and Oly came from the bathroom wearing a pair of butter-colored boxer shorts and nothing else. He carried his toothbrush and toothpaste in one hand and a motel glass in the other.

He said, "Might I bother you to open the bottle, son?"

A pint of Captain Morgan rum sat on the nightstand between the beds. A pint was all Lydia had been willing to spring for, and it took the threat of blackmail for Oly to get that.

He'd said, "*I'll tell the prissy woman,*" and Lydia said, "*I see this threat business turning into a never-ending nightmare for the rest of my life.*"

Oly said, "*My life.*"

Lydia said, "*That better not be much longer, you old goat. If you don't back off, I wouldn't feel an iota of shame about shoving you into traffic.*"

Now, Oly humped over to his wheelchair and more or less fell into it. He screwed around with his hearing aid, either turning it up or down, Roger couldn't tell, then Oly said, "Turn the TV to an exercise show, if you please."

Roger tore the seal off and twisted open Oly's rum. "I've been around the dial more than once, and I've haven't seen an exercise show. All they have are regular shows and sports. There's a news–all-the-time channel, and a station to tell you what's on the other stations."

"Those ladies on the exercise shows are hired for entice-ment." Oly held out his glass while Roger poured. "I watch them before bed. They improve the quality of dreams."

Roger said, "I don't think this TV gets exercise shows."

"I'll settle for Weather Channel if there's no exercise," Oly said. "Weather girls are hired for enticement too, but the dreams they bring about are not near so entertaining."

A knock came at the door and before Roger could say, "Who is it?" the door opened.

Shannon stood in the dark rectangle of the doorway. She said, "I can't stand this anymore."

Roger and Oly looked at one another. Roger said, "Can't stand what?"

Oly assumed it had to do with the TV. "You don't even know what we're watching."

Shannon walked toward Roger. "We have to talk."

"Uh-oh." Oly gulped from the motel glass. "I've run into that one before."

Shannon nodded at Oly. "Without him around."

"Whoa there." Oly affected offense. "I'm harmless."

Shannon picked Oly's overalls off the floor. She held them at arm's length, between her thumb and index finger. "Get dressed, Oly. You're going to my room."

Oly stuffed the glass between his floppy thighs and dug his

hands into the wheelchair handles. "I just took my clothing off. I'm not putting it back on again. At my age, you don't waste time undoing what's done."

Roger finally caught up with the situation. "Lydia will fly off the handle."

Shannon knelt to peer under Oly's bed, searching for the shirt, but she didn't find it, because he'd washed the shirt in the sink and left it to dry on the shower-curtain rod. She said, "Lydia's long gone."

Roger turned off the TV. "What's that supposed to mean?"

"Soon as we checked in, she changed her clothes, grabbed her keys, and took off."

"Where to?" Roger asked.

"What I don't have here is a clue." Shannon gave up on the shirt and stood with one hand on her hip, hovering over Oly. "It's a warm night, compared to back home, anyway. We'll take him like that." She raised her voice to a near shout. "You ready to roll, Oly?"

His mouth chewed on itself, then he said, "Only if I get to keep my bottle."

"Of course you can keep your bottle. We'll set you up in front of the television with your bottle. You'll have a ball."

Roger leaned over to put on his shoes. "Lydia will come back and find him."

Shannon dropped Oly's overalls back on the floor, where she'd found them. "I don't see that as a problem."

——

Together, Roger and Shannon pushed Oly's chair down to the girls' room, which looked exactly like the boys' room, only messier. Lydia's traveling outfit was thrown across her bed, along with most of the clothes from her overnight bag. Makeup bottles and tubes cluttered the top of the TV. Roger was amazed at how quickly women fill up a room.

Shannon placed a pillow in Oly's lap and draped a blanket over his shoulders. She clamped the remote in one claw and the bottle in the other.

"You're set," she said.

Oly twisted his skinny neck and cocked his head into an ogle position. "Can I have a good-night kiss?"

Roger said, "No."

———

"I understand how we're almost but not really related and all, Roger, but I was wondering how much you know about me." They were back in Roger and Oly's room. Roger was sitting in the motel chair that came with the little desk squeezed between the TV and the heater. Shannon sat on his bed. She had kicked off her cowboy boots and taken the tie out of her hair and was twisting it between her fingers. Shannon likes to twist something whenever she talks about matters that are important to her.

Her immediate problem was where to look. Straight eye contact was too intense for a serious conversation. It tended to turn into a who-blinks-first contest, and besides, Lydia always looked you right in the eyes when she lied, so Shannon had been raised not to trust the ones who overdid sincerity. But she couldn't just stare into space. He might think her mind was elsewhere.

"I know we've been in the same state as each other eight times in the last ten years."

Shannon stopped jiggling. "You kept count?"

Roger crossed his right ankle over his left thigh. He didn't waste any angst on where to look. He stared straight at Shannon.

"The first was Uncle Pete's funeral. That's when we met, although *met* might not be the proper word. Nobody introduced us, and I wasn't talking yet, so we didn't come in contact with each other, except once when I left the bathroom and you were waiting to go in. You said, 'What took you?' "

"I don't recall that."

"A couple years later, you flew in for Christmas and stayed a week. That's the first time we spoke back and forth. Maurey and I went down to North Carolina when you graduated college. The other times were in Wyoming."

Shannon absorbed all this. She didn't remember any of it. Roger had just been there, for ten years, part of the family, but not a part she'd taken notice of.

"Those are charming memories." She twisted the hair tie back into a high-riding ponytail. "But that's not what we're talking about."

"What are we talking about?"

She inhaled, glanced up at him, exhaled, looked away, and jumped in. "Has anyone ever told you about my boyfriends?"

Auburn had told Roger about Shannon's short-term serial-monogamy tendencies, although that's not the way he worded it. Auburn had said, *Our sister is a tramp.*

Now, in the Lompoc Comfort Inn, Roger considered Auburn's word and said, "No."

Shannon gave a joyless laugh. "I've had many boyfriends." She ran through a quick inventory to make certain that statement was correct. "The truth is I fall in love too quickly and then I fall back out too soon. It's a problem. I guess. It makes me feel inconsistent. I'm always in flux."

Roger nodded as if he understood. "If you were a boy, that wouldn't be a problem."

Shannon thought, *Isn't he sweet?* Then she said, "That's not true. Boys take pride in sex without emotional ties more than girls do, but falling in and out of love indiscriminately is a problem for either gender."

Roger said, "I didn't know that."

They fell into a comfortable silence. Even though she still wasn't sure where to look, Shannon felt much more at ease than she usually did when getting to know a new man. It was as if Roger wasn't a new man. He'd been around a long time, like when you discover the perfect shirt that has been hanging in the closet for years, but you didn't remember it, so it feels new even though it isn't.

Roger was wondering if he'd gotten Shannon's ears right in his portrait. He liked her ears. They were not like other girls' ears in that the top fold was softer and less pink, and the lobe didn't hang down. Roger had a theory that a girl's breasts were reflected in her earlobes, and Shannon had tight earlobes.

Shannon sighed, looking at her hands. "The truth is—I'm a mess."

Roger started to disagree, but he stopped. That's what anyone would do, and he didn't want to be just anyone. Besides, she was right.

Shannon spoke with her head down. "If I don't break the pattern, this will end badly, especially for you. We could ruin every Christmas and family reunion for the rest of our lives."

Roger recrossed his legs the other way. He cleared his throat. "Shannon, I know we're talking about something important, but you'll have to define what you mean by *this* if I'm going to know what."

Shannon blinked in surprise. "*This*? This is us. Don't you want to be a couple?"

Roger's response—after thinking his dream was coming true and not knowing whether that's a good thing or not—was to wonder if couples always lived together and, if so, where in the cabin he was going to put Shannon's stuff. He hadn't built storage for two.

"That's what I hoped you meant," he said. "Being a

couple with you has been a goal of mine since middle school. It just seems so sudden and far-fetched, I wasn't sure what you meant."

Shannon frowned. "Sudden is the problem. I've done sudden. Sudden ends in a train wreck, for me. We have to go slow."

Shannon bit the corner of her lip and considered ways to slow down courtship. In the past, she would meet a guy, sleep with the guy, move the guy into her house, and start choosing bridesmaids, pretty much simultaneously.

"The future has to be unique with you. It can't be like it was with the others. I have to handle every detail in this relationship different than what I've done before."

She stared hard at Roger, noticing he wasn't scared or nervous. She was scared and nervous and took it as a good sign that he wasn't.

"How do you normally go about relationships?" Shannon asked.

In his mind, Roger pictured the girls he had been with. "I've never had a relationship, that I know of."

"What about all those pregnant teenagers you sleep with?"

Roger shrugged. She liked his shrug. It was disarming without pretension or arrogance. He said, "None of that was a relationship. I was a familiar sex object, to them."

Shannon nodded, understanding what he meant. "And what were they to you?"

"Hell, Shannon. I'm twenty-one. No twenty-one-year-old guy is going to say *No* to a girl who wants him."

He could see right off that wasn't the right tack to take.

Shannon said, "When we're a couple, you better learn how to say no right quick."

Roger backed up. "Unless he's in true love with another girl. Which I will be. If we're together."

Shannon tore out of the stare. Eye contact had gone just the way she was afraid it would—all ego and want, none of it certain. "But you were already in love with me, before you slept with the hordes."

"That doesn't count. I never dreamed I had a shot with you. If I'd known you might like me back, I would have waited."

"Is that an excuse for promiscuity?"

"It's better than yours, for sleeping with your hordes." Roger put both feet on the floor and leaned toward her. "If you want to be a couple, we should start over fresh. Dwelling on the past will only cause hard feelings."

Shannon knew that was true. She'd been with guys who were jealous of former boyfriends. They always thought the exes were losers, dorks, jocks, poets, or any of the categories they considered themselves vastly superior to. They were insulted that Shannon could have ever liked such a poor choice for a man. It made them doubt themselves.

Shannon could tell from the leaning forward that Roger wanted more of the meeting-of-the-eyes thing, and she didn't. She didn't trust eye contact. She trusted skin contact, so she walked over and sat on Roger's lap. She sniffed behind his ear. He put his right hand on her lower back. Now they could talk without soulful looks. She could be honest without seeming to be evasive.

She murmured into his neck. "The reason I fall in and out of love so often is because I sleep with the guys too soon."

Roger enjoyed the breath on his neck. "In novels, sex leads to love. I never experienced it that way, myself."

"It does with me. Every time. One orgasm and I think I've found my prince. If we're going to be different and make this work where it hasn't before, we have to not sleep together."

Those were surprising words, coming from a girl sitting on his lap, breathing into his Adam's apple. Not what Roger had expected to hear. "You think the love will stick if we don't have sex?"

"It never stuck when I did have sex. We'll try it the other way."

Roger placed his left hand on Shannon's back, below her shoulder blade, and pulled her into him. For Roger, this was the most intimate moment of his life. He'd never felt a true connection before, and since he'd never felt one, he didn't know what it was or what he'd been missing. This was good jazz, a genre novel, a cup of coffee, and an early-morning piss outdoors all rolled into one—a person. This was deep satisfaction.

He said, "Forever?"

Shannon laughed and bit his earlobe. "Oh no. We'll fuck like cats someday." She felt his erection beneath her and wondered how long she could hold out. It would be intriguing to watch. "In the meantime, we'll date. Talk and eat, go for walks and neck ourselves into a frenzy like normal kids did back when Mom and Dad were young, so when we finally do it, the sex won't swamp the special thing between us."

This wasn't exactly Roger's dream of being a couple with Shannon. "I'm already in a frenzy over you."

Shannon hopped off his lap and walked over to the mirror to check herself out. "That makes me so happy." She met his eyes in the mirror. "We're going to have the longest foreplay in modern history."

MAUREY'S FIRST CLUE WAS THE TIFFANY-STYLE LAMP. IT LAY on the carpet—base, stem, and stained-glass shade pieces—but that was not necessarily conclusive. Lydia had a flair for the dramatic gesture, which often led to broken furnishings, and that was okay, so long as the trash job stayed in her own home. The results, however, tended to remain where they fell. Lydia couldn't see the point of throwing an object against a wall if she was the one to fetch the whisk broom and dustpan. Cleaning the mess was an admission that the gesture had been in vain.

So, the Tiffany-style lamp hinted at the breaking and entering Maurey expected, but it didn't confirm a crime. Vanilla soy milk on the kitchen floor did. No matter how off-the-handle Lydia let herself go, she wouldn't dribble. Then Maurey saw the rest of the milk and the carton on the counter and the broken pane of glass from the back door.

Leroy had been here. The fact he'd broken in when the door was unlocked only proved how stupid the yahoo was. A neighborhood kid looking for tranqs would have used the door. Anyone local would have used the door.

Maurey went through the house, searching for clues Leroy might have found. The closets had been rifled, and several of Lydia's two-piece outfits thrown on the bed. That seemed strange, even for Leroy.

She found the DuPree manuscript in the trash can and took it out. Maurey read the first page—a fairly graphic description of castration—then returned it to the trash.

Back in the kitchen, Maurey found a wadded-up sheet of yellow legal-pad paper on the floor beside the garbage pail. She carried the paper to the table, smoothed it out with her palm, and read Reasons Life Is Good written across the top left of the page and Reasons Life Stinks across the top right. No doubt Shannon's reckoning. Lydia wouldn't have left the right side of the page blank. From the corner of her peripheral vision, Maurey noticed the steady red light on the answering machine. On her machine at the TM Ranch, a blinking light signified a message no one had listened to, an unblinking light meant there was a message someone had played but not erased, and no light meant no message. Operating on the assumption that Lydia's machine worked the same as hers, Maurey reasoned that whatever message was on the machine had been heard, probably by Leroy.

BEEP.

"Hi, Lydia. It's me. Shannon. Shannon Callahan. I'm flying into Las Vegas this afternoon, and I need you to pick me up. I'm on Delta. The plane gets in at 4:10 p.m., which should leave you plenty of time to swing by and—"

BEEP.

"Get me. If I miss you guys, I'll fly on to Santa Barbara and leave a message on your phone as to when I'll be there. If I miss you in Santa Barbara, I'll go on to that writer's house. I'm sure I can track down anyone famous as Loren Paul."

BEEP.

"Don't let Roger get away."

Maurey picked up the phone and punched in the Madonnaville number.

I answered on the third ring. Because I held Baby Esther in my right arm and picked up the phone with my left hand, I dropped it—the phone—on the floor. Maurey waited while I shifted Esther from right to left and retrieved the phone.

I said, "Hey."

Maurey said, "The kids are in trouble."

"Do they need money?"

"Tell Gilia we're flying to Santa Barbara."

Esther yanked my glasses off and put the earpiece in her mouth. "All of us, or just you and me?"

"This isn't a vacation, Sam. There won't be any flights tonight, but I want you at the airport first thing tomorrow morning. And I mean my definition of first thing, not yours."

I got my glasses back and managed to put them back in place. I'm not one to handle a crisis blind.

"Can you pick me up, or should I meet you at the terminal? We're kind of short a vehicle."

"Have Gilia drive you down. We don't have time to carpool."

22

The Refried Boogie Bar was typical central California coast style—squishy asphalt, heavy neon, cinderblock, more pickups than cars out front. Greasy burgers and onion rings to the right, bar and tables to the left, dance floor the size of an elevator, soundless TV set to a Giants game. Juke box playing CDs. The bartender was an aging hippie who told Lydia his name was Red, he had a pot farm out in the national forest, and two kids in Head Start.

He said, "You want another of those?"

Lydia said, "How's your life turning out, Red? Things going about the way you expected?"

He eyed her a moment, flicked a bar rag toward her empty Jack Black on-the-rocks glass, and said, "You need anything, let me know."

"I'll do that." Lydia spun the bar stool to face out toward the tables and surveyed the room like reading a fast-food menu. It was mostly men, mostly not out hoping to hook up with a woman. This wasn't a singles bar. Two girls in cowboy hats and designer jeans line-danced to whatever country song was on the jukebox. Lydia didn't recognize the song or the female singer lamenting love for a man whose wife treated him poorly but he was too honorable to forsake her. Lydia was way beyond that. Country music couldn't touch her these days.

She zeroed in on a table of five working men, drinking beer and idly watching the line dancers. Four had on baseball caps that said things like CAT and DASH. The cockiest-looking one of the bunch wore his cap backward, but the others wore them straight. The kid without a cap had clunky glasses, a San Jose Sharks windbreaker, and curly hair and looked too young to be in the bar. He was nursing something either stronger or weaker than beer. Lydia couldn't tell which, only that it came in a glass instead of a bottle.

The cocky one saw Lydia watching them. He pointed a bottle lip in her general direction and said something that made the others chuckle. Nothing overtly aggressive. The scene was low-key as ladies sewing a crazy quilt.

When Lydia reached the table, she discovered they were discussing the benefits of an I-beam suspension. The guy with his hat on backward held strong opinions. He hated Ford trucks with a passion normally reserved for interpersonal relationships.

"Ford ain't been worth flying horse manure since 1982," and the others nodded knowingly, all except the young one in glasses, who looked at Lydia.

"You fellas up for a test?" Lydia asked.

"Urine or blood?" the oldest one said, and none of the others smiled. Lydia realized he wasn't being cute.

"History," Lydia said.

The old guy looked nervous. The cocky one with the backward hat said, "What do we get if we pass?"

"A surprise," Lydia said. "Now, can any of you tell me who Valerie Solanas was?"

The four in caps looked at each other with beats-me eyes. The young one took a sip of whatever he was drinking and said, "She's the woman shot Andy Warhol."

"Who's Andy Warhol?" asked the old guy.

"Artist," the kid said.

The cocky bastard leaned his chair back on two legs. "How the hell do you know who this woman was who shot him?"

The kid pushed his glasses up on his nose. They were the boxy, thick-framed type made popular by Elvis Costello. "My grandma was a bra burner."

The others laughed. Lydia thought, *Grandma?*

"My sister and I stayed summers with her in Monterey. She knew the whole history of bra burning. Used to talk about the crazy things the women would do to get at men."

"Did she ever tell you about Lydia Callahan?" Lydia asked.

He scratched his wrist and thought. "No. I don't think so."

"That is immaterial," Lydia said. "You know the answer, so you win the prize."

"What prize is that?" Backward Cap asked.

Lydia tapped the kid on the head. "Come with me."

He said, "Yes, ma'am."

"Call me *ma'am* once more, and the deal is off."

———

Shannon and Roger lay on his queen bed, on top of the spread, fully clothed except for their shoes. Shannon had insisted Roger take off his shoes. He wouldn't have had the nerve on his own. They'd doubled the pillows, and he lay on his back with Shannon's head on the stretch of chest below his shoulder. His arm was around her, and her hands were curled together on his sternum. They were both more comfortable than they could remember being before, with members of the other gender. Roger was almost asleep.

"Tell me about the first time we were alone together," Shannon said. "Did you know I was the one then, or did it come to you later?"

"Some then, but mostly later," Roger said. "I was too young to think of anybody as *the one*. I just remember I wanted to see you naked."

Shannon smiled and poked a finger into Roger's ribs. "I bet you thought that about every girl you met."

"Maybe." Roger tried to recall the girls he'd met in his early years in Wyoming. "We didn't have a lot of girls at the TM Ranch, and the ones we did have were recovering alcoholics or drug addicts or something. Maurey was always taking in lost souls. That's why I was there."

"You were a lost soul?"

"I was a little kid who couldn't take care of himself, and no one else wanted to, besides Maurey. I wasn't speaking out loud back then. People treated me like I was retarded, or whatever the word is now. Maurey's the only one acted like I was a person."

"What about me?"

Roger stared at the ceiling. "By that second time you came—a couple of Christmases after Uncle Pete died—I'd started talking. We had a conversation."

Shannon snuggled deeper into Roger. It felt natural as the sun coming up. "What'd I say?"

Roger dropped his head so his chin momentarily rested on the top of her head. He ran his fingers up her back, then back down. "Christmas Eve, I went out to the barn to check on Rip. He had a lung infection, and we'd put him up in a stall for doctoring."

"Rip's a horse?"

"Don't you remember Rip Torn?"

"Sorry."

"I found you in the tack room, sitting on a saddle, smoking a joint."

Shannon flattened her right hand on Roger's belly. "Oh my."

"You seemed lonely."

"I don't smoke joints anymore, Roger. You should know that about me. I'm more interested in caffeine than marijuana."

"You said, 'Don't tell Mom. She'll freak out and pull an intervention on me,' and I said, 'I won't tell.'"

"Did I offer you a toke?"

"No. I sat on a bale, and you told me the right way to make divinity. You said in Carolina, every house you went to had divinity at Christmastime, and all anyone had in Wyoming was candy corn, and you hated Wyoming."

"I was so self-obsessed back then. I must have been a total pain to be around. It's the family curse. My greatest fear is I might grow up like Lydia."

"Lydia's not so bad."

Shannon raised her face off Roger's shirt and looked at him. "She dragged you all the way out here on false hopes, just to catch a ride so she could talk to Hank in prison."

"What makes you think my hopes are false?"

Shannon lowered her head to his chest again. This was comfortable. She felt like she could say anything true, and Roger wouldn't turn mean on her. "No one let me in on the trip details, but from what I've picked up, she wants you to believe you're a little boy in a novel."

Roger hadn't faced it quite so bluntly before. He'd said as much to Lydia, but not with any conviction. The idea that he was a character in a made-up story was ridiculous. He began to wonder what had possessed him to come on this trip. Was he so desperate for a past, he'd been willing to take off across America with no more evidence than what Lydia had dug up in an old book? That was pathetic.

Shannon sensed she'd made him unhappy. She reached across his body and squeezed him. "I'm sorry, Roger. I don't want to be a spoilsport. It's just, what are the odds?"

His thought process went on to the next conclusion. "If I

hadn't let Lydia bring me to California, we wouldn't by lying here. We might not have become a couple."

"That still doesn't make me want to end up like Lydia."

The door opened without anyone knocking, and Oly rolled in, still wearing boxers and nothing else. He had the now-empty rum bottle between his flappy legs. Lydia was pushing the chair.

She said, "Look who got lost."

Shannon said, "He wasn't lost."

"Your turn to baby-sit." Then Lydia was gone. She didn't even shut the door.

Roger slid out from under Shannon. He stood and moved over behind Oly. "You ready for bed, Pard?"

Oly was worked up. His eyes popped in a cross between drunk and stimulated. He said, "She brought home a boy."

Shannon sat up and stared at him.

Oly's mouth was a drooly crack. "Lydia went out and got herself a boy to play with."

———

His name was Warren. He was standing right where Lydia had left him, in front of the air conditioner. He would have been staring out the window at the parking lot, had the curtains been open. As it was, Warren appeared lost in curly-haired introspection.

Lydia said, "How old are you, Warren?" She'd kicked off her shoes and was sitting on the bed with her legs crossed, almost, but not quite, seductively.

Warren turned away from the curtains. "Twenty-three."

Lydia arched an eyebrow at him.

He said, "Twenty."

Standing in the motel room, away from the bar and peer pressure, Warren looked to have more confidence than he had earlier. In the car, he had asked no questions about where they were going. At the Comfort Inn, he asked no questions about why they were there or where she was taking the ancient gnome in the wheelchair. He seemed to know instinctively what was expected of him.

To Lydia, no one able to tell you the story of Valerie Solanas could be a total idiot. That's why she had given the men the test. She wasn't simply searching for an anonymous dick—not at her age.

"How do you spend your days, Warren?"

"I hang Sheetrock for my uncle Mark." Warren made no move to come toward her or to sit down. He hadn't even taken off the Sharks windbreaker. "He was at the table there. The whole crew was at the table. I'm kind of nervous about what they're going to say Tuesday, when we go back to the job site."

Lydia patted the bed next to her—an invitation. "You'll be a hero, Warren. Trust me on this. They'll make jokes and tease you about robbing the grave, but each and every one of those good old boys will wish he'd been chosen."

Warren moved over and sat where Lydia had shown him. He kept his hands on his thighs, palms down. "I wonder if Uncle Mark will tell Mom."

"Not likely. Men tend to cover for each other."

"You know a lot about men, for being a woman."

"Studying men is a hobby of mine. Always has been, since I was a child. I take it quite seriously." She reached over and brushed a curl of hair off his forehead. He reminded her of a boy she'd known in high school, a boy she knew was secretly smitten by her. For two years, the kid tried to work up the nerve to ask her out, and she would have gladly gone, but he never did ask, and for some reason she couldn't explain to herself, Lydia didn't take the step necessary to help him. It was as if she wanted to know him better, but if he was too much of a coward to make his move, she was willing to pass. Now, she regretted her lack of initiative. Lydia firmly believed it's the ones you could have had and skipped that haunt you more than the ones you had, no matter how good or bad they turned out to be.

Lydia said, "You know the drill here?"

He stared down at the carpet between his feet. "We're supposed to do the dirty, right?"

"That is correct." She took his glasses and placed them on the bed, on the side away from Warren. "Have you ever had sex before, Warren?"

He blinked in his new near blindness. "Of course."

Lydia waited.

He said, "Do blow jobs count?"

"Yes," Lydia said. "Blow jobs count, Warren, no matter how much men pretend they don't, blowjobs do count."

He nodded. "Well then, I guess I have. Had sex before."

She reached across to help him out of his windbreaker. He held up one arm, then the other, not exactly cooperating, but not resisting either.

Lydia said, "Let's take this slow and easy, okay, Warren? I'm out of practice, and you're new to the game. We want the experience to be something you'll remember fondly when you're my age."

Warren finally turned toward Lydia. He looked into her eyes and said, "What should I do first?"

———

Shannon and Roger had moved under the sheets, facing each other, wearing nothing but boxers on him and panties on her. In the next bed, Oly made the sounds of an old man sleeping, although they couldn't be certain that's what he was. Oly's breathing always sounded like a bugling elk, even when he was awake, or to be precise, a bugling elk on the inhale and a train whistle on the exhale. Awake or asleep didn't affect Oly much.

Shannon held her right palm flat against Roger's chest. His hands lay inert at his sides. The arm on bottom was not only inert but also prickly dead.

"I need you to do me the biggest favor in the whole world," Shannon said.

Roger tried to think of the biggest favor in the whole world. His ideas on the subject were much too complex. "Sure. I'll do whatever you want."

"I want you to smell me."

"I can do that."

"Down there." Her eyelids blinked in the direction she had in mind. "Someone recently wounded me deeply by saying I smell badly. Down there. He compared me to rancid shrimp."

"That's cruel. He must have been in love with you."

Once again, Shannon marveled at Roger's intuition. How could a kid his age with practically no experience at relationships always come up with the right thing to say? It was like he was throwing out lines, only they were original and sincere coming from Roger where they wouldn't have been coming from a man of the world. She said, "It's awfully sweet of you to say so, but I think he only wanted to cause me pain. I'd rejected him, and he struck out with whatever he had."

The prospect of going down there wasn't nearly as intriguing as you would think for Roger. For one thing, he wasn't certain what it's supposed to smell like. He'd tried a couple of times, at the urging of his pregnant girls, and the logistics had been insurmountable.

"Hurting me was his way of regaining his pride," Shannon said, "but now I'm totally paranoid. I saw people sniffing on the plane, and I was sure they were sniffing me. I worry about it all the time."

"You shouldn't let assholes control you."

"I know that. What I don't know is how he came up with the idea. Sometimes when people say things to be cruel, they're telling the truth."

"Okay." Roger didn't move. He was wondering what life would be like with this woman, if they were fated to be a couple, which evidently was what she had in mind. She seemed to have been raised to think abnormal behavior was normal. Roger had little experience distinguishing normal from abnormal. He was, after all, the boy whose entire sexual history consisted of pregnant teens. But he had some grasp of what regular women do and don't do, and asking a man you've only gotten to know that day and never been with conjugally to smell your snatch didn't seem regular.

Shannon blamed me for her way of accepting bizarre behavior as commonplace, and I blamed Lydia. Lydia didn't think about such things.

"Well," Shannon said.

"Well, what?"

"Will you?"

Roger glanced over at Oly and started shrugging down into the sheets.

"It's vitally important that you be honest," Shannon said. "No matter how much you may think I don't want to hear the truth, you have to give it to me. If I can't trust you on this, I'll never be able to trust you and I'll go on being paranoid. I might turn into one of those high-strung women who can't leave their house and communicates with folks through a mail slot."

Roger's voice came from deep under the covers. "I'll tell the truth."

Shannon lifted the sheet with her fingertips to give Roger air. "You'd better, or we might as well call it quits right here."

Roger's cheek brushed Shannon's breast as he scrunched low in the bed. In the pitch-blackness, he felt heat rising off her stomach. She was soft as a rose petal down there, not like the over-inflated volleyball skin he'd felt on the eight-months-along girls. Most of them had not encouraged Roger to go down. They were too young or too pregnant to feel comfortable with the procedure, so Roger had little experience at slithering down a bed. The sheets were tucked tightly. He had to crumple his legs in an uncomfortable way. Shannon did nothing—such as sliding toward the headboard—to help.

She said, "Well?"

He said, "Just a minute."

He found the hem of her panties and lifted it away from her skin.

"Don't touch," Shannon said. "We don't want to start something we can't stop. Just smell."

Roger sniffed. He smelled talcum powder and maybe some fabric softener, but not much else. He said, "I'm coming up."

After Roger hunched back up Shannon's body and into the original position, she said, "Give it to me straight."

"Lemon drops," he said.

"Don't mess with me."

"And fresh snow on sagebrush."

Shannon smiled. She couldn't recall smelling fresh snow on sagebrush, but it sounded pleasant. Damp, maybe, but not too damp. More of a bracing chill. She liked sage. "What else?"

"The tiniest hint of clove, or cinnamon. I'm not sure which, but whatever it is reminds me of pies on Christmas."

"No fish?"

"No fish. Just clean air after a spring rain."

They cuddled quietly. Shannon didn't buy clove, cinnamon, or spring rain, but she was reassured about the fish. He wouldn't have been nearly so quick with the answers if he'd had to lie in a bad way.

Shannon said, "All men are full of shit, Roger, but you carry it off with style."

———

The kid slept with his mouth open and one hand under his cheek like a curly-haired angel child. A drool track traced off his lower lip edge. His neck sported a bruise the size of a Mandarin orange. Lydia wondered when she had inflicted the bruise. It had been a long night, and she'd introduced him to new concepts. The boy was a quick study.

There's good sex and mediocre sex, and then on an entirely separate plane, there's sex that makes you feel good about yourself and sex that makes you feel bad about yourself. Warren had started as mediocre, but after training, he'd evolved into decent. His technique with young girls would never be the same, anyway.

But good, mediocre, or decent, the sex had not made Lydia feel good about herself. The truth is, she felt like a monster. Her stomach gorge rose up against the gag reflex. Her sinuses throbbed.

She blamed Hank in every way. Hank had ruined all forms of pleasure for her by asking for nothing. If he'd ask her to stay monogamous while he was in prison, she could have said, *Fuck you,* and stayed monogamous without his knowing it. He'd never asked, so she never had a wall to strike out against.

She sat, nude, in the plastic, flesh-adhering chair with her feet propped on the air conditioner, watching Warren sleep and wishing she still smoked. She could smoke if she wanted to. She couldn't remember why she quit. Everyone had been quitting back then. Not quitting felt stupid, but she'd never been motivated by what everyone did or what wasn't stupid. She simply hated dependencies. Lydia had a talent for walking away from dependencies.

And now there was Hank Elkrunner, her husband, her protector during the fugitive years, and the man in prison because he stood by her. Screw that.

The strong woman does not allow love to confine her. The strong woman does not feel guilt. The strong woman does not grow old needy. Lydia lived by these words, and she was worthless without them. Throughout her own years in prison, she had repeated them like a personal Ten Commandments. *Thou shalt not be rescued by a man.*

The losses started with Sparkle Horse. Sparkle Horse was a stuffed pony—fake velvet or plush, as Lydia recalled—and Sparkle Horse was her best friend when she was four, five, six, and seven. Lydia carried Sparkle Horse everywhere. She couldn't possibly sleep without him. She chewed his ear to the point where his head was misshapen and someone first seeing him would not have recognized a horse.

Then, one fall day, Lydia's father, Casper, invited Lydia to his golf club for lunch—a daddy/daughter affair. A big deal for both of them—only Casper wouldn't let Lydia bring Sparkle Horse to the club dining room. Lydia spent the entire lunch sobbing. Casper said he would never bring her again.

That night after supper, Lydia threw Sparkle Horse into a huge pile of post-oak leaves. She lit a safety match, the first of her life, and dropped it onto the leaf pile. Lydia stood in the front yard in her blue jumper and T-strap sandals and watched the flames lick Sparkle Horse. Soon, thick smoke obscured him from her sight. She turned to see Casper watching from the library window. Lydia went around the house to the back door, went into her room, and lay on the bed.

Lydia never thought about Sparkle Horse again, for fifty years, until dawn at the Comfort Inn in Lompoc. Now, the grief broke through her chest. Lydia knew her entire life, from the day she burned him, would have been different if she had saved her friend. She would be different. She couldn't understand why she had killed Sparkle Horse—Lydia didn't think in terms of why she did what she did. In her memory, it had not been a choice. It was what she did. Tonight—Warren—was what she did. To ask why was to waste thought.

"FRIDAY NIGHT, AFTER FREEDOM TOOK HIS HOT LITTLE HUSSY AND left, I couldn't sleep. I got myself all worked up from wondering if I may have helped cause this mess," Maurey said. "I don't see where I had a choice, but still, if I hadn't taken Mary Beth to Oklahoma, Freedom's son might not have run away, and Freedom might not have snatched Roger. Fred."

We were on a morning flight from Salt Lake City to LAX, and because we'd bought our tickets at the last possible moment, I was stuck in the middle seat of a three-seat row, between Maurey and a young woman who was weeping. The woman in the knit pantsuit was not only weeping so fiercely tears streamed down her cheeks and dripped from her pointy chin, she also had a mirror propped on the food tray and she was frying her hair with what looked like twin prongs on the end of a flashlight. Curling her hair into blonde ringlets meant sticking her left elbow into the side of my face, and between that and the weeping, I was too distracted to follow Maurey's odd confession.

In order to keep Maurey talking, I said, "What's that?"

"The trip I made with Shane and Lloyd in the ambulance, smuggling Coors to the South that time. We picked Mary Beth up hitchhiking in New Mexico and took her to a house full of hippies and drug fiends in Comanche, Oklahoma. Freedom was there. He was Mary Beth's old man back when she was called Critter."

"Boyfriend?"

Maurey nodded. *"He had a kid named Hawk that he treated like trash. Hawk hid in the ambulance, and we found him a hundred miles later, near Arkansas. He changed his name to Brad and stayed with us to Carolina. He lives in France now. He's an artist."*

Maurey had never told me much about that drive from GroVont to Georgia. It was when she jumped from practicing alcoholic to recovering alcoholic. She's been recovering ever since. I always wondered what prompted her to stop drinking, and I was interested in finding out, but the blubbering woman kept whacking me with her elbow. She swung the prong things close to my ear, and I've had enough experience with teenage girls to know you don't want to get poked by curling iron prongs.

"I've tried to calculate when Freedom kidnapped the child," Maurey said. *"According to what Roger told me about the* Disappearance *book, Fred was five at the time he was snatched, and Roger was eleven, maybe twelve, when Mary Beth brought him to the ranch. That would mean Freedom stole him the summer after I helped Brad run away. What if there's a cause and effect? What if me taking one boy pushed Freedom off the deep end so far, he kidnapped another boy? That would mean I am partially responsible for Roger's mother's suicide."*

"That's a pretty far guilt reach," I said. *"Ouch."*

The weeping woman had swung her curling iron into my right earlobe. I said, "Watch out."

The woman gave me a look of helpless contempt and continued weeping and curling.

Here's one of the big differences between living in Wyoming and living in North Carolina. A person sitting beside a weeping woman in North Carolina will offer consolation. Can I help you, honey? *Whereas a person from Wyoming will figure the cause of the crying is none of their business, and if the woman wants help, she'll ask for it. I'm from North Carolina, but I live in Wyoming, and we were in the air over Nevada, so I wasn't certain what I was supposed to do. As the woman worked her way across her scalp, the weeping escalated into moaning. She was difficult to pretend to ignore.*

"What are the odds of you causing a kidnapping, then raising the victim?" I said. "It's too random to be believable."

Maurey sipped from her rank cup of airplane coffee. She made a face and said, "It's not random if you factor Mary Beth in as the link. She was with Freedom in Oklahoma. She brought me Roger. Freedom must have gone to Mary Beth and found out where she left the boy. But he doesn't seem to remember I was at the house the day Brad ran away. Hell, the way that house operated, Brad could have been gone a week before Freedom noticed. He might not know I was the one who helped the kid escape."

After one particularly gut-wrenched snivel, I broke down and intervened. Turning to the weeping woman, I said, "Are you in trouble? Do you need any help?"

The woman swung the curling iron into my face and yelled, "Stay away from me, you stupid pervert!"

I jumped away from the hot iron, bumping Maurey's hand and spilling coffee.

Maurey said, "Jesus, Sam, what did you do this time?"

23

No wall topped by barbed wire, broken glass, and machine-gun turrets, no electric doors slamming shut with the finality of death, no purse search or body pat down—federal minimum security is about as intimidating as a Tucson fat farm. Loved ones don't even meet the inmates indoors. A khaki-clad guard with all the authority of a doughnut led Lydia out back to the landscaped grounds and pointed across the grass to Hank, who sat at a picnic table next to a pecan tree, reading a book.

Lydia stood, momentarily frozen in place. She didn't know where to start. For one thing, they'd cut his hair. I should have prepared her for Hank in a crew cut, but the damage had been done years ago, before his trial. I'd been afraid to tell her then, and after a while, I got so used to the new look that her reaction slipped my mind. The thing is, when you throw the fear of God into people, to the point where they are afraid to say anything you don't want to hear, you risk missing out on vital information.

Lydia thought short hair made Hank look foolish, in the same way he would have looked in Bermuda shorts at the rodeo. Blackfeet warlocks had always been such a part of him, they had become mixed up in her notions of who he was. The new Hank seemed white.

Lydia fell back on her standard method of dealing with anxiety. She turned her obnoxious side loose. "Have you lost your manners in this country club?"

Hank looked up from his book and smiled. It as all Lydia could do not to launch herself into his arms.

"Lydia." He stood up and came around the picnic table and hugged her. They were both shy, after three years, and the hug came off as awkward. First, Hank held too tightly while Lydia kind of clutched and sniffed, then Lydia melted into him and held tightly herself, when Hank was ready to break off and study her from arm's length. Neither one of them came from a family background of easy hugs. They were both better at sex than affection.

"You've gained weight," Lydia said.

Hank patted himself on the belly. He was wearing a denim shirt and green pants, nothing vaguely close to a prison uniform. "They feed me regular-like."

"No, your new weight is muscle. They've turned you into one of those prison jocks who spends four hours a day in the weight room."

"It's either that or television," Hank said. "I never was much for television."

They moved back to the picnic table and sat facing each other, touching fingertips across the table. Lydia was frightened. She'd thought about the moment for so long that she didn't know what angle to come from. She knew she had something important to explain to Hank, but she had no notion exactly what it was that was so important or how she would explain it to him even if she figured out what it was. The hair had thrown her off her rehearsed attitude.

"Are they treating you like a dirty Indian?" she asked.

Hank shook his head. "I'm older than most of the others. There's a rumor around that I'm a wise medicine man. The kids ask my advice on spiritual matters."

Lydia blew air out of her mouth, up toward her bangs. "You're about as spiritual as Burger King."

"You'd be surprised." Hank grinned. One thing about the federal penal system, you come out with better teeth than you had going in. "If I cross my arms and say"—*deep voice*—"'It is a good day to die'"—*normal voice*—"they think I am a Vedic seer."

Lydia wondered when Hank had discovered Vedic seers, and if he knew they were not his sort of Indian. She had trouble telling when he was ignorant and when he was being funny. The Blackfeet sense of humor tends to be so low-key most people miss it. She picked up the book and turned it around so the title was facing her—*Okla Hanali* by R. A. Lafferty.

"It's about a Choctaw," Hank said.

Lydia said, "How sweet."

She swiveled around the picnic bench to check out the grounds. A couple of men—she couldn't tell whether they were inmates, guards, or dining room help—jogged along a path through the trees. A guy in tennis shorts and no shirt rode a lawn mower back and forth over by an outbuilding. The place seemed fairly deserted.

"Where are the dregs of society?" she asked.

"Work. Everybody has a job, and those who won't work spend fifteen days over in maximum." Hank nodded toward a white block of building in the distance. To Lydia, it had the architectural charm of a Costco. "That cures the lazy ones right quick," Hank said.

Lydia turned back to Hank. "You have a job here?"

"I'm gardener to the warden. His house is down that way."

Lydia frowned. "That makes you the head screw's farmer."

Hank chuckled, a low, throaty chuckle that hadn't changed in thirty years. "I grow flowers, mostly. And trim shrubbery. He has a huge fig tree in his yard, big as any tree in Teton

County. Tiny wasps live on it. They're born in the leaves and eat the old figs. Far as I can tell, those wasps never leave that one tree their whole life."

Lydia drummed her fingers impatiently. "What's the metaphor, Hank? I don't get it."

Hank frowned down at his book. "No metaphor. Just a tree and wasps. I take care of them."

Lydia said, "I didn't come all this was to discuss figs. We're here to talk about me."

Hank sat with his fingers in the shape of a net. His unblinking gaze appeared aimed at Lydia's breasts, but it wasn't. He was focused about six inches this side of her, considering the options. Hank knew Lydia better than anyone else ever had, including Lydia herself. He'd made Lydia studies a life-long quest, and he knew she hadn't risked a parole violation to drive a thousand miles just to say hello.

"So tell me," Hank said. "How have you been?"

Her face flushed a dark shade. "Terrible. Wretched." She searched for a more forceful way to put it. "The status quo is unacceptable. I cannot live this way, and you know that I am not exaggerating for the sake of drama. I will not tolerate this, Hank."

"And this is?"

"You in here." Her body language took in the entire penal system. "And me out there."

Hank's voice was maddeningly calm. He'd always reacted to her hysteria with maddening calmness. It was the single trait she hated most about him.

Hank said, "That's not something we control."

"It's not fair that I committed the crime, but I'm free and you're not."

For the first time since she'd arrived, Hank registered surprise. "Fair? Since when do you demand fair? Your life has never been fair. You were born white and rich. Why did you wait till now to start complaining?

"I've always complained."

"Not about fairness."

She thought. "Okay, it isn't fairness so much as guilt. And shame. And hatred of addiction." Lydia looked in the distance toward maximum. "I'm so afraid of losing you, I'm terrified I'll be forced to destroy you, like Sparkle Horse."

"Who?"

"I cannot risk holding on until you come back home and then losing you again. What if you die? I'd rather kill you than take that chance."

Hank reached for Lydia's hands, but she wouldn't cooperate. She pulled them away.

He said, "The possibility of loss is what gives life depth."

"Just because the scum thinks you're a Vedic seer, don't let it go to your head." Lydia stood up, turned around 360 degrees, and sat back down again. She looked Hank straight in the eyes. "I'm Lydia Callahan. I cannot be defined by a man, even someone as wonderful as you. That would mean my life's work is meaningless, and after seven years on the run and three in prison, I cannot stand for my life's work to be meaningless."

Hank stared back for a full minute. In the silence, the distant mower grew louder as it crossed the rolling lawn, heading toward the main prison block.

Hank blinked first. "Why are you telling me this?"

"I screwed a boy last night."

Hank said, "I know."

"You don't know." Lydia balled her fists. "All right, you do know, but how?"

"Lydia you have a gift for hiding emotions, but you've never been able to hide getting laid." Hank reached over and touched her hairline at the temple. She flinched. He said, "In here. There's a tension line that runs through here. When you make love it relaxes for a few hours." He ran his finger down her temple toward her earlobe. "I know you."

Lydia's eyes glistened like oil on a puddle. "It was the first time. Since you."

"I know that too."

She slammed a fist on the table. "Christ, I hate it when you say *I know*. You're so smug you make me barf."

"I know."

The last *I know* was Hank's way of defusing tension, and Lydia almost fell for it, but instead she leaned back, not willing to give him control over the mood. "I just couldn't see you today knowing I'd never betrayed you. I couldn't do it."

"Proving you could sleep with anyone anytime was the only way you could face yourself."

"It's more than pride. I had to smash your *fucking face you bastard*."

The shout shocked them both. Neither knew where that level of anger had sprung from. Lydia's skin had gone Spearmint gum gray, and her hands shook so badly she hid them in her lap. "Everyone I ever loved was destroyed because of me. I can't deal with it being random. I have to cause the pain before it comes from outside."

Although her line of reasoning twisted about and doubled back on itself, Hank was able to follow Lydia perfectly.

"So you had to destroy me on purpose before you destroyed me accidentally."

"Yes."

He turned his palms over and spread his hands. "It didn't work. Look at me."

Lydia looked at him.

"Do I look destroyed to you?"

Hank looked the same as he had when they sat down, before

she dropped her bomb. "Hell, Hank, you're so good at that wooden Indian face, no one can tell."

"I can tell, and the way I care for you hasn't changed."

"How can that be? I fucked a kid named Warren. He got me off, eventually."

"We've been together thirty years," Hank said. "Don't you figure I know who you are and what you are capable of, and more important, what you're not capable of, by now. You're God's own woman, but remorse doesn't become you."

"Become?"

Hank nodded. "It's missing from you like a blind colt missing its sight. The colt can't comprehend what it would be like to see. When you try faking remorse because you think that's what a normal person would feel, you get all screwed up inside."

Lydia started to weep for the first time in Hank's memory. He was so stunned he almost shut up. But she'd come this far to disillusion his heart, or whatever the hell she thought she was doing. He couldn't very well stop short.

Hank said, "I love the mountain lion. Does that mean I want to pull the teeth from the mountain lion to make it safer?"

"If you married one, you might."

"Then it would no longer be a mountain lion. If I demanded—or expected or even dreamed of—normal behavior from you, you would no longer be Lydia."

Lydia didn't try to stop the tears. She didn't touch her face or sniffle or any of the gestures most women make when crying. Maybe she was so new to tears she didn't know how to use them.

"So you don't care who I sleep with."

"Of course I care. But me loving you and you loving me loses every shred of truth if you are confined by duty."

Lydia thought about this a long time, long enough to cry

herself out. Finally, she said, "There's a really good chance that you're nuts."

"Probably."

Neither of them spoke for ten minutes. Lydia watched the man on the riding lawn mower pull up before a door, get off the mower, and scratching his belly, he went inside. He came back out with a bottle of what, from Lydia's perspective, looked like Calistoga water, and stood staring at the mower, drinking.

Hank's eyes were on a pair of hummingbirds fighting over a feeder. Even though the feeder had four fake flowers with holes leading to sugar water, neither hummingbird would allow the other to drink, so they battled like fiends and both went hungry. Hank didn't see a lick of a life lesson in this. He wasn't thinking in those terms.

Lydia said, "I've lost my power."

Hank looked from the hummingbird feeder back to Lydia, whose lower lip puffed out like a child who's been told *No*. He said, "I don't think so."

"No one pays any attention to me anymore. If I scream, they treat me like an elderly eccentric. 'Oh, that's just Lydia. Don't bother about her. She's harmless.'"

Lydia thought about the Mexican at the gas station the day before. She still couldn't get over how he'd deflected her charm. He'd behaved as if they had no common ground, as if she were the enemy. Even gay men paid attention when she wanted them to. There wasn't a man at that table in the Refried Boogie Bar who wouldn't have gone with her. Why had the gas-station attendant been so mean-spirited?

Lydia said, "I'm hauling around this ninety-nine-year-old geezer. Nobody in their wildest imaginations would ever think he has deep emotions. People *humor* him. I *humor* him. I hear the story of his past, and it doesn't matter who he loved and hated and lost, because all those people would be dead by now anyway. What does it matter if he lost them at thirty or eighty? They're gone. It means nothing that the old fart once took up space."

"He still does."

"Not space anyone cares about." Lydia frowned at the thought of Oly Pedersen. It offended her no end that he could stand what he'd become and the way people viewed him. He should be enraged, but he wasn't. What was all that about?

Lydia's hands formed into fists, thumbs inside fingers. "That empty bag doesn't want to die. He's got no one. He can't do anything he used to do, and no one who remembers his youth is still alive, but he's not ready to get out of the way."

Hank touched her hand, and this time she didn't flinch. He said, "I can make you a guarantee, Lydia. You will never be harmless."

Her eyes flashed with a hint of the old flame. "I sure as hell wasn't harmless last night. I hurt myself but good. It was like self-rape. It was filthy."

"But you didn't hurt me."

The flame left Lydia's eyes. Her shoulders slumped. "That's the cruelest thing you could have said."

24

LYDIA LEFT A NOTE ON THE AIR-CONDITIONER CONTROL BOX:

I'm taking two hours, maybe three. Make yourselves useful by recording the next round of the old man's hogwash. Be prepared to leave before checkout. That is 11 a.m., Pacific Time.

———

The winter of 1923 to 1924, I went insane. It wasn't pretty neither. People talk about craziness like it's a vacation from responsibility, but in my case, anyway, it meant a horrid loss of perspective. I howled to the coyotes. My insides rebelled, and I vomited upon the earth. I tore flesh from my skin. And to make the situation worse, I did so in secrecy.

Here I was, in what should have been the happiest part of my life, and I was in the miserablest. Around Evangeline, I acted the proud husband and father-to-be. Always a smile. Never a whine. While away from her, my guts were being eaten alive, like in the dream of the bear. If Evangeline was keeping secrets from me, I was keeping just as many secrets from her. Try it sometime: try acting thrilled to the core when you're about to die of doubt.

Rangering in Yellowstone in winter holds no correspondence to rangering in summer. November, I was stationed on and off at Buffalo Ranch in Lamar Valley, cutting hay and fixing fence knocked down by the tame herd. This was awful, as my imagination ran rampant wondering what Evangeline and Bill were up to in my absence, but at least there were people around. Keeping appearances up will get you through most hard times, simply because faked sanity is superior to insanity. When I worked, I could block out the pictures in my head. I could not block the pictures at night, although the cabin where I slept was shared with others, so I had to keep quiet—no screams at midnight. Some mornings I awoke to find I'd bitten my arms to alleviate the pain.

I spent Christmas home with Evangeline. Pregnancy suited her. A peace descended over my wife that was a marvel to behold. Her skin glowed. Her hair shone. She must have felt the nausea and discomfort inherent to her condition, but if so, she never complained. She showed complete satisfaction with the moment.

Only once did she ask how I was holding up. Our first anniversary, New Year's Eve 1923, we were lying in bed, faced together, lost in one another's eyes, and she said, "Are you content?"

And I said, "Of course, I'm content. Why do you ask?"

"You looked worried this afternoon, when you carried in the firewood."

I hadn't known she was looking at me then. "I was concerned I'd get enough cut for you and the baby before I go on patrol."

She smiled, more to herself than me. "Crow women split wood till the day the baby is born. The next day they get up and split more. You shouldn't spoil me with white ways."

I said, "I'll spoil you any ways I can."

Then, while Evangeline slept I imagined her naked in this very bed as Bill Cox mounted her and the both of them laughed at my innocence.

After New Year's, the park put me on snowshoes and sent me back to border patrol south of Lewis Lake. I was alone. The temperature hovered between thirty and forty below zero, some-times dropping to the point where it fell below the calibration line on the thermometer. At night, the trees cracked like gunshots.

Those were the weeks I crossed the line from overwrought to full-blown crazy. Ofttimes, I was so paralyzed by terror I was unable to rise from bed for thinking of Bill Cox and what he said he did and what I should of done to him for saying it. Luckily, I went to ground at a line shack up on the Thoroughfare, and I could have stayed in bed for weeks with none the wiser.

On my better days, I was certain Bill was lying—hell, he lied all the time in France—and on my worse days, I was just as certain he spoke true. Worse days outnumbered better ones. I thought of asking Shad since a big part of diddling women for Bill was going back to brag to Shad. I think he enjoyed the bragging more than the diddling. Only I wasn't sure I could believe whatever answer Shad gave me, and if I did believe it and it confirmed my fears, I was fairly sure to die. Some nights, death felt preferable to uncertainty, and I might have chosen the coward's way had that not meant leaving Evangeline and the baby to fend for themselves. I could never go that route, whether the child was from my seed or not.

—

Full moon, early May, I came to myself barefoot and drooling along the ridge that looks down on the Old Faithful Geyser. My rangering shirt was tatters, although still on my back. The pockets of my trousers were inside out. Needless to say, on top of madness, I had broken my sacred vow to Evangeline—the only vow she'd ever asked for—and reverted to drink. I'd found a bottle of white hooch the man before me hid in the Upper Basin Station.

The reason I came to was I'd walked into a lodgepole pine and knocked myself over. I lay there in the needles and melted snow puddles, staring up at the night sky. I had no excuse for walking into a tree. The moon was so bright it threw shadows. Stars twinkled off toward the horizon, but only the brightest of planets shone through the immediate moon glow.

From my back, flat on the earth, the realization arrived that I had a choice between death and action. Not knowing the true father of my wife's oncoming child had become worse than the pain of knowing—or even worse, letting Evangeline know I doubted her. I had to ask Evangeline, and I had to try my gut best to believe whatever answer she gave. The alternative was no longer bearable.

So I walked home. We were in the midst of a warm snap. Often May is as much winter as January in those parts. The temperature breaks freezing, but the snow falls deep as ever. But in 1924, some of the roads were so clear you could get through in an automobile, and I walked mostly on gravel. My brain was a blank slate, which was a far cry better than what it had been. Now I'd committed to asking Evangeline for the truth, I'd settled into not peace so much as a vacuum. The boiling tar was out of my head, only nothing had come along to replace it. It was like in the War, the night before a battle. No feelings. No thoughts. No nothing.

Hours went by while I walked, until I passed into a mist by the old Fountain Hotel, that wasn't in use anymore. Due to hot runoff, the Firehole River is warmer than other high mountain streams and the fog is thicker. Tree stumps hovered ghostly. I could barely see the ranger station as I trudged by in the light of dawn and only made out our cabin along the basin edge when I was right up on it.

A four-door Model T Ford touring car was parked in front of my doorstep. My nightmare had come to pass.

———

I sucked a deep breath, yanked open the door, and crossed the threshold. My eyes went straight to the bed, but they weren't in it. Bill sat at the table before a steaming coffee mug, while Evangeline stood at the stove, feeding a stick into the drum. They both looked at me, amazed by my sudden appearance.

Bill recovered first. He boomed, "Come on in, hoss. Have some coffee," like it was his home and not my own.

I could see Evangeline was surprised, but not so much overpowered by shame as I expected. She was wearing a sleeveless cotton dress and moccasins. Her belly had expanded since I last saw her. Her hair hung down to her elbows. It had been washed recently.

She said, "What happened to your feet?"

I looked down at the blood clots between my toes. My feet were torn up and I was tracking the floor, but to my mind, we had more important matters to hand.

Evangeline's eyes traveled from my feet to my face, and what she saw there gave her cause for concern. "Oly, what happened? Why are you here?"

I stepped forward into the room, hoping to menace Bill. He grinned and drank coffee. I figure he was glad to have me catch them out. He couldn't have plotted it better.

"I came to ask you a question," I said. "I guess I got the answer."

Evangeline caught up with the train of my suspicion. I don't think she'd realized till that moment the conclusions I had jumped to. What was I supposed to think at 6 a.m. with them together while they knew I would be gone?

"You have chosen the wrong answer," she said. "Mr. Cox was driving by and his radiator boiled over, so he stopped while it cools."

Bill winked. The jerk. He must have been the first that spring to drive over the road from Gardiner. No way could this be a social drop-by. He knew her words for a lie, and he knew I knew. The bastard was enjoying himself no end.

Evangeline said, "Bill was about to leave."

"No, I wasn't," Bill said. "I wouldn't miss this for a hundred dollars."

Bill was too rotten to waste time on, but Evangeline was my wife. I ignored him and addressed her. "You took advantage of my absence to wallow with this sleazy excuse for an animal."

"Watch your mouth," Bill said.

"You cannot believe that," Evangeline said.

"What else am I to believe?"

There followed a long silence. I hadn't expected her to deny the evidence, and it brought my righteousness up short. Against all that I could see, what if she was innocent? Her stare bored into me. She was almost, but not quite, angry. I didn't know what to do next. Outside the open door, a spring robin went into that trill of theirs. The coffee that was already made started to boil again. You have to watch that with a woodstove.

Bill stood up and said the last words I expected. "I'm in love with Evangeline."

Evangeline swung her attention to Bill. She said, "That is stupid. You cannot love anyone, and even if you told yourself you love me, it wouldn't matter. Oly is my husband."

Bill sniggered. "Not for long."

I nodded towards Evangeline's belly. "Which of us is the father of that child?"

She covered her womb with both hands, palms in, toward the baby. "How could you ask such a thing?"

"Bill's been telling everyone who'll listen that he's the true father. I need to know."

She stared at me like I'd grown a snake's head and rattle. "You would dream truth could come from such a mouth as his, while I lie? Haven't you grown to know me by now?"

I looked from her to him and back. I was spent. It'd been too long a winter, and I was exhausted, confused, and lost. I wanted to believe her, but how could I, with him standing there? Someone was playing me for a fool, only I didn't know who.

I said, "I'm starting to think I have no idea who you are."

Bill turned sidewise to face my wife. He stared at her while using his fingers to pull points into that mustache of his. "Tell Oly who you are, Evangeline."

Her face went stricken. All the dread she could muster leaped suddenly into her eyes. Beyond stricken, she flashed panic.

She held a hand out to me and took a step forward. I took a step back, away from her. We were in a tunnel with only us on both ends and no one else anywhere near.

Bill's voice came from outside the tunnel of us. "Remember that prostitute lived up on Burnt Wagon Draw. The one gave you the dose."

I was so wrapped in Evangeline it took a moment to catch what he meant. I said, "The fat whore who made us all pee broken glass."

Evangeline exhaled. "Oly."

Bill's voice was happy. "This is the whore's daughter."

I stared at Evangeline, not believing at first. Swamp Fox's child had been a little girl. Bone thin, malnourished, much younger than me. How much? It'd been ten years ago. Maybe eleven.

Evangeline watched as I did the arithmetic. Her mouth looked torn. She clutched her belly like holding a lifeline.

Bill didn't let up. "Syphilis killed the mother. Little Evie's been on her own ever since, living by her wits and"—he paused—"whatever."

I asked, "Is this true?"

She didn't speak. Didn't even nod. I saw, anyway. Before me stood the daughter of the biggest mistake of my life, the mistake that cost me Agatha. This woman used me to escape Paris. She was the lover of my enemy.

I said, "Evangeline."

I'd never seen fear in Evangeline. It took a few moments to

realize that's what she was—afraid. When I didn't say anything more, her eyes flickered with hope. She must have thought I would behave with honor.

I didn't. "I guess you had to follow Mama's moccasins. Once a whore, always a whore."

Evangeline gasped. Wet slickness sprung to her eyes. She advanced quickly, and I thought she might strike me, but instead she pushed past and rushed out the door.

———

Bill said, "You handled that well."

What I'd done hit me like a maul to the chest, and I turned and took off after her.

Evangeline was headed toward the basin at a good clip. I made her out through the fog, walking fast, holding her belly, her shoulders twitching up and down from the weeping. Even seven months pregnant, she had the posture of a dancer.

"Evangeline!"

She glanced over her shoulder at me and then hurried faster.

I ran. *"Wait. I'm sorry."*

She was fixing to disappear in the mist, so I picked up my speed. I could hear Bill's footsteps pounding behind me.

"Hold on one second," I called.

I never have figured out exactly what happened next. Evangeline fell forward on her hands and knees, and she screamed a curdling scream. As I ran, she floundered, trying to turn herself. The screaming stopped, but the silence was worse.

I yelled something and ran up to find Evangeline in a hot pot, at the edge, fighting to pull herself out. I grabbed her by the shoulders and fell back, pulling her out and over my body.

She whimpered, "Oly," and, "Help the baby."

Bill was pulling her off me. He moaned, *"My God."*

When I scrambled up and lifted her in my arms, the skin

peeled off her feet into the moccasins. It was the awfulest sight I ever saw. Her hands and arms were burned, and her stomach and breasts. From knees to thighs, she was coming apart.

"Start the car," I said.

"Let's take her dress off," Bill said.

We stripped Evangeline, poured cooking oil over her, and wrapped her in a sheet. I had a morphine tablet left from the bear incident that I forced down her throat. She wasn't conscious, but she wasn't unconscious either. Her head lolled back, and all that showed was the whites of her eyes.

She said, "I'm sorry."

I said, "Hush."

She didn't say more till we'd loaded her in the car and were moving toward headquarters. I had her in the backseat, afraid to touch her, but needing to keep her from rolling. She raised her head to look at me full in the face.

She said, "Promise you'll save the baby."

"I promise."

—————

Evangeline lost the baby before we made the headquarters hospital. Coming through Golden Gate—me holding her head in my lap and keeping her from rolling with my right arm—she suddenly gasped hard and started to breathe fast and deep. She emitted a series of animal-like exhalations—terrible sounds—and a great quantity of blood and fluid burst from between her legs. There was tissue and a skull, then a body but not a body connected by the pulsating cord to a floating, gelatinous mass. I grabbed it—him—and he cried out once. He choked air for maybe thirty seconds, long enough to catch his soul, before his face turned bruise purple and he died again.

Bill glanced back at us. "What's that?" he asked.

"Keep going."

I placed the child on the floor, below the seat, so Evangeline wouldn't have to see him. This was to be the one offspring I would ever have, and I lost him before I knew him, to my eternal shame. I didn't tell Evangeline what had happened. I'm fairly sure she knew, though, because after that, she settled—stopped thrashing and arching her spine—and closed up within herself, I suppose concentrating on bearing the pain. Being boiled alive comes with horrible pain.

"I'm all mixed up here," Shannon said. "*He died again?*"

Oly passed his bony hand over his bald head. "My son wasn't alive, and then he was, and then he wasn't."

"What's the part about catching the soul?" Roger asked. "I'm interested in soul theory."

"Genesis, second chapter. Eve has a body but no soul until she breathes air. The soul enters the body with the first breath, so my son got hold of a soul before he left." Oly lifted himself off the wheelchair by his hands, then lowered himself again. "I've had plenty of time to study on this. You mind if I finish? Thinking about this part of the story tires me out."

Shannon said, "Go ahead. We won't interrupt."

They put Evangeline in the same room I'd been in after the bear cuffing, only where I was alone, Evangeline had a roommate, an old woman named Parthenia who'd cooked up a mess of wild mushrooms and got the wrong kind. She spent her days and nights down the hall at the toilet or asleep.

Evangeline did get a real doctor instead of a horse vet. He said there wasn't much could be done for her. He said she needed skin grafts, which I'd never heard of, but he couldn't do them from Mammoth, Wyoming, and anyway, there wasn't enough proper skin left on Evangeline to graft from. I had little to no idea what he was talking about. Bill pretended he did.

Bill stayed with us most of the time there. He seemed to think him pledging his love to Evangeline gave him the right to be part of us. I didn't have the strength to run him off.

Two days into the ordeal, Bill went away to eat or sleep or something—I didn't ask what—and Shad dropped by. I was sitting in a hard chair by Evangeline's bed, talking quietly to her about our future. Her fingers were too messed up to hold. It upset me there was no way to touch Evangeline without hurting her. More than once, I reached over and pulled my hand back at the last moment.

Her eyes were open. They shifted back and forth, and she blinked, but she didn't move her head. Maybe it's selfish of me, but I thank God her face didn't go under the way the rest of her did. Evangeline still looked like herself.

Shad stood in the doorway, holding his left wrist with his right hand. He said, "How is she today?" He looked awkward. Shad never seemed at ease indoors.

"Better, I think. She had some water a while ago." To Evangeline, I said, "Look who's come to visit."

She didn't show any sign of hearing.

Shad moved in and stood on the far side of her bed. He looked down at her, but I couldn't read his face.

I said, "You knew she was the woman's daughter."

Shad said, "Yes."

"How is it you and Bill recognized her, but I never did? I keep going over the past in my head. I had no idea. I think maybe she hinted at the truth, in Paris, but I missed it."

I glanced at Evangeline, whose only sign of life was the rising and falling of her chest. It felt strange to talk about her in front of her, knowing, or at least being fairly sure, she could hear me, but there were things I needed to talk about. I was more trying to explain myself to her than Shad, although I can't tell you what I was trying to explain.

Shad said, "Bill and I saw more of Swamp Fox than you did."

"Bill, maybe," I said. "But you only used her the once."

"I went back to chop wood for them a time or two. Bill was there quite a bit."

I'd seen Evangeline blink when Shad spoke the words *Swamp Fox*. "I hate referring to her mother that way," I said to Shad. "Do you know her name?"

Shad shrugged.

Evangeline said, "Helen." It was the first word she'd spoken since she lost the baby.

"Helen," I said. "That's a nice name."

We waited for Evangeline to say more, but she didn't. The old lady with mushroom poisoning came back from vomiting in the bathroom down the way, glanced at Shad and me, but not Evangeline, and climbed back into her bed. In thirty seconds, she was snoring like a fat miner.

Shad looked up from Evangeline to me. "Bill isn't the father. He never took her, even once."

Evangeline blinked again, but that was her one reaction. I felt an amazing weight lift from my forehead. It makes me more ashamed than ever, that I should feel relief while she lay there in pain.

Shad cleared his throat and went on. "He tried to force her to bed him. Said he'd tell you who her mother was if she didn't. She was terrified you'd find out and leave her, but she never gave in to his demands. She kept putting him off with excuses." Shad left the bed and walked to the window. He looked down on the lawn area where I'd watched him circle my motorcycle last summer. When he talked, he looked neither at me nor Evangeline.

"She let him come to the cabin when you weren't there—she couldn't stop that—but he didn't so much as touch her."

"You know this to be true?"

"Yes."

I waited for more, but he didn't give it. "Why didn't you stop him?"

Shad exhaled a sigh. I saw he wasn't looking out the window. He was looking at his reflection in the glass. "I've never been able to stop Bill. I used to try." His voice drifted away.

Shad turned from the window to face me. We held the contact a long time, searching for answers to questions over fifteen years old.

"You're thinking when all this is over, you'll kill him," Shad said. It wasn't a question.

I left off Shad to study Evangeline's face, looking for a clue as to what she felt. Who she blamed.

"It's on my list of possible outcomes."

Shad placed his hands on his hips, thumbs back. "He really does feel love for her. I think he's hoping you'll kill him."

"I don't believe that."

Shad nodded at Evangeline's boiled body. "Dying for this might be easier than living with it. For you or Bill."

———

After Shad left, I stood at the foot of the bed with my hands on the iron bedposts. My hope was to memorize Evangeline. I wanted to know, intimately and with clarity, every shadow and plane on her face. I wanted the two of us to be a single person.

I found myself talking. "I would never leave you, I could never leave you on account of your mother or what life you used to lead or any other excuse. I wasn't even a true human before you came along. I didn't know how to care."

She didn't move, other than shallow breathing and the occasional blink. Due to the way she fell in the hot pot, her backside was spared, so lying straight still without twitching a muscle was probably the best method of making the awful pain less awful. Even today, however many years later, I suffer not knowing what Evangeline thought at that time. I've never given myself the benefit of the doubt that her thoughts toward me were not bitter.

"I am so sorry I spoke cruel words to you. I would cut off my legs if that could undo the damage, and I don't mean you falling in the water, I mean you being disappointed by me. For not living up to my vows." By now, I was rambling, not making sense even to myself. I don't know if Evangeline was catching what I meant as opposed to what I said or not. Having her understand felt like the difference between life and death.

"You could have told me the facts. You should of. I would not have thought badly of you, Evangeline. I could never, ever think badly of you."

She stared hard into my eyes. Her voice came as a whisper. "I could not take the chance."

———

Evangeline passed at dawn, on the third day after I'd called her the daughter of a whore. Shad and Bill were in the room with us. Bill wept like a baby.

———

I buried my Evangeline on a hillock at the point near where Nez Perce Creek and the Firehole come together. Nez Perce was high and brown from spring runoff, but the Firehole, being primarily hot spring fed, flowed clear. The day was brisk and blue, a spring day Evangeline would have loved. The balsamroot was blooming, and larkspur off across the river along the tree line. You can see some expanse from that point which is a mile or more from the hot pot that took her life.

A mix of park employees stood around the gravesite, talking amongst themselves. It was kind of them to come. Being as Evangeline kept to herself and our cabin, not that many had actually met her. They attended to support me in my grief, although some no doubt were present for something to do. By May, the permanent park employees are climbing trees from cabin fever. They'll show up for any group outing.

We had a Lutheran minister down from Gardiner. I suspect Evangeline was baptized Catholic, but I can't say where I got that idea. Most of the Crow were, as I recall, so maybe I assumed she was too, but I didn't ask for a priest. I was afraid he'd feel testy toward her, on account of no last rites. I don't care what the Catholic Church says, Evangeline had done nothing she needed forgiveness for.

The minister said some prayers while I watched ravens working a winterkill downstream. I'd stuck the baby's body in the box with her during the night. No one knew but me. He'd been in the hotel icehouse for four days, and I didn't know what else to do with him.

The minister had us sing "Nearer My God to Thee" while four motorcycle rangers, including Snuffy, worked this rope rig to lower Evangeline into the hole. Half the park people didn't know the words, and the other half made for poor singers. If Evangeline heard, I imagine she took it as pitiful. By the end, the Lutheran was singing alone.

Then he shook my hand and called me Otis—he never knew my name—and got into a horse-drawn buggy with a canvas top and left. In groups of one, two, or three, the others also shook hands with me, put on their hats, and said whatever you say at those times. The words are lame, but the thought is wholesome.

The rangers picked up shovels and started throwing dirt onto the box. That was the point where I about died myself.

Bill and Shad were the last to offer sympathy, after most of the park folks had wandered away. Bill held out his hand, but I didn't return the gesture. Ever since the conversation with Shad, I'd been thinking about what he said, how living with this might be harder than dying for it. What I did next will make no sense to some. Others—the ones who have felt the grief that I felt—will know it was reasonable.

The throwdown was I had to punish myself as much as Bill. We were both to blame.

Bill said, "I feel badly that this had to happen."

I said, "It didn't have to happen."

He shrugged and put on his floppy cavalry hat that went with his mustache and fringe jacket. I think he was hoping to get through the funeral without an ugly scene. Slim chance of that.

He said, "I, for one, will never forget the part I played in this tragedy." What bull. Anybody who could say *I, for one* wasn't properly sad.

I turned from the ever-growing pile of brown earth on Evangeline's box to stare hard at Bill. "You won't forget," I said, "because I won't let you."

Bill looked across at Shad, who'd taken a shovel from Snuffy and was throwing dirt into the hole. Shad wasn't one to watch while another worked.

Bill had no such compunctions. "That's what I said. I'll never forget."

"Without my help, you would," I said. "Inside a year, Evangeline will have no affect on your daily mood. You'll go about your business as comfortable and irresponsible as when you were a child."

I reached into the dirt pile and scooped up a handful of dark soil in the palm of my hand; then I held my hand out and let the dirt trickle down between my fingers onto the box. I'd seen it done in a moving picture once, in Paris, and it impressed me as a solemn way to say good-bye.

"I'm not going to allow that to happen. You want to hear what I'm aiming to do to make certain neither of us goes a day without dwelling on the truth that we killed an angel?"

Bill came across as uncomfortable. I think if Shad hadn't been present as a witness, Bill would have walked away before I could finish. As it was, he turned his back to the hole that held the box that held Evangeline. He turned toward Nez Perce Creek so he wouldn't have to look me in the eye.

I addressed his profile. "Here's what I propose to do, Bill. I propose to remain by your side, every day and every night for as long as we live. When you travel, I will travel. When you stay put, I will stay put." I glanced over at Shad, who'd stopped throwing dirt and leaned on his shovel, looking at me with curiosity.

I said, "We're back to being the three brothers, just like we were when we took advantage of her mother. Every morning when you wake up and see my face, you're going to think of Evangeline. Every time you drink water, I'm going to remind you that she can't. When you warm yourself by the fire, I'll be there so you can't forget she died in terrible, burning agony given her by you and me. Together. No one else."

The upshot of my resolve didn't sink through Bill's thick hide right away—he had to work out the nuances. He went from thinking me funny, to disbelief and dismissal, to wondering if I was serious, to realizing I was. I could see the various thoughts flicker across his face as he progressed to the point of seeing the future. At the end, he took on a look of utter horror.

He said, "I won't let you."

"Try and stop me."

He turned to face me full-on. "You're not man enough to ruin both our lives."

I said, "Watch me."

—⋅—

And I did. I stayed with Bill from that day forward, till 1964 when he suffered a stroke and fell over dead in the White Deck Cafe there in GroVont. He would have gotten over her without me. Hell, I might have gotten over her without him, although I hope not. But the way we lived our lives, neither of us had a chance to move past Evangeline's death.

Bill and I were a pair spot-welded together at the hips. Local folks thought we were the apex of male friendship, sidekicks like Robin Hood and Little John, or Butch and Sundance. They never suspected there wasn't a day of those forty years that Bill Cox and I didn't hate each other.

Shad died in '58. An avalanche up on Togwotee Pass took him out. He'd been crippled for four years, on account of a tree accident, so I don't think he minded dying when it came. He's the only one among us who married and bore children.

"Your Mama Maurey Pierce is his son's daughter."

Shannon said, "Then Shad was my great-grandfather?"

"Yep."

"Why didn't somebody tell me?"

Agatha Ann went on to spawn a family with eighteen grandchildren. She spent the last ten years of her life in a nursing home in Muncie, Indiana, of all places. I drove out to see her in 1982, the year she turned eighty-five, but she didn't know who I was. She didn't know who anyone was. She just lay twisted and shriveled on a chaise lounge in front of a color TV tuned to game shows she didn't understand.

"I will now reveal what I have learned. You two pay attention. I'm happy Mrs. Elkrunner isn't here, because she thinks she has nothing to learn from her elders. You kids know better."

"What have you learned, Mr. Pedersen?" Shannon asked.

"This here is the important fact you must accept, should

you live a hundred years, as I have. No matter how long you pass on this Earth and in this body, you will look back on your time and say, 'It went by in a heartbeat. How did that happen so quickly?'"

Roger said, "That's the most important thing you've learned in a hundred years?"

Oly's voice was angry. "The most important thing—time is short. Don't toss it down the toilet."

On the tape, there follows two minutes of silence. You can hear someone—Shannon or Roger—shifting uncomfortably and Oly's asthmatic breathing. One of them coughs. Papers are rattled.

Finally, Oly's voice comes back. He says, "Let that be a lesson to you."

25

LOREN PAUL LIVED UP A STEEP SLOPE OF LUSH GREENERY. THE third switchback above the state highway, Roger got his first glimpse of the Pacific Ocean. It was gun-barrel silver and not what he had expected an ocean to look like, although Roger couldn't say what he had expected. Blue, maybe, or a deep green. This ocean was so flat it didn't quite look wet.

He sat in back, holding hands with Shannon, who'd found a stick of Doublemint in her back pocket. She gazed out the window and chewed with her lips pressed tightly together. Lydia drove. She was in the foulest mood of a lifetime of foul moods. Her eyes burned. It took no imagination to see the black cloud hovering between Lydia and the roof. The other three were afraid to make small talk. Oly had been waiting all night to bait her over the boy she'd seduced, but even he knew that right now, any sound could prove fatal.

Roger wondered what had gone wrong. The possibilities were so endless he couldn't think up a decent guess. Lydia hadn't spoken an unnecessary word since she came back to the Comfort Inn. Roger didn't expect thanks for setting up the next session of Oly's history, but acknowledgment would have been appropriate. Lydia didn't even criticize the way he'd packed the recording equipment.

Roger thought of poison ivy. The hillside came across as reeking of poison ivy. And snakes. Sure enough, they drove by a roadkill snake on the shoulder. It was long as a jump rope and banded in fall colors. Northwest Wyoming didn't have poisonous snakes, spiders, or ivy. Roger was comfortable wandering the mountains where nothing smaller than a bear might kill him. He wouldn't have been comfortable wandering the Santa Barbara hillside. All that life made him claustrophobic.

At the top of the rise, a pickup truck hooked to a horse trailer sat parked with the right tires up on the curb. The trailer had Wyoming ranch plates. No one but Roger seemed to notice, and he was too afraid of Lydia's wrath to point it out.

A half block later, they pulled up in front of Loren Paul's address. The house looked pretty much like any other house on the hill—white stucco with red semi-circular tiles on the roof. The front yard was mauve gravel. A couple of varieties of cactus and a willow pushed through rocks. Alongside the house grew a decorative border of red and yellow big-blossomed flowers. Something about an existence between mauve gravel and white walls made the flowers more forlorn than festive.

Shannon said, "Is this it?"

Lydia more or less sneered. "No, I just stopped for the fun of it." She got out and said, "Let's get this over with." Then she slammed the door.

In the quiet of the car, Oly said, "I wonder who planted a scorpion up her drawers."

Shannon said, "Right."

While Roger went around to pull Oly's chair from the trunk, Shannon searched for a gum-dumping site. The street was too clean. Someone might step on it. Finally, she stuck the gum up under the mailbox on a post. Lydia glared at her but didn't speak. It occurred to Roger that Shannon had chosen the mailbox for gum dumping as a ploy to yank Lydia from her malaise. It didn't work, but the gesture struck him as noble. Everything about Shannon struck Roger as noble that morning. Without Shannon, he wouldn't have been able to cross the yard. As it was, Oly got stuck. Lydia did nothing to help Shannon and Roger wrestle Oly through the gravel.

Shannon said, "They must go in through the garage."

Oly leaned forward to take some of the weight off the back wheels. "Doesn't look like these folks want company."

The four travelers stood—or in Oly's case sat—on the front porch, looking at each other, until Lydia growled. "Are you going to knock, or what?"

Roger rang the doorbell. His mind felt blank. Not clear so much as empty. Would Loren appear at the door, recognize Roger for who he was, and throw his arms around his long-lost stepson? Or would he shriek and bolt? Maybe the lost child had been recovered years ago, and he would be the one to answer the door, and Roger would feel like a fool. The only thing that kept him from running back to his cabin in the woods was Shannon's hand on his back.

She said, "Breathe."

Oly said, "No one's home. Let's go."

The door opened. A girl, eighteen or so, stood there draped in a UNCG Spartans basketball jersey, spooning yogurt from a carton. She was pole thin with flattop-cut watermelon hair and a nail protruding from her cheek.

She said, "About time you guys showed up."

"What?" Roger said.

"The gang's out back by the pool. Come on through here," and she turned to walk away.

Roger sought out Lydia for guidance. "What do we do, Callahan?"

"You heard the tramp."

Roger said, "But."

"Don't stand there like a buffoon. Go in."

The house was dark and tasteful—hardwood floors, weavings on the otherwise-bare walls, a minimum of places to sit. There were some Lladro pieces on the fireplace mantel and a huge Chinese vase in the corner. Through French doors, Roger made out a library with floor-to-ceiling bookshelves. No photographs of family. It wasn't a personal living room, but it was comfortable. The people who lived there didn't care what professional designers thought of them.

Roger's first urge was to peel off from the group and sneak into the library. He was curious as to what a mid-list novelist reads. Besides, after coming all this way, he was in no hurry to meet Loren. The illusion of hope would be no match for the reality of disappointment.

Shannon was guiding Oly's chair. She nodded toward the back of the girl leading them through the house. "That's my shirt."

"Oh, please," Lydia said. "This isn't about you."

"How did my shirt beat us across the country?"

Roger believed her. If Shannon said an impossible event had come to pass, in his mind, an impossible event had come to pass. "When did you see it last?"

"Yesterday morning."

"And your shirt miraculously flew a thousand miles to reappear at this house on that grotesque woman," Lydia said. "Give me a break."

"UNCG Spartans, number 12, Sambotini. They don't sell Sambotini shirts at the mall. He wasn't that good."

"Is that another one of your boyfriends?" Roger asked.

Lydia said, "Shannon has so many ex-boyfriends, they've saturated America. I imagine we'll run into evidence of Shannon's love life wherever we travel."

Oly bobbed his head up and down and *meowed*.

Lydia said, "Clam up, old man."

They cut through the kitchen that was lighter than the living room, but just as organic. There was a stand-alone cutting block the size of a picnic table and an array of copper pots and pans hanging from a rack on the ceiling. A walk-in pantry sat off next to the stainless-steel side-by-side refrigerator-freezer. The stovetop was smooth.

"They're out here," the girl said, pushing through the Dutch door that led to the backyard.

"That shirt isn't random," Shannon said. "It came from my closet."

———

While Bruce Springsteen didn't record Roger's favorite music, he could tolerate pounding rock. Lydia couldn't. The first thing she said when they filed into Loren Paul's backyard was, "Would somebody please turn that dreck down?"

"This isn't our house," Shannon said. "The music is their choice."

"Even if it is dreck," Oly said.

Leroy said, "Haven't seen you in a while, son."

Roger's chest twitched, and nausea swept through. His focus swung from the CD player on the stone table to the salamander grinning at him from the hot tub. The man had the look of a Hindu god-man. No chest hair—hell, no chest to brag about. No muscles in his arms or shoulders. No teeth. This was the man from his nightmares, the one who stood too close and smelled of rubbing alcohol. This was the man who had silenced Roger's voice.

"Are you Loren Paul?"

"I'm Loren Paul." Loren spoke from over by the pool, in his pajamas and bathrobe, next to a beautiful woman on a chaise lounge.

The beautiful woman—mid-forties, silk caftan, bare feet—lowered her sunglasses to stare at Roger. "Who the hell are you?"

"I might be Loren Paul's son. Fred." When she didn't react, he said, "Buggie."

Loren had the slightly stunned face of a writer whose real world is elsewhere. You would think a man confronted by the child he lost so many years ago would react visibly. Loren had more of a tornado-victim-in-shock demeanor.

The beautiful woman was angry. Roger could see tension in the tightness of her forehead, although he couldn't tell if it was caused by him or the freak in the hot tub. Her anger wasn't the general irritation toward everything and everyone he was used to from Lydia. This woman's anger was more specific.

She said, "I see you brought an entourage."

Lydia had been left out of the conversation as long as she could stand. She said, "You must be Lana Sue. We met once, back when you were a young trophy wife."

Lana Sue dropped her sunglasses back into position and studied Lydia with what Roger assumed was coolness behind the lenses. The mutual disdain was instantaneous and palpable.

"I'm still a trophy wife."

Lydia snorted.

The skeleton in the hot tub sloshed water over the top, dangerously close to swamping Bruce Springsteen. "You're my son. He's a fraud."

Roger's confusion was about what you'd expect in a kid who suddenly went from having no fathers to having two.

"I don't get it."

The scary man's left hand came into sight, over the lip of the tub, pointing a pistol at Loren. "That scumbag is a liar."

"Can I borrow a swimsuit?" the girl with the nail in her cheek asked Lana Sue. "My neighborhood back in Trinidad is too normal for pools in the backyards. I'd be so thrilled to work on my tan and swim some laps while Charley decides which one of you to kill."

The word *kill* threw a pall over the gathering. Until then,

Roger had been interested in the father question and wondering what he was supposed to feel. Whatever it was, he didn't feel it. All he felt was mixed up. The death threat only added to the conflicting swirl of information.

Lana Sue said, "Nobody's getting killed on my patio."

The girl smiled at her. "I'm afraid that's out of us girls' hands. Can I borrow a bathing suit?"

Leroy—who's going to be called Charley until someone corrects the misconception—snapped. "Zelda, you pig. You want a bathing suit, go in the house and get a bathing suit. Don't ask permission. We have guns. They don't."

Zelda said, "I forgot."

"God, you are stupid," Leroy said.

Shannon said, "That's no way to talk to your girlfriend."

"That's okay," Zelda said. "Charley doesn't mean it. It's the way he was raised." She left her yogurt and spoon on the table and scooted inside. There was a moment of silence while the Springsteen CD stopped playing and Talking Heads started. It was a multiple-disc machine.

"Let's go back to the who-the-hells?" Lana Sue said. She spoke to Lydia. "Who the hell are you, and why have you people invaded my home?" Then she glanced at Oly, who had rolled around the pool and over to the back fence and was standing up to relieve himself on the slats. "And what is that?"

Shannon said, "She's my grandmother, Lydia."

Lydia said, "Shannon, there's no call to define ourselves."

Shannon kept on going. "Lydia got out of prison on Mother's Day. She brought us to Santa Barbara to meet Roger's dad. And he's Oly Pedersen. He's turning one hundred pretty soon, and I have no idea what he's doing."

"I need a hand here," Oly called.

Roger walked over to the fence and Oly.

Loren said, "Your name is Roger?"

Roger was bent over, helping Oly with his zipper. He spoke without looking back. "That's my name now. It used to be something else."

"I'm not his sister." Shannon sat in one of the lawn chairs scattered about the lawn. They were high-end redwood like the fence, not cheap webbing like most lawn chairs. "Not genetically speaking. Even though we both call my mother *Mom*."

"You people have invaded my home. I don't care about your inbred love life," Lana Sue said.

"I care. I'm going to sleep with Roger after we get to know each other better. Only not yet. I have a history of sleeping with men too soon."

Leroy fired a shot into the air. *Bang!* "*Shut the fuck up.*"

"The neighbors heard that," Lydia said. "You'd better pack up and go, before they call the police."

Loren looked distractedly at Lydia. As far as Lydia could make out, he wasn't attracted to her. It was one more nail in the coffin.

He said, "You must not be from California."

"We drove in from Wyoming yesterday," Shannon said.

"The neighbors won't be calling the police."

Leroy shouted over the music, "I'm the boss here. No one talks till I say so."

Everyone stopped talking and turned their attention to the hot tub. Oly shook and tucked, Roger zipped him up, Oly fell back into his chair, and together, they came around poolside.

"Well?" Lydia parked herself in a lawn chair beside Shannon. She'd had enough of standing and waiting.

Leroy said, "What?"

"Isn't it time you explain why you are holding us at gunpoint?"

Leroy's eyes shifted back and forth from the pool to the house to the group before him. When he swallowed, his Adam's apple hopped like a frog in panty hose. To Roger, it was obvious Leroy didn't have a plan. He'd taken hostages with no real idea what to do with them.

Leroy's gaze fell on Loren. "Where's the book?"

Whatever Loren—or anyone else—had expected Leroy to say, *Where's the book?* wasn't it.

Loren pulled his bathrobe tighter. "What book is that?" No matter how befuddled Loren came off—whether from a stranger with a gun in his hot tub, or the return of Ann's child, or maybe Loren always came across as befuddled—he didn't show a hint of self-consciousness about the pajama thing.

Leroy waved the pistol vaguely toward Roger. "The book where you exploited my boy. I have to read what you wrote about me."

Lana Sue swung her legs off the chaise lounge and sat up. "Are you saying this mess was caused by one of Loren's novels?"

Lydia said, "I don't know about Charley the Sociopath, but that novel is what brought us to town."

Lana Sue stood. She was shorter than Roger had envisioned. For some reason, he didn't expect short, beautiful women. It's a flaw in Roger's character.

"Nobody asked you," Lana Sue said to Lydia. "I still don't understand why are you at my house."

"I told you, she's my grandmother," Shannon said.

Lydia's voice was a slap. "*Shannon.*"

Loren said, "I have no copies of *Disappearance*."

Zelda came from the house wearing a creamy white bikini so brief it only had laces on the sides and between the cups. The bottom was a thong. None of the Wyoming contingent had ever seen a thong, not in person. Lydia and Shannon had seen photographs. Roger didn't even know such attire was possible.

Oly groaned. "Jesus and Mary Magdalene."

Lydia scowled at Lana Sue. "That belongs to you?"

Lana Sue was a bit embarrassed—Zelda had chosen the suit

Lana wore in the privacy of their enclosed backyard—but she hid it well. She said, "Are you going out of your way to offend your hostess?"

"This is California," Shannon said to Lydia. "All older women dress like teenagers."

Zelda walked to the pool and stood on the side, bouncing on her toes. She'd never shown this much flesh in public. It was thrilling yet terrible. Her own swimsuit was a one-piece her mama bought at Target a size too large because she still bought clothes Zelda was supposed to grow into. Zelda decided against the dramatic dive. That would be too much. Instead she turned around and worked her way down the ladder.

Oly said, "I only wish I was eighty years younger and had two dollars."

Loren missed the Zelda saga. Without so much as a glance at her, he said, "I'm clear out of copies of *Disappearance*."

"*Filthy liar.*" Leroy cocked the pistol. "What kind of crock is that—an author with no copies of his own book?"

Loren was more embarrassed over the book than Lana Sue was over the swimsuit. He didn't expect anyone to believe he'd published a novel and didn't have a copy. "I gave them all away when the movie was being made. The cast wanted to read it, to research their motives. It wasn't in print, of course, so I lent them copies, and they never gave them back."

He stared down at the cobbles on the patio, sadly. "No one ever returns a book once they borrow it."

"Movie?" Lydia hadn't been paying much attention since she left Hank. Lana Sue was an irritation that normally would have driven Lydia to alert bitchiness, and the girl had said somebody was likely to be killed soon, but today Lydia didn't have the energy it takes to reach righteous firepower. She didn't truly snap to until she heard *movie*. "That book got itself made into a movie? I never heard of a movie called *Disappearance*."

"It had a different title," Loren said. "*Floating Away*. It showed on Lifetime." If possible, Loren sank even further into his funk. "I can hardly believe they took my deepest pain and turned it into a Lifetime Network original."

"What an odd title," Lydia said.

"It was voted on by a focus group." Loren sighed. "They wouldn't tell me the other choices."

Leroy uncocked his pistol and lowered it back out of sight. "Who played me? In the movie?"

Loren was stumped, but Lana Sue knew. "Your character was cut from the first draft of the screenplay."

"Ann told me the father's name was Chuck," Loren said. "You were the ex-boyfriend who got jacked up on meth and hit her. We decided you weren't germane to the story."

Leroy brought the pistol back up. "I'll show you germane, asswipe."

Roger jumped in before Loren got shot. Roger had gone to a lot of trouble to track down his stepfather. He didn't like the idea of losing him ten minutes later. Roger had questions only Loren could answer.

He said, "I have a copy. I remember your character. He was called Freedom, in the book."

"Where is it?"

"Come again?"

"The damn book. Is it back in Wyoming, or where?"

"It's in the car. Out front. I hoped maybe Loren would autograph it, especially if I'm the missing boy. It would prove who I am if he puts it in writing."

Leroy called across to Zelda, who was dog-paddling up and down the pool, "Zelda, drag your bare fanny out of there."

She stopped churning her arms and treaded water, squinting at Leroy in the light. "I only just started."

"You're done now. I want you to walk with my kid to his

car. Take the rifle. If he tries to use the phone or run off or anything but go there, get the book, and come back, shoot him."

Zelda swam to the ladder and pulled herself out. "I forget where I left the rifle."

"You'd best remember, right quick."

"I think it's in the laundry room. I'm washing my panties."

"Hell, I can't trust you." Leroy turned to Roger. "You try anything fancy, and your girlfriend and grandma are dead. You understand?"

Roger said, "I understand."

From the lawn chairs there rose an indignant voice. "I'm not his grandma."

———

Zelda led and Roger followed. He didn't dare glance down at the thong, or the flesh on either side of it, until they were in the house out of Shannon's sight. In the kitchen, though, he couldn't help himself.

There were dimples. The right cheek had a rash.

"Is that thing comfortable?" he asked.

She stopped and twirled around. "Do you like it?"

From the front, the thong was wider, but it still didn't hide all her pubic hairs. "It makes you walk like you've got a wedgie."

Zelda pouted. "You're no gentleman."

She left the kitchen, turned right, and went through a door. Her voice floated back from what must have been the laundry room. "Is that your girlfriend out there—the chubby one?"

Roger waited in the hallway, feeling put-upon. He'd never aspired to be a gentleman, not if gentleman meant *liar*. She'd asked a question, and he answered. She was too young to go snippy on him.

"She's not so chubby."

"She's a hundred years older than you." Zelda reappeared in

the doorway, the .280 Remington they'd taken from Barnett and Rowdy cradled in her arms like a baby. It wasn't the proper way to handle a firearm. She said, "She's not good enough for you."

"You just don't know her yet. Shannon's good enough for anybody."

"She acts like my mom's friends who make fun of my eyeliner. A bunch of snobs."

"I'm pretty sure Shannon isn't a snob."

Zelda cut back through the living room. "I hope she's the one Charley decides to shoot."

Roger took another peek into the library. He wondered how long the nutcase in the hot tub would give them before he turned psycho. "So that guy is planning to shoot someone?"

"He has to now, or you'll think he's a wimp." Zelda stopped at the front door. "I'm not showing myself out there like this. You've ruined my confidence."

"I'm sorry."

"Too late for sorry now, isn't it?" She cracked open the door and peered out into the yard and street. "You go to the car alone while I watch from here. Come right back with the book. Charley flies off the handle when people don't do what he says."

"Why are you with him?"

Zelda seemed offended by the simplemindedness of the question. "He's my man."

"Oh."

"Go get the book."

———

Leroy balanced *Disappearance* in one hand and the pistol in the other. He'd found the gun stuck in a leather holster behind the seat in Barnett's truck. It was a Taurus .38 Special with a two-inch barrel loaded with five rounds. Leroy hadn't found any more. If this bunch rushed him, he'd run out of ammunition before he ran out of bodies, and he'd have to switch to the rifle to finish the job. He had felt secure enough, though, to send Zelda on errands with the rifle in hand. This didn't strike Leroy as a rushing bunch—one guy in a wheelchair and another in pajamas. He felt safe, so long as neither of the two old women got in behind him.

The disc changed from Talking Heads to Willie Nelson. Lydia groaned in a way no one was likely to miss her meaning. "Are you planning to make us sit here like mannequins while you read a novel?"

"That's right."

"I've got places to be."

"It took me five hours," Roger said, "not counting bathroom breaks."

Leroy studied the title page. It was signed to Marcie VanHorn and said something inane about a Cornish game hen. "I'll read the parts about me."

"That's all of a paragraph. You want me to find it for you," Roger said.

"Then I'll skim the other parts. I'd like to know what he wrote about the day I rescued you."

"The verb is *kidnapped*," Loren said.

"Watch your mouth there, writer fella. From my end, it was a rescue. That evil woman was holding Fred against his wishes."

"She was his mother. He was five and worshipped her. I've never seen a child so attached to his mother."

"You've only been on one side of the deal. Every custody disagreement has two sides. I'm hungry." He searched out Zelda, who was hiding under a towel. "Zelda, take the rifle and that rude woman who lives here."

Lana Sue fluttered her right hand. "That would be me."

"Zelda can watch while you whip up lunch. This won't take long, but there's no point in murdering on an empty belly."

Oly said, "I don't cotton to being murdered hungry either. How about letting the rude woman fix us all some grub."

Lydia said, "I hate it when he calls food *grub*."

Shannon said, "What's cotton got to do with it?"

Lana Sue advanced on Leroy, until he swung the pistol her way. "Do I look like a servant to you?"

Leroy closed one eye to focus on her. "You look like a rich bitch with a stick up her tail. Now go and cook up lunch, woman."

Zelda said, "I can do it, if you're too good for us. You'll just have to show me where things are. I make a swell boxed mac and cheese."

Lana Sue said, "I'd rather cook than have you rooting around my kitchen."

"That's the spirit," Lydia said.

Zelda, still toting the rifle the wrong way, followed Lana Sue back inside. Everyone else settled into the lawn chairs to wait for lunch, while Leroy read the book.

"You want me to show you where Ann first talked about her history with you?" Loren said.

"I'll find it. You stay put."

Oly rolled over to the very lip of the pool and sat, staring into the deep-end water as if it held the secrets to the past and future. Sometimes—often—his face took on a sunken-eyed wizard likeness. Roger thought the look conveyed wisdom or the ability to delve into another dimension. Lydia said it wasn't wisdom, but a self-induced lobotomy.

Oly's so old he can slip into white noise, she had said. *If he's thinking at all, he's planning his next bowel movement.*

Lydia herself leaned back in her lawn chair, her eyes closed and her arms crossed over her chest. She'd had in the range of three hours sleep since Friday, and the pace was beginning to wear. There'd been too many emotional extremes. All her choices were unacceptable.

Shannon sat next to Roger, across from Loren, clutching Roger's hand. It felt important not to let him go. She had him and had no intention of losing him.

Roger decided it was question time. There might not be another chance. "So, how true is the book?

Loren knew what Roger was digging for, but he needed time to compose himself. It was vital, he knew, to give this boy truth and nothing but, only in his need to gather his thoughts, his first answer was a lie.

"I'm not sure what you mean."

"Is the book true?"

"It's a novel. I write novels, or at least I did before I started screenwriting. I enjoy the novel form more than scripts, but the pay doesn't compare." He nodded, as if confirming something to himself. "I gave up work I love to make money."

Roger didn't care about Loren's soul-searching. He wanted to know where he stood. "Then you made up *Disappearance*?" Roger nodded toward Leroy, who was reading and keeping them covered at the same time. "Why is he here, if it's not real?"

"The book is based on a true experience. All books are based on experience, and that book is based on more reality than most. I've just never been comfortable with the nonfiction label. It seems so…limiting."

Shannon squeezed Roger's hand. He glanced at her, and she smiled encouragement. Roger had a flash of what it would be like to be Shannon's mate, and a quick qualm as to the worth of quizzing Loren, when he could be back in his cabin in the mountains, making love to Shannon.

"I need to know about my mother," he said. "Is the mother in the book anything like my mother?"

Loren plunged into telling the truth. It didn't come naturally. "I was married to a woman with a son. The boy disappeared. My wife committed suicide. I was too much of a coward to die, so I wrote the story. You can release pain by writing about it, at least to some extent. You can make the unbearable bearable." His eyes seemed to beseech Roger, but Roger couldn't tell what he was being beseeched to do.

"Did you know he kidnapped the boy?"

Leroy had set the pistol on the hot tub lip and was picking his nose with his free hand. As Roger and Loren watched, he pulled the finger from his nostril, licked it, and used the wet tip to turn the page.

"I still don't know he kidnapped you. Or whomever he kidnapped. None of this makes sense to me. I don't understand what led you people to come here."

"Lydia read your book in prison and decided I might be the boy. Her evidence was pretty weak and based on coincidences, but she talked me into coming to California." Roger bored in with heavy eye contact. "Do you think I might be Fred?"

Loren studied Roger a long time. He closed his eyes and tried to overlay his mind's picture of the child Fred onto Roger's face. His physical remembrance of Fred was fuzzy. There were a couple of photographs that had replaced his real memories, but he and Ann had never been big on photographs. There hadn't been a need to freeze the moment, at the time.

Loren opened his eyes. "I don't know. We lost our baby when he was only five. That man's presence"—meaning Leroy—"leads me to think you must be Fred. He certainly believes it."

Roger sat back. It was too much for him to absorb. He'd planned on a *yes*-or-*no* answer. *I don't know* was hard to swallow. But then, Loren was probably right about Leroy's presence. Why had Leroy shown up when he did? Shannon's basketball jersey proved Leroy had followed them here from Wyoming. It wasn't just bizarre timing that brought them both to this house on the same day.

Lydia was right. He was Fred. "What was my mother like?"

Loren sighed. That was the question he feared most. "It was so long ago. I was a different person then."

Shannon said, "It wasn't that long ago."

Loren looked at Shannon, glad for an excuse to break away from Roger. "We lost Fred in 1975. Ann died in '77."

Roger asked the question he'd wondered about for ten years: "When was my birthday?"

And Loren knew this one. "February fourteenth. You were a Valentine's baby."

Roger made a sigh-like squeak sound. This much alone made the trip worthwhile. "I've never had a birthday before."

"You didn't choose a day to celebrate?" Loren asked.

"There wasn't much point."

"Everyone deserves a birthday."

Roger automatically started pulling down his bandanna, before he realized it wasn't there. "That makes me twenty-three. My parents—the people who raised me—guessed I was eleven when I came to them. They think I'm twenty-one."

Shannon did the math, comparing her age to Roger's. This was closer to socially acceptable.

Roger said, "I couldn't talk the first two years that I have memories."

Loren blinked three times in succession. Guilt rose like gorge. All those years, he'd felt responsible for whatever happened to Fred after they lost him, and his imagination had come up with horrendous scenarios. In spite of that, the true pain had been the idea that reality might be worse than his imagination.

"Why couldn't you talk?"

"Ask the asshole."

Leroy cracked the spine and placed *Disappearance* on the hot tub lip beside the pistol, with his hands braced on either side of the book. He lifted himself into a crouch, obviously passing gas in the hot tub.

"Tell me about my mother," Roger said.

Loren shrugged and looked down at his hands. Ann left no photos behind. He hadn't realized that until her face started to fade, a year after her suicide, and he went looking for one. He found a few pictures of Fred in a drawer, but none of Ann. He couldn't even locate her driver's license. He suspected she had destroyed every trace of herself before she died.

"She was short, with dark brown hair."

"In the book, she's blonde," Roger said.

"I had to change something." Loren's mind drifted back, searching for a memory he knew was true. The real Ann and the fictional Ann were intertwined in his head. He was uncertain where one left off and the other began.

"She had nice eyes. I remember her eyes being soft, but I can't swear as to what color they were. She was thin, but not anorexic or anything. Just thin."

Eyes and weight—Roger needed more. "What did she act like?"

Loren sighed again. This wasn't something he wanted to dwell on. "You were Ann's life. I don't know why she married me. She was never interested in anyone but you. She had a day care when you were a toddler. Started teaching preschool when you went into preschool. Ann couldn't relax around adults."

Roger waited quietly while Loren searched the past. Loren hadn't brooded over what went wrong with Ann in years. Even when he had been with her, he had been writing novels that were more immediate to him than she was. He mostly thought of her when he needed a trait for some character in one of his books.

"Ann was one of those women whose life matters during pregnancy and when the child is a baby. Nothing else felt quite real to her." Loren twisted the loose ends of his bathrobe belt into a clockwise coil. He wasn't looking at Roger anymore. "I've met men who survived wars who felt the same way, as if only one short period of their lives is relevant, and everything else is going through the motions."

"Why did she kill herself?" Roger asked. "If she'd lived, I might have come back. I mean, I did, eventually. Wouldn't it have been better if she'd waited?"

Loren's attention came back to Roger. The young man reminded him of Fred. So serious. So earnest. Fred had been a five year old who rarely laughed or cried. "She couldn't face another day without you."

Roger hadn't thought Lydia was listening, but she suddenly snapped out of her trance. Her eyes flew open. "What about you? You faced another day."

"I wrote the book. It got made into a movie."

"You took the tragedy of your wife and child and turned it into a career move," Lydia said.

"Writing about Fred was the way I kept going. Ann didn't have any defense."

26

"BALLS!" LEROY SIDEARMED *DISAPPEARANCE* ACROSS THE patio, where it bounced once and slid under Oly's chair, stopped by a wheel before it fell into the pool. "I should break your knees and elbows, you maggot." He glared at Loren. "Not one sentence of that pile of stink is what really happened."

"What do you expect?" Loren said. "It's a novel."

"That's an awfully convenient fall-back position," Lydia said. "The book is true when you want it true, and a novel when you don't."

Leroy wasn't listening. "I am the father. Fred—pay no mind to the villain. Chuck claimed it was his jizz, but Ann knew better. She knew I lit the fire. She told this fool idiot of an author a lie and he put it on paper. Now the lie is taken for history. I won't stand still for being cheated out of my due."

Roger went over to Oly to retrieve the book. At the moment, he'd had it with men claiming to be his father. Leroy, Loren, Chuck the Dead Guy—hell, Pud Talbot brought him up. If anybody deserved his due, it was Pud.

"Did you kill Chuck?" Roger asked.

Leroy grinned. "What do you think?"

"In the book, he gets murdered in the hospital parking lot, the day I was born, but it doesn't say who killed him."

"Ann didn't know who killed Chuck," Loren said.

Leroy's eyes narrowed into glittering lizard slits. "You think I could let that weasel live, claiming his sperm had been inside my property? Claiming he had bred with her? I have ethics. Justice must be served."

"You think killing serves justice?" Lydia asked, which strikes me as a bit hypocritical, coming from a woman who sent a poison chew toy to a dog.

"Killing is justice when I say so, and I'm about to say so."

The back door banged open, and Zelda's cheerful voice came from the kitchen. "Look what I found."

Maurey Pierce came out the back door, resplendent in Levi boot-cuts, a yoked shirt, and stitched black cowhide boots with inch-and-a-half heels.

Shannon said, "Mom."

Roger said, "Mom."

Lana Sue followed Maurey, carrying a tray pyramided by little triangular sandwiches and a plate of baby dill pickles. Zelda brought up the train, her rifle leveled properly on the other two women. Zelda was beginning to worry over the numbers of women in the yard. Without the rifle, she would have been the least memorable of the bunch, and she knew it.

Maurey said, "How's it hanging, Leroy?"

Leroy said, "You've got the nerve."

"Who's Leroy?" Zelda asked.

Maurey nodded at Leroy in the hot tub. Leroy was almost, but not quite, abashed at the exposure of his lie.

"This one," Maurey said.

Lana Sue brought the tray to the stone table and left it next to the CD player, which had gone on to Van Morrison. Leroy reached over, lifted a half dozen sandwiches, and stuffed one whole between his gums. He chewed with his mouth open.

Lana Sue left the food for the others to serve themselves. She wasn't about to circulate the tray.

"How many more are we expecting?" Lana Sue asked. "I'm not volunteering to feed an army."

Zelda was so confused she pointed the rifle at Leroy instead of the hostages. "His name is Charley Manson."

Oly spit into the pool. "My God, woman, you are stupider than you look."

"I am not. He told me his name was Charley Manson. I had no reason to think he's a liar."

"You know he's a killer and a kidnapper," Lydia said, "but you saw no reason to think he might lie?"

Maurey picked up one of the sandwiches and examined it. The bread was dappled, like an Appaloosa. "His name is Leroy and he broke into my barn night before last." Maurey lifted the tray and took it to Lydia and Shannon. She wasn't above the role of serving wench. "He was in your kitchen yesterday, or it could have been Friday night, after he left my place. He broke your back window and threw milk around the counter."

Shannon said, "Was she with him?"

"She gave Auburn dope and he told her how to find Roger."

Shannon refused a sandwich but took a handful of pickles. "I knew that was my shirt. Lydia, you owe me an apology. The tramp stole my shirt, and I knew it, and you belittled me for saying so."

Zelda held the rifle in her left hand and her sandwich in her right. "Who you calling a tramp, bitch?"

Shannon cupped her hand over her lips until she'd swallowed her mouthful of pickles. "Well, you. Nobody else here has a face full of iron and a strip of nylon up her butt crack. Nobody else has been stealing clothes but you."

"One lousy shirt was all you owned worth taking. This

woman"—Zelda nodded toward Lana Sue—"has a better wardrobe than you, and she's ninety years old."

Lana Sue nibbled a bite of sandwich. "I have to be honest here, Zelda. You are a tramp."

Maurey kept on task. One thing Maurey can do is focus on what matters and avoid peripheral catfights. "Leroy got the author's name off a message Shannon left on your answering machine. Then he beat it here. For some reason I haven't figured out yet, it looks like he brought a horse."

"That was an accident," Zelda said. Leroy himself was stuffing more sandwiches down his gullet.

Lydia held hers on a dainty napkin. She nodded, putting together the two and twos. "I've been trying to figure out how he knew we would be here."

Loren walked over with his left hand holding his bathrobe in place and his right hand extended. "Loren Paul. You look familiar."

Maurey shook his hand. "I live up the Gros Ventre River. Fifteen years or so ago, back when you had that place on Ditch Creek, I helped after you'd gotten stuck."

Lana Sue appeared at Loren's side. "How is it you can't remember what you wore yesterday, but you recall a woman you flirted with fifteen years ago?"

"The Toyota slid off the road," Loren said. "She pulled me out of the snowbank."

"Of course she did."

Shannon said, "I can't believe you're jealous of my mother."

"Mother?" Lana Sue compared Maurey to Shannon. They were fourteen years apart, but Maurey's lived the healthy ranch life while Shannon'd let herself go a bit lately. It was a stretch to see them as different generations. "Is this mother real, or imaginary like the boyfriend-brother?"

"She's real," Shannon said. "Where's Daddy?"

"We don't talk about your father, Shannon. And what's this about a boyfriend-brother?"

"Roger and I are a couple now. Isn't that cool?"

Maurey gave Roger the look, and he concentrated on his pickle. He'd hoped to break the news to her in private. He wasn't sure how pleased Maurey would be, and the whole public spectacle of being in a stranger's backyard with guns and Van Morrison and stupid little wedge sandwiches struck him as outside his zone of comfort.

Oly more or less erupted. "You're poisoning me with lawn clippings."

"It's olive tapenade on Pepperidge Farms Rye and Pump," Lana Sue said. "I was fresh out of boloney and white bread."

Lydia made a lemon-sucking face. "Would you call this a California fad or an upper-class affectation?"

"It's food. And you can go back where you came from if you don't like it."

Leroy finally swallowed his last glob of sandwich paste. It was time to regain control. "You people shut up, or I'm going to shoot somebody just to get your attention."

"It's not so bad," Roger said to Oly. "I'll take yours."

Zelda the Social Climber said, "Roger and myself just adore your sandwiches, Mrs. Paul. You must give me the recipe."

"The ancient pervert is right," Lana Sue said. "You are stupider than you look."

Leroy said, "We're all going to play a game."

Zelda flounced. "They're making fun of me, Charley or Leroy or whoever the heck you are, just because I trusted you. After everything we've been through, you lied to me." She touched Lana Sue above the wrist. Lana Sue flinched.

Zelda said, "He burned up my brother's car."

Roger ignored Leroy. Everyone ignored Leroy. There were too many uncontained relationships crisscrossing back and forth across the yard for anyone to care what the naked freak with the gun had in mind.

Roger said, "I understand how he came from the TM barn to here, but how did he know to come looking for me at the ranch?"

Maurey looked at Leroy, which was more attention than anyone else was giving him. "I'd say he tracked me down through Mary Beth. She was his girlfriend a long time ago, in Oklahoma, and she's the one who brought you to Wyoming in the first place."

"Your friend Mary Beth was with this crazy man?"

"Mary Beth is sweet, but Leroy has a way of finding innocent teenagers and corrupting them."

"Don't look at me," Zelda said. "I'm not corrupt."

Leroy hissed an unpleasant laugh. "Mary Beth wasn't innocent. Who do you think helped with the original rescue?"

Loren said, "Kidnapping."

Maurey said, "I don't believe you."

"Mary Beth drove the van while I grabbed the kid." Leroy's toothless grin was reminiscent of a jack-o'-lantern a month after Halloween. "I'll bet she didn't tell you that part."

Maurey was shocked. And hurt. She liked Mary Beth. Maurey had trusted her and helped her when she was in trouble. The idea that Mary Beth knew Roger was kidnapped and hadn't told her was a terrible disillusionment.

Lana Sue said, "Are we expecting this Mary Beth person for lunch? I'll have to make more sandwiches."

Oly said, "She can have mine."

Roger said, "I'll take it."

We have now reached the point where I come back into the story. You no doubt think I'm the hero of my own life, or at least my own novels. You think I'll take action, save the day, and find inner peace. If so, you haven't read my other novels.

In my actual real life, as in my novels, I play the part of comic relief. It isn't by design. I don't plan to be the man who farts in a crowded elevator. It just seems to happen.

What happened at Loren and Lana Sue Paul's house was this: I had the opportunity to come to the rescue, and I flubbed. I'd never in my life seen broken glass embedded in concrete on top of a double-redwood fence. Nobody expects broken glass on top of a fence when they go vaulting over to save their loved ones from horrible danger. No one from Wyoming, anyway. Hank's prison didn't even have a fence lethal as the Pauls'.

So I cut my hand as I came across, caught my pants leg on a shard, and hung for a moment, suspended upside down, bleeding. Leroy snapped off a shot that splintered wood next to my ear.

I yelled, "I surrender."

Lydia said, "I knew he would do that."

Lana Sue said, "Oh fuck, another one," and Roger came over to help me down.

Roger said, "Smooth move, Ex-Lax."

"You're the last one I expected to turn tacky."

"Did you call the police before you jumped the fence?"

I squeezed my shirttail in my cut fist. It wasn't a terrible cut, but like always, I couldn't remember the last time I had a tetanus shot. I can't ever remember how long it's been since my last tetanus shot. I can't even remember how many years they're good for. Three, maybe. Or seven.

"Not exactly," I said.

Roger guided me around the pool over to the waiting group.

Lydia was scornful. "What was your plan, Sam? Did you expect to fly over the fence and disarm the ruffian?"

I looked at Maurey, who was, of course, disappointed. She hadn't fared any better than I did. I don't see where she had room to criticize.

"I wasn't expecting a gun," I looked at the gash on my palm. It wasn't deep enough to milk for sympathy from this bunch. "Maurey told me when he was in her barn, he didn't have a gun. I figured if he had one, he would have shown it then."

"You figured wrong, numb nuts," Leroy said.

"I'm afraid so."

The Wyoming contingent didn't seem overly terrified at the nearness of death. Oly was staring angrily at something made out of bread on his lap. Roger and Shannon wore semi-goofy grins, as if me falling over the fence had been expected all along. Maurey stood beside Loren Paul and they seemed to be discussing old times, which didn't make sense, but there you are.

Only Lydia had the face of one who's lost their last friend. She wasn't frightened, but she was depressed at a depth I'd never seen before, and I've seen Lydia depressed many times in my life. She'd never been a mother who hides despair from her son.

Her posture was so beat down, I asked, "What's wrong?" which may sound stupid, considering Leroy, Zelda, and the firearms, but it wasn't. Lydia had concerns beyond the immediate and obvious.

She said, "None of your damn business."

I said, "That's fair."

———

Leroy stood up. Nobody wanted Leroy to stand; he was grotesque from sternum to head, which is what he showed sitting in the hot tub. Leroy from the knees up was worse than anyone I'd ever imagined, and I'm a professional imaginer. He looked oily, even though he'd been soaking in hot water for several hours. It was as if the grime had sealed off his skin, and not even Zelda could face his penis without queasiness. He would have commanded more authority if he'd stayed where he was.

It was evident, to me, anyway, that Leroy was set to make a pronouncement. The assembled crowd gradually grew quiet as his eyes strayed off, above the fence top I'd recently fallen over.

He spoke. "I have taken a sacred oath to God Almighty that I will have vengeance on the evil Ann for stealing my rights as the proper father to this child. Too bad, but the scheming slit offed herself before I was able to recalibrate the natural order. I cannot renege on my oath. While the Bible demands an eye for an eye, it doesn't say whose eye I must pluck out. We are gathered here today to decide that question."

He paused, waiting for more sick thoughts to flow through his head, or maybe waiting for comments. I don't know why Leroy paused, but he drifted away there for a moment.

I expected one of the women to jump in with a scathing cut, and Lana Sue had that alert face like she wanted to, but surprisingly enough, she held back. I believe it had finally sunk in that this was for real and someone was likely to die in her backyard. She'd lived in Los Angeles before coming to Santa Barbara, so she knew what crazy looks like. She knew the danger of smart remarks or eye contact.

Lydia had never recognized the survival skill of shutting up, at least, not before she went to prison. Maybe she'd learned how to be silent in the face of insanity there, but I doubted it. Lydia was staring off into the mid-distance, not listening. Her distraction factor gave me cause to worry.

Leroy continued. "My death chart is one name short. There can be no peace, no balance or justice, until someone pays Ann's debt."

I couldn't help myself. I said, "Death chart?" I turned to Loren. As a fellow author, I figured he would be the closest one present to my sensibilities. "Do you keep a death chart?"

Loren said, "Not me." I don't think he knew who I was.

I said, "What kind of person keeps a death chart?"

Oly said, "I used to, but ever'body on it died, so I gave it up."

Leroy shouted, "I am the last righteous being. I demand that one of you sacrifice your life to restore the balance."

Oly said, "Don't look at me."

I guess people were looking at him. I'm not sure why. My eyes just wandered that way of their own accord.

Leroy said, "These are the rules."

Lana Sue finally broke her extended period of not butting in. "We're going to play by rules? I don't think so."

Zelda said, "Don't be a party pooper."

Shannon said, "This is no party."

Leroy lifted his arms for silence. "America is a democracy, so everyone has one vote, except me. I'm God, and God doesn't vote. God scourges the land."

Loren put his hands on his hips. He would have come across as masculine and forceful, had he been wearing pants. "I refuse to play."

Leroy glanced down at Loren from above. The CD moved on to Pink Floyd. It seemed to me that whoever had programmed the background music was living in bygone times.

Leroy called out, singsonging his voice like a preacher or a bad poet giving a reading. "If any of you refuses to vote, the holy law shifts and I kill the whole Goddamn lot." He stared slowly around from person to person. "Is there any among you who doesn't realize what a thrill it would give me to wipe out each and every one of you yuppie scum?"

No one spoke to that one. I knew Leroy would have a ball killing us, but what I wondered at was capability. Us novelists pretend vast knowledge when it comes to how many bullets go with each firearm, only I wasn't familiar with the pistol in

Leroy's hand. I'm not familiar with any real pistols. I just do the research when it's needed. I figured there weren't enough bullets to nail all eight of us—who ever heard of an eight-shooter? Nine, since you have to count the bullet he'd wasted on me. At some point, he'd be forced to switch to the rifle, and Zelda might not give it up.

The problem struck me as theoretical, more than immediate. I don't know about the others, but I was in denial of the bloodbath outcome. We were in Santa Barbara, for Chrisssake.

Zelda said, "That's not a fair game. They'll all vote for the old fart. He's about to drop dead any minute, anyway."

"You can vote for someone else," Oly said. "It won't hurt my feelings."

Shannon pointed a finger at Zelda. "She shouldn't even get a vote, unless she's on the death list like everyone else."

Leroy said, "We'll cast secret ballots."

"Hold on, hoss," Zelda said. "I want it clear that voting for me is not a choice. You tell them. These snobs will vote me in over the fossil. They know I'm your squeeze."

"Squeeze." Leroy stared at Zelda, long enough to make her uncomfortable. She wrapped the towel around her body, over the bikini, and under the armpits, in a maneuver that women can pull off, but men can't.

"Okay," Leroy said. "You cannot vote for me, and you cannot vote for Zelda. Killing her is separate from Ann. The only ones who can settle Ann's debt must be connected to her son there."

Lydia snorted derision at Zelda. I was glad to see Mom had some scorn left. She said, "He plans to slice your zitty little throat later, honey."

"Does not," Zelda said. "We haven't even had sexual congress yet."

Roger spoke for the first time since he'd pulled me off the

fence. "Does sexual congress with a maniac mean he's more likely or less likely to kill a person?"

Zelda tucked her towel in so tightly it gave her a hint of cleavage. I don't think she'd considered Leroy's plans for her future. The dangerous-man thing would be fun to throw in her father's face, but she hadn't spun the adventure out to its logical conclusion.

Leroy focused on Lana Sue. "You there, hostess. Go inside and fetch nine pieces of paper and nine pencils. Zelda, go with her. You know the drill."

"Yeah, yeah," Zelda said. "If she tries to escape, shoot her. If she uses the phone, shoot her. I'd be more in the mood for shooting if you'd promise to take me home after we leave here."

"Just do what I say, you stupid weasel, or risk going back on the list."

—

I was at a loss as to what to do next. My hand throbbed, and the blood had soaked through my shirttail, but the bleeding seemed to have stopped. None of the women offered to help me wash or find a clean towel. Women in my life are like that.

Maurey was on the patio having an intense yet quiet talk with Roger and Shannon. Something I didn't understand was going on there. Shannon was staring at Roger, who had turned a flushed color. I can spot heightened emotionalism from afar and those two were deeply involved in a situation.

Oly was taking a nap. His head had fallen back on the headrest of his chair. His mouth was open, revealing cracked gums.

That left Leroy or Loren for conversation. I chose Loren.

I said, "I'm pleased to meet a peer."

Loren was a bit taller than me, and maybe a year older, but he came across as much taller and much older. Literary respect improves a person's impressions.

"What do you mean by that?" he asked.

"A fellow author. I write novels too."

"I haven't written a novel in fifteen years."

"Yes, but *Yeast Infection* changed my life. That book is a twentieth-century classic. It defined a generation."

Loren said, "It's out of print."

"American publishing is blind and tone deaf." I have a give-away pen with that printed on the side. If anyone wants one, drop me an e-mail. "My books are out of print too. I've published eight novels so far, mostly young adult."

"I only put out four."

"Four masterpieces are better than eight hack jobs." To be honest, Loren's first two books before *Disappearance* and *Yeast Infection* were Westerns and not masterpieces, but it would have been rude to say so. "Your use of symbol and dynamic imagery is breathtaking."

"I wouldn't touch symbol and dynamic imagery with a stick. I tell stories. I was successful enough to get myself kicked up to screenwriter, but not successful enough to circle back to novels. What's your name again?"

"Sam Callahan. I wrote the Bucky climbing series, and the RC Nash detective stories. I also penned a Plucky Woman in Jeopardy novel, but I had a pseudonym there."

Lana Sue banged her way out the back door followed by Zelda, who trailed along with the demeanor of a puppy packing a rifle. She'd put a men's white dress shirt on over the bikini. The tails hung below her crotch, covering the thong some, but not much. She'd lost her sandals along the way.

Loren said, "I never penned a book. I was more of a typist."

"Typist of what?" Lana Sue asked as she crossed the yard. "I found index cards and pens. We don't have pencils, that I know of."

"Novels," Loren said. "I felt more like a typer of novels than a penner."

"Look where literature got us," Lana Sue said. "We've never had a killer in the hot tub over those tacky MTV reality shows you type."

I realized who Lana Sue was. The name should have tipped me off, but I don't think her last name was Paul back when I'd seen her perform. I said, "I saw you sing once, at the Cowboy Bar in Jackson. You were with a band called Thunder Jug."

"Thunder Road."

"That's right. You were remarkable, considering how drunk the musicians were. It was one of the finest nights I've spent in a watering hole."

Lydia said, "Hell, Sam, how many more asses are you planning to stick your tongue up?"

"I was just telling the Pauls that I admire their creative work. When I do admirable work, I want random strangers to tell me."

"Lucky for us, you've never done admirable work."

Lana Sue passed out pens and index cards. When she handed me mine, she said, "Is that woman really your mother? With this bunch, I can't tell what's real and what isn't."

"I'm afraid so. She had me young."

"Is she always this negative?"

Okay. That was a little odd coming from Lana Sue. She might be the only woman I've met who could give Lydia competition at ironic negativity.

Speaking of which, Lydia said, "You should talk to me when I'm in a bad mood."

See. Ironic negativity on parade.

"Vote," Leroy barked.

Lana Sue poked Oly with the point of a pen. I could tell she didn't want to touch him. "Wake up, Grandpa. Write your name here."

Oly came to with a long, whistling snort. He looked from

the index card to Lana Sue. "You spell Lana Sue as one word or two?"

Loren said, "I'd rather not choose. I don't do well at making decisions."

Leroy said, "You know what'll happen if you don't write a name on the card."

A CD by a band called Yes was playing. I hadn't heard Yes since college, and I wasn't overly keen on them back then. I snuck a peek at Loren and Lana Sue, wondering which of those two was trapped in a bygone era. My money was on Loren. Lana Sue didn't strike me as a stagnant woman.

Shannon, Roger, Maurey, and Loren cut their eyes around the group, weighing probabilities. It was the old game of *who do we throw off the life raft*. Lana Sue, Lydia, and Zelda kept their heads down and pens scratching—no wishy-washiness as to who to kill there—although, at the end, after she'd placed her card facedown on the hot-tub ledge, Zelda looked at Shannon and smirked.

I couldn't come up with a justification for choosing. I mean, it mattered. A lot. Someone was likely to die here. Logically, it had to be the ninety-nine-year-old Oly. His life expectancy lacked the potential of the rest of us. But then, I'd known Oly thirty years, and I hated to sentence a man I'd known for so long to death.

I was related to all the others, except Loren and Lana Sue. I figured the immediate family—Lydia, Shannon, Roger, and I counted Maurey, even though we weren't technically related, because we shared a child—wouldn't choose each other, which left only Oly or the new strangers. Lana Sue was the closest anyone came to innocent. She had no connection to Roger or Leroy, other than her husband had once been married to Ann. Loren was present at the original abduction. To read the book—and I had read the book, years ago—if

Loren had been paying attention he might have stopped the kidnapping. If anyone should die for Ann, it was Loren. But then, how could I condemn him? He'd written literature. Society at large would be less without Loren Paul. The rest of us would be grieved by friends and family, but that was the extent of our reach. Loren mattered to people who didn't know him.

In the end, I wrote my own name, hoping no one else would think of me. What if everyone used the same thought process and wrote their own names? It could happen. Zelda had voted for Shannon. By the rules, Shannon couldn't write *Zelda*, so if everyone who could named themselves, we'd all have one vote, except Shannon, who would have two. And that would up the bloodbath factor, because Leroy could only kill my daughter over my dead body. I had no doubt Maurey would throw herself into the breach for Shannon also.

That brought us back to Oly.

Leroy said, "Zelda, collect the cards."

Lydia stepped forward. "That's my job."

"Who died and made you boss?" Zelda asked.

"I'm the oldest and wisest. It's my responsibility."

Oly spit between his skinny legs. "What's that?"

"I'm the oldest who isn't senile. It's my fault we're in this mess. I'll collect the Goddamn cards."

So Lydia circled the yard, picking up votes. Roger took Shannon's card, placed it with his, and passed them both over. Loren passed his face down, while Lana Sue passed hers face up. Zelda wouldn't touch her card. She made Lydia take it off the tub ledge. When I gave Lydia mine, she brushed her fingers on mine, looked me in the eyes, and winked.

Scared the holy beJesus out of me.

"Read the names," Leroy said.

That's when the CD player ran out of CDs. The timing is

hard to believe, I admit, but sometimes timing in life is hard to believe. All I know is the backyard was suddenly quiet. A bird—sounded like a magpie, but then, what do I know about Santa Barbara birds—called from the far side of the fence. Water gurgled from the pool pump. I could hear Oly's wheeze, but the absence of music made the yard feel eerie.

Lydia stood in front of Leroy, cards in hand. One by one, she flipped them over and read.

"Shannon."

Zelda giggled.

"Maurey."

I looked at Maurey, who gave me a weak smile. She'd voted for herself. I could tell.

"Oly."

Oly blinked. He was trying to pull of his absent-from-reality act, but it wasn't playing, this time. He came across more as a toddler, spoiling for a fight.

"Oly."

Lydia glanced at Oly and turned another card.

"Oly."

She stopped and faced him. Their eyes locked in a long stare-down. I hadn't been around for the recording of his oral history, but I can imagine the link that is formed when one person hears another person's life story. Something crucial passes between them.

Lydia said, "You don't want to die, do you, old man? That's why you keep going when anyone with any sense would have called it quits long ago."

Oly nodded. The bone plates under his temple rubbed against each other. His goiter turned splotchy.

Lydia said, "You don't want people to say"—her voice changed ever so slightly—"'He had a good life. It was his time to go.'"

Oly's lips moved like chewing his tongue. He said, "Fuck that."

Lydia stood frozen, staring at the old man until Leroy grew impatient. "Move it or lose it, woman."

Lydia turned over the next card. "Lydia."

She moved on quickly. "Lydia."

"Lydia."

One card was left, with Lydia and Oly tied, and I'd voted for me. I didn't know what Leroy planned in case of a tie—kill them both, I supposed, unless that screwed up his balance of nature as much as not killing anyone. Leroy's spiritual logic was so convoluted, you'd have to be as nuts as he was to predict it. I scanned the pool area for a decorative rock or a loose brick. Anything blunt. The Paul's backyard was clear of all weapons bigger than a coffee cup. There was an aluminum pole with a net on one end suitable for fishing leaves out of the pool. I didn't see what good that could do me, even if I got hold of it before Leroy commenced firing.

Lydia looked around at Shannon and Roger. They were standing by the back door, Shannon's hand clutching Roger's arm like an anchor. Loren and Lana Sue were on my right, between the stone table and the pool. Zelda was up close to Leroy. Oly hadn't moved from the edge of the pool. No one seemed on the verge of rushing the hot tub.

Lydia flipped over the last card. She studied a moment and said, "Lydia." Then she folded all the cards together and slipped them into her back pocket.

"Wait a minute," Loren said, at the same moment I said, "Bullshit!"

Roger said, "Let me see those cards."

Lydia faced Leroy. "Your turn, asswipe."

He shot her.

Shannon screamed, Maurey yelled, "*No!*" I caught Lydia as she fell, and Lana Sue threw the CD player into the hot tub.

There was a hard electrical *Pop*. Leroy started to rise. His face twisted into a grin, and he died.

———

I lowered Lydia to the ground and held her head against my chest with her body across my lap and her legs sprawled on the grass. I'm not sure if I'd ever held her before, other than a quick, awkward hug. She seemed too light to be my mother. Leroy'd hit her in the sternum. There was a lot of blood. I clamped my cut hand over the hole in her chest, but it didn't do any good.

Her eyes looked up at me, or past me—I couldn't tell which. Her eyelids fluttered.

I said, "You didn't have to do that."

"I did." She coughed a wad of blood. "I'm too vain to age with grace."

I held her and cried. Maurey knelt down beside us. Then Shannon and Roger came in on the other side. Shannon arranged Lydia's legs so they weren't crumpled, but Lydia didn't notice.

Maurey said, "Hold on. The ambulance is coming. You'll be okay."

Lydia almost laughed, but the laugh turned to a spasm of pain. After it passed, she said, "Maurey, you always were such a liar."

After that, we were quiet. Lana Sue was talking on her cell phone. Oly rolled up to Lydia's feet and looked down at her.

Lydia raised a hand to touch my face. She said, "Tell Hank."

"What?"

Her eyes grew cloudy. Her hand lowered back to her side. She said again, "Tell Hank."

Oly said, "I'll take care of it."

Then Lydia left me.

No one spoke for a while. Loren came up and touched my shoulder. He said, "Can I do anything?"

I said, "No."

From the outer edge of the circle, I heard Zelda's voice. "Would somebody take me home?"

Loose Ends

Why do we treat those we love so much worse than those we don't like? Lydia would starve before not tipping a waitress. She'd go back home if the alternative was parking in a handicapped slot, yet she lied to and browbeat the family she loved. The truth I can't get around is this: Lydia slept with a stranger the night before seeing the husband she would rather die than live without. Maurey may know why. Or Oly. I cannot find a way of understanding the last day of my mother's life.

For the past twenty-five years, whenever I've had a question I couldn't answer, I'd write a hundred-thousand-word novel in which people acted out my problem, and by the finish of the book, the question was either answered, or it had vanished into the pages. But this time I'm way over my one hundred thousand words, and I'm no closer to understanding than I was back when I typed *I am that I am.* I still do not know the answer, and I still wish I did.

———

Hank's parole came two months after Lydia died. He took a bus to Idaho Falls and I drove the van over to get him. He had no luggage. We drove back over Teton Pass, mostly in silence.

He asked about a horse I wasn't familiar with. He commented on how early the fireweed was out.

Hank had me drop him off at Haven House. He went in and talked to Oly for a couple of hours. Even as a novelist creating the parts where I wasn't there, I can't conceive of what they said to each other. Later that week, Hank disappeared up into the Bitterroots. The next spring, eight months later, Maurey went out at dawn to check on a foal, and Hank was in the pasture, fixing a head gate. He's worked and lived at the TM Ranch since then.

A year after her death—Memorial Day 1994—Hank and I took Lydia's ashes to the top of Miner Creek and turned her loose. Human ashes aren't what you'd think, if you haven't spread them before. They're crunchy, with bits of bone mixed into the ash pack. I hadn't expected to see pieces of Lydia when we dropped her into the creek. It brought her back all in a rush. I could hear her telling us we were doing it wrong.

You spread ashes downwind, you idiots, she would have said. *You dickwads don't piss against the wind. What makes you think you can scatter me that way?*

Hank said this was the place he'd brought her on their first date. Lydia climbed off the snowmobile and fell through the ice rime, ankle-deep into the creek. He had to pull off her boots and warm her feet between his thighs. He'd been embarrassed no end to have the white city girl's bare toes up against his crotch. Lydia laughed till tears froze to her cheeks.

I said, "You should have known she'd be trouble."

Hank and I watched her ashes swirl in an eddy, and then gradually, they spread and disappeared downstream like sugar in a glass of iced tea.

He said, "I knew."

Mary Beth and her family drove up from Albuquerque last summer so she could beg forgiveness for the kidnapping all those years ago. Lonnie and the girls went into Jackson to see the shoot-out while Mary Beth stayed at the ranch and wept. Maurey hugged her and said she wasn't to blame for the awful trauma of Roger's childhood; Roger patted her on the shoulder and assured her she didn't cause his mother's suicide.

I'm glad she didn't ask me. I wouldn't have been so nice.

———

Roger and Shannon moved into Lydia's house in GroVont. He commutes up the river to Madonnaville five days a week. The Home for Unweds couldn't make it without him. Shannon has discovered ceramics. Her dream is to own a tourist trap where she can sell pots and authentic Indian goods.

Three months after Shannon and Roger moved in together, Shannon announced to Maurey that the waiting period closed with a crash. Maurey asked me if I wanted to know what that meant and I said, "No."

Christmas, they flew back to Santa Barbara and stayed a week with Lana Sue and Loren. Roger tells me he still has nightmares, but not nearly so often, and when he awakes after one, Shannon is there to hold him. He no longer fears uncontrollable suicide.

———

I wrote this book in his old cabin.

———

There never was an Oly Pedersen Day in GroVont. The week before he turned one hundred, Oly and Irene Dukakis ran off to live in Greece. I didn't even know Oly had a passport. We had no clue as to where they were for a month or so, until

Roger got a postcard with a picture of Delphi on the front. The back—in a scrawl like a bird scratching blood—read:

Irene and I are hitched. We would prefer cash to wedding gifts. Send money orders to...

and then came an address in Amfissa, Greece. I mailed him two hundred dollars, in Lydia's name.

———

Last Mother's Day—two years after Lydia got out of prison—Gilia and I took Esther to Yellowstone to look for Evangeline's grave. We found it too, right where Oly said it would be. There's a picnic area, now, on Nez Perce Creek. Her marker sits thirty yards or so beyond the bathrooms. The park service has placed a low pipe fence around the site, so kids won't climb on the stone, I guess. I can't think of any other reason.

If you stand with your back to the picnic tables and face the Firehole, the view must be close to what Oly saw seventy years ago—the blooming balsamroot and larkspur, ravens soaring the updraft, juncos in the sage. It helps that our visit came within a week of the funeral date. The similarities were easy to see.

The stone is a yellow-white slab, not marble, maybe quartz. Rock identification always has been a flaw in my nature lore skills. It's that rock from over by Canyon that gave Yellowstone its name. The words read

Evangeline Pedersen
July 10, 1902–May 15, 1924
Our Angel Has Flown

Gilia said, "That sounds just like Oly."

"The man is a born poet," I said. "Or was. He'd be pushing one hundred and two now, if he's still alive."

"He's still alive," Gilia said. "That old blowhard is unkillable."

Gilia took photographs of the grave and the surrounding land, so when I wrote this scene I wouldn't screw it up while I worked out the relationship of beauty to death and how one meant nothing without the other. Esther did cartwheels around the fence. Cartwheels are her new method of getting from place to place. She doesn't walk, run, or skip much these days. She cartwheels. It's a skill she picked up in Mighty Mite Gymnastics. As she cartwheeled around the circle, Esther sang a song in which a woman swallows a fly and tries to figure why. It wasn't one Lydia taught me. I don't remember Lydia teaching me any songs when I was young.

My daughter was so heartbreakingly alive I gave up on the deep thoughts to watch her circle the grave. As Lydia pointed out more times than I wanted to hear—for a person who thinks deep thoughts for a living, I'm not very good at it. I don't have the discipline. I'd rather watch my daughter, or a cloud, or listen to running water. I start out with a thought chain and end up with white noise.

With each loop, Esther's dark hair brushed the dirt, and sooner or later one of her palms was going to come down on a sharp rock. I knew I should say something, but I kept putting it off. Gilia was more interested in photography than parenting. The day was too nice to criticize. My women were happy; therefore, I was happy.

Finally, I couldn't stand it anymore. "You ought to stop that before you get hurt."

Esther glanced over to see how serious I was, and decided I wasn't.

"Her hair is getting dirty," I said.

Gilia's next line would normally have been *So what?* but

this time it was so obvious she didn't bother to say it out loud. Instead she shifted closer to me, so our shoulders were touching as we watched our daughter cavort. The things that are simple to other people—sunlight on skin, spring air, family close by—floor me when I suddenly recognize their value. I have trouble breathing.

Esther yelped and twisted her arm back to avoid touching elk scat, and she went over backward in a crash. She sat on the ground, legs akimbo, eyes flashing, glaring at me.

"That was your fault," she said.

I laughed. Big mistake.

"*Daddy. Don't laugh at me!*"

"I wasn't laughing at you. I was thinking how much you're growing up like your Grandmother Lydia."

Gilia socked me hard on the upper arm. "Good Lord, don't say that."

"Why not? Lydia was my mother."

"I wouldn't brag, if I were you."

Esther stood up and brushed sage and elk scat off her shorts. "I want nachos."

I said, "Okay."

With no more thoughts of death and dying, the three of us loaded into the Madonnaville van and drove off in search of nachos. Lydia would have approved.

Author's Note

YOU YELLOWSTONE STICKLERS WILL NOTICE I SWITCHED THE Midway Geyser Basin for Fountain Flats. There is a good reason for this. Fountain sounds better in a sentence than Midway. Try it. Other than that, the history and geography are more or less correct, at least as Sam and Oly would have remembered them.

Acknowledgments

MUCH OF THIS BOOK WAS WRITTEN IN PEARL STREET BAGELS and the Center for the Arts. I wish to thank the fine folks at both for their patience while I lived in one world and existed in another.

Valley Books, as always, kept me going.

My family gave me time, space, and optimism.

Todd Stocke and Flip Brophy had the faith.

Thanks to the Sandlinistas, especially Curt Pasisz and Army and Aero Feth. You too can join at timsandlin.com.

I thank the board of the Jackson Hole Writers Conference, particularly Nicole Burdick and Linda Hazen.

I have now been with Maurey and Sam through four novels, two movies, and twenty-seven years. My loved ones say that's enough. Even though, when pushed in a corner, I will admit they aren't real, I still want to thank those two for giving me their travails and deepest needs. It's been more fun than folks who only live one life can imagine.

About the Author

Rebecca Stern

REVIEWERS HAVE VARIOUSLY compared Tim Sandlin to Jack Kerouac, Tom Robbins, Larry McMurtry, Joseph Heller, John Irving, Kurt Vonnegut, Carl Hiaasen, and a few other writers you've probably heard of. He has published nine novels and a book of columns. He wrote eleven screenplays for hire, two of which have been made into movies. He used to write reviews for the *New York Times Book Review* but was fired for excessive praise. He lives with his family in Jackson, Wyoming, where he is director of the Jackson Hole Writers Conference. His Sandlinistas follow him at www.timsandlin.com.

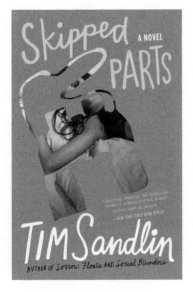
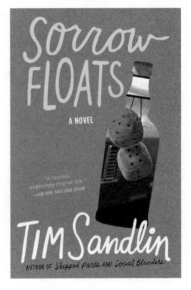

Tim Sandlin's Complete GroVont Series

Social Blunders

978-1-4022-4175-8
$14.99 U.S. / $17.99 CAN / £7.99 UK

Lydia

978-1-4022-4181-9
$24.99 U.S. / £16.99 UK

Don't miss these releases
coming soon from Tim Sandlin and Sourcebooks Landmark

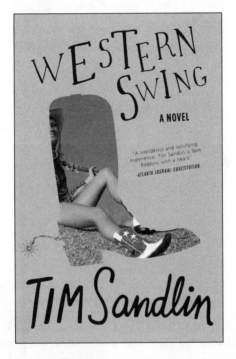

Western Swing

L ana Sue has had too many husbands and too little success as a country-western singer. Loren Paul's a semi-successful writer presently sitting on top of a western Wyoming mountain while waiting for Cosmic answers.

Together or apart, Loren Paul and Lana Sue are modern folk heroes in this deliciously ribald saga of the new wild West—a spirited tale of love and loss, of country music and coming home.

May 2011 | 978-1-4022-4177-2 | $14.99 U.S. / £9.99 UK

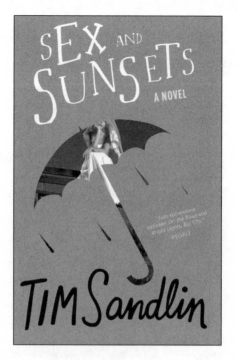

SEX AND SUNSETS

A NOVEL

"falls somewhere between On the Road and Bright Lights, Big City."
—PEOPLE

TIM Sandlin

Sex and Sunsets

At twenty-nine, Kelly Palomino's a little off-kilter but settled into his career of professional dishwasher. His big, blonde, ex-hippie wife has left him for good.

So it's with no particular purpose that Kelly positions himself on his porch across the street from an Episcopal church in Jackson, Wyoming, to witness a singular sight: a dark-haired bride in full regalia punting a football over the rectory before turning resolutely to walk down the aisle.

It's love at first sight for Kelly, and he'll do absolutely anything and everything to get his girl...

May 2011 | 978-1-4022-4179-6 | $14.99 U.S. / £9.99 UK